Slave to the Wolf King
Volume 1

By Aimee Lynn

For Alan,

Thank you for always being my protector and never my betrayer.

1.Call the Reapers

Behold, I was brought forth in iniquity, and in sin did my mother conceive me.
- Psalms 51:5

~ CASIMIR (Pronounced "CAZZ-uh-MEER") ~
I woke up needing to piss.

One of my toys slept face down with her arm thrown across my chest. The second was curled like a puppy on top of the furs at my feet.

Tossing the fur—and the unwanted arm—back, I turned to sit on the edge of the bed, elbows on my knees, running a hand through my hair while I blinked my way awake.

The toy who'd been embracing me rolled away with a tiny protest. I watched her over my shoulder for a moment, considering punishing her. But she only rolled to her back, her beautiful breasts bouncing slightly as she slumped back against the pillow. The strands of her dark hair that lay over her face fluttered when she began to snore quietly.

I shook my head and pushed to my feet, walking naked towards the bathroom.

Our underground chambers meant there was no morning light. No dawn at the window. No windows at all. Nothing to tell my body it was morning but sheer discipline.

Other wolves might have chosen to give in to the bestial urge to become nocturnal. We were creatures of the dark, after all. But I didn't will it. And while I didn't will it, the packs did not do it.

Our wealth was reliant on trade with the humans, who mostly kept what they called *office hours*. So I had determined that we wolves would, as well.

Of course, almost everyone slept late. Except me. A habit from my youth, at the urging of my father, the previous King.

The wolf of power plans while his enemies sleep.

My rage crackled at thoughts of my father, so I dismissed them.

The only other wolf more disciplined than me was my servant and advisor, Ghere.

Small and slight, Ghere was the runt of his litter. He should have been nose to the dirt—never hold the ear of the King. But in order to make up for his fine frame and delicate constitution, God had given the fucker a mind larger and sharper than any I knew.

And he never failed to step into my room the exact moment that I arose.

I suspected he stood at the door, his ear pressed to the frame, waiting. How he heard me pad across the stone floor every morning, I would never know, but he never failed me.

This morning, though, he scuttled towards me even faster than usual as I crossed the chamber, heading for the bathroom.

"Good morning, Sire."

"Is it?"

"Perhaps not," he said quickly, licking his lips in a nervous habit he had that always made my nose wrinkle.

I stepped into the bathroom, leaving the door open for him so he could follow. I was desperate to piss. The man had shadowed me into far darker spaces than this.

"What is making your balls retreat this morning, Ghere?" I asked, sighing with relief as I began to relieve myself into the bowl.

The humans had so many things wrong, but indoor plumbing and electricity were not numbered among them.

"Sire, the Queen is dead."

I went very still, only for a breath, guarding against the rush of rage and frustration. It wouldn't do to lash out at Ghere. He was necessary.

I cursed under my breath. "Did she leave a note?"

"Yes."

Fuck.

When I had finished and turned from the toilet to see him holding a piece of paper, I snatched it out of his outstretched hand. Walking slowly back into the bedchamber, I opened and read it, scanning it quickly. But there was nothing new.

Pitifully weak.

Crying for attention.

Miserable. Depressed. Unable to cope, blah, blah, blah.

Just like the last one.

Fuck.

I crumpled the paper and tossed it at Ghere, who snagged it deftly out of the air, but the tension in his features didn't ease.

"Sire—"

"She was too weak. Just like the others."

"Yes, obviously. But—"

"Call the Reapers."

"Of course, but I just wonder—"

"This time tell them to hunt the poor areas. The trailer parks and slums."

"Sire?"

I reached the bed and shook the toys awake. Miraculously, the blonde curled at the end of the bed was still wearing the wisp of lace and silk I'd given her yesterday. When she sat up, frowning and blinking, one side of it fell away where I'd bitten through the strap last night.

There were marks on her shoulder, scrapes in the shape of my teeth leading from her collarbone to the top of her full breast.

I smiled and reached for her, taking the weight of that pale globe and teasing her nipple with my thumb until it stood proud.

Flushed and messy from sleep, she still bit her lip, smiling, and leaned back on her hands, pressing her chest up for me.

Good girl.

I put one knee on the bed and her eyes brightened, so I crawled forward to kneel on it, nodding when she reached for me with a question in her eyes, burying a hand in her hair when she leaned down to take me in her mouth.

I let my head drop back and growled my approval of her talented tongue.

"Sire," Ghere said, averting his eyes from my toy. "I think—"

"Tell them to hunt the poorer areas, Ghere. The women there have suffered already. They'll be stronger."

"But... your offspring must be of the noble bloodlines. Taking a human I understand, but—"

I hissed and tightened my grip in the toy's hair, guiding her as pleasure coursed through me, lighting my veins. My second plaything was waking and crawling over to join us. I cut eyes to her to keep her from interrupting. The blonde was doing her work well. I would meet this dumpster fire of a day with my skin thrumming.

"There will be no noble bloodline if they keep dying before they bear young," I said through clenched teeth. "Find women who have lived in the darkness before. My blood is noble enough for both of us."

Ghere hesitated.

He was threatening to stifle my pleasure, so I let the power rise with the blood coursing in my veins and snapped a thread of compulsion at him—just a bare taste. But his breath rushed out of him and he bowed so low his hair brushed the tops of his feet.

"Yes… yes… of course."

"Do it now."

He scurried from the room as quickly as he'd arrived and I turned my full attention to the women.

Or tried to.

Something itched at the base of my skull.

Frustration.

Anger.

And something… shakier. But I shook it off. We'd already been through this twice before.

Women killed themselves every day in the modern human world. One more sad story wouldn't cause so much as a ripple in the thin veil that guarded our world from theirs.

I wouldn't let myself be disturbed. I'd find her, the woman capable of this. I would force her to submit, bear an heir with her and no longer be tormented by the clock ticking over my head. The clock that counted down to my defeat.

"What's wrong, Cazz?" the dark-haired toy whispered, coming to kneel next to me and leaning in to kiss my chest while her friend continued sucking me.

I hadn't compelled either of them this morning. Yet the blonde was remarkably dedicated to her task.

But despite her talent, my thoughts were too disturbed to let me focus. We'd played late into the night, so I was sleep-deprived. And now I was… tense.

And I had things to do.

"Fucking human women," I muttered. "You're always more trouble than you're worth."

Thrusting into the blonde's mouth, ordering her not to gag—her body would obey me, even to the point of stopping her heart if I instructed it—I took a handful of the brunette's hair and tugged her head back to bear her throat.

"Do you know why I bother?" I whispered to her.

She shook her head as best she could with the grip I had on her. She gasped as I leaned over her, pulling her head back until the tendons on her neck stood proud.

Her breath hissed in and out of her teeth and her chest rose and fell quickly. Unable to lift her head from my grip, she followed my progress with her eyes as I opened my mouth over that vein, pulsing thick, hot blood just under the surface of her flawless skin.

I latched on, sucking hard, needing to leave a mark. But I wouldn't let her relax into the pleasure of my touch thinking there was no danger. I let my teeth graze her skin and she shuddered.

Then I kissed the skin, laving it with my tongue to soothe the pain where the beads of blood rose.

"Every time a human submits to me, my power grows," I murmured breathlessly, the combination of the blonde's attentions and this toy's fear ensuring that my body was prickling with promised pleasure. I was beginning to sweat.

"I s-submit!" the brunette gasped. "I do!"

I tipped my head, staring down at her and her eyes widened further.

"You do," I murmured, pretending to soothe her.

"I'll always submit," she breathed. "Always. I'm here for you, Cazz. You can trust me."

A jolt of pleasure from the blonde's ministrations rocked through me and my eyes closed. I tipped my forehead against the brunette's, my breath rushing between my teeth and over her face.

"And you human bitches also… confuse lust… with love…" I growled. "Every. Fucking. Time." I dropped her hair, but whipped the hand around to close it on her throat, squeezing hard enough that her eyes bulged. "I don't need a lover," I hissed. "I need a fucking bitch in heat."

She opened her mouth but no sound came out.

"I didn't compel you, so why did you ask me what was wrong?" I snarled.

She was trying to shake her head, but I had her neck clamped in my hand, just one hair away from cutting off her air.

"Every fucking one of you decides that you have given your heart, and then you break, and then you die. I am *sick* of your failure."

I closed my eyes as the blonde redoubled her efforts and my body responded. For a moment I couldn't speak. But then I opened my eyes and caught the terrified gaze of the brunette.

"Good thing you're delicious," I rasped.

The brunette gave a little sob and my orgasm detonated at the base of my spine.

2. All Hail the King

"Beware those who come to you in sheep's clothing but inwardly are ravenous wolves."
- Gospel of Matthew 7:15

~ *JESSE* ~

The guards tipped us out into the room like puppies out of a bag.

I landed heavily on rough stone, scraping my knees and palms, hissing against the pain. But they'd freed my hands and ankles before they shoved me in here, so, with my heart thudding in my chest, I scrabbled to pull down the blindfold that was over my eyes and get my bearings quickly.

Dark room. Stone walls and ceiling. Warm lights. Cold air. Damp. Shadows my eyes couldn't penetrate—and more shadows behind us I wished they couldn't.

Left and right, women shrieked and sobbed, hitting the floor, some rolling, one planting face-first into the rock and laying there, unmoving.

Behind me, a cluster of guards filled the doorway, with more spreading out along the wall. They didn't carry weapons, but they didn't need to. They were all well over six foot and huge with it. Strong and rugged... feral. Brows and jaws heavy, and bodies that moved in that fiercely controlled way the wolves had that was riveting and terrifying at the same time.

So, when a low voice muttered, "Really? This is the best you could do?" and the guards shrank like they wanted to disappear through the wall, I whipped my head back around to see who was capable of scaring these monsters.

Then I couldn't breathe.

The back of the room was swathed in deep shadows so that at first it was difficult to make anything out. But as I blinked and tried to breathe, slowly he became clear, walking towards us out of the dark like an apparition manifesting out of hell itself.

He stood easily as tall as the guards, his shoulders just as broad and draped in thick fur from an open vest that fell almost to his knees. His chest was bare revealing warm-brown skin, the wide, flat planes of his pecs, and rippling abs so defined they cast their own shadows.

He stood staring down his nose imperiously at everyone in the room, one side of his upper lip pulled up in smug derision, and yet, somehow the ugly expression only emphasized the razor edge of his jaw, the full lips, and the dark hair that fell in loose waves around his face and to dust his collar at the back.

But that wasn't what made my lungs deflate.

His eyes glowed.

Incredible, stunning eyes, a blue so deep and shining it should have felt like staring into the waters of a tropical ocean. And yet those eyes were coldly cruel. Arctic waters, deep and flickering with shadows. Yet, glowing like moonlight through a sheet of ice.

Like all humans, I'd heard myths about the Wolf King and his packs—mostly the kind that were whispered at sleepovers or around a campfire. But as I watched him materialize out of the darkness, it was suddenly clear that those were not stories at all.

This man was very, very real.

Something deep and primal screamed that a predator was stalking me. Pushing to my feet, ready to run, I was forced to watch him because there was no room to move, stumbling back a step as he advanced on us, the dull, warm light that bathed half the room from lanterns on the walls finally falling on him, cutting hollows into cheeks shadowed by stubble and revealing him more clearly.

In the shadows he looked almost tribal—all leather and fur, with three necklaces at his throat.

But in the light, the perfect cut of his pants became clear, the sheen of soft, durable leather, the thick lushness of the fur around his shoulders, and intelligent disdain in those eyes that scanned each of us with such impatience...

This was no animalistic warrior.

Beast he might be, but he was a King. He exuded a fiercely masculine presence. A weight, as if the air around him was thicker. And a tingling, fascinating glimmer of power, light on the horizon that flickered in the corner of your vision, but disappeared when you turned to see it.

I couldn't take my eyes off of him.

And my guts trembled.

The creak of leather and rustle of heavy weights moving behind us told me the guards were all bowing, or offering some kind of acknowledgement to him. But he ignored them, instead scanning each of the women—there were eight of us—his expression growing more and more contemptuous with each passing moment.

"What the fuck is this mess?"

"They're from the poor neighborhoods, as you requested," one man, presumably the leader of the guards, offered tentatively.

Male. I had to remind myself, they called themselves males, not men.

Then the guy's words sank in and I bristled.

Indeed, they were not men. Taking women like commodities, herding them like sheep.

When I'd been thrown into their arms I'd been certain I was about to die.

Or worse.

It had taken hours of pretending to be asleep or catatonic with fear, to catch enough snippets of conversations between the guards to understand that they were wolves. And that I was one of what they called a Reaping.

That none of them would touch us, as long as we obeyed.

Not because they were honorable thieves, or had any scruples. But because we had to be untouched. Because we'd been chosen for the King.

I'd hoped I had that part wrong.

Clearly I didn't.

A snarl ripped through the room and the King bared his teeth.

The women around me cried out, or sobbed, all of them curling in on themselves, turning back and forth, shrinking from the King, but unwilling to get closer to the guards behind us, either. They turned impotent circles, shaking and crying. One even wailed like a child.

SILENCE.

I jolted as the word echoed inside my skull just as clearly as his voice had echoed in the tall chamber around us a moment earlier, an eerie thrust of power with it.

And the room obeyed.

All of it. All of us. Every one.

The noises from the terrified women stopped as if someone had muted the television.

I'd already been quiet, but I felt the conviction settle in my chest. I would not speak. My jaw clenched of its own accord, and any words on my tongue faded like smoke on the wind.

Then he looked around, those incredible eyes glittering with frustration and something I couldn't identify, and it was as if the air shifted.

Four of the women were still on hands and knees, bodies convulsing with tears, shaking with terror. Two had made it to their feet like me, but remained hunched. Cowering.

And one still lay unconscious where she'd fallen when the guards dumped her in the room.

The King shook his head slowly, then sighed, as if he carried a great weight.

"There's no need to cry. You have nothing to fear," he crooned. And then he smiled and the world tilted.

Power wafted off of him like a rich perfume, rippling as he moved and I felt myself changed.

My body thrilled.

He was King. He was male. He was everything I had ever wanted. The earth answered his voice and the sky stormed at his bidding.

Awed and breathless, everything within me ached to throw myself at his feet.

I wrestled it with the corner of my mind that understood that something was happening, something outside my control. That the thoughts suddenly clamoring in my head, admiring his beauty and strength, hadn't started in my mind.

And yet... I wanted him. Wanted to slide hands up his torso, curl fingers into his hair. I ached to hear that deep voice hushed in my ear, to feel those hands on my body.

My mind overflowed with images that stole my breath.

Images of him in the dark, our bodies entwined. Images of him in the light, standing over me and staring murder at any that would harm me. Images of him smiling, laughing, sultry and sweet, then dark and demanding, eyes glowing and breath hot—

14

I blinked, more terrified than I'd been even when the guards took me because while they might have forced my body, this man—this male—could control my mind?

I felt the desire to kneel before him like a hand planted between my shoulder-blades, yet no one was close enough to touch me. I shook with it, watched the woman to my right who'd made it to her feet, drop to her knees, then bow herself, face almost to the floor, as she crawled towards him, eyes shining and jaw slack.

He watched her come, tipping his head, though his expression remained blank. And then she reached a trembling hand toward the toe of his boot, her breath heaving in her chest like she was seeing the face of God.

My knees almost gave, my body wanted to give in. I wanted to tear her away from him and put myself in her place—

Please, I begged God. *Please... I can't...*

The King's sneer returned and he glided back a step, out of the woman's reach.

And just like that, the spell was broken. Nothing in the room had changed, and yet everything was different.

The women around me all froze, blinking, as if coming out of sleep.

I shook my head, more scared than I had ever been in my life.

That power he held... that compulsion... the intensity of it. Dear god, if he'd held that thrall a few more seconds I would have fallen to it as well.

We'd all heard the stories of his unquestioned authority, of his influence over others. But what I had just seen wasn't persuasive. It wasn't even intimidation. That was *control.*

He *possessed* others?

A cold chill prickled, like death breathing down my neck.

I looked at the women around me and saw it in their eyes... even as their minds cleared, even as they shuddered and breathed again... they'd stopped crying, stopped struggling. Even as their fear returned, something in them was drawn to him. Their eyes flicked to his face again and again, and they worried at their clothing as if they were suddenly self-conscious. A piece of that had stayed with them. A piece of them now belonged to him.

They had given in.

I began to tremble uncontrollably, my head screaming, my heart pounding so loudly it was all I could hear, drums beating in my ears.

I would not be a puppet to any man—any male—ever.

I could not lose myself to this!

When his eyes fell on me and he smiled so I could see the predator in him. I flinched.

Then he shifted his gaze to the others and I slumped.

"Now that we're all a little calmer... Welcome to the Sifting," he said, his voice low and gravelly as he scanned each of us in turn. One of the women sighed. "Before this day is done, one of you will be my mate."

He sounded like the idea made him want to vomit.

3. A B*tch in Heat

~ *CASIMIR* ~

I was horrified.

When I'd told Ghere to order the Reapers to find women from the human slums I had imagined the wicked types, like my toys. The women who embraced their fate and it made them bold. Instead I'd been sent a box of poorly bred puppies suitable only for drowning?

What the actual fuck?

"God help us," one of them murmured.

I snorted.

"I assure you, God abandoned this place long ago," I drawled.

The woman looked at me, shocked. It was the one at the center who'd stayed on her feet. She'd been staring around the chamber in horror, murmuring to herself, clearly forgetting that we wolves enjoyed heightened senses.

She remembered now.

The guards laughed, but the women's eyes snapped down to her feet. She dropped her chin. Her hair, a rich mahogany brown, the kind that would spark red in sunlight, fell around her face in long waves, though it was messy and matted now.

She was a thin little thing, though there was evidence of muscle under those terribly fitting clothes.

Then—noting the tear at the neckline of her shirt—I started paying attention. Which made me scan the others and grind my teeth. The Reapers clearly hadn't been gentle.

I cursed again. None of the women were even clean. I saw torn shirts, ripped jeans, even bruises. And one of them had hit the floor and remained there, as if she were already dead.

"Who is responsible for this shitshow?" I growled to Ghere below the hearing of the humans.

The male stepped up to my side, responding in kind so they wouldn't hear us. "Khush led this foray," he muttered.

"Order ten lashes. I asked for women who'd met darkness, not poorly freighted dolls."

"Consider the restrictions, Casimir: those who are virgins at this age are likely more timid in their approach to life."

"Timid? These women are helpless." Some of them, including the one who'd stared at me, looked malnourished. I was tempted to simply send them back and tell the Reapers to try again—with more stringent instructions on who and how to select targets. "Are they even fertile?"

"Impossible to know for certain with virgins, of course. But we know they all cycle regularly," Ghere provided.

I shook my head. "Look at the bruises on that one."

"I believe some of them fought—"

"I don't give a shit, Ghere. You want me to believe the guards couldn't control these frail birds without tearing their clothes?"

The male hesitated, obviously wanting to correct me, but unwilling to risk my ire.

I rolled my eyes and gestured at him to speak—I wouldn't punish him for raising truth, if he had it. But how the fuck was I supposed to name a mate from among these pitiful creatures without walking straight into yet another failure?

But Ghere must have read my wave to proceed as the signal to begin the rite, because he stepped forward and cleared his throat.

"Ladies, I know the day has been difficult, but I assure you, you are safe here. The King Himself, Casimir Augustus Klane, is here to greet and assess you. Despite our, er, unconventional beginning, I hope you understand that it is a great honor to stand here today. The King of Wolves seeks a mate. A human mate. You alone have been selected from among your kind for his consideration."

I was considering very little. If this was the best the human race had to offer, we were all in much deeper trouble than I had imagined.

"A mate?" the same woman asked quietly. "I thought... the stories said he was already mated?"

Ghere opened his mouth to reply, but I spoke first. No point avoiding the truth. "She died," I said baldly.

"May… may I ask how?" Her eyes were wary, but accusing. She was brave, this one. The others were all staring at the floor, though two of them seemed to still be at least partially in the thrall of the compulsion, because their eyes were glazed, and one was loosening a button at her throat.

I raised a brow, partly-amused, partly-impressed. "She suffered a mental breakdown and killed herself," I said with a warning smile. The woman blinked. "Being the Wolf King's mate comes with many privileges. But few humans are strong enough to live in my world. Hence, the Sifting."

Ghere leaped in then, as if he was afraid I'd give away too much. "Of course, we will provide everything you need to advance in this process. The King only wishes to identify which of you is most likely to thrive."

Thrive? These women didn't know the word existed. I stopped listening as Ghere continued to explain the process of the rite, the tests and challenges, and their role in them.

I was fast determining that this entire idea had been a poor one. These women didn't even have the *physical* strength to live here, let alone to keep up with me. Chances that they'd be capable of enduring the inevitable trials to come were miniscule.

The women's eyes grew wider as Ghere explained the wealth and opportunity that would be afforded to them, as well as the expectation of delivering an heir, and a second child to ensure the succession of the throne.

The two who hadn't shaken the compulsion began to shiver and stare at me with hopeful eyes.

I'd barely touched them with the power, but their minds were so weak, they were already more than half mine. It was pathetic.

"…our main concern is for your wellbeing," Ghere went on kindly. "The King's power relies on his utter domination of the packs. But especially those highest in the ranks of the hierarchy… which includes his mate. I am aware that your human society does not function similarly—but please, understand… the power you felt from Casimir when you entered was only a taste. He is the most potent ruler the wolves have enjoyed for centuries. You will not need to worry for your safety or provision. Our King is… formidable."

One of the women who'd given over to the compulsion shuddered and clutched a hand to her chest.

Holy fuck. Weak didn't cover it.

"Actually, Ghere, I think this has been a mistake," I said abruptly, interrupting him. "I don't believe my mate is here."

I began to turn away, muttering to him under their hearing. "These minds are far too weak. It's a waste of my time. We need a new pool."

"But, look, Casimir!" Ghere grabbed my sleeve, pulling me back to face them. "They're receptive, see? You've always said that a willing partner is worth more than someone who must be... urged."

It was true. I had. But only when their commitment rose from strength in themselves. Not wounded puppies who rolled over and showed their bellies to the Alpha with tails wagging.

I could see that the two women who'd never fully released from my power were beyond willing. They were already halfway in love. Which was our entire problem with these humans. This would not do.

"The position of Queen requires three things," I snapped impatiently. Let them hear the terms and reject them, then we could move on and find a new group of women. "Firstly, the ability to bear heirs. Secondly, submission to me as King and Mate. And third, acceptance that I will not offer love. Love is a sacrifice of self. My power relies on dominance. It weakens when I yield to another. I cannot offer it and remain King."

I was growing impassioned, so I stopped for a moment and took a breath, dropping my voice for the women who were all listening avidly. I met their eyes one by one until I landed on the warm-haired beauty who'd spoken up.

"My Queen will receive anything material she wishes. But she will submit to me, and I *will not bow*. She will share my bed, my power, and my wealth. She will not share my heart."

I'd been glaring down at them, impatient and determined. I lifted my chin and waited, but none of them spoke.

Good.

Too weak—or perhaps, strong enough only to see that they had frail hearts in desperate needs of the affirmation of a male's—

"What happens to the others?" the mahogany-haired one asked quickly. "You have eight women here. What happens to the other seven when you... when you choose?"

I smiled. "I assure you, mate or not, by the time the sifting is complete, all of you will *desire* to stay here with me. And if I find you appealing, I will not turn you away." Though, looking at this lot, most of them would be thrown back to their own world. I wasn't interested.

Ghere nudged me, but the two who'd already given themselves both looked ecstatic.

The one whose hair was so rich and warm frowned at the floor, her eyes flitting back and forth as if she searched her mind, her lips moving though she made no sound.

She was a strange little thing—courageous to speak to me without permission. She might be fun to break if she turned out to be strong-willed.

Ghere was dry-washing his hands, looking at each of the women in turn, clearly nervous about the direction this had taken. I wasn't sure why.

He cleared his throat. "As you've heard the King explain—"

"Are you violent?"

I turned back to the woman with a flat smile. "Show me a wolf who isn't. And I am the King of the others. What do you think?"

Her throat bobbed. The tear in the neckline of her cotton shirt offered a fleeting glimpse of plump cleavage. My cock twitched.

"I meant... I meant with women... um, Sire," she said uncertainly. "With your Queen. You said you have to dominate, that she has to submit. What is she submitting to?"

An image flashed in my head of that day just weeks ago when my second mate had killed herself. I'd had my toys, one of them by the neck.

I smirked. "I don't make a habit of leaving bruises," I said, letting a dark promise seep into my tone. "But they've been known to happen."

The woman flinched and I sighed, rolling my eyes. "I take no sexual pleasure from violence. I am a wolf, not a beast. A loyal, submitted female has no reason to fear me."

It was, perhaps, a *stretching* of the truth. But the woman looked relieved.

I was intrigued. Of them all, she'd shown the strongest spine when I compelled them. Not that that was any guarantee. The last two had been the strongest in their bunches as well, and look where that had gotten me.

Dark frustration washed through me again as I looked over this group of thin, dirty women and I shook my head. "Ghere, this is pointless—"

"I'll volunteer," the mahogany-haired one said quietly.

"You see," Ghere nudged my side nervously. "One offers to be sifted already. I'm sure the others will as well. There is no need to—"

"No," she said, then licked her lips and stepped forward. "I volunteer to be your mate."

4. Fascinating

~ JESSE ~

As I'd listened to the King's pompous tirade, it had become clearer and clearer to me that it was not just bad luck that I was here.

The question was, would I step out of the flames of one man's making, and straight into another? Or was this truly an opportunity for escape?

"I will be your mate… if you'll have me."

The King's eyes narrowed.

His servant's brows rose and he raised his hands. "Oh, I don't think you understood—"

"Why?" the King asked, his voice deep and skeptical. But I didn't miss the glimmer in his eyes. I'd surprised him.

I swallowed hard and prayed I'd understood all of this correctly. "I think… I know, I can give you what you want. And in exchange, you can give me what I need."

The King's brows rose then. "How very presumptuous of you. But I will take the bait: What is it that you want?"

"I propose… an exchange."

"Of what?"

"You take me as your mate and you keep me safe like you promised. Away from my world and… and anyone I knew. When I bear you an heir, you give me a house somewhere remote. Somewhere no one can find me. A couple of servants to run it and enough money to live modestly. You can have your family, and I can have solitude. And... and safety."

His eyes narrowed again. "Why would you offer yourself to this? To me, when I have not compelled you to do so?"

I hesitated, but couldn't find any reason to hide the truth. "Because you're the first man I've met with the power to free me from all the others."

The King stared at me as if I'd confused him. He tilted his head, his eyes pinning me to the floor. I was terrified he was about to unleash that power on me and steal me from myself.

I couldn't let it happen.

"I have terms, though," I blurted.

The King looked indignant—also a little amused. "You think you're in a position to set *terms?*"

I hurried on, praying he'd listen. "No violence. At all," I said, swallowing the pinch that was rising in my throat. "If I'm going to get pregnant, I can't be hurt. And... until I'm pregnant, you only have sex with me. No one else. You give me every chance to... to bear you the heir." The King snorted and fear jittered through me. "If you do, I'll submit. Truly. You won't have to use that... that power. I will do anything you say. I'll give myself to you. Willingly. Like... like a slave."

The room was silent except for our voices so at that word I could hear him suck in a breath. Flames flickered in his eyes—fire beneath the ice.

"Slave?" he rumbled.

I nodded, hands clenched at my sides, praying. Because it was better to humble myself than to be forced to it. I couldn't let him steal my mind. I had to keep myself. I knew if he used that awful power on me, I would lose myself completely with time.

"You said... you said your power was about dominance?"

"Yes."

"Well, surely, if someone gives themselves willingly... That must offer you more power? More than if you have to... make them?"

His face went open with shock, his brows rising as if they'd climb into his hair.

"You promise me a home after you have your heir, and that you'll never hurt me, or use that... that power on me. And I will give you everything you've asked. If I don't, well... it sounds like I'd be dead anyway."

He was still gaping, but as if he'd caught himself doing it, his eyes suddenly hooded and his mouth snapped shut. "That you would," he muttered.

I nodded. "So... what do you have to lose?"

*****

~ CASIMIR ~

It was a fascinating proposal.

The moment she'd said she'd give herself to me willingly, my cock had twitched. Then, when she named herself a slave... my power *surged.* Even now, it raged in my veins as if it could reach through my skin to take her.

It was impossible, and yet, it couldn't be denied. Her choice to submit sent power coursing through me.

What would it do when she actually gave over?

Without compulsion?

I'd never thought... never even considered...

Fascinating.

I had to work not to swallow like a boy at his first mating. "And if you defy me?" I asked, indulging myself, because all I wanted was to know what she'd say—and see how it affected my power.

She raised her chin. Her expression was sad. "I won't defy you. I'm sacrificing myself to you. But in the end... in the end it's your choice. If I ever say no... well, it's not like I could fight you. Or your power. I'd be trusting you to... to keep your word."

"You can't actually be considering this?" Ghere hissed at me below the humans hearing, through unmoving lips. "What about the rite?"

"The rite hasn't worked for us so far," I snarled back.

Her eyes hadn't left me.

She was too small, too thin, too wiry—though I suspected all of that would change if she was properly fed. And yet...

When our eyes locked, a jolt of desire and a correlating wave of power washed through me.

A slave. She would *make herself* my slave? Willingly?

"Do we have an agreement?" she asked, her voice shaking as if she were losing her courage.

"We certainly do."

Every wolf in the room gasped, but I couldn't have cared less what they thought.

I didn't take my eyes from hers—hazel eyes, I realized. Brown at the center, bleeding to a soft, gray-green at the outside of the iris. I inhaled, picking out her scent from the crowd, drinking it down.

She would be my mate.

She would be my Queen.

She would *choose to* be my slave.

I physically shuddered. God, I was going to come.

Without breaking eye contact with her, I snapped my fingers. "Take the others away and bring the Cleric," I muttered.

Ghere bowed stiffly, then gestured to the guards, who immediately gathered up the other women—shrieking, crying, some pleading for me.

But I barely heard them.

As the room filled with the noise of moving bodies, of guards muttered orders, and women's cries, my new mate's eyes widened.

"Cleric?" she asked hesitantly. As if she were afraid of the answer.

I frowned. "Did you think we would conceive the royal heir out of wedlock?"

5. What's in a Name?

"Therefore what God has joined together,
let no man separate."
- Mark 10:9

~ *JESSE* ~

I stood there, stunned, while the guards cleared the room. The King spoke briefly with the man who'd been at his side this entire time, then he gestured to me.

"We have a short time before the Cleric arrives. You should bathe."

The words seemed so alien in the middle of this surreal and terrifying day, for a moment I just stared at him. But he either didn't notice my stunned silence, or didn't care. Because he and the man turned and started toward the end of the room from which he'd first arrived.

A moment later, realizing I had no choice, I stumbled after them.

The two men never spoke to me, though the King looked over his shoulder a few times to make sure I was following, and his servant tried to give me an encouraging smile that just more terrifying than when they weren't looking at me.

At the end of the room we'd been in there was a door that led into a wide corridor—much more obviously a cave tunnel than the other rooms we'd been in. The ceiling was rounded and the space clearly cut out of the rock.

I walked after them, staring around. There was no one behind me. I could have fled, darted down the hallway back into that room, or tried one of these other large wooden doors we were passing. But their casual acceptance that it wasn't a risk to leave me to follow only affirmed my conviction that while the King wasn't actually watching me, he'd know the moment I tried to flee, and I wouldn't make it more than a few steps.

He walked with the casual grace of the predator, and even in the hubbub of that crowd of people he'd heard me mutter to myself. This wasn't a man I could easily flee.

If I tried to run now, I'd probably be dead before I reached that room.

Still talking quietly, the two men led me to a small chamber off the hall, like a bathroom in a cave. It was a small, elongated semi-circle shape with rounded walls and ceiling. Small lanterns nestled in tiny self-alcoves in the wall all the way around a huge bathtub, already full and steaming—how had they done that? The copper basin was easily big enough for two people—even if one of them was a large wolf-man, which made me nervous what he thought was going to happen right now.

But as soon as I stepped inside, the servant opened a small, freestanding cupboard against the wall and brought out two massive, fluffy towels, and some soap.

"You'll have about twenty minutes," the King drawled. "I trust that is enough time to... improve yourself." He smirked.

I gave him a flat look, then took the towels. "I'll do my best."

He nodded as if that was only expected. "I will prepare for the vows. Ghere will remain outside. You can call him if you have need of anything."

"I... okay."

He turned on his heel and started for the door and it seemed so strange to look at him—the man was about to become my husband—and I knew nothing about him except that he was beautiful and cold.

"Wait," I said quickly, lifting one hand.

He stopped abruptly, then turned to look at me, his forehead pinched with disapproval.

"What?" he asked impatiently.

I swallowed. "What... what do I call you?"

He smirked. "Majesty? Lord? Master? You can choose."

My heart sank and frantic fear began to chitter in my head. I wasn't sure I could do this.

"We're going to get married and… and mate and… you want me to call you *Master?*"

He sighed and folded his arms, his lips twisting as if he was considering me. "My name is Casimir. Those who are… intimate, call me Cazz. You may. If you wish."

"Cazz-uh-meer?" I asked hesitantly.

He nodded. "And you are?"

"Jesse," I said, and had to swallow a humorless, hysterical laugh as it came home to me that I was *introducing myself* to a man that I was about to vow my life to.

He frowned. "Isn't that a male name among your kind?"

Why did that make me bristle? "It's… it's both."

His forehead pinched again, but then he sighed as if he didn't care enough to pursue it. "Well, Jesse, our time ticks away. Please, clean up as best you can. I will have a gown brought for you in twenty minutes, and then we'll return to the chamber for the vows."

I nodded, speechless with his casual reference to what was going to amount to our wedding.

"Do you prefer hair up or hair down?" I asked quietly as he turned away again. And this time he froze for a moment before turning back to me again slowly, looking at me suspiciously like he was anticipating a trap.

"What did you say?"

I frowned. "I was asking if you'd prefer my hair up or my hair down? For the vows?"

His eyes narrowed. "Why would you ask me that?"

I was confused. "You're going to be my husband. This is our wedding, right?" How ridiculous that sounded coming out of my mouth. I didn't even know this man! "I… I guess I thought you might have a preference?"

He glanced at the servant who was watching our exchange nervously, then returned his gaze to me, scanned me once, from head to toe, then back up.

"Hair up," he said suddenly. "I'll have some combs and clips brought with the gown." Then his voice dropped to a deep, silky gruffness. "I'll enjoy taking it down for you."

A clench of heat gripped me low in my belly. A shocking jolt behind the fear and confusion. His eyes remained on mine, that eerie glow behind them flaring, though I didn't feel any of that horrific power coming off of him, thank God. Then with a small, lopsided smile he turned again and prowled out of the door.

I was left standing there with his servant.

A moment later the man sort of flinched, then stepped forward like he was leaping to it. "I'll leave you," he said, ducking his head without meeting my eyes.

"I'm sorry… but what's your name?" I asked him quickly as he darted for the door. He drew to a halt, one hand on the handle of it, turning only his head and smiling at me. "I'm Ghere."

"Gear?"

He nodded. "And might I say, Jesse, that I think… I think I am looking forward to this."

"To what?"

He looked out the door like he was checking that no one was there, then he whispered, just loud enough for me to hear. "To seeing someone offer him… humanity."

He was still smiling when he bowed his head quickly, then left, closing the door behind him and leaving me alone.

6. Give You My Word

~ *JESSE* ~

When Casimir had used the word "Cleric" I'd imagined some stuffy old man in a suit with a black collar—like a priest.

Instead, the man—wolf—who showed up was young, handsome, and vital. I couldn't have picked him out of the guards if they'd lined up.

Maybe all the wolves were like that? Big, strong, *hot?*

I'd heard the legends about women having wolf-lovers before, but again, it was always a whispered story at a sleepover, or someone's fantasy fiction. A naughty, forbidden kind of story. Never something I'd taken seriously.

But after I'd hurriedly bathed, surprised by the pleasant smell of the soap that felt different in my hands to what I was used to, and twisted up my hair as best I could with only a small mirror and dim light, and put on the strange-but-beautiful dress that Ghere handed me through the door. When Ghere led me back to the first chamber where Casimir had appeared, it occurred to me that, perhaps, all these stories I'd heard weren't fiction at all.

I couldn't imagine any of these men being left alone if they appeared in public in my world. Any one of them would turn heads. And Casimir was... stunning. Terrifying, too. But if I hadn't seen him use that power, if I'd just looked at him, he'd dry the roof of my mouth.

He'd changed his clothes and now stood in a slim-fitting black tunic-jacket that looked like it belonged in some historical romance. But it also revealed that he was every bit as powerfully built as he'd appeared.

The fur vest he'd been wearing before hadn't increased his size, only complemented it.

He wore tight fitting black boots, beige pants that clung to the muscles on his thighs, and a white shirt, open at the throat, but otherwise very stiff—the collar stood high and cuffs with cufflinks peeked out of the jacket sleeves whenever he raised an arm.

The jacket itself was embroidered in thin gold and silver thread that blinked and flashed in the low light whenever he moved. At first I'd thought it was just a pattern, some kind of design. But when I was ushered to the front of the room to stand next to him, I realized the embroidery depicted scenes—wolves hunting, wolves fighting, and men… men taking women.

I swallowed and prayed.

I'd done my best to make myself look good with the things they'd given me. The dress was strange, but beautiful—light and airy so that I barely felt the weight of it. Thin spaghetti straps held a wide round neck that dipped low enough to bare my collarbones and show a hint of cleavage at the front, and below my shoulder-blades at the back. It was gathered at front and back, but the beautiful, flowing material and the way it had been cut meant that even though it was technically a loose dress, it fell against my body, cascading from my breasts and hips in ways that were almost suggestive.

Casimir's eyes blazed when he caught sight of me approaching, and I was half flattered and half terrified by the sudden hunger in his gaze.

"No longer the dirty puppy, but suddenly very much a woman," he growled approvingly.

I just stared at him, still taking in the subtle images on that jacket. He raised one brow and opened his arms, turning slowly for me. "Do I meet with my Queen's approval?" he asked smugly, not a hint of doubt in his tone.

I nodded, but was still swallowing the choking fear that punched me right in the guts the moment I'd entered the room, because holy shit, this was actually happening.

There was the wolf he'd called a Cleric—dark haired, dark eyes, broad shoulders, and a gaze that seemed to see everything, and approve of little. There was Ghere, standing behind Casimir, also in a new suit, though nothing as fine as the King's. And there were several other wolves milling around near the door where we'd been brought in here, to be witnesses, Ghere had said.

No women. No females at all.

My knees felt like they might give.

Then the Cleric cleared his throat and called all the others to pay attention. His eyes cut between me and Casimir, dark and disapproving, but he made a hasty introduction of why we were there that wasn't unlike how I imagined a real wedding in my world would go. Except, without the smiling and hope.

Every man—male—here was focused and attentive, but the feeling in the room was as if we were there for a business meeting. Everyone concentrating on reaching a goal, but no one even remotely emotional about it.

I stared at Casimir, whose gaze was raking up and down my form, his smile growing more predatory every second. My heart raced, then pounded, until it felt like it was trying to flee my chest.

But then I realized all eyes were on me, including the Cleric's.

"I… I'm sorry…what?"

The Cleric glanced at Casimir, but spoke to me. "Do you honor the King as Dominant?"

"I… yes?"

"And do you accept him as mate, embracing your fate both together, and apart?"

"Yes…"

"Do you open yourself without reservation, accepting the bond and stepping to the throne with the duty and honor required of the role?"

"I do."

"Will you serve your people, your mate, and husband, without hesitation?"

"Yes."

The Cleric's eyes grew darker, as if he was angry, and I couldn't figure out why.

Casimir looked hungry, but otherwise bored.

"And will you give yourself without boundary, give your womb to produce the heir, and your body as a vessel to the King until the day of your death?"

I blinked.

Casimir's eyes, which had been lingering on my breasts, suddenly snapped up to my face and he went very still.

Our gazes locked and my breath got thinner, faster.

Body as vessel.

Womb for the heir.

Given. Taken. No boundaries.

I started to shake. But there was no choice. No other option. He'd kill me now if I didn't say yes—and frankly, I'd rather be dead than go back home after all of this.

So, I released the breath that was tense in my lungs and held Casimir's eye-contact. "I will," I said, as clearly as I could, glad that there was only a small tremor in my voice.

7. Bound

~ JESSE ~

Behind Casimir, Ghere relaxed, like he'd been holding his breath.

The Cleric's jaw flexed.

Several wolves who'd been watching, chuckled or grunted.

But then it hit me: It was done. I'd done it. I'd vowed myself to him until the day of my death.

Nerves trilled in my chest. Should I be glad, or would I soon want to hurry eternity along?

Only time would tell.

I was in a fog, barely hearing as the Cleric led Casimir in a vow of protection of my person and my throne, promising to use his power to uphold me as Alpha Female, and to give me the heir.

And then…

"…And will you give yourself to her as a vessel, your body for hers, serving her pleasure?"

Casimir's eyes narrowed and blazed. "I will."

The Cleric raised his voice slightly. "And do the Witnesses agree and let the vows bind? Do you accept her as his mate? Do you bow to her as your Queen?"

"We do," they growled in unison.

And something in my chest flared.

I sucked in a breath, swaying forward as something came alive inside me—a curling heat that seared a hole in my heart, but immediately filled it as well.

I could barely breathe and clutched a hand to my chest, pressing on the place, right at the center, where it felt as if the bottom had just fallen out of my world—only to be stuffed full of sensation and darkness and light and…

I blinked and staggered.

Casimir quickly took my upper arms in his hands. His lips were moving, his brows heavy and forehead pinched. He was saying something, but I couldn't hear him.

But I could *feel* him.

Instinctively, I grabbed for him, fisting the front of his crisp, white shirt, swallowing, and trying to catch my breath as, inside me, something took shape. Something that was very clearly *him.*

Strength. Power. Determination. A roaring fire of need. And a hollow, bone-cold, echoing dark.

"Jesse?"

My head snapped up and our eyes locked. I was gripping his shirt in both hands now.

A flash of concern shifted behind his eyes, but he didn't move, still holding my upper arms like he was afraid I was about to fall.

I was about to fall.

He had no idea.

I was going to pitch headlong deep, deep inside that well of pain and darkness that was him.

It made me want to weep. It made me want to scream—could none of them see it? Feel it in him?

This man, this wolf… his heart was a wasteland. Empty, dusty, dark and cold.

And weeping.

I was blinking rapidly, my brain struggling to define the boundaries between what was me and what was him. For moments I'd feel the desert of his heart, convinced it was mine. Then I'd feel myself again and look into the canyon of him as if I stood above it.

Back and forth, flickering between the urge to rush to him, to soothe him, and to run screaming, the urge to plead, and a crackling need that threatened sanity.

"Jesse?!"

His eyes were dark with something angry and afraid.

This man felt fear?

"Jesse, can you hear me?"

I nodded, still sucking at empty air, still trying to find my feet on the shifting sand under the line that danced between us.

And then… rushing, warming comfort. A third presence. There was another hand on me, on my shoulder, and it brought clarity. Brought strength. Drew the lines between Casimir's heart and mine so that I could see where I stopped and he began.

I looked up, startled, to find the Cleric, one hand clasping my shoulder, staring at me intently as his lips moved and I tried to take in what he was saying...

"...You are one. Two hearts made one. Before God, and wolf. Before male and female. Before time... you are one. What God brings together, let no creation tear apart."

I sucked in a deep, cleansing breath and came back to myself with a jolt.

Both Casimir and the Cleric were leaning closer, chins low, eyes intent.

But I'd found myself again—and I understood now. Understood why I was here and why God had let all of this happen and what He was asking me to do.

I shook my head, clearing the last of the fog.

"Jesse?" Casimir muttered. "Are you well?"

I nodded. "Yes. Yes... I just... this... inside me..."

"The bond," he growled.

I swallowed. "I can feel it."

"Good," he said, and even though his voice was tight, his grip on my arms softened. "Good."

There was a moment when everyone sort of waited, a hanging kind of silence, poised on the edge of action. Then the Cleric straightened and let go of my shoulder. Cazz didn't let go of me completely, but his fingers loosened, and his eyes...

The fire in those startling eyes was joined by a low, simmering warmth that I hadn't seen before.

"It is vowed, and it is witnessed," The Cleric said softly, his tone somehow defeated. "Let every man, every wolf, see and acknowledge the King and his Queen. Casimir Augustus Klane takes Jesse Hudson as his mate. What God brings together, let no earthly hand separate."

The wolves in the room repeated the line, and then everything went silent again.

The Cleric swallowed audibly. "Your Highnesses, as God's hand here, I declare you vowed. Mated. And married. Sire... you may kiss your bride."

I stared up at Cazz, sinking into those eyes, still breathless at what I could sense of him, of what his heart revealed, still reeling.

Casimir hesitated only a moment, one hand lifting from my arm to take my chin as he leaned in.

"God is not here," he muttered. "But we are." Then he lifted my chin and took my mouth in a slow, deep kiss that stole my breath all over again.

His lips, so full, softened against mine. His tongue flickered, teasing and tempting. And then, instead of pulling away, he sucked in a breath and tilted his head and pulled me up on my toes, into his chest, as he wrapped those steel arms around me and devoured me.

I was still gripping his shirt, trying desperately to catch my breath, but overwhelmed with the sensation of that kiss—the promise of it, the urgency and… something I couldn't define.

As if it was a place I was meant to be.

When Cazz sucked in and pulled away his hair was messy, falling over his face—had I done that?—and his chest was heaving. He stared at me, eyes wide and startled, the warm flames licking at the surface of the ice, as if they threatened to burn through.

Then he blinked, and that beautiful gaze shuttered like he'd slammed a door.

We were left clinging, staring, blinking.

And then he stepped back, eyes still locked on mine, but giving nothing, before he cleared his throat and turned, tearing his gaze from mine to the wolves gathered to witness.

"Leave us," he hissed, and I felt that power detonate from him.

Soundtrack for the following chapter is
Eternal Flame by Atom Music Audio, with Randall Jermaine and Alexa Ray.

8. Mine for the Taking

~ *CASIMIR* ~

This was my third vow-forged bond, and it never got easier, feeling my soul entwined with another like that. Each one had made my skin feel too tight, as if I wanted to claw out of it.

But this one... Jesse... dear *god*.

The moment the pack leaders acknowledged her as my mate and the bond was forged, I was ripped out of myself. Left flailing.

I fought as I'd fight a hurricane, leaning in and forcing my body to weather the pummeling blows that seemed to come from every direction at once.

Mate.

Wife.

Mother.

Soul.

Twisting, turning me, flipping my heart on its head like a babe in the ocean tide as I fought, wrestling for control of my own fate.

Because that was the source of my power—dominance always won. The more I owned, the more strength I gained.

That must be the difference this time—she'd come to the vow willingly, choosing it without compulsion from me. And so it struck as true and deep as a fated bond.

But the moment I got my head above those waves, it only plunged me back under the surface of *her*.

Gold, warm light that wanted to suck me in. A lush forest of a heart, bursting with life. Where cold and shadows existed, they retreated in the face of a blazing sun.

She fought, too. Ignorant and unprepared, the arctic desert of my soul threatened to suck her down.

I felt her fumble, felt her almost fall into the dank pit of my dead heart.

It was instinct to catch her, to keep her on her feet, to grip her and call for her…

As if she scrabbled at the edge, being pulled over into the unending dark of me, and I clasped her wrist, leaning with all my weight to bring her up and out of it, pleading with her to hear me and to fight.

And she did.

Fucking hell, did she fight.

Her eyes clamped on mine and her heart grasped mine and she fought the suck of that death hole.

And yet, for a moment it seemed we would lose.

I growled through my teeth, gripping her arms, demanding that she not let go, that she crawl up and out of the darkness within me that threatened to consume her already. But I wasn't certain I wouldn't lose her until Rake clamped a hand to her shoulder and leaned in, like the hand of God Himself, reaching for her, showing her the way through the forging of the bond—until I was almost tossed aside.

"…You are one. Two hearts made one. Before God, and wolf. Before male and female. Before time… you are one. What God brings together, let no creation tear apart."

Then, finally, she saw me, heard me, and I felt the braid of our souls snap tight.

The three of us made a triangle, and the wolf within me snarled a warning to Rake—he touched my mate!—but a smile threatened on Jesse's face, her beautiful lips tipping up at the corners as she shook her head and blinked rapidly.

"Jesse?" I muttered. "Are you well?"

She nodded. "Yes. Yes… I just… this… inside me…"

"The bond." The humans never understood it, never expected it.

"I can feel it." Her voice was hushed, awed.

"Good," I said, surprised by the jolt of relief that rocked through me. "Good."

I took hold of my power, though it wanted to slip through my hands suddenly, and Rake must have felt the rage growing in me at his hold on my mate, because he let go of her like he'd been burned.

I kept my eyes on hers, but held her more lightly, testing to see if she'd lose her feet. But she didn't. She'd almost lost her soul, but she stood her ground.

Fucking brilliant.

"It is vowed, and it is witnessed." Rake sounded like he was declaring the victory of the Devil, my wolf snarled. "Let every man, every wolf see and acknowledge, the King and his Queen. Casimir Augustus Klane takes Jesse Hudson as his mate. What God brings together, let no earthly hand separate."

The witnesses repeated the line, and then I could breathe.

"Your Highnesses," Rake ground out, his eyes blazing with a righteous anger that made me want to snap my teeth. "As God's hand here, I declare you vowed. Mated. And married. Sire... you may kiss your bride."

Jesse's eyes widened as I took her chin in one hand, pinching her chin gently between my thumb and forefinger.

She seemed still unsteady on her feet, but her eyes had focused and she was breathing again.

"God is not here," I warned her. "But we are."

Then I kissed her and almost lost my own soul.

I'd meant to take her. To own her. To brand her. Remind her and everyone else in the room that she was mine.

And yet... that first taste... like honey on my tongue.

Heedless of witnesses or any need beyond my own, I pulled her in and devoured the velvet joy of her mouth.

And, as if she felt the pull just as strongly as I did, she clung to my shirt, her fingers clawed and fisted as she leaned into my chest.

My body responded to her touch with such force, I was at risk of tearing that butterfly-fart of a dress off her with my bare hands and revealing her to all these male eyes.

Not fucking happening.

And so I pulled away, startled and off balance, my chest heaving to find her staring back at me looking as shocked as I felt.

Mine.

The thought was as undeniable as it was invasive.

And utterly counter-productive.

With every ounce of the power and strength I'd earned, I clawed back control, slamming the door on my heart and cutting her off from feeling anything more than my presence.

I blinked once, twice, breathing carefully, testing the strength of my own defense before stepping back, away from her.

And yet, I couldn't take my eyes off of her.

We remained locked together that way, even as I doused myself in cold, hard control.

I sucked in a breath to speak, to *demand* submission from the other males. And I would have it, whether they wished it or not.

"Leave us," I hissed. Rake stepped back immediately as I unleashed my power on all of the others at once… except her.

And when each of them yelped and retreated like reprimanded puppies, I swept her into my arms and carried her out, towards my chambers.

The bond had taken hold and my need could burn down the world.

9. The Need

~ *JESSE* ~

I'd flinched when that wave of power left him, felt the impact in my bones like a sonic boom. And yet, when I took a breath and blinked, I was still myself, while every man around me cowered or knelt, all their eyes on the floor, every head bowed. Except Rake.

As if the wolf had seen it coming, he'd stepped back and away, and was obviously untouched. Stunningly, so was I.

Cazz hadn't touched me with it.

I looked up at him, trembling. What was he doing?

He didn't even look at me, just swept me up like I weighed nothing and carried me from the room without a backward glance.

His breath was harsh in my ear as he stormed through the maze of tunnels and hallways outside. Voices raised in protest behind us. But he ignored them completely, one hand under my knees, the other curled at my ribs, his chin low and brows pinched, eyes glaring—and glowing again.

I would have felt afraid because he looked *enraged*. But from the moment he'd let go of that power, I could feel him again. Could sense the tangle of anger, jealousy, thrill and desire that twisted together inside him.

I stared at him and saw him as the others must—cold, calculating, disdainful. And yet, it was the strangest sensation to also *feel* him from the inside, to *know* that alongside those cold things he was carrying that dark, aching abyss.

Then he muttered a curse, and the sense of him disappeared like he'd slammed a door on it.

I tensed, pulling tight against his neck where I'd laced my fingers when he picked me up. But moments later I realized he wasn't gone entirely. That I was still aware of him. But like a voice through a thick door: Muffled. Unclear.

I peered over his shoulders, watching as a handful of the men stumbled out of that chamber, calling after us.

"Do you like what you see, Jesse?" he snarled without turning his head.

I looked back at him, his stunning profile—jaw tensed and muscles flexing, eyes shining, lips peeled back slightly from his teeth, which were gritted.

He looked like a fallen angel, about to rain hell on someone who deserved it.

Thrill and nerves coursed through me. "Yes," I breathed, stunned by how different it suddenly felt to be close to him.

As if I *knew* him. Understood him. As if we were already… intimate.

I blinked.

"It's the bond," he muttered, turning a corner so tightly my toes brushed the wall. "Do you feel the pull of it?"

I nodded slowly, still stunned and trying to understand what was happening. "Why are you running? Is there danger?"

He huffed, his lips curling up into a wicked half-smile that made my stomach flutter. "The only real danger in your world now, Kitten, is *me.*"

I should have been terrified. Should have been screaming, fighting him, running… But despite the nerves and thrill, despite the uncertainty and sheer desperation of this entire day… since that bond had snapped into place it was as if I'd found my purpose.

I understood why I was here. Why it had to be me. And what I was supposed to do.

If he'd let me.

Then the door he'd slammed on that link between us cracked open and a jolt of desire came at me through the bond. I gasped, suddenly aching.

Casimir gave a low, throaty chuckle and smiled again, shaking his head. "It's always fun at the beginning," he murmured.

"What is?" I asked breathlessly.

"The bond. The need. The insatiable appetite…" He finally turned his head to meet my eyes and if I hadn't been in his arms, I think I would have sunk to the floor under the weight and promise of those eyes. The flames roaring behind the slick, frigid ice he placed between himself and the world.

And every tongue of flame that licked at the ice of him, also flickered at the core of me. My breath was coming faster, the hair rising on my arms.

"Yesssssss," he hissed. "That's it. Dear god, it's going to be good between us."

"You need to show me... I haven't..." I stammered, uncertain how to say it. But he cursed again.

"I know. I told you... you do not need to fear me."

And yet, at those words, it wasn't fear *I* felt, but a chill that turned in *his* chest. It was muffled and distant, the roll of thunder far enough away you weren't sure where it came from. And yet...

"Stop blocking me," I whispered. "I understand better when you don't."

"Kitten, you understand *nothing.*"

He was practically running up a flight of stairs now, taking them two at a time, carrying me effortlessly. Then he took the turn to a landing at the top and suddenly, we were in a massive, echoing space, with triple-height ceilings and a plunge off to his right to another level below. A thick, hand-carved banister kept us safely on the wide mezzanine, but while I marveled at the massive chandelier hanging from the tall ceiling and the grand pillars and double, arched doorways, he only fixed his eyes on a door halfway along the mezzanine and picked up his pace until he was practically running.

Shouldering the door open, he kicked it closed behind him, then walked me to the center of the massive room and finally, with some care, put me back on my feet.

The moment I had my balance, he let me go, muttering again, but it was only to stalk back to the door and lift a large beam from where it leaned against the wall, slotting it into braces on the thick, double-doors with an echoing boom... and we were locked in.

10. It's Time

~ *JESSE* ~

Cazz stood in front of the door for a half a second, hands still on the beam, head cocked as if he was listening to something. There was a strange tension in him that made the hair on the back of my neck stand up. But then he turned and found me with his eyes.

In that space in my chest where I'd been connected to him, I *felt* the spear of desire that rocked through his body. It made my breath catch.

When he began to walk towards me, it was with the slow grace of a predator, the fire in his eyes burning inside me as he locked on, only the rapid rise and fall of his chest outwardly giving away the tension in him that I could feel. A few strands of his hair fell over his eyes, but he peered out at me through them, like a wolf in the grass and when he spoke, his voice was guttural, so deep it seemed to come up from the stone beneath my feet, and barely loud enough for me to catch the words.

"You're stronger than I gave you credit for," he murmured, prowling towards me.

I swallowed, but my heart was racing and my breath shallow. "Don't underestimate me," I breathed.

"Why do you submit? Why choose it?" He'd reached me again, stopped right at my toes, looking down on me. He was so tall, his chin was almost on his chest when he held my eyes from this close. That hair fluttered around his face, framing the diamond-sharp cut of his jaw and making his light eyes seem even brighter.

I couldn't resist, I reached up to trace the line of that jaw, felt the steel of it under his butter-soft skin.

"You shaved for me." The words sounded so pathetic, but he gave a one-sided smile.

"If that is all it takes to please you, this will be easy," he said dryly. Then the smile fell and he reached for me.

My breath caught again when he began to slowly trace the neckline of the dress with one, calloused finger. But I made myself stand there, not try to push his hand away or cover myself.

The material of the dress was so light that when he trailed that finger down, over the fabric and my nipple stood to meet him, his touch on the sensitized tip felt as thrilling as if he'd touched my skin.

But instead of pulling the dress down, or kissing me, he took hold of my shoulders and turned me around so my back was to him.

I was tense at first, unable to see him. But then he stepped in, his warm chest pressing right at my back, his breath fluttering on my ear.

Then he lifted his hands and began to trail the tips of his fingers from my neck, to the point of my shoulders, then down my arms.

"There is a lie among the males of your kind that seduction is centered on... sacred places."

I shivered as the skin under his fingertips *bloomed*, the hair on my arms rising to meet his touch as he trailed them softly, slowly down my forearms. "Every square inch of your skin hides one thousand nerve endings. Each one a tiny seed of pleasure. Did you know that?" His voice was rough, guttural.

I shook my head and he chuckled and dropped his chin so his breath puffed, hot on my neck. Then he opened his mouth on the skin under my ear and sucked, sliding his tongue as if he tasted the salt there.

My breath caught. Closing my eyes, I tipped my head back and aside to give him better access.

A deep, approving rumble began in his chest, vibrating against my back. He rewarded me by lightly dragging those fingers back up my arm, so slowly that the goosebumps rushed ahead of his touch to sensitize the skin before he reached it.

I shivered.

"Do not be afraid, Jesse. I will paint you in pleasure," he rasped, his touch trailing all the way up my arms, then to my shoulders, then down to trace the lines of my collarbones... and when I bit my lip, he took my chin in one hand and turned my head, forcing me to meet his eyes. His stunning, sapphire eyes that glowed so chillingly cold it was like being doused in ice-water. "But do not deny me."

"I won't," I whispered. "I don't want to."

He shuddered then, his eyes closing for a moment and his chin dropped so his lips brushed the top of my shoulder. "How you feed my power so acutely, I do not know. But it is... stunning, Jesse. If you can do this before we've completed the bond... I barely dare to hope how it will be once we have."

I tensed, then, knowing what that meant. And he felt it.

With a low growl, he let his hands slide down to my waist, then my hips. He kissed the side of my neck again—softer, slowly, but his breath was getting faster, and I could feel the hardness of him against my back.

"Submit to me, Jesse, and I will show you pleasure you didn't know existed." His hands slid down to the outsides of my thighs, then he began slowly furling up the skirt of my dress on both sides, concertinas of fabric gathering in his hands as the hem slowly climbed my legs.

My breath got faster too, goosebumps pebbling my back and raising the hair on my arms again.

"I will," I whispered. "I told you... protect me and I'll give you everything you want."

He groaned like he'd been struck and leaned into me so I felt the heat of him from my calves to my neck.

"Then it is time, Kitten. Now... prepare yourself," he rasped. "We're going to make you truly mine."

11. Let Me Teach You

~ CASIMIR ~

Standing behind her as I was, I had a perfect view down her cleavage as her chest rose and fell very quickly. I looked forward to plunging my length down that dark valley.

I'd been furling up the skirt of that spider web of a dress and now I set to my task with focus. As the hem drew up to her thighs, I let my fingertips brush her skin as I continued to raise it slowly, slowly, smiling when her skin pebbled under my touch.

She shivered when the cool air of the room met her hot skin, then shuddered when I grasped the skirt in one fist and reached for her with the other, urging her to spread her stance a little wider.

"Tell me everything," I whispered in her ear. "What you like, what you don't. What makes you tremble. Tell me if it hurts or when you want it to hurt more. Tell me when you're going to come."

She gave a short little huff, but then I slid two fingers into her folds and she tensed.

"Relax," I growled, and had to remind myself not to give her a taste of the compulsion to make her obey.

She didn't, of course, because I'd sounded angry, so I made myself breathe and rethink my approach.

I was startled to find myself anticipating the challenge of bringing her through this without the use of my power.

"Relax, Jesse," I repeated, but softly this time, letting my lips play on her neck while I played with the rest of her.

Her breath was already short, her heart racing. But it was hard to know how much was from desire and how much from fear.

I continued nuzzling and kissing the sensitive skin of her neck, nibbling at her earlobe teasing with the tip of my tongue.

Her breath was coming in puffs now, but I was gratified to find her wanting me.

Delving deeper, slowly, only teasing her, never penetrating, I began the slow, rhythmic slide between where she wanted me, and that sensitive nub, stroking her like a cat, beckoning, smiling when her hips began to lean into the peak of each stroke.

"That's it, beautiful... that's it. Tell me where it's good. Tell me what works."

"I can't. It's embarrassing."

"Your pleasure isn't embarrassing, it is... delicious." Then I didn't speak again for a moment but continued to stroke her until she relaxed into my touch again. Then I whispered, "Tell me."

She swallowed. "Like that. But... a little harder?" she breathed.

With a low growl, I rewarded her honesty, pressing a little more, but continuing the slow pace, because I wanted her asking for more.

She'd been passive to that point, but as she grew more wet her eyes closed and her head tipped back against my shoulder and one of her hands came up to curl around my upper arm. I changed the rhythm with two faster, beckoning curls with my middle finger in tandem with my thumb over that bundle of nerves, and her fingernails dug into my bicep.

Got her.

Her breath was louder now, her nipples both standing proud under the thin material, and her hips beginning to roll into my touch.

And still I didn't move, but let her fall into the experience, not be reminded of the world around her... or me.

But feeling her come alive under my hands was raising my own need to an urgency I hadn't experienced for years. My own breathing grew harsh and I cursed as my erection became extremely uncomfortable still contained by my trousers.

Then she shifted her weight, widening her stance again and tilting her hips so that my fingers passed over her core.

I chuckled, breathlessly. "I told you to *tell* me what you want, Jesse."

"I want... inside."

I bit down on her neck as I finally penetrated her with only one finger first, groaning when I slid inside so easily, and then, after a moment, I found the angle that allowed me to keep teasing her flesh with the pad of my thumb, while I buried a finger inside her, curling to almost pinch between the two. She jolted the first time and her other hand came up to grip my other arm.

"Now," I growled. "Pull down the front of your dress so I can see you."

My breath was hot against her ear, watching her as she lifted one hand from my arm to grasp the gathered neckline of the soft dress and then tugged it down until her breast on that side popped free.

"More," I rasped. With a deep inhale, she pulled the top of the dress down until she was revealed, her skin pebbled and both breasts high and tight and calling me.

Her nipples were a deep pink, small and hard. I wanted to suck one. To bite it.

Seeking some release from the urgent ache, I rubbed myself against her ass, but there was little pleasure in it with my trousers still on and my shaft so tightly constrained.

So instead, I dropped her skirt, letting it catch where my other wrist pinned against her and with my free hand, I reached for that beautiful, round breast, taking the weight of it, my breath hitching when I felt the hard rivet of her nipple against my palm.

I rubbed it with the side of my thumb, enjoying the hard press against my skin. But to my joy, Jesse gasped too and her back arched a hair, leaning her shoulders back into my chest and pressing her breast into my touch.

I was still stroking her and she was beginning to shake, panting hard enough that she swallowed now and again, her hips jolting when I found the right spot within her.

I lifted my head to stare down at her for a moment, thrilled to find my mate already quivering for my touch.

I hadn't even had her yet.

My mind conjured images of her riding me, her head thrown back in exactly this way, but her hands in my hair and holding me in place as she arched, pressing her breast into my mouth and—

My body shuddered, hot, urgent need stabbing through me. Removing my hand from between her legs I grasped the skirt again, both hands this time, pulling it up and all the way over her head, tossing the whole dress aside then snarling as it registered that she'd been naked under it the entire time.

She'd been in that room with all those males, only this scrap of material between her beautiful body and their eyes?

"Turn around," I rasped through my teeth. "Now."

It was instinct with females to follow an instruction with a touch of the compulsion, and I had to catch myself and wait impatiently while she blinked back to reality, registered the order and turned, hesitantly, to face me, her cheeks as hot as the rest of her.

When she finally did, it took another moment for her wide eyes to slide up my chest to meet mine.

I licked my lower lip. I did love them uncertain.

"Unbutton my jacket." I tried to make the order sultry, but my breath was coming too fast and my need too urgent. It sounded harsh.

She blinked and some of her fear returned. I cursed myself, but again... I anticipated the challenge of seducing her until she was abandoned, surrendered to me. And my body surged with hot, hot need again.

12. Tell Me

~ *CASIMIR* ~

"Quickly," I rasped. She was keeping her body just clear of mine, reaching up to pop the brass buttons at my chest, but her eyes were on the bared skin at my throat and collarbones.

"Tell me," I whispered. "Tell me while you undress me."

"I-I like the way you look," she murmured, her eyes flicking up and down between my face and the buttons as she worked them loose.

Then my jacket was open and she slid her hands up my chest to my shoulders underneath the stiff fabric, pushing it off and back, her hands following the rounds of my shoulders, then down my arms.

I hadn't told her to take it off, but I was too impatient to correct her—and this first time it was better to encourage her when she was bold.

Then she leaned against me to push the jacket off my arms and her body brushed against me and I groaned.

Had she been more experienced, I would have had my trousers off in seconds and plunged into her. But it was important to train her body to trust that each new step would be one of pleasure. So, I gritted my teeth as the jacket slapped to the floor behind me.

"You work on my belt and trousers," I growled as I reached for my shirt buttons because even if there was a reason to step carefully, I *needed* to be skin-to-skin with her.

She blinked, then nodded and dropped both her eyes and hands to my belt, pulling it through the buckle until slapped against her hand, then tugging it back to release it.

Her hands were shaking when she got the belt undone and reached for my buttons.

And then she struggled. My erection was pressing hard against the fabric, pulling everything tight and making them harder to unbutton.

My breath was a harsh cloud in the room as her tentative fingers brushed my most sensitive flesh through the thick fabric of my trousers while she tried to free me.

I had the shirt unbuttoned and was tugging it out of my pants when she got stuck on the third button down and I lost my patience.

I reached down to free the last two buttons, groaning when I finally sprang free, but cursing my luck that it was my hands there, rather than hers.

Her chin dropped and she looked down at me, blinking, eyes wide.

"Have you ever seen a man before?" My voice was rough and guttural with desire. Let her hear what she did to me.

She nodded, then hesitated, then shook her head. "Not in light," she said, her voice high.

"Have you touched a man?"

She nodded, but her body squirmed.

"Are you lying to me?"

"No, I just… not very much," she said, sounding embarrassed.

Gathering my control by the shreds still available to me, I reached for her chin, lifting her head and forcing her to meet my eyes. "There is no shame in sex, Jesse. If you feel the urge for it, soothe yourself that you are my mate and my wife. Between us, nothing is off-limits."

I waited until she nodded again, slowly at first, then faster. But her eyes dropped back to look at me before she lowered her head.

I dropped my hands from her, let my arms hang loose at my sides and waited, letting her look her fill.

Her chest still rose and fell quickly, her cheeks were still flushed, but the glaze in her eyes had been replaced by a curious light. She lifted one hand, then hesitated again.

"Touch me," I ordered her. "Take me in your grip—not too tightly at first—and slide your hand up and down slowly, passing over the head and letting your fingers close at the top each time. The underside is the most sensitive. Be careful not to use your nails."

Biting her lip in a way that made me want to suck it, she did as I asked, at first just holding me in her hand, her eyes widening when she carefully began to draw her hand up, then slowly back down again.

Pleasure coursed through me, my skin tingling far more than the simple touch would usually warrant. But the matebond was always potent at first, and for whatever reason, her voluntary submission was thrilling me in a way nothing had for a very long time.

My heart began to pound, sure that it would be very good between us.

My breath grew coarser as she continued to stroke. Then, frustrated by how slowly she was moving, I pumped into her grip twice, groaning, then catching her wrists, because despite her lack of finesse, she was going to bring me to my limit very quickly.

When I caught her hands she froze, and her head snapped up, her eyes measuring me.

But I was smiling and already walking her backwards towards the bed. "Tell me," I said. "Tell me what you think. What you feel. What you see."

She swallowed, her throat bobbing deliciously, but that was another bridge for another day. The marking brought with it a raft of complications. I wasn't sure I would even do it with her.

"It's... I'm surprised how soft it feels," she whispered. "Silky. But hard underneath."

"You make me hard," I told her quickly.

She gave a little huff and licked her lips, which made my cock pulse, and she felt it. She startled, looking down, then up.

"That's what you do to me," I growled. "You make me want. And when I want, I get harder. Fuller. And then I want to fill you."

She swallowed again. "I know how sex works," she said breathlessly. "I just haven't... gone that far."

Another conversation for another time. I was still stepping her backwards slowly, teasing hands up and down her arms, letting the backs of my fingers brush the sides of her breasts, my thumbs tease her nipples.

She looked down to my touch, shivered, and sucked in a breath and *dear god* I wanted her.

"Always look at me, Jesse," I muttered. "Watch me. Tell me what you like."

"That feels good," she whispered.

Virgins, I thought dryly. "Your breasts are so soft and heavy, they call to me. I want to suck on them," I rasped, tracing the width of her nipple with my thumbs. "I want to bite…" Then I cupped them both and pressed them up and together. "I want you to hold them together while I fuck them."

Her eyes widened at that, but I smiled.

Another joy, another day.

Then the backs of her thighs hit the bed and she stopped dead, staring up at me. Through the bond I felt her adrenaline spike and it only served to shove more through my own veins.

Sensing her fear through the bond, I took her face in my hands and lifted her chin, taking her mouth slowly and deeply, letting my lips drag on hers, tracing under her lip with my tongue, then sliding the flat of it against hers until she'd stopped tensing and begun to pant, and both her hands had come up to my chest.

Then I tilted my head and sucked on her tongue and she sighed into my mouth.

Oh yes, it was going to be *so good* between us.

Soundtrack for the next couple chapters is
Breathe by Kansh

13. Never Hide

~ JESSE ~

Somehow, when Cazz kissed me I felt it in my belly. An ache started down low and I didn't just get breathless, I got a little bit desperate.

Then he straightened, locking eyes with me—and his were glowing—and he growled, "Get on the bed. Now," and his voice vibrated against my chest, but I felt it all the way to the soles of my feet and started scrambling backwards, trying to get my ass up on the high bed.

I tried to jump and missed twice.

Cazz gave a chuckle and shook his head, dropping to squat, his hands sliding all the way down the backs of my legs, then cupping the back of my calves.

There was a moment he just knelt there, looking up at me and I looked down on him and everything in me that was aching gave a *stab* of desire, right behind my navel. My breath rushed out of me and I started to shake. His eyes flashed and I braced my hands on the bed behind me and heaved, and this time he helped lift my weight until I was sitting on the thick fur, and it was the most luxurious, erotic feeling I'd ever had against my skin.

Soft, thick fur under my hands, under my ass, brushing my skin all the way down my legs.

My breath caught and Cazz caught it, his eyes snapping to mine as he stood, his gaze intent. "What is it? Tell me."

My breath was quick and shallow. "The fur," I murmured. "It feels… really nice."

"Where?"

"Everywhere. On my skin."

One side of his mouth twisted up in a wicked smile and his eyes gleamed. "Kitten likes a soft touch. Noted. Now back up and lay down, beautiful."

I started moving immediately, crawling backwards as fast as I could and still burying my fingers in that thick fur. But my heart was hammering for more than just the intensity of his gaze on me and the fact that when I backed up I'd be bare to his eyes.

The thrill inside me made the urge to follow his instructions so deep, so powerful, I was worried he *was* using that compulsion on me, because I wanted to literally jump to do as he said.

But then I got distracted, because as I crawled backwards on the bed, the soft, smooth fur sliding under me and raising goosebumps on my skin, Cazz was crawling up after me, looking exactly like a wolf prowling up on its prey.

Chin low and eyes up to stay on mine, his pupils were huge and dark, but the bright blue around them glowed. One side of his lip curled back from his teeth in a wicked smile as he pursued me all the way up the length of that massive bed, until I felt the pillow bump my arms and I stopped, then lowered myself so my head rested on it.

I was afraid he'd just crawl right up on me and this would be happening, but to my relief, he stopped at my toes, kneeling, one hand on my ankle, the other grasping himself and pumping slowly.

"So fucking beautiful, kitten," he growled, letting the hand that was on my ankle slide up my leg, then cup behind my knee.

I'd kept my knees together as much as I could, and he smiled again as he grasped me there and pulled my right leg up, so it was bent high.

"Do not hide yourself from my eyes. You're a stunning woman, Jesse, but this is the most beautiful part of you," he hissed, his voice deep and rough. Then he'd pulled my other leg up too, so both were high and bent—and wide—then moved himself to kneel between them, staring at me, his lower jaw slack as he stroked his hands down the insides of my thighs, a feather touch that he repeated, up and down, his fingers teasing—so lightly—at my folds just for seconds at a time, but never pushing between them, until all the skin between my knees and hips was sensitized, all the hair standing up, every inch of me quivering for more.

"Tell. Me."

Oh. Right. I swallowed. "I love that," I admitted, my voice high and a little thin.

"Why? How does it feel?"

"It's... tingly. Like... like waves on my skin. Like butterflies on the outside," I gasped as his fingers found the places I didn't shave and he teased through that hair too.

"Keep talking, Jesse."

"I don't know what to say!"

"Tell me what you like. And how it can be better."

"I like all of it, exactly as you're doing it, Cazz. Just... don't stop!"

He gave a low growl of approval, then continued stroking. I didn't know what to do with my hands, so I buried them in that fur, spreading my fingers, then closing them to fists, over and over, the softness another pleasure against my palms.

"Yes..." he murmured, his eyes raking over my body, then returning to my eyes again and again. "Look for your pleasure, Jesse. Seek it. Don't be scared to pursue it. I will follow you to it."

"This is... this is nicer than anything I've done before," I admitted, because the truth was, it felt like my bloodstream had become thousands of tiny butterflies, rushing through my body, under my skin, their fluttering raising tingling pleasure across all my skin. It was tantalizing and overwhelming. The ache growing deeper and harder within me.

Then, the next time Cazz stroked me between my legs, I widened my knees and lifted my hips slightly, to press into the touch, silently pleading.

"You want me there," he whispered. It wasn't a question. But I nodded anyway. "Have you ever felt that kind of want before?"

I nodded again. "But not so strong."

My head was spinning, my body reeling. Every so often I'd blink and realize where I was and what was going on—what was about to happen.

I was somewhere in a cave, being seduced by a *wolf*. A wolf that I'd just married.

And that was the only fact that kept me sane, because I'd seen inside him for those desperate, dangerous seconds after the bond took, and... I'd seen my purpose.

I'd never imagined, though, that my purpose could be so... consuming.

Finally, finally, he started touching me again, sliding into me with one finger first, still rubbing with his thumb on the most sensitive skin until I was panting and gripping the fur, rocking my hips onto his hand and starting to make noises in my throat.

"Yes, yes, yes…" His eyes flared and he smiled, his own chest rising and falling quickly as he shifted, opening his own knees wider and scooting closer.

14. Chase It

~ *JESSE* ~

A flash of fear speared through me because I thought he was going to cover me then, and take me. I screwed my eyes tightly closed and gripped the fur, bracing for the pain that I'd heard would happen this first time.

But Cazz tsked and his hands returned to stroking up and down my thighs, from knee to hip, top, then back, then inside until I was shaking again.

"No, Kitten. No. Don't tense. Don't do that," he cautioned, sounding a touch frustrated. "Just relax and seek your pleasure. Leave the rest to me. Watch."

I opened my eyes to see him take himself in hand. His jaw flexed as he rubbed himself against me, softly at first, just separating my folds and drawing himself up in a very similar way to the way he'd used his fingers, but... it felt very, very different.

There was so much more of him and he touched so much more of me. He started slowly, right where he'd enter me, and that made me tense. But then he'd draw himself slowly up, pressing slightly harder as he reached that nub of pleasure to send fizzing pleasure coursing through me.

The first time it felt good and made my breath catch.

The second time it felt even better and made me hope he'd keep going.

Then he kept going, and I got lost in it, each slow draw of pressure against me raising the heat and joy in my belly a little higher, peaking when he drew himself over that bundle of nerves, then easing off when he pulled back down, but leaving me gasping a little more desperately each time.

Then, without stopping that delicious draw of himself against me, his other hand took my ankle and lifted my foot, bending my knee up and back, resting the back of my heel on his shoulder, opening me wider as he began kissing the inside of my calf and ankle, his lips soft and tongue teasing. And suddenly the pleasure in my veins crackled between the two places he touched me, until it felt like that entire side of my body was going to explode with it.

His fingers trailed up the outside of the leg he had bent up, his lips on the inside of it, and he continued that slow, heavy glide against me—but picking up the pace just a hair.

"That's my girl, that's it," he hummed against my skin, sliding slightly faster against me, his own breathing growing rough.

"Cazz…"

"Tell me."

"I… I'm… I'm going to…"

"Yesss."

The pleasure in me was growing, building pressure between my thighs and low in my belly, making me jerk and twitch when he passed over my sensitive, swollen skin.

Oh… oh god… I was…

The ache became a need and that began to drive me forward to reach for him, but I gripped the fur on either side of me instead, grounding myself as I suddenly understood what he meant about chasing my pleasure.

I bent that knee harder, pressing down on his shoulder to tilt my hips up and pull myself against where he slid against me. He passed over my core where he'd enter me, and my hips bucked reflexively, seeking, *needing* something inside me to ease the ache.

"Cazz!"

"Focus on the pleasure, beautiful. Chase it. Seek it. Ignore everything else…" he hissed, his own breath hitching.

I was starting to make noises, little mewling cries at the peak of each slide. Twitching. Growing frantic, tilting my hips, pulling for him, shivering, my breath stopping.

Please… please… please…

As if he'd heard me, Cazz began to move faster, but still sustaining that pressure, that incredible slide against me from my core, to my clitoris.

And with each stroke, earthquakes shook me. My body vibrated from the inside out and I worried I was going to lose control of myself.

"Cazz!"

"I'm here."

"I'm going to... I'm..."

"I know... let it happen." He sounded like he spoke through his teeth, his breath tearing in and out around the words. "Embrace it, sweetheart. It's here just for you—oh *god!*"

Three things happened at the same time.

Cazz drew himself up and over that bundle of nerves that set my blood alight.

The wave of pleasure crested, then hung there, as if waiting for a signal from him.

His hand tightened on my leg and instead of drawing himself against me again, this time he slid into me, filling me.

A guttural cry broke in my throat as everything in my body exploded in pleasure—at the same moment a jangle of pain tore deep inside me. But it was overwhelmed by the sheer, incredible joy of being taken.

That ache that had been building was suddenly a wave of ever-increasing bliss at the sensation of his flesh entering mine, inch by inch, shoving pleasure through me until he filled me with a bellowing roar of my name.

Dropping my leg, he fell over me, fisting the fur next to my head, his arm going rigid, all the tendons standing proud from his fist to his jaw as he threw his head back and swore, fighting for control as he drew himself out slowly, then plunged back in—and my orgasm finally peaked.

Unable to breathe, mouth open in a silent scream, I slapped one hand to his neck, gripping him in a desperate plea for him never to stop, the other still gripping the fur. And now, as every hair on my body stood tall and pleasure rocked through me, he drew out again, then thrust into me, guttural moans and tormented cries breaking in his throat as we began to move together and he milked every last wave of my orgasm from me.

And even when the wave began to suck away and I thought I would breathe, I was stunned to find that he was still moving within me, still slow and intentional, but now his trembling body covered mine, our hips rolling together, our cries echoing through the room in unison.

Then, still taking me, he put a hand to my face and when I opened my eyes it was to find him watching me.

"Hold on," he graveled. "We're only just getting started."

15. In This Together

~ CASIMIR ~

No one had ever come so close to stealing my control.

She was stunning. Skin flushed and pink, lips soft and open, she clawed one hand into my neck and I could have howled.

When she came, I'd swear I heard God in her cry.

And even when she was blinking and stunned, swallowing, I didn't let up.

We weren't finished.

"Hold on. We're only just getting started."

Her eyes—glazed with pleasure, but clearing—locked on mine and her mouth opened like she'd speak, but then I rocked into her again and her jaw dropped.

She was twitching, her body over-sensitized. The risk of course was that she'd grow desensitized, so I lowered myself to my elbows, cupping hands over her head and finally indulging the urge to be skin-to-skin with her. As we rocked together slowly, I groaned and dropped my chin, our cheeks brushing and even that sweet contact was heightened.

When her hands came up, her fingers sliding on my scalp, I kissed her and she clung, taking my tongue as readily as she'd taken the rest of me. And her eagerness, her joy in it was so hot, I was fighting for control again, even though I was only pressing my hips against her and letting our bodies roll together while she found herself again.

"Beautiful," I whispered, then kissed her neck below her ear. "So beautiful when you come, Kitten."

She gave a shaky little laugh, but then I took her mouth again, and was gratified to feel her tighten around me again.

But still I didn't rush. Bringing her to that peak again would be harder the second time, especially if the adrenaline of her orgasm hadn't been enough to cover the pain of losing her innocence.

Holy shit, she really *was* a virgin. At twenty or more? That was a story I needed to hear. Another time.

But those thoughts fled because she was lifting her knees and gaining confidence to meet me with each stroke. I was nearly certain she wasn't feeling the pain at all.

When her body was supple again, and her breathing was steady, but still harsh, I pushed up on my hands again, arching my back so we didn't lose contact where it mattered most, but staring down at her.

"Look at me," I growled.

Her eyes flew open and locked on mine—then darted away, then returned.

Again and again as we moved together, she looked away, licking her swollen lips.

"Do not flee me now," I muttered. "Look at me, Jesse."

Biting her lip, she snapped her eyes back to mine and this time, didn't look away.

"Good girl."

Something hungry flickered behind her eyes, and I felt her shake, but she didn't drop eye-contact. Instead, I went to war against my own body, because having her this way, so willing, so eager, having her watch me as avidly as I was watching her... it all conspired to steal my wits. And my restraint.

Needing a moment to center myself, I leaned down to kiss her, then realized my mistake when she threw her arms around my neck and clung, her kiss desperate and deep, our breaths mingling and every sensation shoving me closer and closer to my own climax.

Desperate, I fisted both hands in her hair and tugged her head back until her neck was bare, kissing down her chin, then to that soft, warm skin of her throat.

The wolf in me snarled, snapping, rushing for her, but I pushed it back. It wasn't time.

Instead, I kissed all over her neck, slowly, matching the drag of my lips and flick of my tongue on her skin with the rhythm of my hips.

And then, still keeping her head locked back, just as she began to clench around me and her nails bit into my skin, I drew all the way out of her.

She froze, a tiny cry of disappointment breaking in her throat—just as I plunged into her again, thrusting hard so that my thighs slapped on hers and she sucked in.

Then I did it again.

She bowed under me, pulling herself up on my neck, arching, her breasts pushing up so that I could curl and take her nipple in my teeth and flick it with my tongue in time with my pounding.

And then she began to keen.

And those beautiful, thin, wordless cries finally snapped my leash.

"Come for me, beautiful," I snarled, biting down carefully on her nipple until she jerked in my arms and sucked in a deep breath.

Then, letting go of her hair, I pushed up on one arm, clamped a hand at the back of her neck and used my own wrist against her shoulder for leverage as I plowed into her. And when she began to buck and arch, I slid my other hand to her lower back and lifted her to meet me.

Low, guttural growls rolled in my throat as her cries grew higher, thinner, then cut off as her eyes rolled back in her head and she clenched around me, her body jolting.

"Yes! God, yesssss…!" The call rolled off into a guttural snarl as my own climax hit right at the base of my spine and my body screamed with ecstasy. Waves of sheer bliss rocked through me again and again and I stared down at her, bellowing her name as, in my arms, Jesse shuddered and shocked, her body bucking and jerking.

And then, in what was always life's greatest disappointment, those short moments of sheer pleasure sucked away like a wave on the sand, leaving only the residual pulse of joy and grief because it was over.

Bracing on my elbows so I wouldn't crush her with my weight, I dropped my head, my forehead on the pillow next to hers, our sweaty temples pressed together, sucking at the air over and over to catch my breath.

I was trembling, I realized. That bore examination later when my head was on straight again. But for now I'd just—

I went still as a mouse under the eyes of an owl as a sweet, tingling sensation began just behind my hip, then dragged slowly up my back to my shoulder-blade where it looped… then slid slowly back down.

I gaped, still gasping for air, trying to get my head around it.

Then it occurred to me... Jesse was stroking me. Her little fingers dragging up and down my body in a sweet, simple expression of... what?

And then she dealt a stunning blow.

"Thank you, Cazz," she croaked. "That was amazing. Thank you."

16. Time to Breathe

~ JESSE ~

Laying there with Cazz's weight pinning me to the bed, my head was reeling. My insides were at war because half of me was already halfway in love with him. I wanted to hold him to me, keep him there, lay under him and just soak him up like a good smell.

I knew—I knew—that I was never going to be the same. And that was scary, because something I had never anticipated was suddenly very clear: Having sex really did affect my feelings.

I'd talked to my friends over the years. I'd shaken my head over and over again, baffled about why they were so attached to some douchebag who was inconsistent and insensitive at best—sometimes downright abusive.

And they'd always talk about how they wanted him. Couldn't get enough of him. And how rare that was...

I'd been skeptical—naively, as it turned out—that this kind of connection had anything to do with it. I'd never had a man make me feel anything close to what Cazz had just wrung from my body, so I assumed they were just trying to romanticize their own messed up issues.

But now...

Now I could appreciate that, at least in this area, I was very, very blessed.

So few of my friends had even enjoyed their first times at all. And I didn't remember a single story where they'd laid there afterwards like I was—poleaxed with bliss, my entire body thrumming in time with my pulse because the waves of pleasure had sensitized everything.

That sex had been incredible. Mind-blowing. Stunning. And even though there was an ache of pain deep inside me, the curl of pleasure and desire was stronger.

I wanted him again. Soon.

I swallowed hard. I'd felt sexual desire for a man before. But nothing like this. Not this… irressistable drive. Had he used that compulsion on me when I was in the throes so I wouldn't notice the power coming off him? I prayed he hadn't.

"Thank you, Cazz." My voice was rough, but the sentiment was genuine. "That was amazing. Thank you."

I'd been absentmindedly stroking a hand up and down his back while he was panting and recovering. But after I spoke he froze.

"Did you just… thank me?" His voice was muffled in my shoulder, but he sounded slightly shocked.

He pushed up on his hands, still panting, staring down at me, his angular face framed by his loose, dark curls, stunning even with sweat dripping down his temples.

His shoulders turned to rounded rocks, and his forearms got those gorgeous lines in them—while his chest turned into moving plates of steel as he propped himself high over me, staring down at me like he was analyzing me.

I scrambled, trying to figure out what I'd said that made him look affronted. "I… yes? Is that bad?"

His eyes narrowed and he rolled off me to prop his temple on his fist and stare at me. "I can't decide," he said darkly. "I can tell you that it isn't the usual response."

"You've done this enough times to have a usual response?"

He smiled wickedly. "Seduction is a skill, like any other, Kitten. You think just any man could make you shake and scream?"

I already knew they couldn't, so I ignored that.

"So, what is it? The normal response?" I asked him, not wanting to admit that I was feeling the niggle of jealous unease. And insecurity. My eyes naturally followed the line down his arm to where his bicep flexed, then to his carved torso.

For a moment an image flashed in my mind of that beautiful chest as he sat back between my knees, my heel propped on his shoulder, his eyes cast down as he opened his mouth on my calf and his hand trailed slowly up my leg and I shivered.

When I blinked the seductive memory away, it was to find Cazz staring at me, his lips curled up at the corners like he could see exactly what was playing in my head.

"That's closer," he purred. "Though you lack the salivating adoration. Pity."

I stiffened. "I guess that's the cost of not turning a woman into a mindless robot," I snipped, rolling my eyes to cover my nerves. Inside my stomach was trilling. I kept swinging between being drawn to him, and afraid of him. But when he looked at me like that, my cheeks heated and I felt suddenly very visible. And vulnerable.

I didn't like it. "So... you do this a lot? With a lot of different women?" I asked, hating myself because I knew no matter what he said, I wasn't going to like it.

"Practice makes perfect," he purred.

Oh, ugh. "Have you ever been tested? You know, for diseases?" A question I should have asked before all of this even happened, I was suddenly realizing.

Cazz's lips thinned. "That isn't necessary."

"You can't know that, Cazz. Maybe that's why your mates didn't get pregnant before. If you were carrying—"

"I carry nothing but power and nobility," he sharply, his eyes blazing with a different kind of heat. The fist he leaned his temple on tightened.

I held his gaze, my breath coming faster again, but for all the wrong reasons. "Cazz," I tried to sound reasonable. "Unless you're using serious protection, and nothing happens—"

"I am not diseased, and neither are any of my partners," he snapped. "Understand this and know it to your bones: They would not. They could not. I tell their bodies to eradicate anything that could be harmful—to them, or to me. They cannot deny me. They are clean, as am I. You have nothing to fear."

I blinked. He couldn't be serious? But then... then I remembered the way those women who had been terrified for their lives had suddenly become... pleading. Eager. Worshipful. I remembered how I had felt the desire to do the same.

Could he...

"Seriously?" I breathed. "You can... you can make them heal?"

Cazz's chin dropped and his eyes locked on mine. "Kitten, I can make them do anything. I can heal—or I can stop their hearts with a word. I could, if I wished, tell you to die, right here. Right now. And you would."

17. The Power

~ JESSE ~
Holy shit.

It was suddenly hard to breathe. The immensity of his power, of what that meant… of what kind of man it made him was stunning and utterly horrifying.

As my head spun with the implications of what that meant, instinctively I pulled the blanket up and over my chest.

"Don't," he said darkly, reaching out immediately to tug it back down to bare my breasts. I was about to slap his hand away when I remembered our agreement that I would submit, as long as he didn't use that power on me.

That power that could literally make my heart stop?

What else was he capable of?

I swallowed back the fear—then quickly forgot it when his eyes zeroed in on my breast and he gave a small smile, reaching out to trace the nipple closest to him with a touch so soft I wouldn't even have felt it if my nipples hadn't still been hard.

"You're a beautiful woman, Jesse," he said, as if the fact surprised him, his tone quiet and suggestive, as if his prior anger had simply melted away. Then he frowned and scanned the length of me. "But you're underweight. Pregnancy is very difficult on a female's body. We need to fatten you up. What are your favorite rich foods?"

I didn't like his casual tone, like I was some kind of broodmare to be conditioned. But I doubted I was going to achieve anything by arguing with him. And besides, when it came to food, that was easy.

"Cheese."

He waited, then his eyebrows rose. "That's it? Cheese?"

I thought about it. "I mean… I like a good steak. Oh, and fried chicken and french-fries."

He nodded. "Several fruits and vegetables a day as well. Your body will respond quickly because you've been deprived. And that will help you conceive quickly as well. What day are you at in your cycle?" he asked casually, as if that was a normal question.

Ew. "What do you mean, what day?" I wrinkled my nose.

He frowned like that should be obvious. "Do you know nothing of your own body? Your cycle should be twenty-eight days long, beginning on the first day you bleed. When did that cycle last begin?"

Double ew. "Why does it matter?"

His smile got suggestive. "By knowing your cycle we know when we have to… concentrate our efforts."

My mind filled with that image of him again, heated and ecstatic, and my mouth went dry.

"Yes, that," he said with a sly smile.

I had to think but then… "Day eight… or nine, I think?"

"Excellent, then the next few days are very important to us," he said, and the smile on his face was so predatory it made me cold and my skin prickled for very different reasons.

"But, if you know so much about women and you can just make their bodies do stuff… I mean, why can't you just make them pregnant?" Then I realized what I was saying and shrank back from him. "Or have you? Are you saying all this about an heir, but there's a dozen little Cazz's already running around? Is this about some stupid royal ego boost—"

"You are bold with your tongue, Jesse," he said dryly. But he didn't sound angry. If anything, his flat expression seemed a little defensive. "But no, I have no offspring. As assiduously as I protect mine and my partners' bodies, so do I also ensure that they do not conceive. I will not bring offspring into this world that do not carry my power—and only the royal bloodline, a child of the bond-forged Alpha Male and Alpha Female can receive the inheritance."

I licked my lips. My kid was going to be able to do this awful thing he could do? "I see… but, how would you even know—"

"It simply is," he said flatly. "Trust me, generations before me have tested every route. The offspring of unmated pairs do not receive the gift, and any offspring that is the result of compulsion is… twisted by it," he said with a shudder. "My power is not infinite, Jesse. I am not God, though my will is closer to His than any other you know. It is an undeniable truth that I am forced to wait on natural conception to find and make an heir—which is precisely why you're here."

It was a strange, heady mix of relief and fear that coursed through me then. Relief because at the very least he wasn't going to get me sick. But… what would happen to me if the problem with conception was actually him? What if all these women weren't getting pregnant because he was firing blanks?

Did wolves even test for that stuff?

All his talk about cycles and focusing efforts seemed like they must know the medical side of these things. But what if he was some kind of sick sadist, who got his kicks from bringing some woman in as a breeder, then blamed her when the barrier to conception was actually him?

I tensed, and Cazz, his gaze distant and distracted, reached for me. I wasn't sure if he was even aware that he was doing it as he started stroking my body almost thoughtlessly, drawing his hands up and down my skin in a way that gave me tingles. But his eyes were focused on the middle distance, as if he was deep in thought.

But either he didn't notice my tension, or didn't care, because he licked his lips and continued to stroke me.

Despite the chilling darkness in his gaze, that flutter began again, low in my belly, when he let his hand play all the way down to my knee, then dragged those talented fingers up the inside of my thigh, I found I didn't want to move.

And that seemed to please him as he continued stroking. I wondered if we were going to "concentrate efforts" right away.

He was just leaning into my ear, about to breathe whatever thoughts he'd had that had lit flames in his eyes, when there was a thudding knock on the door and we both froze.

18. A New Rulebook

~ JESSE ~

"Ah. Food," Cazz said with a sigh, then rolled off the bed and walked towards the door, completely naked.

It took a moment to realize it wasn't a joke, or a ploy, that he was walking towards the door to open it, buck naked, while I lay there in the same state.

I yanked the blankets up and over me, praying he wouldn't see that as defiance when it was obvious he was about to invite other people into the room.

"Cazz!" I hissed.

"What?" His back and shoulders rippled with strength as he lifted that massive beam out of the brackets holding it across the double doors.

"I'm not dressed!"

"So?" He glanced at me over his shoulder as he leaned the beam up against the wall behind where the door would open. "Neither am I."

"But—"

But then he opened the door and suddenly four women dressed in dark leather pants and white linen shirts walked in carrying a massive tray between them spilling with food—I saw fruit meat, breads, cheeses... like a buffet. Except for two.

Ignoring Cazz's naked body, they walked it over to the table in the corner of the room. It was so large it filled half the round table that was made to seat four.

Once they had the tray situated, they each hurried to turn and gaze at him, keeping their chins low but their eyes avid on him. But

Cazz didn't even look at them. He was frowning at the food, as if he were ticking off a mental checklist, then he nodded and waved them off, towards the door.

"Thank you. Now leave us—oh, Daisy, will you please see that a bath is drawn in my bedchamber?" he added as a second thought.

The woman, a pretty blond with muscular arms that threatened the limits of her sleeves, nodded, her eyes alight with eagerness to please as she hurried from the room ahead of the others, all of whom appeared to be dragging their feet, glancing at Cazz over their shoulders as they made their way out in a line like they were hoping he'd give them a reason to stay, or a new task to do that would bring them back.

When they were gone, he closed the doors again. "Come. Eat. You need to keep up your strength—and gain weight," he said, striding towards the table, snapping his fingers at me.

My jaw set at being called like a dog, but I reminded myself I was *choosing* to follow his orders. And that he was my husband now.

Which was when his words to the servant hit me.

"Wait," I said, halfway out of the bed and tugging one of the furs off it to wrap around myself. "Isn't this your bedroom?"

He'd just taken a seat at the table and was picking through a bowl of fruit. He frowned when he saw me covering myself, but thankfully he didn't demand that I stay naked. The room was cool, though not cold. And I didn't feel comfortable just walking around naked now that the door was unlocked and anyone might walk in.

"No, of course not," he said impatiently. "This is your room now. It's the largest, except for my own. But if it doesn't please you, you can be shown others and select one."

I stopped halfway across the floor to him, uncertain how to feel.

He was a stranger. And a dangerous one. Having my own space to relax in when I wasn't forced to be with him would be a good thing.

And yet...

I remembered the yawning chasm of darkness in him that I'd sensed when the bond appeared. Remembered my purpose. And the fact that, regardless of whatever else he might be, he was now my husband.

"We're mates. And married. Why would we have different bedrooms?" I asked.

He looked up at me, his expression amused. Then he smiled again. "I assumed you'd rather not witness my... interactions with others. Don't worry, you do not need to worry that I will have offspring with one of them—I will not allow it."

Horror, deep and jangling, rocked though me. "You're going to keep having other women too? I said no sex with others—you said you agreed!"

His eyes narrowed. "Not sex, since you requested that I didn't. But there are plenty of options that remain to us."

I was horrified, gaping at him. But he grinned and gave me a suggestively arched brow. "If you'd like to, you're always welcome to join us. Learn a few things." Then he popped a grape in his mouth.

I spluttered, frantic. "But... I married you! I volunteered—I said no other women!"

He frowned. "I assumed you meant no bastard children, which as I've told you, is already taken care of. I assure you there's a great deal of release that can be gained without penetrative sex—"

"Cazz... You can't *do* this!"

All sense of casual grace disappeared. His eyes flashed and he was on his feet faster than I could see, crossing the carpet in aggressive strides to loom over me.

"And I assure you, Jesse," he muttered with cold fury, "as King, I can do *whatever I wish*. I know that your human leaders are far more lax in the boundaries of respect for authority, so I will let this pass—*once*. But do not presume to tell me what I can and cannot do."

His eyes glowed and that power began to cloud behind him. I was suddenly terrified he was going to compel me.

"No, no! That's not.... I didn't mean..." I put my hands up to soothe him. "I only meant... you said you want an heir. If you're... sowing your royal oats with others, it lowers my chances of conceiving. You should give me every opportunity."

He stared at me, hungry, but dark. "My appetites are... substantial. I doubt you would wish to be the only recipient of them."

Another flash of that moment when he'd loomed over me in the bed.

"Try me," I said, determined.

His brows popped up for a moment. Then he laughed. I was a little confused. He had seemed angry, but now he was chuckling and for the first time I thought I saw warmth in his gaze.

He was stunningly handsome when his eyes crinkled like that.

I waited, swallowing. Definitely *not* laughing.

Still snickering, he wiped his eyes. "I haven't laughed in a long time. You are full of surprises, Jesse."

"But—"

"I must go and clean and—"

"But, Cazz, *please!*"

He stopped, frowning, his gaze snapping. But he didn't speak, only raised an eyebrow for me to go on.

I swallowed. "I said I'd submit and I have. And I will. I will have your babies, and… and do whatever you need." The light in his eyes flared at that. I swallowed again. "But you… please… I don't want to risk a disease or… or miss a chance to get pregnant. Please. Can you just… just use me for all that… just until the babies?"His jaw tightened and he stared at me like a… well, like a wolf.

19. How Did You Know?

~ *CASIMIR* ~

Jesse, my newly deflowered *wife* was begging.

Had I only heard the words, so earnest and needy, I would have thought she was compelled, but my loins stirred because unlike those I had used my power to compel, she was no shrinking worshiper, slavering at my feet, grateful for any crumb I might drop.

She stood with a pride that far exceeded her actual strength. And yet... her posture gave no hint of her fragility. Her chin was high. High enough to reveal the bob of her throat that underlined the stink of fear on her. Yet she didn't cower. Didn't throw herself at my feet like the others would. I would not have thought it possible, but somehow she managed to beg with dignity. And her eyes, when they met mine, walked the line between pleading and challenging.

Her stubbornness and insolence might have irritated me, but I admired her courage. Of course, it also made it extremely clear that she had no concept of the true depth of my power. None whatsoever.

She held the knowledge, but had not yet seen the truth that there would be no disease in any partner of mine, because at my command, any that might have existed within the body of one of my toys was eradicated.

She knew, but did not truly grasp, that I could instruct their hearts to stop beating, and they would. Or hers. Or any living creature. That I held death in the palm of my hand and could dispense it at will.

And she *truly* did not comprehend that she was not in any way equipped to take the brunt of my sexual appetite. And yet, she wished to try.

The tiny kitten, hissing in defiance at the wolf.

How fucking adorable.

She did, however, have a point about the odds of conception being improved with increased opportunity. Certainly for the next week it was a good idea to give her body every chance to conceive, and relieving my stress with another would only deplete my body in ways that could otherwise be beneficial to us both.

I was surprised that the idea wasn't entirely repulsive to me.

A virgin she might be, but her body had responded eagerly, and she clearly possessed a heart of passion. Perhaps this cycle was the only one it would take. Perhaps I could impregnate her immediately, and then we could shed this façade of a marriage. She could have her little cottage. I could have our offspring. I would visit her during the times most likely to impregnate her again until we had a second. Then we could both be alone and happy.

Why hadn't I seen it this way before?

Suddenly buoyant about the possibility, I nodded to myself. I was a grown male. I could restrict myself for a week or two.

I'd gone so deeply into my thoughts that I hadn't thought about the fact that she was watching me. And growing more and more nervous. Presumably because I hadn't answered her, she swallowed for a third time, closed her eyes, and offered that stunning sacrifice once more.

"I am… your slave, Casimir," she breathed, eyes screwed tightly shut and forehead pinched. "If what you want isn't violent, I will… I am willing to *try*. Please."

The words should have made me furious. She made demands on me?

Yet, she begged. She submitted. Against her own will—she herself into my hands, choosing it even when everything within her clearly recoiled…

Power jolted through me with such force it stole my breath. I was forced to wait a moment to respond, pretend to consider her words, rather than staggering to find my balance until my blood stopped fizzing. Because, right alongside the wave of power that threatened to consume me, there was a tiny, whispering urge in me to… give *her* what *she* wanted. The very anathema to my dominance.

Rage and fear roared in me and I held that power back by my claws, barely delivering her from the lash of it.

What was she doing? Had this all been a trick? Had I finally fallen to the machinations of my enemy?

Who the fuck had explained my power and how did she know where to erode it?

She opened her eyes as I swiftly closed the last feet between us, grabbing her arms and pulling her close. I snarled down at her and her eyes went wide and frightened at my sudden aggression.

"How did you know?" I demanded.

She shook her head, blinking rapidly. "Know what?"

"How did you know that offering yourself in that way would increase my power?" *And how did you know how to steal from it?* I would never speak that thought, never confirm for her that she'd been successful. Because she *had* also strengthened me.

My breathing was too fast.

How had she known that giving herself up voluntarily would light a fire in my blood unlike any I had ever experienced? And while it increased me, it would also fight to take me down?

She frowned, her forehead pinching. "I didn't really. It just seemed... logical."

Logic? She rationalized this when I'd lived with this power for three decades and never seen that?

"Who told you?" I demanded. "Who brought you here to tempt me?!"

Was this a trap? Had she been planted by my enemies?

Her head jerked back and she looked horrified. "No one! I just... I know about men and... and power."

"Oh?" I growled. "And what do you, a poorly bred human, know of a wolf's power?" I seethed.

Anger flashed alongside her fear. "I don't care what you are, power is power. And I know power isn't really about what you take. The real power... the real strength is in what you choose."

"Stop speaking in riddles! Answer my question!"

"I am! No one told me this, I learned it from my life!" she shrilled.

"How? Who taught you?"

Her face got hard then, revealing the spine of steel that explained why she hadn't bowed when the other women fell to my power.

When she spoke it was in a vicious hiss. "My asshole father and my bastard brothers that he's molding into his own image. And trust me, they don't know a damn thing about you. They just wanted the money they could get for selling me to the wolves!"

20. The Snack

~ CASIMIR ~

Jesse's frantic insistence gave me a moment's hesitation. And then her words landed and gave me even greater pause.

She'd been sold? I frowned and made a mental note to have Ghere look into her family and see how they might be tangled up with wolves in a plot. While she seemed guileless, we could never be too careful. I didn't remember being told that some of those we took were purchased. That left an itch between my shoulder blades.

Then I was distracted from my thoughts because she raised her chin, so even though I was taller, she managed to look down her nose at me.

"You don't have to worry about me, Cazz. I'm going to give you whatever you want." I almost groaned as my power surged again, but she wasn't done. "I'm going to do that, choose to do it, because then you've taken nothing from me. You only get what I give. And when I get out of this hell, I'll still... I'll still be me."

There it was again... the faintest of echoes, a whisper of poisoned claws against my heart.

I considered her again, measuring her for truth. She showed none of the signs of a lie—and I was incredibly perceptive with humans who did not have our senses, or awareness of the many ways they gave away their true intentions. And yet... it seemed too coincidental that she, a cowering virgin, would not only understand exactly how to empower and tempt me, but also threaten the very power she was fueling.

I frowned down at her. I could kill her. Just rid the world of her. If she had been planted, or was part of a conspiracy, that would put an end to it.

But with the bond still so new and unbreached it would be very... uncomfortable for me.

And while I hated to admit it, she was fascinating. Though, I would never tell her so, because that would give her power, and *that* made her dangerous.

She continued to stare defiantly down her nose at me, but she didn't pull out of my grip.

"I'm not certain you understand the definition of a slave," I muttered.

She arched one brow. "You don't seem to understand the definition of *wife* and *mate*, so maybe we're even?"

Surprised, delighted laughter bubbled in my chest, but I swallowed it down. *Dear god,* I thought fatalistically, *I am going to have to find more like her. At least if we fail we'll enjoy the process of burning down the world. And if we don't...*

I rubbed my face to cover the grim smile I was hiding. "I accept your... eagerness," I said carefully. "And I understand that you prefer me to remain faithful."

"Yes. Please."

I nodded, twisting my lips and considering my options. "Very well. For now I will bring all my appetites to you. But now the terms will be mine."

Her eyes widened. "What terms?"

"I will agree not to breach the bond as long as you continue to want my... attentions. If you give me your word that the day you do not, you will give me your permission to seek attention elsewhere."

She swallowed hard. "Okay, I think... I can do that."

I tilted my head and gave her a dark smile. "Trust me, Jesse. I may not read your mind, but I can read your scent—and sense you through the bond. You believe you will not wish it. I have lived this before. I assure you that you will. I am asking you to be honest with me when you do—and not to hold off out of some petty sense of revenge."

"I... okay, Cazz. I said if I stop wanting you—your attention— I'll tell you."

He shook his head. "No, Kitten. You'll do better than that. You'll *ask me* to go elsewhere. None of these female games—you will not double-speak, or half-speak. You will not later accuse me of misreading the situation. You will be very clear with me, and tell me to take another. And rest assured, I will."

"But only after I tell you to... right?" she said shakily.

Reluctantly, I nodded. "I have been advised that breaching the bond can be... detrimental to our shared goal," I said dryly. "So you have my word, I will not seek another in my bed until you ask me to."

Her relief was palpable and brought with it a rush of renewed desire, strong enough that I could smell it on her. Good. We would need that if she was to be my only plaything for the next week.

Pleased by her response, I cupped her face for a moment, smiling with anticipation. "Now, I really must go. The servants will bring clothing and anything else you might want. You have only to tell them. Other than that, I will return to you this evening. Rest while you can."

Then I stalked out of the chamber.

It was gratifying to feel the kick of her desire as she watched me leave. I wondered which part of my body pleased her most. I would have to ask.

The dark grief that descended on her when I was out of sight was more worrisome, and yet, not unexpected.

Because, while she may have found a new way to add to my power. She was apparently ignorant of the whole of it. And I would not be the one to educate her.

She thought she would not lose herself simply because I didn't apply the compulsion? I shook my head.

I could inflict my power on her, compel her to my wishes. But even if I did not, simply giving herself to me would not make her immune to my dominance. If she believed she'd provide me an heir, then walk away unshackled, she was a fool.

And yet, it would be fun to watch her fall to my graces, rather than my compulsion, to watch my power slowly erode her will without her awareness.

And it would be the greatest of my triumphs, the crown jewel to my throne, to watch her become a slave in truth without ever compelling a single step.

I smiled then, and laughed again.

This little kitten was going to be a very, very tasty treat.

21. Help Her Thrive - Part 1

~ CASIMIR ~

As I walked further from Jesse's chamber feeling smug, but still a little sweaty, something itched between my shoulder blades. I tapped into the bond, careful to hold myself apart, yet open myself enough to measure her... and to my irritation, discovered her emotional descent becoming more drastic.

I'd felt the pang of her desire for me—which was a good sign—but this sudden plunge into fear, while perhaps natural, was frustrating. And as I held her heart on that glowing string between us but kept myself blocked, all too quickly her fear threaded with hints of despair.

Already? Already we were back to this... this *failure?*

I wanted to bite something. What had happened? What was she thinking to make her so scared?

Far from being the strongest I had found, was she going to fail me even faster than the others?

I stopped in the middle of the corridor, turning to look over my shoulder in the direction I'd come from, suddenly tempted to return to her, a combination of frustration and impatience urging me to shake some sense into her. I could go back, remind her of the truth I'd spoken to her before the wedding—reassure her that despite the fact that I would not give my heart, she would continue to have my body and every resource available to me as King.

But then my hackles rose.

We had an arrangement. And worse, I had *adjusted.* Surely she could at least get through the first day without falling apar—

"Cazz? Is there a problem?"

I turned quickly to see my Cleric, Rake, striding from deeper within the castle. The relief I felt in response was... out of kilter with the situation.

"I was just looking for you," I lied.

His eyebrows popped up. "Oh? Was there a problem with the ceremony?"

"No, no, nothing like that. But I think the rush to our union and mating has... unsettled my mate. I hadn't thought about how she would need to be alone in these hours. I wonder if you might have a word with her?"

Rake stared at me darkly for a moment and I stared right back.

Rake was the only other wolf I had ever agreed not to compel, but not because he wouldn't challenge me. Rather, specifically because he would.

It was tradition in our bloodline... a heritage passed down seven generations, and a strategy for war: Whoever held the power to compel others risked losing sight of the truth and becoming his own echo-chamber because he was capable of turning the minds of everyone around him.

The power to compel was not foolproof. It did not solve issues that were unseen or heard by its holder. If I believed something to be true, and told those around me to believe it, with compulsion they would, whether facts bore out or not.

And while compulsion could heal, or end life with a word, it could not give it back.

It was a running joke in my family line that God knew a wolf with the power to give life would kill too many, knowing he could always get them back. So, He'd hobbled us in that way.

Whatever the purpose, it was believed that if a wolf with that level of power didn't have *someone* in his ear that would question or challenge his thinking, the King would grow beyond arrogant. He would begin to see the world through broken eyes, simply because he could make everyone else believe whatever he wanted to. And he would mentally decimate those who followed him. In the end, the King himself would eventually reach levels of stupidity and self-service to surpass even those under the compulsion.

And so... each King before me with the power to compel had chosen a servant. Someone of a sound mind, self-control, but true strength, who could be their unadulterated voice of reason. That wolf would never be compelled, and his service would be measured in his courage to be honest.

Rake was the wolf I had vowed never to compel. And in the years since I had taken him, I had never found reason to regret the decision.

He was a male of integrity. Boringly righteous—even utterly celibate, though his faith did not require it. *That* had been a shock the day I'd learned that. I had assumed his resolve to never take a mate—or relieve his body with *any* female—was a requirement of his devotion. But he assured me, it was a step he had taken willingly. Choosing it for himself to allow himself to better focus on his work, and the service he offered.

Admirable, but unnecessarily noble, in my opinion.

Still, the male had not wavered. Six, perhaps seven years, and I'd never seen him even tempted to give in to a female's invitation. And I had been present to witness more than one.

He was an enigma in the pack, and some of the females saw his discipline as a challenge.

I had stopped betting against him.

If any male could ever convince me that God was more than just a tyrannical despot, it would be Rake.

I'd never tell him that, though. He'd never let me hear the end of it.

No... Rake did not need to know that I considered him more brother and friend than advisor. I had vowed never to compel him—and had never had need to even consider rescinding the oath. And Rake, in turn, had vowed to always speak his challenges or concerns to keep me humble.

And he did a fantastic job, I thought dryly. *The fucker never stopped looking at me sideways, or sniffing his disapproval.*

"Cazz, you want *me* to have a word with *your* mate?" Rake asked quietly.

"Yes. She's... struggling already. I suppose since we skipped the rites, things did move a bit quickly. She's probably in shock. It might help her to feel she has an ally of sorts. And she seems to speak to God quite a bit, so perhaps you'll have that in common?"

"Perhaps. But... what was it, exactly, that you wanted me to speak to her about?"

"I don't know, just..." I waved my hand. "Help her feel less afraid of us, I suppose."

"Wouldn't it be more beneficial for her to have that kind of comfort from you?"

"Well, of course," I snarled. "I meant for you to be an additional reassurance, Rake. Perhaps you could tell her, from your vast personal experience, about how I *don't* just kill or compel everyone who pisses me off?"

Rake gave a half-smile. "I can do that."

"Well, thank God."

"Apparently, that's what she said," he snorted.

"More than once," I shot back with a smug smile as I started walking again, half-amused, and half-irritated.

Rake groaned. "I didn't need to know that, Cazz."

"Vows of celibacy creating some fiction, Rake? Burning a little? You know, if your palms are chapped, the humans make this very effective lubricant—"

"It's wonderful to speak with you, as always, Sire."

"I know."

Then I turned the corner and stepped out of sight. I would have smiled again, but the part of me that was now Jesse took a sudden plunge into panic.

I ground my teeth and mentally linked with Rake. *'Get to her chambers now. She's in crisis.'*

Then I cut off all contact with him, and blocked Jesse. But even unable to feel her spiraling fear, I walked away uneasy.

I did not like it.

She'd been in my life a matter of hours and she was already causing trouble.

Fucking women.

22. Help her Thrive - Part 2

~ CASIMIR ~

"I need to know if you've discovered any more hints about the human female fertility," I muttered a few minutes later to Ghere as I picked through the strange items spread all over his desk.

He watched me cautiously. "We discussed it, Cazz. I told you that their emotional and mental state is incredibly central to their likelihood to conceive—and to sustaining the pregnancy also."

"Yes, yes," I muttered, flapping a hand at him impatiently as I turned away from the detritus on the desk to face him.

His brows were high and he eyed me warily. He'd been shocked when I walked in. I supposed it wasn't common for me to come all the way down to his study cave under the Palace. But after that delicious taking, I'd needed to move to wake my mind back up. So, I'd come to him rather than linking to summon him.

"It's all well and good to speak of emotional and mental health. But how do we improve our chances after the last two fuck-ups?" I muttered.

Ghere scratched the back of his neck. "Well, primary concern is her health, of course. Simple nutrition and strength-training—"

"Taken care of," I snapped, then opened the link with Rake long enough to shoot him an order to make certain that Jesse ate from the tray I'd had provided before slamming it closed again. "What else?"

"Lowering stress levels," Ghere said with a pointed look.

I frowned. "Be more specific."

Ghere turned away, and for a moment I thought he was rolling his eyes, but his tone was even when he spoke. "It's quite stressful for the women being torn from their normal lives and thrown down here with us." He walked towards a cabinet against the wall and opened a drawer, flipping through papers inside. "It might be good to look for ways to help her feel safe and cared for, as well as... well, just giving her things to do that she can enjoy. Just like us, the humans need a purpose, otherwise they can despair. I've told you before I felt your mates got bored—"

"I am not boring," I snapped.

"No, Cazz, *you* aren't," Ghere answered blandly without turning to look at me. "But you are... busy. Perhaps... consider setting aside a couple of hours a day to speak with her or... undertake some kind of activity in which she feels she has your full attention."

I smiled. "Oh, I plan to." She'd been delicious—and for her first time, showing a naturally passionate and eager approach. I was looking forward to training her both for my pleasure and to find her own.

Ghere sighed. "That's *not* what I meant, but it is actually the other aspect of this picture. The human experts agree that orgasms assist in fertility, both as a stress release and because it encourages the... er... seed towards the egg, as it were."

I snorted. "You can just say it, Ghere."

He did roll his eyes then. He was turning towards me, flipping through a sheaf of papers until he found what he was looking for and handed it to me. "That will tell you in detail, but as an overview, orgasm can help reduce anxiety, and raises the level of dopamine in the blood—which can help guard against depression. But it's not the *only* form of relaxation a woman needs," he said dryly. "She needs other ways to unwind and have a good time."

"I assure you—"

"Hobbies, Cazz. I mean *non-sexual* hobbies. Entertainments. Things she enjoys doing that don't require her to attend *you*. And if it's fertility and the improvement of the sexual sphere you want, you'll need to spend at least some of that time with her. She needs to feel safe with you outside the bedroom, in order to trust you in it."

I frowned. "Give me an example."

Ghere stared. "You should ask *her*. I don't know her, so I couldn't tell you what she likes."

"I know that, I meant—nevermind. I'll just ask her."

Ghere looked like he wanted to say something, but then he pressed his lips together, and walked back to the filing cabinet to close the drawer.

"What?" I asked him flatly.

"I didn't say anything."

"Exactly. What did you want to say and decide not to?"

He turned around, leaning back against the cabinet and watching me like a prey animal wanting to keep their distance. But to his credit, he didn't balk. "If you really want to give this one a chance to be different, you can't do to her what you did to the others."

"Oh? What did I do, Ghere?"

"Breached the bond with other women."

I went very still, eyes locked on his. "We have discussed this."

"Yes, we have. And I know where you stand. But you asked me how to make better certain that this mate succeeds in conception. And I'm telling you, *most* human women prefer a secure relationship—especially those who have never given themselves to men before."

I had a flash in my head of the look on her face when she learned I'd thought to only avoid actual intercourse with other women.

"You can't do this, Cazz!"

I growled in frustration, for some reason unwilling to tell him that I had already offered her this concession.

"She is utterly secure. I fucking married her! Made her my Queen!"

"Seriously, Cazz? Don't pretend to be stupid. You know what I meant. These women aren't accustomed to matebonds at all— they are quite enthralled by them. Add to that, the matebond allows her to feel your presence even when she isn't physically near you. When the time comes that she wants to be near and instead has to feel you with others and enjoying things without her... that becomes *torturous.* You and I both know the fastest way to break any mind is unrelenting torment. So... don't torment her."

I folded my arms and glared at him because he was making sense and the truth was, I didn't want to hear it. I didn't want to think about being the reason the previous two had failed. And I didn't want to think about... well...

I'd always sworn I'd never allow myself to go the route of my father and vent anger just because I didn't like that a person was right. I'd felt the injustice at the end of his fangs too many times to rationalize it for myself.

The battle here was not whether or not Ghere was correct in his facts, only whether I was willing to give up my toys completely for the sake of the bloodline.

The thought made my skin feel too tight.

"I will think on it," I growled. I didn't tell him I'd already agreed to do so for the immediate future.

Ghere nodded placidly, as if it were no big decision to him.

Smug fuck.

23. The Endless Dark

~ JESSE ~

Watching a naked Cazz walk away from me was a feast for the eyes. His body was perfect—broad, thick shoulders and chest, narrowing to a muscled and lean waist, an ass you could bounce a dime off of, flawless skin and perfectly cut lines... everywhere.

The thrill of watching the muscles on his back roll and twitch as he walked, my *sense* of the sheer masculine power of him as he moved away from me, distracted me for a moment from the sinking feeling that started as soon as he turned to go.

But then he disappeared out of the room.

I stared at the door for a minute, suddenly feeling sick as I turned that last conversation over in my mind.

He'd agreed to leave the other women alone, which was a huge relief. But it also seemed like he believed it wouldn't be a permanent arrangement. My head spun with images of laying alone in the dark while my husband had sex with someone else...

I wanted to throw up.

I wanted to believe he really would wait until I told him he could—which I'd never do—but... But there was nothing I could do about it just then, I realized, and I was still naked except for the blanket. And the servants might come back at any minute.

At that thought, it hit me like a truck what a strange and dire situation I was in.

Panic fluttered in my chest and my thoughts began to race.

I'd just married a wolf. A wolf *king*. He was promiscuous, arrogant, powerful, and terrifying... and attractive, and delicious, and fascinating and... and terrifying.

And I'd *married* him? Given him my virginity? *What the hell just happened?*

I shook my head. I could feel the anxiety rising. I needed to focus on something normal.

Before he'd left, Cazz had mentioned a bathroom. I really did want to get cleaned up... but what was I going to wear?

Keeping the fur tight around my body, I cast around looking, then hurried over to pick up the wedding dress from the floor where Cazz had tossed it when he'd taken it off me.

As I leaned down, there was a flash in my head of that moment before he'd whipped it off, when he'd been touching me, and the ache he'd inspired deep inside. I felt my cheeks heat as my pulse rose.

I straightened to look for the bathroom, but there was suddenly a thrum in my chest, something warm and... actually, something *hot.*

I stopped moving and put a hand to that spot, right at the center of my chest. My heart beat even faster.

There was something strange. A space within me that hadn't existed before. A tangible sense of something else... of some*one.*

It dawned on me that I could feel Cazz there. And as I concentrated, I could discern his smug satisfaction from his determined strength. I could feel that he was moving away from me. And the pulse of his desire.

Did that mean he'd felt mine?

As I walked slowly to the bathroom, my hands full of fur and wedding dress—which was a situation I'd never imagined I'd find myself in—I considered what this bond they'd forged between us meant.

He could feel me. I could feel him. We were linked.

Was that only because we were close here, in this cave they'd made into a palace? Or would that always be the case? If I had his babies and he sent me away as I'd asked, gave me my own space, was I still going to have to *feel* him lusting after his other women?

Or worse... what if he kept his word and didn't sleep with them, but I could feel him wanting them and resenting me and...

Panic didn't just flutter then, it stabbed.

I'd thought tying myself to him was a way to get free. I'd thought if I could stop him from compelling me with that awful power, I could eventually get free of him, and everyone else.

Was I going to feel this man and his *urges* inside me for the rest of my life?!

As I closed the door on the bathroom, my breath shuddered out of me.

There had to be a way to block it, right? Or close myself off? Or something?

I needed to ask Cazz—and pray that he'd tell me the truth. Or that I might find another ally here... perhaps some of the servants, who'd tell me?

Then I remembered the way those women had looked when they'd brought the food in for him—adoration, eagerness, mindless devotion.

It was chilling.

The guards hadn't looked at him like that, but they'd shrunk when he appeared. So even the males were under his thumb.

I stopped dead in the middle of the bathroom's slate floor.

With sudden, heart-rending clarity, the terrifying months and years to come fanned out ahead of me: Me, a wife and eventually mother, surrounded not only by people who weren't entirely human, but who were all utterly in the thrall of my husband.

I could see myself surrounded by people, but not a single ally or friend who could be trusted to have only my best interests at heart among them.

That picture of the future stretched before me, a hollow wasteland, whistling with nothing but loneliness and isolation.

My throat began to pinch.

Memories and injustices, frustrations and fears... it all suddenly bore down.

Twenty-four hours ago, I'd been a poor woman with a low-paying job, four asshole brothers and a father who bordered on sadistic. I'd been secretly saving cash to get myself out of state and on my own feet. Determined to build a life in which no man ever had a controlling hand on me again.

Now I was married to a man with the power to steal my mind. I was no longer a virgin. And even if I was successful in fulfilling his demands, I was probably years from having any kind of independence—but even then, always under the threat of the sudden appearance of my husband and his undeniable power. That was assuming he didn't just steal my mind at some point anyway. Or that he didn't *break* my mind by igniting this fire inside me, then burning with someone else, while I had to stand by and feel it.

God... please...

Panic ripped through me. I'd thought I'd been clever, coming up with a way to curb Cazz's influence over me, and use his strength to my advantage.

Instead, I'd completed the death circle of my family and had put myself in the path of an actual predator?

What the hell had I been thinking?

24. Predator Panic

~ *JESSE* ~

Self-loathing and injustice burned in my chest. But it soon twisted into gut-wrenching fear.

What was I going to do? How was I going to survive this?

And how did this man, who I barely knew, have such a grip on me? Why couldn't I shake free from him?

My entire body shook and I wondered if I was going to lose my mind even without him compelling me.

I had thought it was odd when Cazz said human women didn't survive in the wolf world. I had thought he must mean they couldn't fight off other wolves and got killed or something. But then, why would his wife commit suicide?

But now, as my chest constricted and my heart pounded, and no matter how I tried to *think clearly* I couldn't get free of this sense of impending doom, I feared I might have an inkling of what pushed the poor woman over the edge. I mentally ticked off the reasons why she might have reached her limit.

Unknown culture.

Strange people who aren't just people.

Nothing but darkness underground.

Violence or actual magic used to control her mind.

Emotional isolation without end.

The one male who should be your greatest advocate, actually posing the greatest threat.

And through it all, looking over your shoulder at everything, watching every word, because anyone could be his spy or ally, programmed to betray you, even if they might not choose to.

It was… impossible. What the hell had I been thinking, giving myself to this man?

No matter which way I looked, there was nothing good. No connection. Nothing that made a life… a life.

I wanted to weep. I wanted to scream. I wanted to demand God let me do this day over and just pretend to be dead like that woman who'd fallen when the guards brought us.

But then there was a flash in my head of Cazz staring at me, his eyes burning with that sultry heat that also flared in the space in my chest that was shaped like him…

My heart rattled behind my ribs and my body flushed, overwhelmed for a moment with images of the way he'd touched me, how he'd made my body feel. And for a moment, it was soothing. There was *one* good thing here.

But then I remembered his casual reference to the other women and wanted to weep.

So, the sex was great… but not sacred.

And I was supposed to make a life out of *that?*

The urge was there to just put the robe on and crawl into bed, to cry and wallow and generally feel sorry for myself, but I had learned a long time ago that self-pity achieved nothing. So, why was I so affected? I was stronger than this!

It had been a strange and terrifying couple of days. Was it any wonder I wasn't at my best? I needed a distraction. I also needed to get cleaned up. So, I stumbled over to the bath, fighting tears, twisting my hair up into loose bun, and running the water into the massive basin, just enough to get in and wash myself hurriedly. I didn't even bother with my hair, just got myself clean, then crawled back out, hands trembling, and asking myself how I was going to endure this bleak future.

I dried and wrapped myself in the robe that had been hanging on the hook, grateful that it was long enough to go to my knees and it had a hood I could pull up over my head against the chill I was suddenly feeling.

I had just flopped onto the top of the bed, trying to get a grip on myself as images of a dark, friendless, joyless future yawned before me, when there was a knock on the door.

Was it a servant?

Clearing my throat because it was pinching, I tried to make my voice sound normal as I called out, "Who is it?"

"It's Rake," a deep but smooth voice replied, muffled by the door.

Rake? Who the hell was Rake?

"The Cleric," he added, as if he'd heard me.

I blinked. "I… oh. What do you want?" It was rude, but I wasn't sure—

"Cazz sent me. May I come in?"

I stared at the door. "Why?"

"Because… I think I can help."

Help? With what?

Not really feeling like a conversation with a stranger, but remembering how his grip had sucked me back from the edge of that dark pit in Cazz that had almost overwhelmed me, I crawled off the bed and walked to the door, opening it enough to peer through.

Sure enough, it was the large, handsome Cleric who'd married us, standing there looking like an Instagram model in dark jeans, a tight-fitting shirt, and thick, leather boots that wouldn't look out of place in a biker gang, or maybe at a rock concert.

He peered down at me, his expression a lot softer than it had been during the wedding.

"Are you okay, Jesse?" he asked quietly.

I just frowned at him. "Why are you here?"

He sighed, then looked left and right down the mezzanine level behind him. "Cazz sent me. I've been… a resource for his former mates. He thought I could—"

"Wait… mates? Plural?"

Rake tipped his head, frowning. "Yes. He's had two. You didn't know?"

I gaped. "What happened to the first one?"

His expression got dark. "The same thing that happened to the second."

Holy *shit*. How many women had killed themselves over this man?

That panic quietly speared through my chest again and it must have shown on my face, because Rake put a hand to the door, though he didn't push it.

"Please, Jesse. I really think I can help you. I don't want to see another woman face that fate. Can I come in? Just to talk? I believe… I believe perhaps we share a faith? And if so… I think I can be a very real help to you here. Please. Just… let me explain?"

I stared at him, but realized, what did I have to lose? So, I backed away from the door, then turned and walked to the table where the tray of food was still waiting.

Let him come in if he wanted to. I wasn't going to stop him.

What would be the point?

25. Something New

~ *JESSE* ~

"So, what did he make you come here for?" I muttered, taking a handful of grapes and popping one into my mouth sullenly. It was surprisingly sweet.

"He hasn't *made* me do anything," Rake replied.

I looked at him skeptically as I ate a couple more grapes. They were actually really good. Then I saw berries in a bowl next to them and chose one of those too, eating it—then having to awkwardly catch the juice before it dripped down my chin. Rake smiled. I stifled embarrassment, but waited for him to actually answer the question.

Rake sighed and folded his arms. "He *asked* me to come talk to you, to see if I could help."

"Help with what?"

"Understanding that he isn't, perhaps, exactly what you think?" he said carefully.

I sat back in my chair shaking my head as I picked up a little toothpick thingy from a cup, then speared a square of cheese and an olive from the buffet on the tray. I chewed it and swallowed and Rake didn't add anymore.

"He made you come in here to tell me that he's a nice guy?"

"I told you, he didn't make me."

"I'm sorry, but anyone who's under his thumb like that—"

"Cazz has never—and will never—compel me," he said softly.

I blinked. "For real?"

Rake nodded. "He has vowed never to exert that kind of control over me. And I've vowed to always tell him the truth and challenge his thinking. It's literally my job."

I stared at him. "He *pays* you to question him?"

Rake huffed. "It's not quite that transactional, but... as his primary advisor and spiritual guide, it is my job to ask him to think about aspects of his life and decisions that he maybe hasn't considered—or doesn't want to. He thinks it keeps him humble. I think it keeps him honest with himself. I'm not sure they're the same thing."

I just stared. He shrugged.

"Jesse, Cazz is a good King. Mostly. Much better than his father and grandfather were. He is much more... human."

"Human?"

"Thoughtful. Emotional. Rather than reactive—he doesn't just live on pure animal instinct."

I felt my nose wrinkle. "Are you sure? I had to *beg* him not to sleep with other women, and he's still not committed to it in the long run. I had no idea... I thought we'd agreed..."

Rake sighed. "I despise that part of this also. The breaching of the bond is wrong. Evil. I'm glad to hear that he's going to avoid that—at least for now. I'll do everything I can to help you keep him in that place."

"Why?"

"Why what?"

"Why would you do that? Aren't you one of his wolves? Why would you try to work against him—I don't believe you, by the way. But I'm curious why you'd even tell me that."

Rake frowned. "Jesse, I know this has been a shock, and God knows my skin crawled when I realized who they'd brought to him to mate this time... but here you are. I have to believe that has happened for a reason, because it's too late to change it. So, I'll say again: Cazz is a good King. And more powerful than any I have heard from the older wolves."

I huffed. "It must be easy to rule when you just make everyone do everything you want."

Rake's lips thinned. "I told you he doesn't compel me. He asked me to come talk to you, so I am. I can say no to him. He doesn't like it, but I can do it. I'm here because I think what he asked for was good."

"Which was what?"

"For me to give you insight and help you understand our people and how you fit here. I don't want to see you end up like the others. That cycle needs to stop. And you've come to him differently and… with faith, I gather?"

I watched him warily, but nodded to confirm his suspicion. I very much doubted that a wolf had faith in the same God I did. But they did call him a Cleric and he had helped me back there during that ceremony. When I'd almost drowned in the darkness of Cazz.

That thought took me back to that moment, and that made me shiver.

Rake took a step forward, his eyes intent on me. "You aren't like the others. You saw his darkness—and understood it for what it was."

It wasn't a question, but I nodded.

"You're different, Jesse. Different than any other female they've ever brought to him. And even though I would have removed you from this place if I could have, the truth is… you are equipped to deal with the darkness here in a way none of the earlier women have been."

"What darkness? I mean… I can feel it. But… where does it come from?"

"We all have darkness, Jesse. You know that. You can see it. The wolves are dark already, but Cazz…"

"What about him?"

"His story is… difficult. He was not born the way he is." He stopped speaking abruptly. I waited, but he didn't go on.

"What aren't you telling me?" I asked quietly, taking another handful of grapes.

"It isn't my place to tell you Cazz's story. That's up to him."

"It must be really dark then."

Rake shrugged, but his eyes shadowed. "You have darkness behind you as well."

That was only true, but it made me shift in my seat. I didn't want to talk about that either, so I turned back to the food and kept picking at the crackers and cheese.

When I didn't talk, Rake took another step closer, his voice low and probing. "How did you come to be here? I meant it when I said you're different from the others. How did the Reapers find you?"

I shook my head, my appetite suddenly gone. I put down the cracker I'd been about to eat and brushed the crumbs off my hands, avoiding his eyes.

26. The Way of Wolves

~ JESSE ~

"My brothers sold me to them," I muttered, still not quite able to believe it myself. I'd known my brothers hated me, but I'd never thought...

Rake stiffened. "Like the story of Joseph? Sold into slavery by his brothers?"

It was my turn to blink. "You know that story?"

Rake huffed. "The title Cleric isn't an honorific. I am a spiritual advisor, Jesse. Yes, I know the story of Joseph. I also know what your name means."

That made me squirm. "Don't tell him."

"I won't. That won't make it less true."

I gave a one-shouldered shrug, but didn't answer. I didn't think there was really any truth to—

"So, truly, your brothers sold you to the Reapers? In this day and age that's—"

"Human trafficking. Yes."

Rake gave a low whistle. "No wonder you wanted to get away from them."

They weren't the ones I was most desperate to avoid, but he didn't need to know that. "Don't get all starry-eyed about it. I'm *not* Joseph. No favoritism here. They most definitely weren't jealous of me. They did this because they're narcissistic assholes and they wanted the money. They've probably been fighting over it ever since. I'm the only girl, and they all have no respect for women, thanks to my father."

Rake's expression darkened. "Then I guess we pray that your story ends as Joseph's did, even if it didn't start that way."

I looked back down at the food, but I still wasn't hungry. "Honestly, I'd just be glad to get out of here in my right mind."

Rake nodded. "I can help with that. I've often thought the physical darkness in this place leads the heart towards the spiritual shadow as well. What if we were to take walks above ground each day? See the sun. Breathe the air?"

I sucked in a breath. "I... I think I'd like that."

Rake smiled, and he really was very handsome—a wide, square jaw and full lips, dark hair that was long enough to fall into his eyes, but was usually pushed back. "We can walk in the air and discuss... whatever is on your mind. As the Spiritual Advisor, I can offer counsel, or just companionship. I am one of the few unmated males Cazz will allow to be alone with you."

Oh God. What did that mean? I looked at him, fear curling in my chest. "Why? And... what would he do to other... males?"

Rake's lips twisted. "As his mate you are... off-limits. Entirely. But wolves are predatory and they live by their instincts. When a female is powerful she is desirable. Males want to take her—a hangover from our animal heritage, I suppose. In any case, I am vowed to celibacy, and Cazz knows that's real for me. So he's not threatened by me. Other males though... except for servants who are under his compulsion... he'll be very aggressive with any male who seeks your company. Very. With me though... it'll be fine. And it's safer for you to be with me if you aren't with him, anyway."

I frowned. "Why?"

"Because there's a reason Cazz is going to keep all those males from you, Jesse. Wolf culture is very different to human. You just became the most powerful female this side of the globe—trust me, *many* of the males will do their best to tempt you away from him if they're given the chance. They'll be a lot less likely to try if you're with me."

"Tempt me?"

"Attract you. Catch your eye. Seduce you."

Gross. I shuddered and Rake shrugged. "They wouldn't force you—not any of them that are in their right minds. But by human standards a male wolf can be... assertive in his approach."

I almost laughed, remembering Cazz and his arrogance when we met, and dominance in the bedroom. Assertive didn't cover it. But then that thought made me little bit cold, so I pushed it away.

"Well, if I'm allowed to go up into the sunshine with you, I'd like that. As long as Cazz is okay with it. I can't do anything to piss him off."

Rake's expression tensed.

"What?" I asked him.

His lips twisted. "The truth is, Cazz won't even know what you're doing half the time. And he will really only care if it affects your conception of his offspring, or impacts his power. As long as you continue to submit, he will allow you just about any freedom you wish."

"Why does that make you look angry?"

Rake muttered something under his breath that I didn't catch. He looked down at his feet, then raised his chin again and his eyes held a certain glint. He opened his mouth—but just then, the door behind him opened and Cazz strode in.

My heart immediately began to beat faster. Why hadn't I felt him coming?

"Ah, you're still here, Rake. Thank you for keeping her company. You can leave now."

Rake didn't even blink. He stepped forward to take my hand gently, and when I gave it to him, a little confused, he bowed over it, then looked up at me and smiled. "It's a pleasure to serve you, Sire."

It was touching, but Cazz frowned and watched him darkly as he turned on his heel and strode out of the room almost as abruptly as Cazz had walked in.

But the moment the door shut behind him, Cazz turned to me and my mouth went a little dry.

He was still shirtless, and his hair was messy. But he stood in front of me every bit as confident and assured as a CEO in a suit. And he smiled when he caught my eyes drifting down to his chest and abs.

"Do not fear, Kitten, nothing has changed. I spoke with my servant for a moment, that's all."

"About what?"

"About how to give you the best possible chance of... thriving," he said enigmatically. "And I learned one of my former mistakes that I hope to rectify now."

"Oh?"

He nodded and tipped his head like he was considering me. "Tell me, what things do you like to do?"

"What kind of things?"

"Anything. The real things. The things you would do alone when no one was watching. How do you like to spend your time if you have a chance. What helps you relax?"

I shrugged. "I like being outside, just walking around. I like to read. And listen to music. And..." I trailed off because it was embarrassing.

But Cazz's brows rose. "What? What is it?"

I shrugged, and dropped my eyes back to the table because saying it out loud would sound stupid. But Cazz stepped forward, his smile fading, and took my chin in his fingers, lifting it until I raised my eyes to meet his.

"Tell me," he said, a little coldly.

I sighed. "I like to dance. When I'm alone, I turn music up loud and I dance."

I expected him to laugh. Or roll his eyes. But instead he tipped his head and his smile returned. "Music and dance? Hmmmm..." He dropped my chin and turned to pick up one of the little mandarins on the tray, tearing it apart and peeling it as he spoke. "I think I can help with that."

*****

~ *CASIMIR* ~

Jesse sat at the table wrapped in a robe, a fur blanket over her lap, watching me.

I had kept the link stifled so she wouldn't feel how deeply even her gaze affected me. My skin had prickled and my heart raced when I walked in and caught her scanning my body. I would have taken her again, right then—and aggressively—if she hadn't been so new to the act. And if Ghere's words weren't echoing in my head.

But music and dance? That offered opportunities that might please us both.

The visual that arose in my head the moment she spoke of dancing was erotic. My groin strained against the leather pants already. But perhaps I could kill two birds with only one stone— and the delay of our next lovemaking would make the anticipation even sharper...

Heart pounding, I smiled and popped one segment of the little mandarin into my mouth, letting her see my teeth and lips, and smiling wider when her eyes went round.

114

"Eat," I said quietly. "You need the nourishment—especially if we're going to dance."

"Wait... we?" she asked, blinking like she'd been distracted and was only just coming back to the conversation.

"After you've eaten, dress in whatever you feel you can move in freely and won't make you overheat. So, as little as possible." My voice dropped into a deep gravel at the mental image of *that*.

"But... I have no clothes."

I waved a hand. It was a small matter. "I'll have some brought immediately. As many as you wish. If you don't find what you like, simply ask for more."

She narrowed her eyes like she wasn't quite sure whether to believe me, but I was already reaching for the servant through the link and sending rapid-fire mental images of her body and shape, and the variety of clothes I'd like her to have available. They were mentally scrambling, but we had the goods. They'd be here in minutes.

"O-kay," she said slowly. "But... what are we going to do?"

"I am going to present my new Queen to my people," I said with a smile.

"What, like, another meeting?"

I shook my head. "Oh, no, Kitten..." I smiled darkly, reminding her of my predator. "Tell me... Have you ever been to a wolf den?

I could smell the adrenaline that shot through her.

27. Pick Me

~ *JESSE* ~

The minutes that followed were possibly the most surreal of my life—and given the day I'd had, that was saying something.

At first Cazz dodged my questions about a Wolf Den. I'd heard the stories, of course. But once again, I'd assumed they were just that—stories.

Cazz kept smiling and refusing to give any meaningful details, insisting that I would have to see it to understand it, which only made me more nervous.

But then, out of nowhere, another raft of servants arrived. And this time they were all carrying clothes and boxes of shoes.

Hangers filled with dresses, gowns, tunics, sweaters, shirts, blouses, and every kind of skirt and pant I could have imagined.

There was a dozen of them, and they made several trips each, disappearing into a large door off beside the bathroom that I hadn't explored yet. When Cazz encouraged me to follow the second wave of them in and begin considering my selection for the night, that was when things got surreal.

Because, as I took in the vast array of clothes that spanned every possible need or event—including soft pajamas and silky nightgowns—I was left slack-jawed. And not in a good way. I wasn't pumping or excited. I was… numb.

It occurred to me that this moment should have been thrilling. If anyone had told me that I would stand in the middle of a walk-in closet that was bigger than my bedroom back home and watch servants bring in armful after armful of clothes that were all in my size, continually asking me questions about colors and fabrics that

I liked, or styles that appealed—most of which I didn't even know how to answer—I would have thought it was a dream come true.

But as it happened, it just brought home how completely out of my depth I was. How much my life had changed... and how far from anything familiar or *normal* I had been taken.

For a long time I just stood there, staring.

Cazz stood in the doorway, leaning on the frame with his arms folded, watching me. At some point he said my name and I turned to look at him. I'm not sure what he saw on my face, or what he had been feeling through the bond, but he straightened immediately, his face stern.

"Everyone out," he snapped, though his voice was barely louder than the bustle of the servants hanging and folding clothes and discussing positions in the closet.

Not one of them so much as hesitated. They dropped what they were doing—literally—and turned on their heels, marching out of the closet.

Cazz turned to follow them one step out the door, muttering instructions that I couldn't hear, then he came back into the closet and closed the door, then turned to face me and folded his arms again, looking stern.

"You don't like the clothes?" he asked his voice tight with disapproval.

I blinked. "What? No. No, that's not it."

"You feel... displeased. Aggressively so."

"No. This is..." I waved a hand at the glowing room that would have been any girl's dream. "It's just overwhelming. I'm not used to it. It's too much, Cazz."

He frowned harder. "Too many choices?"

"No. I..." I dropped my face into my hands and sighed. There was no way to explain to him how *alien* this felt. And no point trying to get him to see that it was coming home to me that these kinds of dreams could only come true if you had someone to share them with. That it didn't matter if you were dressed like Cinderella when there was no Prince Charming. Or maybe if Prince Charming was a domineering stranger who may or may not steal your sanity.

There was no real point trying to tell him. Because if I was submitting and he was in charge... this was what we were doing. And it wasn't like I hated the idea of putting on some cool clothes. It was just... a lot.

"It's great," I said eventually. I felt the stab of skepticism from Cazz, but then I lifted my head and met his eyes. "I just need you

118

to tell me what to wear. Because I don't know what this place is like. What they'll expect."

Cazz's brows pressed together over his nose. "Wear whatever the hell you want, Jesse. You're the Queen, for god's sake. Plus... it's that kind of place. There will be others there in everything from jeans to a floor-length gown."

Well, that didn't help. I clawed a hand through my hair. "Well... what are you going to wear?"

Cazz had been staring at me slightly irritated—or worried— but now he smiled. "I already told you: As little as possible."

*****

He'd disappeared from the chamber for a time, urging me to look at the clothes and grow familiar with what was there.

I was bent over a drawer full of jeans in every color and cut when his footsteps sounded again. I just found a pair of vintage Levi's that were the coolest thing I'd ever seen, when he spoke from the doorway.

"Have you found anything yet?"

I straightened, holding the jeans, then froze.

There was muffled *whomph* as the jeans dropped to the floor without my permission, but I ignored it because the roof of my mouth had gone dry and my heart was suddenly racing so fast I worried I might be about to have a heart attack.

Cazz stood in the doorway looking like some kind of Lupine *god.*

I scanned him, starting from the floor, to make certain he was real...

He wore thick black boots that looked like they belonged to a rockstar, or maybe a biker. Then there were black leather pants that fit him like a second skin, revealing every muscle and ripple. They were held up by a thick, black leather belt with a metal buckle that had the sheen and weight of luxury. There was a thick leather cuff on his left wrist. And then... nothing else except a few necklaces. But somehow, his torso *shone.* Every muscle carved like it was cut from stone, the shadows between his abs and under his pecs as sharp as a pen-drawn line. And his skin...

"Are you... oiled?" I asked faintly.

My eyes finally made it up to his face—and the wicked, flashing grin he was giving me. I could feel his smug pleasure. He'd felt my jolt of desire when I stared at his cut abs and my mind took me back to those delicious moments when he'd held me and had me and...

His chest started rising and falling, the warm lights from the closet shifting on his muscles.

He licked his lips.

"You're welcome to match me, if you want to," he said slyly.

There was a split second where I imagined it in my mind—a pair of sleek black pants, heels, and... nothing else. Handing him a bottle of oil. The way he'd lock eyes with me and the wicked smile he'd give as he shook some of it into his palm, rubbed his thick, strong hands together, then reached for my bre—

"No," I squeaked, then cleared my throat. "No. I know I can... I'll... find something," I said breathlessly, turning away from him as my cheeks heated and my heart pumped even faster.

Cazz chuckled and it was such a deep and delicious sound, I almost changed my mind and ripped off the robe I was still wearing to throw myself at him.

But I had another jolt of how *weird* this all was.

I lost my virginity today.

To a wolf.

A wolf *King*.

That I had enslaved myself to.

I swallowed convulsively as I turned away from him and started pulling hangers across one of the rails, letting them screech as I tried to catch my breath and get my head straight. But then the hair on the back of my neck rose as I *felt* him move from the door to stand behind me.

The warmth coming off his skin felt like waves of heat off metal, like it might actually blister my skin if I got too close. But then he reached past me, his arm brushing mine as he pulled one of the hangers from the rail.

"This one," he murmured and he must have dropped his chin, because his breath fluttered against my hair, raising goosebumps on my neck.

I took the hanger with shaking hands, as he hooked his fingertips in the neckline of the robe and pulled it back and away, then brushed the softest kiss on my shoulder

I went completely still, desire fighting fear in equal measure. But he had already moved on and was reaching past me with the other arm this time, pulling another hanger from the rail in front of me.

"And this one."

When I took that one, he let the hand drop to the curve of my waist, where the robe tied in tight, then slid it up to cup the underside of my breast through the fabric, and his lips brushed my ear this time as he growled, "No bra."

"B-but—"

But then he was gone, all that delicious steel warmth slipping away so that my back felt cold and I was left standing there alone, my belly quivering and all my alarm bells ringing.

28. All Wrong

~ JESSE ~

It took a second to get my wits back, but when I did I turned around to call after him, he was really gone. No longer in sight of the door. And I wasn't sure if there were servants coming back now that he had left. So I hurriedly whipped off the robe and started pulling on the clothes…

And then I cursed him.

The pants were fine—black leather, though thinner than his. They were a little tricky to get on because they were tight. But the leather was soft and pliable, and once I had them up and buttoned I was surprised how comfortable they felt.

But then I grabbed the top and pulled it over my head—except when I got it down over my ribs I thought I had ripped it.

I looked down, freaking out—I couldn't even put a blouse on without tearing it? But then I realized it was a crop top that had fooled me.

The sleeves fell silkily from the points of my shoulders, but the neckline dropped directly from there to cut square across my boobs, offering quite a bit of cleavage. But the part that had confused me was the torso.

The front fell almost to my belly-button, and even longer on the sides, but the fabric that fell from under the bust was thin and… split. It fell in panels that fluttered against my midriff and hips.

I gave a burst of startled laughter looking down at myself because I felt *ridiculous*. But when I searched for a mirror, discovered an entire corner of the closet was made up of a mirror with five panels, then hurried to stand in front of it, I bit my lip.

I looked... *sexy.*

I was showing more flesh than I thought I'd ever shown. Especially when I moved. The slightest breath of air or shift of my body made those drapes of near-sheer fabric sway and flutter. Yet I know Cazz had been right. Somehow, I matched his sex-deity look without getting naked.

Then I remembered his last instruction: No bra.

I examined myself nervously in the mirror. The fabric was thin and soft, ruched around the bust so that there was enough weight to it that it wasn't see-through. And yet... Even though it hugged tight enough over my breasts that I wouldn't pop out if I stretched, I worried that my nipples were going to stand out like pencil points, and there'd be nothing I could do about it.

Those slits on the sides spread wide enough if I stretched too high that I was at risk of falling out of the bottom. Yet they gave my waist a beautiful shape...

Then I realized it didn't matter how I felt about the shirt.

I'd told him I'd submit. I'd told him I would make myself his slave. And he'd said no bra. That meant... I was dressed for the night.

Heart banging in my ribs and stomach fluttering with nerves, I hunted through the drawers under the mirror and thankfully found some combs and clips and make up. It was all still in packaging and boxes because he'd made the servants leave. I looked at myself in the mirror and almost lost my nerve.

I'd washed my hair, then done nothing with it. It was drying big and a little frizzy.

Desperate, I did the only thing I knew how to do: I braided my hair. Three twists over each ear to pin the sides of my hair back tight, then I flipped the full top back and left it with a lot of body so it sat high over the braided sides, almost like a mohawk. I weaved the lengths of the small braids together at the nape of my neck and let the rest of my hair waterfall down over them.

Then, to take some attention away from my hair, or maybe to match it, I dug out some dark eyeshadow and hurriedly gave myself a smokey eye.

I found a deep red lipstick, then stepped back to view the whole effect and... dear god... I looked like an eighties teen queen.

Queen. Ha.

I giggled nervously. Then lost my nerve entirely. I was scrambling around to find make-up remover or tissues or something, when a deep voice appeared again behind me.

"Don't touch it. Don't... just... leave it. It's perfect."

I turned quickly to find Cazz standing in the doorway again, his face expressionless—but his eyes glittering.

I huffed. "I look ridiculous."

"No, Kitten, you look like a snack. And I'm *hungry*. Let's go."

He snapped his fingers and I bristled. But I couldn't afford to piss him off, and besides, looking in the mirror wasn't going to change what I saw there. I hurriedly found a pair of strappy black heels and got them on, then trotted around the center island full of drawers, to where he stood in the doorway.

His gaze followed my progress and when I reached his side, he caught me, hands at my waist, sliding his fingers inside those slits and under the fabric, letting his fingertips play up my back to tease along the base of my shoulder-blades.

A long, low, puttering growl of approval rolled in his throat, and his eyes sparked.

"Good girl."

The look he gave me then, his gaze raking down my body, then back up until it rested at my cleavage. "Very, *very* good."

The strangest storm of conflicting emotions ripped through me then.

A big part of me was thrilled—giddy about that growl, and the desire that I felt flush through him as he looked at me. I didn't know if the bond was patchy, or if I just wasn't good at reading it, but sometimes I could sense his feelings and other times I couldn't. But at that moment there was no question: He wanted me. And it thrilled me to my core.

And yet...

At the very same time I was sickened with myself.

For the past two years I had been working my ass off, sneaking around, saving money, hiding resources, in an attempt to gather enough to free myself because I had sworn that once I did, I would never again let a man control my life.

Yet here I was, flushed like a middle-schooler because the man that I had *willingly enslaved myself to* had growled at me and called me a snack.

How was it possible that within hours of meeting him I had vowed my *life* to him, and given him my body?

Survival, I told myself quickly. *This is all about survival. Giving up one thing to keep the most important thing... me.*

But was I just fooling myself? Had he already used that compulsion on me and I just hadn't realized? Had he used it and forced me to forget?

Abject terror tore through my chest and crawled up my throat.

Cazz's eyes turned dark. "What is it? Why are you scared?" he demanded.

I shook my head, as much to myself as to him, because it occurred to me that it didn't matter.

Either I had given myself to a monster, but he would ultimately provide me with my independence and freedom. Or I had been tricked and… Eventually I wouldn't care.

"Jesse?!"

I just shook my head and reached up to comb back a strand of his hair that had fallen aside from the rest that was slicked back. He flinched when I lifted my hand, but then caught himself. His eyes were clouded and uncertain, but never left mine as I reached slowly up to catch that little arc of hair and combed it back into the others with my fingers.

His head sank back a little and his Adam's apple bobbed when my fingertips slid along his scalp, but he never lost the questioning expression. And then I took my hand back and smiled.

"It's not you I'm scared of, Cazz," I said quietly. "It's me."

His brows pressed down like he was confused—and irritated. "What? Why?"

"Because, I told you… the real power is in what you surrender willingly. And you… you make me *want* to give myself."

I knew I wasn't explaining myself well. I felt lightheaded and nervous and slightly hysterical. But before I could try again, Cazz narrowed his eyes and instead of holding himself back from me, he leaned in closer and his hands came up to cup my face.

"Kitten…" he graveled, "haven't you realized yet? That's *what I do.*"

Despair. Hope. Joy. Fear. They burst in my chest like fireworks—flaring and fizzing, then dying one by one.

But then he leaned *right* down until his lips brushed mine as he spoke again.

"There's no point fighting. I'll always win."

When I opened my mouth to argue, he kissed me—so deeply and urgently that I forgot what I had been going to say.

And when he finally released me, both of us were panting. I swayed into his chest when he straightened. He just smirked, then took my hand and led me out of the closet, out of my chamber, and into the maze of tunnels of his Palace… where soon I realized he was following the sound of drums.

29. Risky Business

~ *CASIMIR* ~

I had to pull away from Jesse because my need became so desperate I was at risk of frightening her, and that wouldn't help her relax, which was the entire point of this little adventure. It was a frustration. But I had to keep reminding myself she was new to this. That her first experiences with me *had* to be positive to encourage her confidence. It was imperative to condition her body to expect pleasure so that she'd give herself into my hands and continue to submit.

But the problem was, despite her naivete, she showed an eagerness and passion that matched my own.

Dear *god,* her kiss was intoxicating.

Of course, I was less enthralled with the heaviness in her—the fatalistic doubt drenching her. But her childish embarrassment about dancing had given me this idea, and I trusted it would draw her out and hopefully offer her a reason to continue exploring with me, rather than drawing into herself as the others had.

Plus, I was tense too. I also enjoyed dancing. It was an excellent vent of frustrations. A visit to the Den would help me relax, and help us learn each other.

So, without a word I tore my eyes away from her and all that deliciously half-revealed skin that threatened to shred my self-restraint. I took her hand and pulled her with me, out of the chamber and into the halls—and down.

But before we'd even left the Palace proper, we met Rake coming in the other direction.

The moment he saw my attire, and then Jesse's, his brows snapped high.

"Cazz… you're taking her to the *Den?*"

"Yes." I kept walking, pulling her with me, but instead of leaving us to it, Rake turned and fell into step with me.

"Why would you—"

"She's mine. And their Queen. They should see her. Know her."

"Have you lost your mind? It's *far* too early—you're just asking for trouble!"

I cut him a warning look from the side as Jesse hurried her steps so I was no longer pulling her and leaned around me to speak to Rake. "What is the Den? He won't tell me."

Rake gave me a very unimpressed, very dark look and raised one eyebrow. "Seriously, Cazz?"

"She likes to dance."

"That's not the point. Why would you—"

"Because I am King and it is both my right, and her desire."

"You're being reckless and you know it!"

"Bullshit. I have everything that is needed to protect her. She is completely safe under my eyes."

"And when you get distracted with one of your toys? What then?" he snarled.

I shot him a glare and linked with him. *'Keep your fucking mouth shut—I won't be playing with toys tonight—'*

"Cazz," Jesse gasped and pulled back on my hand. "You said—"

I gave Rake a final warning look and growled through the link, *'Question me. Challenge me. But do not unsettle my mate.'* Then I turned to her. "You have my word," I snapped. "Ignore him."

"But—"

She cut off when I stiffened. Then she dropped her head and her shoulders rounded. Something in my chest got heavy, seeing her deflate like that.

I could have disemboweled Rake for putting those thoughts in her head when I was trying to get her to *relax.*

"Both of you need to stop worrying. This is going to be fun!" I snarled.

Rake rolled his eyes when Jesse flinched.

'*Keep your mouth shut,*' I sent, and turned my full attention to Jesse, who was watching me warily. "I'm not irritated at you," I ground out. "Rake is pissing me off, so ignore me. This is going to be fun. It's not dangerous. No one will dare touch you when you're with me."

"Are you going to stay with me, though?" she asked, her hands clenched at her sides. She didn't tremble, but it was clear that she was frightened.

I let my voice drop deep into a suggestive purr of my own. "I'm going to do better than stay with you, Kitten. Don't worry your pretty little head."

Then I took her hand again and started moving, tugging her with me, when Rake muttered something under his breath and to my surprise, fell in step with me and began yanking the buttons on his high-collared, black shirt open and peeling it off.

I stopped dead, gaping at him. "*You're* going to the Den?!"

Rake scowled at me and tore the last of his buttons free, stripping off the shirt and throwing it to the floor.

"You're going to need backup. And no one else is safe to stand for her if there are… problems."

"I will not allow *problems,*" I growled.

"Sometimes even you make mistakes, Cazz," Rake growled back. "Let the record show that *I* believe this is one of those times."

I shook my head and turned, prowling down the corridor again, still holding Jesse's hand. She was hanging back a little, looking back and forth between us. I could feel the unease in her and was tempted to bark at her to stop listening to him, but then I felt it…

She'd been looking at both of us, but then her eyes rested on me. She was still hanging back, like she'd slow our progress if she could. But something shifted in her—equal parts resignation and curiosity. But whatever she thought, a moment later it all just… faded.

She stopped pulling against my grip. She didn't protest. And when neither me nor Rake slowed, she gave up resisting and trotted to come alongside me.

I smiled as my power surged.

She'd given in. Chosen to trust me—or at least, put herself at my mercy.

Submitted, I thought with a delicious smile.

Slave.

This was going to be even better than I'd thought.

Soundtrack for the next chapter is
Wolves by Sam Tinnesz and Silverberg

30. The Wolf Den

~ JESSE ~

Following Cazz into the tunnels below the palace felt like being swallowed by a mountain.

Down levels. Down stairs. Down, deeper into the earth below, where the hallways became caves, and half of the side tunnels didn't even have doors.

My breath got shorter, and not just because we were walking quickly, but because I could feel the immense weight above us and every instinct wanted to scream that we were about to be buried in a cave-in.

But both Cazz and Rake seemed completely comfortable down here. So I just clung to Cazz's hand and kept following.

It was a maze under here, but slowly, as the walls got rougher and more natural, and the ceilings got lower—though still high enough for these massive men to move comfortably through them—I also became aware of a kind of... vibration.

At first it felt like the air was humming, but then I started to notice trembling in the rock under our feet. And eventually I realized it had a rhythm.

"Is that... drums?" I asked breathlessly as Cazz ushered me around a corner and into a cave that sloped down and was very dark, with only torches on the walls spaced far enough apart that we stepped into shadows between each cone of light.

"Drums. Bass. *Music,*" Cazz said with a wicked smile. "You did say you like music?"

"Yes, I do."

"Then hold on, Kitten, because I'm guessing you've never heard acoustics the way God made them before."

Rake shot Cazz a look at that, but Cazz didn't return the look. He was staring forward into the dark, his eyes flashed. His tongue darted out to lick his upper lip and his grip on my hand tightened. Then the air got colder and a little damp. Finally we made it to a set of double-doors made from thick, rough wood with cast-iron braces and Cazz stopped and let go of my hand to lift another of those big beams that fit across the braces, locking the door from this side.

Despite being entirely surrounded by stone—and this door being made from wood that was clearly inches thick—I could feel the pulse of the beat clearly now, vibrating through the soles of my shoes, and in the air. It throbbed under my ribs and made my lungs shake.

"Are you ready?" Cazz asked quietly, glancing at me over his shoulder. Every muscle in his arms and back rippled as he propped the beam against the side of the cave and took hold of the handle on the door. "Stay close to me at all times. If we ever get separated, find me without delay."

Rake cleared his throat and Cazz rolled his eyes. "Rake is also a safe-harbor. If for some reason you can't see me, stick close to him. But that *will not happen,"* he growled, shooting another dark glare at Rake before he yanked the door open.

It creaked and groaned, echoing in the cave, but I barely noticed because as the space opened behind it, the music became... consuming.

Cazz left the massive door open and took my hand, pulling me into the darkness on the other side.

I hung back from his grip, unable to see *anything* ahead of us.

"Don't worry, I can see clearly. I won't let you run into anything that isn't me," Cazz said, and I could *hear* the smirk in his voice.

Rake snorted, but I just hugged Cazz's arm and threw myself at his mercy, praying he was telling the truth as we walked forward just as quickly as we had in the lighted hallways. But now the noise and pulse of that heavy bass, the crash of the drums, all of it was getting louder and lourder until I wouldn't have been able to hear Cazz unless he raised his voice.

But then there was a glow in the tunnel ahead and Cazz drew me to it and around the corner.

When we turned the corner, my jaw dropped.

The first thing I could see was a *massive,* cathedral-height cavern. A ceiling that would have fit a building several stories high.

There were no lights at the peak, so it was difficult to see exactly how high it was.

The music, that had been crashing to a crescendo, stopped suddenly as we continued forward to a platform with a railing around it and I was able to look down.

The cavern was huge at its base, almost the size of a football field, though the sides were irregular and not straight... more like a wide oval but the lights only lined the long sides, leaving the ends in complete darkness.

We were in one of several platform alcoves around the walls, though none of the others appeared to have people in them.

The only lights in the main space of the room were at the floor and pointed up at the walls, so that it was rimmed in wide, soft cones of blue-white light that illuminated every crack and crevasse in the rock, but gave no direct light to the center of the room.

The lights ringed this massive space, silhouetting a huge, seething mass of bodies at its center.

Cazz stared down at it, smiling, as the beat of music began again and I didn't just hear it, I *felt* it.

It thrummed in the air, hummed in the stone under and around us, throbbed in my ribs, and pounded in my head.

The beat started as short, distorted chords on electric guitars, punctuated by heavy drums, then the music began and that seething mass of bodies below began to writhe.

"What *is this?*" I breathed, not really expecting anyone to hear me over the slowly growing music. But Cazz did.

"This is the Wolf Den. It's our playground," he said, loud enough for me to hear. "Our very free... very adult playground." He leaned in then, his breath fluttering against my ear when he spoke. "It's where we go to... unleash."

I looked up at him as he straightened, nerves jangling in my chest just as the music built up to one of those breath-holding pauses—there was no sound in the cavern at all for a second... and then the beat dropped and the crowd below *surged.*

As lights went up at the ends of the room—one end suddenly illuminated a stage with a band, the other what I assumed was a bar—en masse, hundreds of wolf-people convulsed, pitching forward, hair flying, hands thrown, bodies bent in perfect time. And as the beat hammered through the cavern, through the air, through my bones, the lights pulsed and flashed with them, turning that pool of massive, steel bodies into a rippling sea of strength and... dance.

Raw, primal, aggressive, *feral* dance.

Bodies writhed, heads banged, hands punched and clawed the air...

I would have called it a mosh-pit, but impossibly, it wasn't a chaotic boil of individual bodies, but an improbable, unified pulse of humanity—or lupinity?

I'd never seen anything like it. It drew me and repulsed me at the same time. Then I felt Cazz at my side, moving in time with them.

His eyes were fevered, his smile slightly open so his teeth showed, flashing when the lights rose, and his body...

His body barely shifted, but it was as if the beat came alive in him. I could feel his muscles contracting and relaxing, moving in the slightest shifts, in perfect time with the rest of them down there.

Even Rake wasn't unaffected, though his lips were pursed, twisted together like he fought the draw of... whatever this was.

"Ready?" Cazz breathed. I shouldn't have been able to hear that over the blast of the guitars and slam of the bass and drums, but I did.

Cazz took a step away. But I didn't move at all, just stared down at that... thing. Intimidated and drawn and... terrified.

"Jesse?" Cazz's tone was curious, but a little tense. Irritated.

I tore my eyes from that sight below and stared up at him. "I can't do that. I don't..." I swallowed hard. "That's not how I dance, Cazz."

But as the lights below gave a massive flare, lighting his skin and his eyes and the sheen on his skin, he gave another of those wicked, lopsided smiles.

"Don't worry, Kitten. I'll show you the way."

He took my mouth in a heated kiss, his tongue flicking to tease mine. Then he drew back, grabbed my hand, and pulled me down the stairs towards that seething pit of bodies.

31. The Edge of Metal

~ JESSE ~

When we reached the floor of the Den, I was hanging back against the drag of Cazz's hand.

"Cazz," I hissed. "Can you teach me some of the steps first, or *something?* I'm going to make a fool of myself if I don't—"

Cazz turned, looking stern, his mouth open like he was about to snap at me. But his eyes flipped up, over my shoulder for a moment, and he went still. Then he pressed his lips thin, shaking his head as if he didn't like what he saw. But he didn't reply, just turned to scan the space

The music was climbing towards another crescendo. The lights surged, then faded in time with the beat. That mass of bodies writhed. When the lights flared again, they made Cazz's eyes spark.

He was staring at something, and smiling. I started to follow his gaze, but then he turned towards me again.

"I have an idea," he said, leaning down so his breath fluttered in my hair and made goosebumps rise on the back of my neck. "It will help you relax."

I was about to ask what, and how, when Cazz took my hand again and pulled me towards the narrow end of the cavern, away from the stage. I had been right when I was looking down from the balcony. It was a bar. A long, thick slab of impenetrable stone, like a shield between the servers and the rest of the space.

There were wolf-people amassed four thick the length of it, but as Cazz led me closer, those in the crowd would turn and see us before he had even reached them.

I watched the crowd part, people moving aside as if by instinct. But they also watched Cazz, their eyes bright and excited. His name peppered the air. The males would duck their heads when he looked at them. But many of the wolf women reached out to stroke his arm or touch his shoulder as we passed.

There was an uncomfortable pinch between my shoulder-blades by the time we reached the bar, but Cazz acted like nothing had happened, pulling me up alongside him and leaning over the stone to speak to the male behind the bar. A tall, strapping blond guy, leaner than Cazz but just as fit, and just as shirtless.

"...two please, but make one... smaller."

"Yes, Sire."

A moment later two glasses that were shaped like shot-glasses, only larger, were placed on the stone and the male poured both nearly full of an amber liquid.

Cazz gave a wicked smile and picked one up, running it back and forth under his nose, then taking a sip that drained a third of the glass.

Then he smiled and handed me that glass, picking up the full one himself.

I was about to ask what it was when Rake appeared at my elbow, standing close, but glaring at Cazz.

"Seriously, Cazz?"

"I took half of it for her. A child could handle that."

"What is it?" I asked, lifting the glass so I could sniff it.

It had a strange smell. Not sharp like alcohol. But not exactly sweet, either. More spicy.

I looked warily at Cazz. If Rake thought it was a bad idea—

"It's... something that will help you feel more... connected."

He stepped closer then, right up so our bellies brushed and took my chin in his hand.

I shivered. But not with fear—and that blew my mind.

Throughout my life whenever any guy would put himself that close to me, even my brothers, my skin would crawl. I'd flinch, even if I liked the guy. But my body responded differently to Cazz. Was it because we'd had sex?

I didn't know. But it was a rare luxury to feel relatively safe in that position. So I tipped up my chin and met his eyes. He smiled.

I thought he'd tell me something, or maybe lean right in to whisper some erotic suggestion. But instead he locked eyes with me, and as the lights around the Den flared again, I saw his pupils dilate.

As if he'd flipped a switch, out of nowhere I could sense him in the bond, feel the desire ripping through him, the anticipation, the thrill. His breath stopped fluttering against my face. He went so still I would have thought he was a statue. But between us there was a *torrent* of heat. Sizzling, crackling need. It was such an unexpected window into his heart, and so powerful, it hit like a bolt of electric *want,* deep in my core. Like he'd reached inside me and plucked a string that attached behind my navel and between my thighs.

My breath caught. Suddenly... suddenly I wanted whatever he believed was coming. Especially if it was me.

I started to lift the glass, but with a dark growl, Rake stepped up behind me and caught my wrist.

A gutteral, vicious snarl ripped out of Cazz, and his eyes tore away from mine as his body tensed.

"Cazz—"

"Take your paw *off* my mate unless you want to lose it!"

"Cazz, it's okay," I breathed.

"Jesse—" Rake started.

"Is it dangerous, Rake? Will it hurt me?"

Rake hesitated. "Probably not just one, but—"

I lifted the glass to my lips and threw it down my throat. Cazz actually chuckled, low and throaty, reaching for my glass when I came up gasping and blinking, feeling like someone had just lit a fire in my throat. But there were no fumes like alcohol. No tingling from spice. Just an overwhelming sense that I had swallowed lava.

"What the hell was that?" I croaked when I could catch my breath.

Cazz laughed and slammed his larger drink down on the bar. "That, my dear, was your ticket to the pack mind. Now... let's dance."

My head was beginning to spin, but Cazz didn't wait. Twining our fingers, he tugged me towards that roiling mass of bodies. And even though my head wanted to argue, there was something slowly coiling in my stomach. Something that burned in the best way.

The crowd on the dancefloor parted just like those at the bar had a minute earlier, but even as they made way for us, their voices rose, calling Cazz's name, his title, howling, and cheering.

Hands slipped over Cazz's oiled skin like serpents sliding out of sight. But not one wolf so much as brushed against me.

As we got deep in the crowd, Cazz pulled me close and leaned into my ear so I could hear him over the thumping music.

"Are you ready, kitten?"

"For what?"

"Everything you ever heard about a wolf."

He wrapped his arm around the hollow of my back and pulled me against him. Then he started to move.

Soundtrack for the next chapter is
Vertebrae by Allistair and Spencer Kane.
(BANGER ALERT!)

32. The Music Inside

~ *JESSE* ~

Cazz moved like he was made from water. Really muscular, strong water. His torso was a study in sexy perfection.

Sexfection.

I giggled breathlessly and let my head drop back, letting Cazz take my weight in his large hand splayed at my spine.

Cazz's eyes flashed when I laughed, but instead of speaking, he only leaned closer, his flat pecs brushing my chest as he loomed over me and rolled his torso deliciously, the muscles rippling and flexing in the pulsating lights. He touched my face with his free hand as he writhed against me.

I was a little giddy, and doing my best to move with him, to keep time with the music, but my mind kept drifting—and so did my hands.

I was fascinated by the carved lines between his pecs and under them, the ladders of muscle up his abs and over his ribs. Even as I rolled my hips and Cazz ground against me, I ran fingertips along the lines on his stomach, my breath catching when he dropped his chin and nipped at my ear.

"Feel it, Jesse. Feel us. All of us. We're here. Hold onto the bond. Hold onto me. I'll show you."

His rough, deep rasp seemed to reach me down the length of a long tunnel, echoing and surrounding me. When his breath rushed against my ear, the shorthairs rose on the back of my neck. When he traced a finger along my jaw, goosebumps prickled down my arm. When his hips rolled and he rubbed himself against me, my belly clenched.

At first I thought the heady thrill making me feel lightheaded was just adrenaline.

But as I lifted my hands over my head and focused on undulating in time with Cazz's gorgeous ripples, lights flickered at the edge of my vision. Though the music was so loud and bass thumped so hard I felt it in my ribs, I was able to hear his whispered words in my ear, and the calls of the wolves around us.

And even though we were in the middle of a seething, pulsing mass of bodies, every touch, every stroke, even the featherlight brush of a fingertip, or a breath against my skin, tingled.

All of my senses were heightened. I felt more alive than I had ever experienced. A small, fading voice of reason wanted my attention, wanted to warn me that there had been something in that drink. That I might not be entirely in my right mind.

And yet... Cazz was coming alive, too. And as his gaze brightened and his body moved, all that beauty, grace, and strength laser-focused on me, it was the most devastating feeling I had ever had.

It was as if the bond bloomed. As if it increased, expanding to encompass my entire body, not just that spot at my center. And he was open to me—a bright, shining beacon of lust and delight, anticipation and thrill. He'd opened himself so wide it seemed like if I just reached out, I could touch his insides.

I couldn't, of course, but I was thoroughly enjoying touching his outsides. First I let my arms loop around his neck, then I dragged one finger down the hollow of his rippling spine.

Shame and self-consciousness melted away. I stopped worrying that I couldn't keep up with him, or match his skill. Somehow, impossibly, my body knew what to do. And as the beat rose and fell, cut then dropped, I knew. Knew it like someone had told me. Like I too, had learned the dance.

But we weren't all doing the same dance, I realized. We were just moving in time. As one. Cazz had become my north, his body mine to touch and hold. And the dance was... a conversation.

I let my hips meet his and instinctively roll together.

I was breathless. Panting. And not just from the dancing. And though Cazz's eyes were most often on my body, following the curl of my waist, or the twist of my hips, whenever he brought his gaze up to meet mine, it was brighter.

For song after song, we danced. After a while I wasn't even thinking anymore. I just knew. And Cazz was clearly delighted, easing himself against me—turning me so that my back was to his front and his hands followed the lines of my body, urging me deeper into the beat.

Then, I stopped trying to follow Cazz and just let myself *feel.*

Those heightened senses became intoxicating, pulling at me to feel the prickle where his skin brushed mine, to hear the rush of his breath, to taste the salt on his neck…

Then I turned around so I faced him again and lifted my head, intending to meet his eyes… only to find that the space around us had closed in. Those brushes prickling my arms weren't just Cazz. The pack was *here.* We no longer danced in a gap. We had become part of the crowd, part of that pumping, seething mass.

To my shock, something in my mind snapped open and suddenly I could feel all of them. Cazz was the only one who was clear, his undulating body feeling like an extension of mine. But the others were present in my head, and I realized they had been for a while.

This was the instinct telling my body how to move, and soothing my self-consciousness.

It was unnerving and amazing to look around and realize I could recognize that female by the blade of her heart, and that male by his steady warmth. I didn't know their names, but I *knew* them.

"That's it… that's it, Jesse. That's the pack link. Don't doubt. Just let yourself be in it."

I shivered when he kissed my neck, under my ear, then lifted his head to meet my eyes, his bright and glinting with pleasure.

33. The Display

~ *CASIMIR* ~

The moment Jesse tapped into the pack mind I got hard.

Watching her open herself and lose that tension in her shoulders—watching her smile and move as if her own body didn't frighten her. Or mine. It was stunning. I suddenly saw all the strength in her that the reapers must have identified. And I wanted her.

I could have swept her out of there and taken her on the spot.

When she lost her self-consciousness and just let herself move and respond to me... Dear God, the way she stroked me, the *heat* in her eyes.

I was convinced bringing her to the den was the best idea I'd ever had.

When she turned back to face me I took her hips in my hands and pulled her against me, shamelessly grinding on her, keeping her plastered against me. As we moved together, more and more in sync, deeper and deeper in the bond and unaware of anything else, adrenaline flooded my system.

I wanted her so badly my belly ached. And yet, watching her move with me, her sparkling eyes, the way her hair shone in the half-light, especially when she let her head tip back so that the braids and loose tresses fell past her ass...

I could have eaten her.

But unfortunately, I wasn't the only one.

The pack was suddenly very aware of their new female Alpha. The males' curiosity had been piqued since they'd heard that I took her. But now... now she was displaying. Letting them see her, showing herself.

For the first time, I could *see* the wildness in her. The crackle of feral energy—and I loved it. I dropped my head back and howled, calling the world to see what I saw: A beautiful female, finding her place, and her power with it.

But as I salivated at the sight of her, filling my hands, pulling our bodies together, as the blood in my veins heated for her, so did the other males. And now that she was connected, the pack had sucked in around us. They weren't just seeing her beauty and the presence she held. They were *feeling her.*

The first prickle of uneasiness began a slow shiver down my spine. But I shook it off and pawed at her. First cupping her breast over the wisp of a top with one hand, while she tipped back letting herself lean back into my other hand. Taking her weight was sheer lust as her body bent and her ribs were revealed by the panels of that top and my mind was suddenly peppered with the images of all the ways I was going to take her tonight, and all the sounds she would make when I did, the taste of her skin—

Some of the males nearby pressed in tightly, their eyes turning from their own partners in the dance, to mine, that light in their eyes that made my hackles rise.

'This is what I was worried about,' Rake muttered in my head from his position to my right, his eyes hooded as he watched the other males without making it obvious that he was doing so. *'They were already curious and tense at the scent of her, Cazz. This is just feeding them.'*

I knew he was right. I also knew not a single one of them would dare try to tempt her right in front of me.

And I was right.

But I hadn't counted on Jesse tempting *them.* I hadn't imagined that she would bloom with such certainty as part of the packmind. That when she turned in my arms and leaned into me, when her eyes caught mine and she bit her lip in a way that made me salivate, that she'd open herself so completely—to me in the bond, letting me feel the electric sizzle of desire that shot through her at the sight of me... and in the packmind, as she gave in to her desire and began to entertain her want.

*****

~ *JESSE* ~

Cazz and I danced, bodies bending and rippling together, for a long time. I was panting and sweaty and not at all self-conscious as we locked in on each other. And when he closed his eyes it was to

144

lean back and howl, grasping my hips and pulling me hard against him, directing me so that we truly moved as one.

I hooked my wrists over his shoulders and let him drive us.

Then, to my surprise and delight, I saw Rake dancing to Cazz's right. My eyes knew him—his face, his shape, his name—but now there was more… a weighty, solid strength. The certain sense of a compass pointed north. I blinked, my mind struggling to combine the things I knew about him with this newfound *understanding*. But we were all moving together and… and he was there too. And I loved it.

I turned in the circle of Cazz's arms, inhaling his scent and enjoying the way it cut through my lungs and made a path straight to my belly—and yet, at the same time, my sense of the pack was becoming more and more tangible. As if they crowded not just my body, but my mind.

We turned with the rest and now Rake was directly in front of me, eyes closed, face tight, but his body just as lithe and strong as every male nearby.

He seemed lost in the music—or maybe in the pack mind. I wasn't sure, but something about him felt… separate.

The female dancing nearest him seemed to sense it also. She didn't just move in time with him, but I could feel her offering herself, her body responding to his, giving him every signal that she was happy to help him breach his vow of celibacy if he would choose it.

I blinked. Could they all feel that? Then I turned back to Cazz and felt that twang of desire zing through me… and felt the surge of the pack around us as others responded.

34. Packmind

Someone behind me leaned in and I was pressed closer to Cazz, which was wonderful. He'd put that hand at my back again and I leaned into it, letting my head drift

As our hips met and pressed together, as he swept me in a rolling turn, my heart beat even faster. I felt the crowd around us press in again, could sense them and instinctively reached for them the same way I reached for Cazz—my arms hooking around his neck while my mind embraced *everyone.*

A chorus of howls rose, bouncing from the height of the cavern overhead and my heart pounded. My eyes were closed, but I felt Cazz lean into me, felt a puttering growl roll in his chest that was pressed against mine.

The feeling of being so close to him even as others surrounded us was suddenly intoxicating. Images filled my mind, things I'd never thought before, let alone acted on. Hands reaching, fingers stroking, mouths, bodies, everything twisting, pressing, rolling together. And even though I knew they were only thoughts, images, they seemed so real—as if my body was experiencing the thought. Like a daydream you could feel, and it was delicious.

I imagined a thousand Cazz's, each one attuned only to me, continuing the dance, eager and needy…

Cazz growled again and his teeth nipped that sensitive skin under my ear. I gasped and laughed.

Cazz… my mate. My husband. The one who had wrung such pleasure from my body… Cazz in a thousand ways, a thousand smiles, a thousand bodies, each given hands that were desperate to touch, to be filled…

A throaty chuckle broke in my throat and I threw my head back, letting him catch me before I fell—

"Cazz, be careful—"

The voice was deep and disapproving and had no place in this gorgeous, erotic daydream—

"Cazz!"

My body bent almost in two. I hooked one ankle behind Cazz's thigh and let myself go, pressing into his hands when he reached for me…

"Cazz… Cazz, snap out of it!"

Ultra-sensitive ears heard the guttural snarl and suddenly I was spinning in a fog, turning, bouncing… I was in the crowd, pumping, bending, shaking. And there were sweaty bodies and grasping palms and I thought it was Cazz, but—

"CAZZ! She's wide open. Get her out of here!"

There was a surge in the pack again, a shuddering sense of pressure building, anticipation… something.

"Jesse… *Jesse, wake up!*"

His hands found my wrist and I smiled, until I was unceremoniously yanked aside.

There was a horrific, guttural snarl, and my arm was pulled so hard my head snapped to the side. My eyes flew wide and I sucked in a breath—then another as the pandemonium around me suddenly became clear.

I wasn't dancing at the center of a thousand Cazz's. I was in the center of a Wolf Den and being dragged through the crowd by my mate, who was showing his teeth, swiping his free hand with fingers clawed, and threatening anyone who would listen as Rake ushered him through the frantic crowd.

A hand fisted in my hair and for a second I hung, snapped tight like a string between two hands. Then Cazz moved in a way I didn't understand and the pressure on my head just disappeared.

"Jesse, close your mind. *Now!*"

I blinked and inhaled sharply, all my senses screaming. But that just meant I saw the chaos with sharpened eyes. To my horror, the crowd around us that had seemed such a thrill a moment ago, was now a seething horde—grasping hands, bared teeth, bodies pulling closer. I heard the growls and howls and calls with sensitive ears, felt the pummeling of bodies from every direction at once with skin that would have registered a breath.

"Cazz, what—?"

"Close your mind. You're projecting. Hold yourself back. Think of it like a door you're slamming shut," Cazz snarled in my ear, then his body bowed as he threw a punch to my right, turned and swept me into his arms, then began to run.

I gasped and clung to him. There was no time to question, or even to scream. Cazz was fighting his way through the crowd, assisted by Rake, and here and there, a female or two.

"Jesse, SHUT IT DOWN."

That was when I realized they'd all been feeling my fantasy... all those images in my mind of a thousand Cazz's... *oh dear God.*

Doing everything I could think of to tell my mind not to share, I buried my face in his chest and tried not to think as he fought and snarled his way through the crowd. But the pack was trying to reach me—male after male reaching for me, grabbing, trying to slide between me and Cazz.

And as the reality and horror of what I'd done sank in, I came alive, batting off hands, screaming at them to leave me alone, flinching from the pain of clawed fingers and strong hands, as Cazz roared his disapproval, slamming any male who touched me, until finally, he pulled me through a dark doorway.

"Keep them back!" he bellowed over his shoulder at Rake who had followed us as he threw the door closed behind us, placing me quickly on my feet then turning to grab a long, heavy bar that leaned against the wall just inside, and sliding it into the brackets of the doors, just before heavy weights hit it from the other side.

The door shuddered and rumbled, scraped and screamed. Heavy weights slammed into it again and again, and the bar rattled in its brackets.

Cazz braced against it. His back heaved, slick with sweat. His shoulders and arms were marble, the muscles carved from rigid stone. He clamped his hands on that bar and held it, snarling every time weight hit the doors from the other side, making them shake.

I was panting too. My hands were over my mouth as I watched, horrified, while the pack tried to break into the room.

"Did... Did I do that?" I breathed.

Cazz's head dropped and his hands tightened further on the bar, his knuckles turning bright white. There was another shudder, then a barrage on the other side of the door. But Cazz must have decided the bar wasn't going to break, because a moment later, still breathing hard, he turned around to stare at me.

The thunder against that door seemed fitting when I saw that his eyes were glowing again. That incandescent blue, so bright...

But his face was a mask of rage.

I backed away. "Cazz, I didn't know."

"I'm aware of that," he snarled, though his tone said it was no excuse.

"I was thinking about *you*–"

"And inviting every male in the packmind to come to you."

"I didn't realize... I didn't mean to!"

"I said, I'm aware!" He stopped at my toes, glaring down at me, his chest rising and falling quickly, then his hand came up to my face, his fingers holding me so tightly his grip was on the edge of pain as he searched my eyes.

"They all want you now, Jesse. All of them. They *ache* for you. But they can't have you, Jesse. They can't."

"Of course not! I would never–"

"You're *mine!*" he growled, then descended on me with a kiss so deep and frantic, it stole my breath.

35. Needs Must

~ *CASIMIR* ~

If Jesse hadn't been quite so fucking beautiful tonight that she lit a fire in my insides, if my need for her wasn't *quite* so urgent, and if we didn't have the *entire fucking pack* breathing down our necks, I would have given in to the fury. Ignorant of the packmind or not, she was Queen. She was female Alpha. She, of all of us, *had* to control her urges and lead by example.

She, of all people, could do *nothing* to undermine my power.

Instead, she'd enticed males to her. She needed to understand the very dire circumstances she had created, and the consequences of them.

I should have punished her on the spot.

But the door behind me shuddered and rattled as the males, overcome with lust and intoxicated by the challenge, tried to break through to reach *her*.

They would not have her.

But I had to rip myself out of that kiss, still holding her face, panting. Jesse took a moment longer to blink and find herself.

"Cazz...?" she murmured, barely audible over the crashing and pounding behind me. "Cazz, are you okay?"

I was trembling, my jaw aching because my teeth were clenched so tight. They thought they could come for *my* mate?! A big part of me wanted to throw that bar back and start tearing into them, punishing *them* one by one until there were none left.

But I knew, most of them were already drunk and she'd beckoned them. They were brash because she'd given them hope—and undermined me in the process.

Fucking hell.

"Cazz, talk to me, I—"

"You have no fucking clue what you've done," I growled, my voice low and harsh.

Fear lit in her eyes. "I didn't know they could—"

"You were in the pack mind! You felt them—did you really believe they didn't feel you?"

She went very still, watching me, licking her lips which only made them shine, which only made my cock grow harder.

"I… I get that now. I do. But I was… it was just thoughts. I didn't realize anyone else could—"

"Thoughts of need. Of want. Of *sex.* You dove into the packmind, then swam in desire—"

"Thoughts of *you,* Cazz! I was thinking about you—it was… I wasn't even really thinking. It just kind of happened. All the bodies, and you were so hot, and—"

I had to wrestle with a surge of smug satisfaction. I'd kept the bond open between us and even though at this point she had closed her mind to the others, she hadn't managed to cut me out. Even in her fear of my disapproval, she was remembering what she wanted, what she was feeling… and it was making her belly clench.

She squirmed in front of me, torn between the clang of fear, and the thrill of desire. My body responded to the crackle of need in hers and I growled. I'd been holding her chin, but I plunged a hand into her hair, gripping those braids and pulling her head back so her neck was arched and her throat bare to me.

"Cazz, what—"

Dragging my nose along the line of her elegant neck where her blood pulsed so close to the surface, I let my teeth graze her skin and felt her shiver.

I knew what I had to do. I knew the best and fastest way to back the pack off, but I hadn't even been sure I was going to claim her. Now she forced me to it?

Was it a strategy? Was I the fool? Was she deceiving me?

For a moment I turned my chin, examining the fear in her eyes—and that bubbling desire. Was she capable of that kind of deception?

A low, puttering growl began in my chest and Jesse's hand shot up to lay flat on my chest—to push me away, or to cling?

It was unclear. But either way, it didn't matter.

I opened my mouth over her throat and held her with my teeth. Jesse gasped and went completely still. Even her dull human senses shrilling alarms because in that position, I could have her dead in seconds. Could tear through her jugular and watch her bleed out. *Remove* her from the pack. From myself. Free myself of any obligation to faithfulness or burden of provision…

Such a small, simple movement… I hummed as I closed my teeth a hair, pinching into her and Jesse whimpered.

It was a dark thought. Not entirely unwelcome. Yet… uneasiness bubbled through me.

I removed my teeth from her skin, but kept my nose buried in her throat.

"Mine," I growled. "My mate, my Queen, my female… they cannot have you, Jesse."

"I know. I wouldn't. Cazz, you know I wouldn't… don't you?" she breathed.

"Tell me."

"T-tell you what?"

Still gripping her hair, giving her no freedom to move, I opened my eyes and raised my head enough to meet her frightened gaze.

"Tell me that I *own* you… and make me believe it," I hissed. "Tell me why I should let you live and remain my mate." *Tell me why I should claim you to defend you from them, and give a piece of myself in the process.*

She didn't hear the thought, but she could feel my rage. Her eyes widened, white all the way around. Her body was already trembling from the drink, and the dance, and her first connection with the packmind. But now her brows knit together and she shuddered.

Her scent, rich with need and thrill, now pulsed with the jangle of fear.

I tightened my grip in her hair, tugging her head back even farther, snarling at her as her scent became a baffling stew of terror, confusion, and desire.

Behind me, a new barrage of attempts to break through the door, jolted me awake to the tightrope we walked. The impossible corner she had chased us into.

How? How was it possible that the slave drove me, the King, into a corner?

"Cazz… what…?"

"Do you submit, Jesse?"

"Yes, you know I do—"

I yanked at her hair and her mouth opened in a gasp as I leaned over her, seething, my lips almost brushing hers.

"I will tell you what I know, *mate.* I know that you called to the pack, and now we cannot simply walk out of this room. I cannot walk away from you like I would wish to right now. Because the moment that door is open you will either be torn to pieces in the resulting melee, or taken by the males, one after the other, after the other... is that what you want?"

"What?! *NO!* Cazz—"

"My males are in thrall, Jesse—goaded to lust and domination, and working as a pack. Even I can't break through that now. They have no conscious thought, no logic. They exist in instinct, and they will fight to the death for what was offered. They will follow it to its conclusion, whether that means winning you, or leaving this life."

She was blinking quickly, her already racing heart pounding faster and faster. I let that sink in as I stared at her. Because I wouldn't tell her the next part. Wouldn't admit how she had trapped me. If she'd done it on purpose, I wouldn't give her the satisfaction. And if she hadn't, I wouldn't allow her any more leverage.

"Can't... can't you just compel them?" she whispered, and I could feel the twist of distaste in her at the suggestion.

I shook my head. "The wolves on the other side of that door include most of my strongest warriors, and most valuable Alphas. Their instincts are in full force. The intensity of compulsion it would take to override that would turn their minds to water. They would be useless to me for independent thought after. You have no clue, Jesse—"

"No, I didn't! I didn't know! I didn't mean to—"

"And yet, here we are Kitten, and it's because of *you.*"

She swallowed audibly, her throat bobbing right under my chin and I wanted to taste it again. But the thundering and howling, the scrabbling on the other side of that door...

The full recognition of what she'd done crashed over me and I wanted to shake her.

She must have felt my volcanic rage, because her hand on my chest pressed harder, as if she'd push me away. Which only made me more angry.

I fought the wolf inside me then—fought what I knew was a losing battle. But I had to keep my mind clear.

I could snarl about the injustice of it all when it was resolved. But for now, I had only two choices: To kill her, or to claim her.

Stupid bitch was going to leash me. And I was livid about it.

36. Forced My Hand

~ *CASIMIR* ~

Kill, or claim?

Anything less, and the moment that door was unbarred, those males would kill me to take her. Or force me to compel or kill all of them.

The truth was, even after this, I didn't want her dead. She was the most fascinating of the females who had ever been brought to me. I looked forward to awakening her, teaching her, molding her. And the power she brought me when she submitted...

That power throbbed in my veins as, despite her fear, she must have chosen to give herself, because suddenly my blood pulsed with fire and heat *and* power, and my hands were shaking.

But if I wasn't going to kill her, that meant there was only one choice left. And I hadn't planned to claim her. Wouldn't even have considered it until she gave me an heir. Yet she'd found a way to force my hand.

God, I could have smacked her for that. But I refused to become my father.

While I was still working to contain the anger bubbling in my chest, the door bulged with a hammering rush of bodies on the other side. I knew it wasn't going to give, knew they wouldn't break through. But the adrenaline that jolted through me tipped me over the edge.

With a roar of unfettered rage, I let go of her hair, grabbed her shoulders and turned her around, frog-marching her towards the door.

"Do you see what you've done, Jesse? Of course you don't... or maybe you do? Was that your plan all along?"

"What? No! Cazz, I would never—"

I grabbed her hands and planted her palms on the door, flattening my own hands over them so she couldn't pull away, so she'd feel the power of the bodies on the other side, vibrations and rattles, and fully understand the frenzy that was happening outside.

She didn't struggle, but her desire was giving way to fear and I could feel her on the verge of tears.

"Cazz, I didn't know—"

I leaned into her ear, snapping the words off like bones between my teeth. "You made them want you, gave them reason to think they could take you from me. You took power from me and handed it to them."

"I d-didn't mean to—"

"And yet, you did," I hissed. "Do you submit, Jesse?" I hissed quietly, nipping at her ear. Then, leaving her hand planted on the door, I slid mine slowly up her arm, then under, to her chest, finding her breast pressing against the seams of that incredible top, filling my palm with the plump softness. I gave in to the urge to let my nails dig in to her skin as a wave of lust washed through me and my wolf, reacting to the presence of the pack so close, to the threat to our bond, howled for her.

She went very still under my touch. The door banged again, her arms and shoulders vibrating with the force of it.

I let my teeth graze the back of her neck.

"Jesse, I asked you a question. *Do. You. Submit?*"

She shivered. "Y-yes, Cazz... I told you—"

"You did, didn't you? And yet, here we are."

"Can we... can we wait? They'll calm down. I'll explain—"

"You'll explain?" I laughed bitterly. "My god, you really have no idea, do you?" I loomed over her, pressing her with my strength to understand the chaos she had unleashed. "Even if things grow quieter, they will not be *calm*. They will simply be waiting. Prowling wolves on the hunt. They have your scent now.

"If I were to wait an hour, two, five, then open that door, do you know what you would find?" I didn't wait for her to answer. "Jesse, they would be poised. At the first sign that door is unbarred, they would crouch, ready to pounce. Hundreds of eyes, hundreds of bared teeth ready to hold you, to force you. And before you could speak a word of your *explanation,* they would be on you, dominating you, competing for you—for fuck's sake, if you fought they'd tear you limb from limb. Don't you get it—you're not dealing with your posturing, beta human males. My pack are *animals*, Jesse. You went into heat and raised your tail and now they have your scent on their tongues," I hissed.

She shrank back, clawing both hands into her hair. "I didn't…"

"Yes, we've covered that," I growled. "But let me be abundantly clear: Even if we waited *days,* I'd probably still have to compel them… so, no. We cannot wait this out. I have to show them that they can't have you—prove to them that you're mine without equivocation."

"Okay. Okay. But why… H-how? What do I have to do?"

"Oh no, Kitten, it's not you. This is *all* me," I snapped, gritting my teeth as I fought for control against my wolf who sensed what was to come and was bolting for it. Just as instinctively as those males had come for her, my wolf snapped and barked, throwing itself against the cage in which I held it. And now I was being pummeled both from the outside and within.

Jesse was murmuring, her voice shaky and breathless, asking questions and pleading. But I snarled. She was clueless—clueless about what she'd done, and who she had done it to.

I would show her.

Hot fucking damn, would I show her.

I straightened, pressing my erection against her ass as I hissed at her to keep her hands on the bar while I pulled her hips back and planted a hand on her spine, bending her forward.

"Ready yourself," I muttered through gritted teeth as I reached around to unbutton her pants.

"Cazz, just—please explain—" she whispered through shaking lips.

I could smell her tears and it pissed me off—I hadn't brought us here! She was the one who had forced my hand. *No one* would gain more from this than her.

"Lucky girl, when we're finished, you'll carry my mark," I growled, grunting because I'd gotten her pants loose and plunged a hand between her thighs to find her flesh heated and slick. I slipped a finger into her and she clenched. I gave a humorless laugh. "God willing, you'll carry my mark, *and* my child," I panted, then grabbed the waistband of her pants over each hip and forced them down to reveal her round ass and softest flesh.

I wasn't gentle, could barely control myself as I explored and prepared, found her with one hand, and used the other to release my belt and buttons. But the tension was so thick, my body quivering with such need, I was fumbling like a barely adolescent pup.

I grunted when I finally got my own leathers open and freed myself. Then, unable to wait, I bent over her back, tugged her head to the side to bare the tender skin where her shoulder met her neck and licked it.

"Do you think God wills anything good for an animal like *me*, Jesse?" I panted through my teeth as I positioned myself.

"I do, Cazz. But please, just tell me—"

She broke off, hissing with pain as my teeth closed her on her shoulder. In that moment as the predator in me took over, I lost my mind, almost shifted with the sheer ecstacy of tasting her blood—then her head jerked back and she cried out as I plunged into her from behind with such force I lifted her off her feet.

37. In Disarray

~ *JESSE* ~

"Ready yourself," he muttered, and his hand slipped around to tug at my pants. A bolt of fear shot through me right alongside the ache of desire I had been feeling.

"Cazz, just—please explain—" my voice shook and my eyes blurred. I wanted him—had wanted him this whole time, that was why things had gone so wrong. But even though I could feel him through the bond, even though he'd protected me to get me away from the pack and in here, even though I could feel him yearning for me... something was off.

"Lucky girl, when we're finished, you'll carry my mark," he growled, popping the buttons of my leather pants, then plunging his hand between my legs. I shivered, heat and fear braiding together in a way that made my body shake and left me confused. "God willing, you'll carry my mark, *and* my child."

He hadn't blocked the bond, and through it I could tell that something about that statement touched a deep place in him, but he reacted like it struck a nerve. I felt him tense, then realized he was tearing at my pants, pulling them down over my hips and lower.

I was bent in front of him, still gripping that bar, my ass bare to the room and even though a part of me might have been thrilled if he started stroking me and teasing like he had before... something in him felt jagged right now.

His hands weren't gentle.

His tone was gruff.

His body was insistent.

He grunted as he fumbled with his own pants, then I felt him there... *right there*. I was opening my mouth to say his name, to try to draw him back to me, because it felt like he was deep inside himself—almost unaware of me.

But as I turned my head, he took the top of my skull in his large hand and pulled my head aside, opening his mouth at my shoulder and licking it.

I shivered.

Then he spoke, and his voice was low and dark in a way that gave me chills.

"Do you think God wills anything good foran animal like *me*, Jesse?"

"I do, Cazz. But please, just tell me—"

Stinging, shrieking pain sang through my shoulder. My entire body jolted and I might have screamed—he *bit me!?*—but in the same moment I sucked in a breath, he plunged into me with such force that his hips smacked against my ass and he lifted my feet from the floor.

"CAZZ—" The word tore out of my throat in a guttural rush.

But Cazz didn't answer. He was bent over me, teeth still in my flesh, strange animalistic sounds breaking in his throat as he pulled all the way out, then punched his hips forward, and when he took me off my feet again, he wrapped one arm around, low on my belly, until I was held over it like he'd bent me over a steel bar.

I cried out at the explosion of combined pleasure and pain, uncertain whether the cry was joy or fear.

Cazz hissed as he jerked his head back, his teeth sliding out of my flesh in a nervy, horrific feeling. But a moment later his hand clapped over the wound and gripped my shoulder, his fingers pressed flat above my collarbone, his thumb bracing on my back.

I wasn't sure if he was stemming the blood, or just holding me there. But he continued to pump into me with such ferocity, I couldn't find the air to ask him.

I was helpless, both hands clamped on that bar because it was the only anchor left to me as Cazz plowed into me again, and again, my entire body shaking with every thrust—and my whole world shuddering in time with waves of both pleasure and pain.

"Cazz... *Cazz...*"

"You're mine."

"Yes, but—"

"I own you," he spat.

I dropped my head lower than my shaking arms, blinking hard, trying to understand what was happening, what I felt—love? Joy? Pleasure? Pain? Fear?

All of the above was the answer, and that left me so confused—

"Say it, Jesse," he snarled.

"I… I'm yours."

"My what?"

"Mate. I'm your mate—"

"What else?"

Oh God… I shook, something inside me twisting at the word.

"Y-your slave—" I gasped.

A wave of something powerful crackled along the bond and we both jolted.

Cazz groaned and his entire body shuddered. Tightening his grip on my shoulder, he pumped into me again so hard that our bodies slapped. My toes curled, but I couldn't get purchase because he was still holding me up, off the ground. It felt like at any moment I might fall. If he let me go—

"Don't drop me!" I pleaded, gasping.

"Mine," he snarled, his fingers digging into the soft flesh above my collarbones and behind my shoulder.

"I know, Cazz… Yes," I whispered. "You don't have to—"

"I do! You gave me no choice!"

He thrust again and right alongside the part of me that screamed fear, that tingling wave of pleasure began to glitter within me, a climax beckoning on the horizon. But it called as if over an ocean of stagnant waste.

"Why?" I pleaded. "Why are you doing this?!"

"Because you forced me into a corner and it is not your choice to do that to me!"

"But I never meant—"

Still inside me, Cazz dropped me to my feet, growling and catching me when my knees gave and I almost tumbled to the floor. But when he'd pulled me up and I remained standing—still bent forward, still gripping that bar with everything I had—he plunged that hand into my hair and leaned over me again, his lips brushing my ear, his panting breath rushing against my cheek.

"I am King, Jesse," he snarled, his voice ragged and torn. "King of your heart, mind, and body. King of your *soul.*" His fingers tightened over the punctured flesh where he'd bitten me.

"You are my mate, my Queen. The holder of my soul. And so I Claim you, you lucky bitch. *You are mine,* Jesse. Forever."

38. Mine

~ *JESSE* ~

I thought they were just words. Just him asserting himself. That dominance thing he'd talked about. He was moving inside me more erratically, so I thought it was over. That he'd climax and this would be done.

But the moment he said the word *forever,* my breath stopped. The skin under his hand, where his teeth had cut my flesh, flared bright and burning. And just as I began to cry out against the pain, it chilled to ice.

Still fisting my hair in his other hand, Cazz dropped his face to the back of my neck and sucked in a deep, shuddering breath.

Mine.

I *felt* the word. Heard it in my head, though his lips didn't move. And something inside me responded to it, a whip-crack of light and heat so bright it felt like it seared my heart.

"Cazz!" I gasped, my fingers clawing into that bar. His hands tightened on me again, and there should have been pain, but all I could feel was that piercing right at the center of my chest—the light that seemed ready to swallow me whole.

It was coming from him.

Cazz...

Mine. That word echoed in my skull. It was tender this time, but *shredded.*

Then, suddenly, that light broke through, illuminating the bond, like a dark tunnel suddenly bathed in sunlight, and he was there.

He was there, and broken, and dark and...

All the horror and clarity about the state of Cazz's deepest self that had come to me through the wedding vows, reared up again, reminding me why I was here.

A broken, hollow soul. Isolated and afraid—but snarling into the wind of his own destruction. He felt so deeply alone…

Tears rose, closing my throat. I struggled against his hold on me for a moment. I was desperate to turn and reach for him, to reassure myself that he hadn't given in to that abyss that called to him with voices that chilled my blood. But also terrified because it seemed that he would drag me into that cold darkness with him, and leave me there.

But he only braced his arms around me, kept himself curled tightly around me, moved inside me and breathed that word over and over and over again.

Mine… Mine… Mine… mine…

I choked on my own tears, but as his grip on my hair gentled and his lips brushed the nape of my neck, and our bodies sang together, I was lost. Carried away on the wave of power and light and… whatever this was that was manifesting between us.

Because I could feel it. Something was *becoming.*

I'd had a sense of him ever since the vows. But now… now it was as if the piece of him that fought its own freedom, took a grip on me. Snapped a leash on my heart.

And as he curled around me, he called to me in a way I didn't even know was possible.

I was barely aware of my body anymore, barely aware of his. We were one. Our skins fused. Our bones connected. Our minds held the same space.

"Cazz… what's happening?" My voice cracked on his name.

"I Claim you. *You are mine.* Forever."

I felt the surge of it coming—washing towards me… no *us.* That shimmering promise of pleasure was rushed towards us like a curling wave, high overhead that hung there so we could see it. It carried an explosive climax, and something else… *power.* Power that crackled and sang and,

Power that could save or destroy.

I stopped breathing, gazing at the marvel of my mate and his heart and his darkness and why he needed me.

Then the wave broke, crashing over both of us, tumbling, twisting, until I couldn't know up or down, or anything except that Cazz still held me and we were one.

Then the wave sucked away, back into the tide and we were left on the shore of it, gasping. Trembling.

New.

I blinked, and blinked again. I was on the floor of that room, laying on my side, my arms outstretched in front of me, my knees curled up. And the other part of me, *him,* the strength, the steel of him, curled around me—my back, under my thighs, behind my calves... One of his arms extended out from under my head so I could see his hand—the tendons standing proud because his fingers were clawed like he was about to grasp something... His other arm was around my middle, holding me to him.

His warmth at my back.

His breath in my hair.

His soul entwined with mine.

I had thought the bond, when he created it, was breathtaking. But this...

This was devastating.

"Cazz?" I breathed. I felt helpless. Boneless. Weak. My body hummed, electric and ecstatic, but whatever power was growing inside my skin, it sucked every ounce of energy and strength that I had left and fed me... to him.

My heart thrummed, pulsed, warmed... and fed my lifeblood out of me down that chord that tied us together.

I tried to move, but could barely shift one arm.

Cazz let out a long, ragged breath and it fluttered in my hair, and that power inside me glittered and glowed, pulsing back and forth between us.

I thought he would speak, but he didn't. We just lay there together.

One.

I don't know if we slept, or if it was just part of the magic of that bond, but for a time I was unaware of the noise outside the room. Unaware of anything except Cazz—and he was either asleep, or so deeply overwhelmed he remained silent and unmoving.

But at some point, reality returned.

The rattling and thumping on the door had slowed but it was still happening in jolts and sudden barrages.

Cazz left me and I wanted to cry at the aching hollow within me. But even though he didn't speak, he shushed me, crouching over me to straighten my clothes, then pulling me up and into his chest, standing, carrying me as if he didn't even feel my weight.

I Claim you. You're mine. Forever.

I was trembling from head to toe. Overwhelmed and uncertain of everything except that I couldn't bear to be separated from him.

I buried my face under his jaw, locked my arms around his neck, and tried to breathe.

With me curled in his arms like a child, he started to move. I wasn't sure what he was doing until I heard the resounding thud of the bar falling to the floor.

I gasped and clung to his neck, screwing my eyes tightly shut as the doors flew open behind my back and air and noise rushed around us.

But even though the music continued to thump in a bass so hard it vibrated under his feet, and even though there had to be hundreds of wolves watching, I saw none of it.

I kept my face in his neck, trembled, and prayed.

39. The Wall

~ *JESSE* ~

Some time later, the sound of the Den faded. And some time after that, his boots rang on hollow wood instead of dirt or stone. And then he was bending forward, lowering my feet to the floor.

I gasped and clung to him, unable to explain why, but the thought of being separated from him was horrific.

He still didn't speak. But he caught my flailing hands and pulled them down, stroked my hair and waited.

And when I opened my eyes, it was to find him watching me, his bright, arctic eyes ablaze. And his face a tense, expressionless mask.

My heart thunked, falling for my toes, but Cazz didn't hesitate.

I felt his warm, calloused palms on my ribs as he slipped his hands under my shirt and pulled it gently up.

Then he unbuttoned my leathers for the second time, and pushed them down my legs too—but he also knelt and slipped my shoes off my feet, then pulled the pants off until I stood in front of him naked.

When he straightened to his full height, there was still no expression on his face. I reached for that space inside me that was him, but it was hollow… a wasteland. Cold. And the only sound was an accusing shift of air whistling in uninhabited chambers, carrying blame and judgment.

My entire being wanted to shrink and cry.

But Cazz showed none of it. He stripped his own clothing and shoes in seconds, then took my hand and led me to the bathing room off his bedroom.

Because we were in his bedroom, I realized.

I hadn't been in here before. In the back of my mind something said I should be drinking in the sight of this place, growing to know it. But all I could do was stare at him, his muscular shoulders and back as he pulled me forward to a steaming bath.

He didn't pause, didn't ask, just swept me up again, then lowered me into the steaming water. And when I was settled, the water deep enough that my breasts floated, he started at my hair, untying the bands and pulling his fingers through the braids until it all hung loose, falling over my breasts and down my back.

I looked down to see the strands spread in hazy, unfurling tendrils around me, but then he caught it in one hand and pulled it back, baring the shoulder where he'd bitten me.

He'd picked up a cloth from somewhere and he plunged it into the water, tickling my thigh with the tips of his fingers, before he drew it back out, wrung it out, then began to gently dab at my shoulder.

I finally found the courage to look up at him again, hoping for some glimmer of insight, some expression, or better yet, a word.

But there was nothing on his face. As if the act of what he had done had stolen every feeling, every emotion.

He was a shell. He touched gently, but efficiently. He moved without urgency, but also without intimacy.

He cleaned me. He dried me. And he led me to the bed, urging me to get in between the thick, lush furs.

"Cazz... what just happened?"

He stopped in the act of drawing the covers over me and raised his eyes from where he was holding the furs, to meet mine.

For a split second, the bond rang with something—a shriek of emotion. A plea for help, or accusation. I didn't know, because as quickly as the feeling began it stopped.

"Cazz—"

"Go to sleep, Jesse."

I wanted to argue, but something held my tongue.

Reluctantly, I lay back against the thick pillows, piled tall enough that I was sitting against them, my head and shoulders leaned up. But watched him pull the furs over my lap, push my hair back from my face, then drop his hands and sigh as he walked out of the room, turning off the lamp and closing the door to leave me in unbroken darkness.

And as I lay there, silent, my body humming, that strange light still glowing in my chest, I closed my eyes because I could feel him moving. Sense not only which direction he was in, but how near—or far—he was from me.

I held that sensation carefully, testing it. But it was as tangible to me as my sight.

I could feel him. Not just the sense of him, but *him.*

Tentatively, I reached for him in my mind and heart, like a hand stretching to touch the back of someone leaving.

And there was a moment when I brushed against him, and his heart grew full. Something in him turned towards me—the same thing that had screamed.

And then everything went dead.

Like he'd slammed a door between us. But not the door outside the den that you could beat and rattle.

This door was a wall. A steel wall. Thick and impenetrable.

My reaching came up against the cold stillness of it and all sense of him died.

I panicked, mentally laying my hands on that cold steel, first touching—searching for a way through. Then knocking, begging. Then pounding—demanding that he open again, beating my fists against that door, screaming at him to let me back in, pleading—sobbing...

But even though he didn't answer, as I scrambled and scratched, trying desperately to reach him through the door, I slowly became aware of a pulse... a thread. A rythmic, thudding heartbeat.

I went still, laying a shaking palm against that cold metal barrier, reassuring myself that I could, indeed, feel it.

A pulse.

A heartbeat.

Him.

And then I could breathe again.

Cazz was still there. Guarded from me, but not gone.

A cold tear tracked down my cheek. But I could breathe.

Since I couldn't break through that wall, I let myself slide to the floor, resting my cheek against the cool steel of it, and keeping my palm flat on it.

Because that was where I could feel him... still alive.

And that was where I could pray he would remain that way.

40. Battle of the Mind

The moment my teeth sank into her flesh and I tasted her blood, the world shifted.

I almost shifted.

The part of me that was animal leaped for control, teeth snapping, body steel, all senses heightened and focused on only one goal.

Her.

For a time it seemed my body and mind were torn apart and I clung desperately to keep both as my body plunged into her, gripped her, took her... But my mind screamed—desperate need, fear, rage...

I spent minutes fighting not to lose myself entirely. I fought for her—snarling at her to declare the sick truth of us—her power over me, mine over her, the ways that we were tied together, whether we wanted it that way or not.

And then she said it, she gasped the truth that I was master to her slave, and power slammed through my body until I was clinging to her, not to keep her there, but clawing into her to ground myself, because I feared I was lost.

In the wake of that stunning surge, amid her whimpers and pleas, I slowly but surely clawed back control, inch by inch. Blinking back into my body, she was bent over my arm, her nails scraping into that bar at the door, pleading with me not to drop her.

"Mine." It was a bold truth, a fact, an anchor in this battle for clarity.

"I know, Cazz... Yes. You don't have to—"

Rage streamed from every pore—yes, I had to! She had given me no choice!

Every instinct thrummed with need and I took her, again and again, harder and harder, heedless of her cries, because I was driven.

She must be mine. She *must.* If she were not, she had stolen something from me I could never retrieve.

Her pleas and questions only threw fuel on the fire—flames so high and hot my skin blistered. The ancient call of the wolf within could not be denied—would not. The power that sang in my veins belonged to him. Without it I was dead—and her with me.

I forced her to take her own weight, grasped at her, clawed, desperate.

I am King... of your heart, mind, and body. King of your soul... You are my mate, my Queen. The holder of my soul. And so I Claim you, you lucky bitch. You are mine, Jesse. Forever."

That word hit my bloodstream like mainlining electricity. My fingers dug into her flesh as my head threw back and I roared my ownership of her, plowing into her again and again, my body singing... then, even without the ecstacy of orgasm, that electric crackle eased and I was blinking, panting, slumping over her again, tasting the sweat on the back of her neck and sucking in a deep, shuddering breath.

Mine.

If I could have tattoed myself into her flesh, I would have. My nails threatened to pierce her skin as my teeth already had, but I couldn't loosen my grip. Something was coming. Light on the edge of vision. Heat at the center of my chest.

Power.

And if I didn't control it, it would sweep everything in me away to the hell that rose like a cliff over my head—bathing me in shadows, calling for me.

Mine. The word broke like sunrise in my mind and I trembled, because for a moment it sang hope, love, light and peace. My body hummed like a struck tuning fork—and continued to vibrate as if everything that made me was coming apart.

There was a moment when she saw me. I couldn't block it, the veil had been parted. We stood, facing each other in the light of truth and she saw me for what I truly was—a cold, heartless bastard standing in a barren wasteland of a soul, fighting for any sense of power or strength that would stop me feeling helpless.

And I hated her for it, for seeing me like that.

I cowered in that gaze—the power of her, her strength and willingness to simply *give*… it terrified and shamed me. I had no choice but to hide from it, covering her, blinding her, turning her away. And yet, our lives were now irrevocably linked. I couldn't deny her. Couldn't leave her. Not truly.

Mine… Mine… Mine… mine…

I was still taking her body, still making her mine. Unable to face what happened within, I turned my focus to her flesh, pumping into her, owning her, branding her with my scent, my need, my *self,* braiding our souls, until it was impossible to know where I ended and she began.

And as I shuddered and shook, riding the edge of climax, she cried my name.

"I Claim you. *You are mine.* Forever."

Climax and the power she'd always offered me crashed over us in a tsunami, and I was tossed aside like a leaf in the wind, grasping, screaming, clawing for purchase until I was thrown to the shore of her, limp and helpless…

New.

When I opened my eyes we lay on the floor. I had instinctively curled around her when we were thrown…

Holy shit… *The bond…* light in my chest, that tunnel connecting us glowed and threatened to reveal everything I'd locked away.

Screaming, chittering terror froze me in place. As she came alive again and sought me, helpless and breathless, I didn't move. Couldn't. Had to hold every cell of myself together before I was split open like a ripe fruit.

There was no time. There was no space. There was no me, no her, only *us.*

And it was the most terrifying moment of my entire life.

Had I known it was coming, had I understood what claiming her would do to me, I would have let them have her. Would have let them tear her to pieces to save myself.

And in that truth I was revealed to be the coward I had always feared.

Time stretched and slowed and dragged me forward.

At some point I wrestled the abject terror deep enough in the back of my mind that I could move. I covered her, because covering her shame was covering mine and…

I couldn't think about it.

She was helpless, weak, feeble as a sick child, so I lifted her to my chest, my body somehow stronger, despite how my heart cowered.

When she buried her face in my neck and clung, I almost wept—then the fire of fury blew through me so fast it stole my breath. She weakened me. She poured strength into me, and weakened me. I was lost.

I staggered, not because she was a burden, but because the weight of holding her so truly threatened to unhinge my mind.

I stood there with her in my arms, my toes curling over the crumbling edge of a precipice and once again found myself with only two choices.

To give over completely. Surrender to the claim she had on me now, and give my life and body to her service… or to shut that shit down.

41. Blessed Silence

~ CASIMIR ~

There was a moment, a vision blooming in my mind of a different life—a different male. Given, peaceful, joyful... I could see myself as the mate and husband, the reluctant King. The delighted lover and mentor. Happy... and weak. Happy to *be* weak.

Weak to her disapproval. Weak to the loss of her. Weak to her pain.

I sucked in a sharp breath, fingers clawing into her hip, her legs, holding her tightly against my chest as if someone was about to rip her free. Then the terror rushed in on the back of the rest of that image: Me happy and weak, and failing. Impossible to lead the packs, to maintain my strength, to control *anything* if she held such power.

Impossible.

Utterly.

Jesse made a small sound, as if she heard my thoughts, though I knew she couldn't. Her arms tightened around my neck, her nose nuzzling under my jaw, and her body melted into mine. And then I heard them—the snarling and barking, the howls of distress and fury, the thuds and slams of heavy bodies in a last ditch effort because they could feel the claim taking hold, feel themselves losing her.

I saw it in my mind—them breaking through and tearing her from me. Their teeth in her skin, their pricks inside her, their howls of glee and dominance and a wave of rage and fear rocked through me.

No. NO.

I took one step, and another wolf slammed against the door so hard the bar rattled in its brackets. Claws scratched, howls rose, the pack fought... and the fear broke something inside me.

A shiver, a singing pain, like plunging my entire body into a pool of ice-cold, crystal clear water. A shriek in my mind like a dying animal... then resolve returned.

I blinked, and the tumult of noise and emotion faded like vapor on a breeze.

The only thing I could hear was my pulse, pounding in my ears. The only thing I could feel was her heart, hammering against my chest. The only scent was her blood, spilled by me.

And the power... the power sank into my bones and turned me cold, even as it thrummed through me like it was fed in my bloodstream.

Then, taking hold of her, both literally and figuratively, I opened myself fully to the packmind. And finally, finally, as they saw what I'd done, what I'd taken, what she'd given... the chaos on the other side of that door stopped.

There were no more questions.

There was no more hope for her.

No more fear.

She was *mine*.

Wordlessly, still holding her to my chest, I used one arm to lift the bar from the door and toss it aside. And when the doors creaked open, I barely saw all the bodies, all the eyes.

Rake registered vaguely in my strained mind, standing at the center, turned with wide eyes, searching me and Jesse alike, his chest heaving because he'd been fighting—pleading with the wolves to leave us, to snap out of their frenzy. But now even he was calm. Even he could see.

All of them could.

Chin high and feeling the power like oxygen in my veins, I stepped out, lifting my lip to bare my teeth in case any were stupid enough to have missed what she was now.

But though they whined and turned circles in their frustration, though some shifted and ran, everyone who remained stepped aside... and bowed.

They saw the power in me and acknowledged it.

Even Rake.

We passed through the den untouched.

We walked the corridors and steps through the maze under the palace unhindered. We walked the hallways and stairs of the palace itself, *glowing*. I could feel it… feel the power emanating from me—and so could any wolf within sight or scent.

I didn't make a conscious choice to return her to my quarters, but after urging a servant to run ahead and run the bath for us, it seemed right.

I took her into my sanctum, my private rooms, and only then did I lower her to the ground.

When she gasped and reached for me, there was a single, fragile moment where my resolve wavered—my heart leaped in my chest and I almost gave in to the urge to curl her into my chest and hold her, to stroke her hair and soothe the fear that she was feeling, because she *hadn't* resolved against the claim.

She was now more afraid of losing me than anything else in this world. And seeing her desperate, childish fear, galvanized my heart.

I caught her hands, pulling them down and clamping both her wrists in one of my hands, using the other to pet her hair like a child's, to soothe her, to offer the sense of reassurance until she relaxed.

Then without concern, I undressed her and myself, then carried her to the bath where I loosened her hair and cleaned the blood from her skin that I had put there—tipped my head to examine my own finger and palm prints pressed into her skin in her own blood.

But all it took was water, nothing special, and the marks of our new intimacy were washed away, leaving nothing but the reddened scar. Scars, not wounds, because the power that burned through both of us had healed her on the spot.

I pressed one of those half-moon of teeth above her collarbone with my finger and she didn't even flinch.

Very good.

Then I brought her out of the water, dried her, and led her to my bed.

"Cazz… what just happened?"

Her voice was high and hoarse, a frightened child's. It rang something in my chest, but I took a moment and silenced it.

"Cazz—"

"Go to sleep, Jesse."

Then I tucked her in, brushed her hair back from her face, and left the room as dark as my soul.

As I closed the door, it occurred to me that I was supposed to sleep too. But the power was thrumming in my veins, and that still, small voice in the back of my head shrieked alarm. So I would not sleep. I would walk the halls of power, and I would show them all why they couldn't touch her.

Two hallways down from the bedroom, I stumbled a step because I felt her—stretching across the space between us to touch me. It was so unexpected, I hadn't guarded against it. It took a moment—fists clenched, teeth gritted, mind resolved—to close myself to this river of feeling between us.

But I did it. I slammed the door and locked it just as surely as I'd done back in that chamber off the Den.

My breath was quickened, my hands trembling.

I closed my eyes and inhaled deeply, slowly, filling my lungs with the perfect perfume of power and solitude.

And when I began walking again, I was smiling, my heart beat steadily, no longer pounding. And my mind was finally, blessedly silent.

42. Confusion

~ *JESSE* ~

I woke the next morning and the first thing I was aware of was that parts of my body hurt.

I opened my eyes, confused, then blinked and sat bolt upright.

It took a moment to remember that the dark, masculine chamber was Cazz's. I turned quickly, reaching out for the other side of the bed—but it was cold, the sheets and blankets undisturbed, and the pillowcase uncreased.

A pang landed right in the pit of my stomach.

When the door opened, I yanked the quilt up to my chest, but it was a female servant hustling in with her arms full of clothes.

"Here you are, Sire," she said, smiling, but keeping her eyes and chin low. "His Highness sent these for you. If you would like others, he's instructed me to go get them for you." She placed the bundle of clothes on the end of the bed, then folded her hands at her waist. "I'll also bring your breakfast if you'll tell me what you would prefer?"

My head was spinning as I tried to remember everything that had happened the night before—and figure out what was real and what was a dream. Or maybe intoxication? That drink he'd given me…

I blinked, realizing the servant was still waiting.

"I… just some, um, bacon and fruit, please," I said quietly. "These clothes are fine."

She turned and darted away like she was excited to help, and left me sitting there, buried in confusion and aching pain and…

"Cazz, where are you?" I breathed to the room, looking around. But there was no sign of him anywhere—and the bathroom door was ajar. He wasn't hidden in there.

Besides, the servant had said he sent her, right? So he was already up and... I looked back at the space on the other side of the bed, then corrected myself. He was *still* up. Or at least, had never rested here.

Something cold and hollow sank into the pit of my stomach. I felt teary, but I wasn't sure why.

He'd been angry... he'd been aggressive. He'd scared me. He'd also wanted me. Taken me. *Claimed* me.

I sucked in a breath as a memory of that moment when he'd declared the claiming struck me. Then another, of the moment I was falling. My heart and mind full of him—then suddenly blocked. Pounding at that cold wall, weeping, screaming for him...

I shivered and turned my mind away from that memory and tried to focus.

A few minutes later I was dressed, moving carefully because strange places on my body were sore, and sitting at the small table at the side of the room, staring at a plate of bacon with a bowl of fruit and wondering if I was going to throw it up if I swallowed anything.

My body was doing strange things. Because of the Claiming? I could still sense Cazz, still *knew* him, but it was as if he'd built a thick, soundproof wall between us—something that muffled all sound and sensation... and yet that whistling cold slipped under it to chill my chest.

What the hell had happened to me?

To us?

Cazz...?

I picked up the fork for the fruit with a trembling hand, but caught sight of my broken, ragged nails.

Suddenly I was seeing images of my hands, clawed into that bar and the way my entire body shuddered when he pounded into me...

My belly clenched at the same time that my body flinched.

Putting the fork back down, I raised the hand to that spot where my shoulder met my neck, where he'd bitten me... but it didn't hurt at all. I could feel half-moon lines of puckers in the skin, both front and back and I looked around the room for a mirror.

Spying a full length mirror at the side of the room, I pushed the chair back and hurried over to it, tugging at the neckline of the shirt he'd sent me, my breath catching when I reached the shining surface of the mirror. But not because of the bite...

Impossibly, the bite was already healed. Already scarred.

I had a glimpse in my mind of that light and heat, the flare of something impossible under his hand when he'd held me...

I swallowed convulsively, because it wasn't the scarring that scared me.

In the flesh below the scars, but above my collarbones, a perfect row of bruises, each the size of a large, male fingertip—and three of them with rounded scratches below, because his nails had scraped my skin...

I felt sick. I wanted to turn away from the mirror, but I couldn't. My eyes were locked on those wounds—small, though they might be. Wounds they were. Heart pounding, swallowing, swallowing, swallowing, I stared. And the chasm in my guts yawned wider and wider.

It wasn't abuse, I told myself hurriedly. *We were both overwhelmed. I clawed at the wood—then held him so tightly! He was gripping me because we were trying not to be torn apart...*

But the thought felt hollow. Terrifying.

I was never going to be *that girl*. I had told myself my whole life, if a man ever treated me the way my father and brothers did, it would be the last day I let him be in my life.

But Cazz was my mate... my husband.

He'd claimed me.

Heart hammering, I reminded myself of the good things too—that light, that heat, that vision of him in the tunnel, revealed in the brightest light and staring at me, pleading for help—

The knock on the door startled me and I turned too fast, my hip aching.

The door was already ajar, but it swung open slowly. "Jesse?"

"Rake?" I rasped.

He stepped into the room, his dark hair wet like he'd just showered. He was fully dressed again, and back to being the cleric—chin low, eyes searching, voice quiet.

But as I watched him walk warily towards me, the visions of him last night, growling at Cazz, dancing nearby—and putting himself between us and the wolves chasing us...

I blinked back inexplicable tears and he saw it, hurrying faster across the floor towards me.

"Jesse, what's wrong? Are you hurt? Who—"

I shook my head, brushing the tears away quickly, then wiping my hands on my jeans.

"I'm fine. I'm just… tired… and a little confused," I admitted reluctantly.

Rake stopped two steps from me, his forehead pinched and eyes searching me. But I was dressed. He couldn't see the bruises, I told myself. He didn't know. None of them knew…

Oh god, was I turning into one of those women?

43. Sunlight – Part 1

~ *JESSE* ~

With a soft growl, Rake turned and trotted back to the door, closing and locking it before he faced me again and started back, slower this time.

"Jesse… talk to me," he said quietly, soothingly. Like I was a scared little animal.

"About what?" I laughed humorlessly.

"What happened last night? I mean, I know what happened, but… how did it happen?"

I blinked, frowning. "What do you mean, you know what happened?" I asked, my voice barely above a whisper.

Rake turned his chin slightly away from me, but his eyes never left mine. "Cazz claimed you… didn't he?"

Relief rocked through me, and I nodded quickly to cover. "Yes. Yes, you're right. He did. I just… I don't understand exactly… exactly what happened. Or what it means."

"He didn't tell you?"

I was perilously close to tears, which I *hated*. This wasn't how I lived! But something about Cazz had turned me into brittle glass. I felt like the wrong blow—even a soft one—would shatter me into too many pieces to ever hope to heal.

I hadn't felt like this in years. Why had the claiming made it *worse?*

Unable to put words to how I was feeling, I waved a hand at Rake, looking away like it was nothing, but I had to blink too many times, and I knew he caught it.

"Yes, yes. I mean, I was there," I said breathlessly. "I just meant… we humans don't do the… claiming. Not like that. It was a shock. And I don't really understand…"

God, why did I want to cry? Not just cry—*weep!?*

Rake stood in front of me, a little bit of horror on his face, his hands clenched at his sides, searching my eyes.

"I'm sorry," I choked as the tears came. "I don't know why I'm feeling this way. I'm so confused."

Rake jumped forward, taking my arm and leading me to the chair I'd just left, muttering about stupid blind males. He grabbed up the cloth napkin I'd left on the table and shoved it in my hands, urging me to use it.

So I did, covering my face for exactly two choking breaths, then blinking and wiping the tears away and breathing deeply.

"Thank you," I whispered.

"Don't thank me for… god, Jesse. Didn't he explain at all?"

I shook my head. "Not really."

"Can you… did the claiming take? I was certain it had, but—"

"Oh, it took," I said, laughing and crying again as that yawning chasm echoed in my chest again. "It definitely took. But I think… I think he wishes it didn't," I said, finally admitting the low, dark thought that had been haunting me since the moment I opened my eyes. "I think… I think he only did it because everyone was going so crazy and I think… I think he's angry now, because he didn't want to. He said I forced him…"

Rake muttered a curse and reached out like he'd pull me out of the chair and into a hug. But then he yanked his hand back and clawed it through his hair instead.

"I'm sorry, Jesse. I never imagined he'd…" he trailed off, and I almost laughed, because I knew he was stopping himself from lying.

Of course he imagined that Cazz would leave me alone.

I closed my eyes, one hand to my chest where a deep, painful ache wouldn't let me breathe properly.

It took a moment to realize, I was grieving. My body responding as if I'd lost someone. Someone desperately important.

My mate.

"Rake… I think he left me," I whispered through numb lips, the tears flowing freely now. "I don't understand… I don't understand what happened last night, or what I'm supposed to do now, or anything. Should I leave? Just leave him and—"

Rake hissed and did jump forward then, grabbing my arms and pulling me out of the chair, then back to the bed where he picked up the long cloak the servant had left that I hadn't put on because I didn't plan on going anywhere, and threw that over my shoulders.

"You cannot speak those words here, ever," he whispered urgently, pulling the hood up and over my hair so my face was hidden in the shadows of it. "Just breathe, Jesse. We'll go up. We'll see the sun. I'll... I'll explain. I can help just... don't say those words here ever again."

*****

I hadn't realized how oppressive the darkness of the underground Palace and tunnels was until the last moments in the tunnel to the surface, the way I could suddenly smell air that wasn't just clean, but *fresh*. I closed my eyes, still feeling fragile and teary, but as I inhaled deeply the cool, fresh air from the world above, it soothed something in my chest.

We walked out of the cave that I'd never seen because I was blindfolded when the Reapers brought me here. And to my surprise, we didn't emerge on the edge of the city, or town. Instead the cave nestled in the rocky side of a mountain. The ground immediately outside it was dirt and pebbles, but it quickly gave way to grass that wound away down through a meadow that coiled at the foot of the mountain and was hemmed by forest so that I couldn't see the horizon.

High slopes of rock and trees rose either side of where we stood, the scent of pine and dirt and clear air.

I laughed a little bit as I opened my eyes and watched white puffs of clouds skitter overhead because there was a stiff breeze that we were mostly being sheltered from by the high sides of this little ravine, or whatever it was.

"Thank you, Rake," I breathed, shaking my head. "Thank you. I needed this."

He grunted, then started walking, beckoning me to follow him. "This is a safe place to leave the tunnels. Humans rarely come this far, but if you followed that ridge to the east, there's a cabin there that we use when we're traveling to the city. And there's a smaller settlement a few miles north..."

He trailed off, scanning the forest below us as we walked into the widening meadow.

A couple minutes later—sweating, because I was in the thick leathers that were needed underground—we reached a little cluster of boulders and rocks and Rake stopped walking, gesturing for me to take a seat.

"Let's not go too far," he said quietly, turning so he could see the mouth of the cave above us, and the meadow below. "Rest here."

I didn't argue, but took a seat and for a few minutes, just looked down at the grass and the trees, birds sweeping overhead, flowers rippling in the sunlight... and I sighed.

Up here in all this light, what had happened last night seemed like a dim memory. A nightmare that had been scary, but was fading now.

But the moment I felt like I could talk without crying, and I looked back at Rake who was standing with his hands in the pockets of his leathers and saw the expression on his face...

"What?" I asked, a little sharper than I should have.

Rake's expression was dark with concern. "What happened?" When I balked, he raised his hands to reassure me. "I just mean... You said you were confused. Let's try and clear that up for you, because... because I have a feeling you've got quite a journey ahead of you, Jesse. So if I can answer your questions, I will."

I watched him warily, suddenly, inexplicably, very protective of Cazz. And that made no sense. But the more I thought of describing the events of the night before... the harder it got to keep myself from crying.

What the *hell* had Cazz done to me?

44. Sunlight – Part 2

~ JESSE ~

I huffed, pissed because the threat of tears was back, just like that. I swallowed the pinch in my throat and shook my head. "It doesn't matter."

"Of course it matters. You said you're confused. That you think he's left you—that seems unlikely to me. But... what happened? Perhaps it's a difference between wolves and humans? Maybe I can shed some light?"

"You already do, Rake," I sighed and looked down at my lap, picking at the seam in the leather pants Cazz had sent for me.

That should make me feel better, I realized. He'd been thinking about me needing clothes because I was in his room. That was a good sign, right?

I turned my thoughts inward, towards that knot at the center of my chest. The piece of me that had been so open last night. So full of him until the end. I reached for it, stroking it's surface, but recoiled.

It was still cold.

Dead.

An emotionless wall.

"I just... I don't know what I did," I breathed, cursing myself for the choke in my words and the way my sight blurred immediately.

"I told him not to take you to the Den last night," Rake growled, shaking his head and turning to squint at the forest. "I knew you weren't ready for that."

"How?"

"How, what?"

"How did you know?"

Rake glanced at me like he was measuring whether to answer. Then he sighed and reached down to tear a weed out of the ground—a long, thin stalk topped in what looked like grains of wheat or something similar, but they were gray, and a little furry.

He held it, picking at those tiny pieces, frowning.

"You were... enamored," he said finally. "It was clear you still hadn't really grasped what it means to be part of the pack. And they'd had no chance to get to know you. So there was no restraint on their part. They still didn't yet see you as an extension of him. It was always risky."

"So why did he do it?" I asked him bluntly. "If he knew it was a risk—he didn't even warn me about the drink!"

Rake's jaw flexed and he shook his head again. "Jesse, you need to understand... Cazz is... a little twisted."

I snorted. "Trust me, I already got that part."

"No, that's not what I meant," Rake grumbled, rolling his head to the side like he was trying to loosen a tension in his neck. "I meant... his mind was twisted. By his father, mostly. He's... it wouldn't matter if he was King or not—his need for control is just a part of him."

"He already has control over me," I flung back.

"No, he doesn't. And that's what's scaring him."

"Scaring? Rake, I don't know what you think you saw last night, but that man isn't afraid of anything."

"He's fucking terrified of you."

"Why? I submitted to *him!*"

"Because he promised not to compel you—and trust me, in Cazz's world that's unheard of."

"He vowed it to you," I pointed out.

"I hold a formal role in his staff. He gives me that freedom—with a commitment to listen. But without any obligation to act on anything I say. Trust me, Jesse, of the two of us you're the one who makes him sweat."

"How?!"

"Because you make him willing to give a piece of himself. And he's never experienced that before. Or at least, he's never allowed himself to *entertain* it." Rake chuckled dryly and clawed a hand through his hair. "You intoxicated him with the power you gave him. It was a masterstroke, actually. The one thing he couldn't resist—and yet, the power you offer erodes the very thing he wants most."

"What? What are you talking about?"

Rake exhaled, then squatted down so he wasn't standing over me anymore, and we were eye level. He still had that little plant in his hands, but his eyes locked with mine.

"Jesse, hear me: Your submission increases his power to compel others. And that is something that he wants more than anything *except* actual control. Because that compulsion gives him control. So you're feeding right into what makes him feel safe."

"Then what's the problem?"

"Because he can't control *you.* And my guess is, the moment the bond took—even before last night, when you vowed to each other and completed the mating bond—he was faced with the reality that a bond with a person who has a mind of their own is a risk, whether they're submitted to you or not."

"Why? Why is it a risk? I let him make all the decisions!"

"Because at any moment you could decide he's not worth it anymore. At any moment you could reject him, and he won't have anything to blame but himself."

"But... his other mates left—they killed themselves!"

"They were mentally ill before that happened. He'd compelled them, derided them, betrayed them... he had nothing but contempt for them. Their deaths hurt him only because neither of them gave him offspring first. But you? He's taken you as you are. And now you're just... there. He has no control. I thought... I hoped he was going to embrace you. Do things differently. Meet you in the middle. But instead he's reacting out of his fear. I'm sorry he hurt you—deeply sorry. I will talk to him about it. I'm probably the only one who can. I just think it's important for you to understand: If he's pulling away, it's because he's frightened. Deep down, under all those layers of anger and assholery, there's a good man. A tender heart that has been wounded so deeply... he's too scared to give anyone access to that part of him. So he controls *everyone.*"

I bit my lip and thought about that. About those flashes of emotion I felt from Cazz now and again—and the ways he would always disappear immediately after, before I could really get a grip on what he was feeling.

"This sounds like a line," I muttered. "He only hurts you because he cares."

Rake shook his head. "No, he hurts you because he's afraid. He's too afraid to really feel anything else. Except anger. Maybe you've noticed, most of us give in to temper when we're scared or hurting—it feels a lot more powerful."

I nodded, I did know that. But I wasn't convinced anger was always a cover for fear or pain. Some people—men in particular—were just angry anyway.

Neither of us spoke for a moment, but then Rake sighed again. "I don't need the… gory details, but can you tell me what happened last night while you were in that room?"

I opened my mouth.

Then I flinched.

45. Sunlight – Part 3

~ JESSE ~

Cazz pounding into me.

His teeth in my flesh.

His words growled, his hands grasping.

I flinched away from the memories that were so confusing. Rake was watching me intently, so I kept my face as blank as I could.

"It wouldn't have been bad—it wasn't bad. But there was... it was just confusing. He... he told me that he had no choice but to claim me. That they'd tear me—or him—apart if he didn't. But he was angry. Blaming me."

"Because you enticed the males."

"I didn't know that I was doing that!" I snapped. "I was thinking about *him.* I didn't know how the packmind worked—he never explained it. And he didn't even warn me that he was going to connect me to it. When it happened it made him happy—he encouraged me! I just... I was flying blind!"

Rake sighed. "I know. It's okay, Jesse. I'm not blaming you. I just... he definitely marked you, right? Declared his claim on you?"

"Yes," I said emphatically. "And somehow... somehow the wounds from it are already healed."

Rake didn't seem surprised, but he dropped his eyes to the grass, shaking his head. "The stronger the claim, the faster it will heal." But his tone was flat. Almost dead.

"What is it?" I asked him. "Why did you say it like that?"

"Because that means you're both trapped."

I waited but he didn't expand on that. "Trapped in what?"

"In this bond," Rake said quietly. "I hoped... I hoped if he wasn't going to stay faithful this time, he might betray you before he claimed you. Then you could at least live without him. But now..."

"Now, what?!" I asked, curling my hands to fists on my thighs. "What, Rake?"

Rake's eyes snapped up to meet mine, his face tight. "Now, if you want to survive this, it's up to him to remain, Jesse. Because if he breaches this bond, he will destroy *both* of you."

"I'm not going to kill myself—"

"No, Jesse, listen: *He* will destroy both of you. Those females were weak, selfish, and ambitious. They died because they couldn't accept that they were losing the prize, and that made them hopeless. They saw their mate as an achievement. A... possession."

I scoffed. "I think I can understand—"

"No, you don't," he said sharply, his eyes flashing. "Those women were betrayed and used and derided. He had nothing but contempt for them. With you... there's a grudging respect. He doesn't want to admit it, but he sees your strength. He never saw theirs. But that's not the important part.

"Cazz never claimed either of them. He swore he wouldn't unless they gave him offspring. And they never did. Trust me, that bothers him more than he wants to let on. But regardless... he was always in control with those two. Always. Their despair came because he pushed them with the compulsion, against their will, but not so far that their minds couldn't understand what they were doing. He literally made them hate themselves—and then he hated them for being so weak."

Weak. Yes. That was *exactly* how I felt. And that made the tears come back, which just made the point, but still pissed me off.

"I do get it, Rake! He's made me *so weak*. I don't know how he did it, but... Before last night I felt physically weak compared to him. But in myself? I never felt *little*... I was strong. I was sure. I wanted to keep myself—that's why I made him agree never to compel me, so I wouldn't lose who I was. But last night after he claimed me... I couldn't even move, Rake. He *had* to carry me out of there. I couldn't have walked. And now... ever since I woke up this morning I feel like... like I've lost whatever spine I had. I feel like... like that darkness inside him is just hovering at my back, sucking at me. And he could save me from it, but he won't! I'm a mess. This... needy, distressed mess. It's no wonder he doesn't want to be near me—I don't want to be near me right now! I don't know what he did to me, but whatever it is, it hurts—but I can't fight it. It's *inside me!"*

Rake's face was pained. He straightened and crossed the space between us, standing right at my toes, looking down on me with sympathy and concern written all over his face.

"He hasn't stolen your strength, Jesse. I promise."

The tears came thick and fast, blurring my sight of him. I dropped my face into my hands. "Yes he has... look at me! I don't cry! Not like this! I feel like... like I'm falling apart, and I don't even know why!"

Rake's hand landed on the back of my head like he was going to give some kind of benediction, but feeling the strength in him grounded me. I kept my head down and prayed he had an answer.

"Jesse," he said hoarsely. "Cazz isn't leaving you. Claiming you increased his power last night. Dramatically. The entire pack saw it."

"Then why did he leave? Why did he walk away—and not come back?! Why is he blaming for something, like I hurt him?"

"Because he couldn't make that declaration for you without giving up a piece of himself. And now he's searching for it. He wants it back. It makes him feel vulnerable. And that's not a feeling he's accustomed to."

"But that's exactly how I feel!" I sobbed.

"That's my point."

I lifted my face from my hands. "I don't understand."

"Jesse... he's terrified. He feels weak—he's not used to feeling that way. He's literally running scared. That instinct you had to leave? He's fighting that just like you are. Shaky, fragile, confused... Everything you need, he needs too."

"Then why is he running from me? Because what I need is *him."*

Rake nodded slowly. "But his power is entirely dependent on holding control over others. And the moment someone takes that control away from him, they don't just take his power to compel. Jesse... they'll take *him."*

"What are you saying?"

"I'm saying that to Cazz, the idea that he could care enough about you to give himself up for you... it's akin to loading a gun and handing it to you. He's putting his life in your hands. And for the first time in his life, he's now *unable* to change that. He can't compel you and keep you in his thrall that way. And he can't change how he feels, because he acknowledged his claim over you—which means he acknowledged your claim over him, as well."

I blinked, Cazz's hoarse growl from the night before coming back to me.

I am King, Jesse. King of your heart, mind, and body. King of your soul… You are my mate, my Queen. The holder of my soul. And so I Claim you, you lucky bitch. You are mine, Jesse. Forever.

"The holder of my soul…" I breathed.

Rake's head jerked back. "He said that? About you?"

I nodded, watching him. "Why do you look like that? He said he was King of *my* soul, so isn't that the same thing?"

"No, Jesse. No… I don't know if he realizes what he did… but he must—that's why he ran."

"What? What does it mean?!"

Rake took a deep breath. "Jesse, he gave you his power. Every ounce of it. He acknowledged that he needs you. And to Cazz, needing someone else is… a death sentence."

I frowned, wiping my eyes. "What? *Why?* "

"Because he has enemies. And if they ever get their hands on you, he'll lose. And he knows it. No wonder he's running… He just created the only weapon that could literally take his Kingdom from him."

46. Marred

~ JESSE ~

Rake and I were both quiet for a time after that. I thought I understood what he meant, but I was still trying to wrap my head around Cazz somehow being *afraid*. I'd never seen that in him, and I wondered if Rake was trying to soothe me.

It came back to me then, the way I'd seen it right at the beginning—that every person here was a wolf, and belonged to Cazz. That there was truly no one I could trust to be loyal to me over him.

But at least Rake wasn't compelled by him. I could trust that... couldn't I?

I didn't know.

At some point I got up from that rock and walked out to stand looking down the meadow at the trees and the sky, just to breathe the fresh air and stand in the light and... bask. Because I knew pretty soon we'd be back in the darkness of the tunnels, and my stomach quavered at the idea.

Eventually, Rake walked slowly up behind me.

"Jesse, we need to get back—" He put a hand on my shoulder, to turn me, intending to be gentle. But his fingers closed right over the place where Cazz had gripped me so tightly, and I flinched.

I pulled out of his grip, trying to make the flinch look like part of the movement of turning to face him, but Rake's brows were high with shock, then they dropped and his eyes narrowed.

"Jesse... are you hurt?"

"I'm fine."

He stared at me for a moment like he wasn't sure whether to trust me. "I thought you said the claiming marks healed?"

"They did. I'm fine." I tried to walk past him towards the cave, scrambling for something to distract him, but Rake caught my elbow and turned me back to face him.

"Jesse—"

"Just leave it, Rake."

"Did he bite you more than once?" His tone was scandalized and it was reflex to scoff.

"Of course not, I was just surprised—"

"Show me."

"What?!" I turned to face him then, pulling back.

"Show me the marks," he growled. "It's actually part of my duties—I have to witness the claiming and add it to the records. I wasn't going to ask you yet, I was going to let things settle down a little, but... Jesse... show me."

His gaze was strange, shadows and warning mixed with compassion and pleading.

I gritted my teeth trying to find a way to avoid this, but knowing there was no way he was letting it go now. So I prayed I'd judge it right and gripped the neckline of my shirt, tugging it down, just far enough that he would be able to see the scars, but hopefully not the bruises and scrapes—

Rake moved fast, but gently, grasping my forearm and tugging it down, just an inch. I wasn't quick enough to anticipate and unhook my fingers from the neckline, so the shirt pulled lower, just to my collarbones, but Rake's eyes went wide and he growled.

"He *hurt you*—"

"It was an emotional night—"

"—he fucking hurt you!"

My breath caught as Rake leaned in, teeth bared and fear flashed in my chest. I stumbled back a step, tripping over a knot of grass and scrambling to keep my feet.

Heart pounding I straightened, pulling the shirt back up and glaring at him.

Rake had stopped the moment I stepped back and now he stood there, gaping at me, his eyes sad.

"I'm sorry," he said quietly. "I didn't mean to frighten you—"

"You don't scare me, Rake. I just... you startled me."

His chest was rising and falling visibly. "Jesse... that's not okay. He didn't need to hurt you to claim you—except the bite. That was... that was necessary. But the rest—"

Then his eyes scanned down my body, not in a sleazy way, but as if he was trying to see through my clothes to check the rest of my skin.

"That's why you smell stressed," he murmured. "You're in pain?"

I rolled my shoulders and lifted my chin. "I'm fine."

"Jesse—"

"He wasn't gentle, Rake—"

He growled again, but I met his eyes and spat through my teeth. "—but it wasn't... he didn't *hit* me."

Even as I spoke the words, I hated myself a little bit. I knew what I'd think if a woman stood in front of me and said those words.

I understood the pity now shadowing his eyes. And I hated it.

And I recognized the words, because they're exactly what I would have said if our roles were reversed.

"He doesn't have to *hit* you for it to be wrong—"

"Rake, leave it alone."

"—even if he's King, that's doesn't mean he can use you as a vent for his anger."

"He didn't. We were both very tense. It was a difficult night."
Why was I protecting him?!

Rake opened his mouth and the expression that flashed on his face made it clear he had exactly the same thought. But then he hesitated. He looked back towards the cave into the tunnels and took a deep breath.

"There's a physician who can give you herbs to help with the pain," he said quietly. "And stuff they can add to your bath to aid healing."

"I said I'm fine—" The tears were threatening again and there was *no way* I was letting myself cry over this part. If I gave in to that they might never stop.

"Jesse," Rake said as I pushed past him towards the cave, stomping so he'd know not to mess with me.

"We need to get back, like you said," I muttered. "I need you to show me the way. I don't think I can find my room. I've had very little sleep. I'd like to rest."

He didn't deserve the clipped tones and frustration I was showing, but I didn't know how else to move away from this conversation. Because I didn't need him to lecture me on the wrongness of it all... but I was still dizzy about it. I needed to see Cazz. Needed to see how he took it when he saw what he'd done. That would tell me... I thought.

So I stalked back to the tunnels, Rake right on my heels.

I was sad that we barely spoke on the way to my rooms, sheepish because I knew I was the one causing the tension. But I couldn't talk about it. Not yet. Not until I knew...

Not until I'd seen Cazz.

47. Accountability

~ *CASIMIR* ~

I sat on the throne, fuming, as two of the ancient alphas from the regions beyond the city argued in front of me about a territorial dispute.

Both males were aggressive, bristling at each other, stifling growls, but unwilling to do more than bare teeth in front of me.

They were still fit though they were both old enough for their hair to be mostly gray.

Bringing the issue to me for judgment was better than tearing each other's packs apart. But today of all days? Neither had been in the Palace last night. They were clueless as to what had happened, though they'd heard that I'd claimed my mate. And they approved.

So generous of them...

"...Sire, the river is an appropriate border—it makes things very clear so no wolves can claim they were unaware—"

"And grows your reach without battle for it," Aleric, the second alpha snarled. "Sire, you must see that we cannot simply allow a wolf to *take* what he has not earned. In my day—"

"In your day I could take your throat for speaking out of turn," I muttered, letting my voice roll off into a growl.

Both males submitted, dropping their chins, and that pressure in my chest grew.

It was always satisfying to see the older wolves give over so easily.

I rubbed my face so they wouldn't see me smiling, but sighed because my head was too full, there were too many distractions for me to think this through quickly. And yet, what option did I have? I couldn't show any weakness. The sparks of last night's uprising were still fading. I couldn't let these two march the halls muttering in the packmind about an indecisive King.

I had learned early in my rule that simply staring at wolves was usually enough to keep them quiet when I needed to think. So I employed that strategy as I tried to breathe and get my head clear.

But then there was noise at the door, a disturbance. I sat up straighter, ears perked, until a moment later when the door swung wide enough to admit Rake who prowled across the checkered floor towards me. The heads of everyone in the audience turned to follow him.

I didn't miss the rise in the scents of the females as he stalked across the floor, his boots clipping on the tiles. It shouldn't have bothered me—having claimed my mate, the last of the hopes of the packs for attracting me had been buried. The females were on the lookout for their new gateway to power, and Rake was the perfect challenge.

He was celibate, so they didn't have to feel rejected if he said no. But he was also close to the crown and with the ear of the King if they did manage to leash him.

I tipped my head to my fist and watched my friend and Cleric storm towards me in a mood. It was an effort not to roll my eyes.

Rake was a good male, but he was often annoyingly *right*. As he obviously had been last night. And no doubt he'd come to remind me of that fact.

"Sire, I apologize for the interruption, but there is an urgent matter I must attend with you."

If I wasn't so distracted, so tired, I would have brushed him off and sent him to my rooms to wait for me. But this was a way to postpone making the judgment for these Alphas—and the others waiting their turns to hear from me. So I grabbed at it.

"Leave us," I said, low and hard, my voice echoing through the near silent room.

And they did. The audience. The petitioners. Even the guards. They knew when I took the room, I meant it.

Rake stood at the base of the stairs below the dais where I sat, impatiently watching them all file from the room. He waited until the door thunked closed, then turned on me with a snarl.

"Cazz, what the hell were you—"

I was pushing out of the throne, walking towards the door at the side of the chamber as I spoke, knowing he'd follow. "Shut your teeth, Rake. I heard you last night, and I concede that your advice was good. But we can't—"

"You *hurt* her," he snarled.

I froze midstep, then turned to face him, letting my scent carry the prickle of warning. We stared at each other for a moment, and I felt my power swell—then throb, because I couldn't unleash it on him.

I planted my feet, hands loose at my sides, but ready to defend if it was needed. "I don't know what you're—"

"I saw the marks, Cazz—not just the claiming scars. You *hurt* her. The Queen."

Fury roared through me and I descended on him. "You touched my Queen? You bared her skin—"

Rake didn't step back, but he kept his chin low. "I had to confirm the claiming. She tried to protect you—which is better than you deserve. But I saw it, Cazz. How many bruises? How many times did you touch her in anger?"

"It's none of your fucking business what happens between me and my mate—*especially* during the claiming. I know you haven't shared the experience, but trust me… it's *overwhelming.*"

Rake tensed at the barb about his celibacy, but he didn't bite. Instead he took the final inch of space between us and leaned in.

"You injured the Queen and left her—"

"Get your nose out of my fucking bedroom, Rake," I snarled, leaving him no room to question that I meant the words.

"You've invited me into your bedroom while you held a toy down, Cazz. Don't play modest now—"

Something in me snapped.

Finally giving in to the fury that had been bubbling in my chest since last night, I took him at the throat, shoving him backwards, marching him, snarling in his face, and through the link so there was no question he understood his position.

"They were not my mates, nor my Queen, *you self-righteous prick,*" I snarled.

48. Uncertain Days

~ *CASIMIR* ~

By the time I backed him into the wall, he had both hands up in surrender, but his eyes hadn't left mine, and he snarled through his teeth as well. I shoved him once, making his head clunk back against the cave wall.

His body tensed, but he didn't touch me, left both hands up at his shoulders. And never dropped his eyes.

It was a challenge—one another King probably would have taken as a threat.

"Submit," I growled, letting my teeth snap on the t.

"I haven't fought you, Cazz." His tone didn't soften, however. And he still didn't drop his eyes. "It's my job to challenge you. And to advise. It's what you instructed me to do. So here I am."

"Then give your challenge and your advice, and leave." I shoved him back against the wall again and he grunted, but he didn't fight.

His eyes flashed with righteous anger that pissed me off even more.

"You *never* touch her in anger again. Ever. You vowed you wouldn't be your father—told me to press you to recognize when you were showing colors of him. That's now, Cazz. This is the steep and slippery slope to becoming him."

I growled, but Rake didn't back down.

"And you can't just leave her in the dark. She's human. She doesn't understand. She's your mate—bonded and *claimed.* You two are tied together now. She needs your reassurance. She'll feed your power, but only if she's not afraid of you. Go to her. Soothe her. Connect. Reassure her. The packs know her now, show her to them. Give her a purpose. Don't hide her away and treat her like a child. She isn't one."

"Oh, I'm *well* aware of that," I hissed, smiling wickedly.

Rake grimaced.

But now it was my turn. "I know precisely how grown up she is—and after her little show last night, so does the whole fucking pack. Including you," I seethed. I leaned into his face, pressing him, urging him to break. "Did you feel it, Rake? Feel her want? She was dreaming of me. Did you feel how she ached to have me inside her? Yearned for my touch?"

His eyes went flat. "I did. You're a blessed male. But even a King could break her. Maybe *especially* a King."

Ignoring the dig, I tipped my head and held his eyes. "Is it hard for you, the celibacy?" I asked him, taunting.

Rake just stared.

Irritated that he wouldn't bite, I huffed. "Come on, Rake. I knew you as an adolescent, you don't have to pretend."

"I pretend nothing."

"You weren't righteous then."

"I'm not righteous now."

That surprised me. "Then why the hell are you my Cleric?"

"I've tried to tell you countless times, Cazz. I don't follow God because I'm good. I follow him because I'm not. I need him. He makes me better."

I snorted. "Well, see, then you understand… that's why I *don't* follow him."

"Because you don't want to be better?"

I growled. "No, because I don't believe there's anything wrong with me to begin with."

Rake's brows rose as if he feigned surprise. "Seriously, Cazz?"

"Seriously."

My cleric shook his head. "And here I thought we'd gotten past the lies."

He finally broke the gaze then, and even though it was submission, a concession to my authority, it pissed me off, because he sounded… disappointed.

That shouldn't have touched me. Shouldn't have bugged me. But it did.

The moment he broke eye-contact, I released his throat and he turned, slipping away from me towards the door.

I stood there, feeling suddenly off balance, and uncertain why.

Just before he reached the door, he stopped and half-turned. He kept his eyes down, but his posture was... tense.

"If your mother saw what I saw today, Cazz..." he shook his head.

As that rage roared in my veins again, he just turned and walked out, slamming the door behind him.

Which was when I realized I wasn't going to call him back. And I hated myself for this new evidence of my cowardice.

"Bastard," I spat at the door, then turned on my heel and stormed out of the chamber by the side door.

Ghere was waiting outside, head down in his ledger, but he started speaking the moment I stepped through the door.

"Sire, there's been a disturbance with the humans—the Reapers were caught on a security camera and now their Police are asking questions."

"Have they found the caves?" I muttered, my mind only half on the question, the other half following Rake out of the other door and deeper into the Palace as I filed through the many and varied ways I could torture him until he shut the fuck up.

"No, of course not. We have guards in place. But word has come that it's raising alarms and our friends in their law enforcement are warning us that it's difficult to keep—"

"Unless they're actually smart enough to find us, ignore it. They'll get frustrated and leave it alone in a few weeks."

"Are you certain, Sire? The video is quite damning."

"I'm sure."

"Very good. I'll pass it along. Now, since the Queen has been claimed, we'll need to arrange the presentation ceremony, and we'll need to identify who should be positioned as her allies and—"

"Not today, Ghere."

My man hesitated, glancing at me, curious because I was usually quite a stickler for the old traditions. Or at least, to be seen to be fulfilling them.

"Um," he said, frowning at his ledger. "Do you mean you want to meet tomorrow, or—"

"I said, *not today,"* I growled. "Now, leave me. I must speak to my mate. I will tell you when she's ready to step into her role as Queen. Until then, reassure the packs that I am... educating her," I said with a sly smile.

Ghere smiled uncertainly. "Very good, Sire."

I didn't like the implication that he was just humoring me, so I growled. But to my relief, he gave his farewell and peeled off down an intersecting tunnel before I reached the Royal chambers.

Which meant I was able to stalk the rest of the way to her room without anyone hanging over my shoulder.

49. Agenda

~ *JESSE* ~

I don't know what I expected from Cazz when he next showed up, but it wasn't that he would storm into my room in a rage.

"What the fuck are you doing *baring* yourself to the fucking cleric!?"

He'd surprised me, throwing the door open and stalking in. I jumped and whirled, hand to my chest. It took a moment to realize there was no threat, he was just standing in front of me, snarling.

I took a deep breath. "It's great to see you too, Cazz."

He growled and pursed his lips, but he folded his arms and lifted his chin.

I swallowed hard. "Thank you. You don't need to *loom* to get me to answer a question, you know. We're mates. And claimed. Apparently that's... that's important," I said carefully, because that yawning chasm in my chest now inhabited every inch where he used to be. And I wasn't sure if he'd actually removed that bond, or was just so shut down that I couldn't feel it.

His eyes narrowed. "What happens between us is between us. Even I don't speak of it. Why would you share *any* of that with—"

"I didn't. Rake needed to see the claiming marks to enter them into the records. I tried not to show him the rest, but he caught a glimpse of the bruises."

"Bruises?" he snapped.

I nodded. My heart was beating far too fast. I knew if I didn't grip them into fists my hands would be shaking, too. But I wasn't going to cower in front of him. Or beg. Even though there was a part of me that desperately wanted to.

I hated that part. The piece of me that was missing somehow. The piece of my foundation that was suddenly gone. Like if I took the wrong step I'd just fall into nothing.

The abyss. That darkness I'd seen that consumed him. That wanted to consume me, too.

Dear God, I hoped not.

I swallowed again, relieved that he was close even if he was angry.

"Show me," he growled.

I blinked and had to file back through the conversation to remember what he was asking about. Oh… the bruises.

"Cazz," I murmured, suddenly feeling very vulnerable.

"I said, *show me,*" he snapped and stepped forward, reaching for my buttons. The instinct was to fight him, but as my hands reflexively came up to grab his wrists, I stopped myself.

No. *No.* He *had* left bruises on me. And scrapes. Nail marks that cut my skin. Let him see them. All of them. Because I had realized it wasn't just on my shoulder. There were fingerprint bruises on my hips, my thigh, and my side as well.

So as Cazz's eyes blazed and he stripped me naked with no ceremony, and no seduction, I let him.

And then, when I stood in front of him, bare as the day I was born, I lifted my arms to show him, turning my body so he could see all the ways he'd left his mark on me—so many that had nothing to do with claiming.

After tossing away my leather pants, his eyes went dark and he folded his arms again, scanning my body from top to toe. Then his eyes snapped to mine, a question in them, but also… heat.

I hated myself for the simmering that began low in my belly. For the way my breath sped up.

"You're a beautiful woman, Jesse. But *far too skinny.*"

"Said no one, ever—"

"Do not bait me!"

I snapped my mouth closed and folded my arms too—not missing the fact that his eyes dropped to my breasts when my arms pushed them higher. He yanked his gaze back up to my face a second later.

Then he turned on his heel and began to pace, his eyes nowhere near my body. He prowled the room like he was readying to pounce on something, clawing a hand through his hair, muttering to himself too quietly for me to make out what he said.

I was still shaky and uncertain, so I just stood there, waiting, but hating myself for it.

"I... apologize for the bruises," he muttered finally, his eyes cutting to me to make sure I'd heard him, then away again. "It will not happen again."

"Okay."

"The claiming... my instincts because the males were fighting for you... it was a more powerful battle than I had prepared for."

"I believe you."

He paced back and forth a couple more times, then turned to me, rolling his shoulders like he had to brace for it before he held my gaze again.

"The claiming should improve our chances of pregnancy. Please eat more. Please sleep as much as you can. Rest. Do things you enjoy so that your body is less stressed. If there is anything you need to feel happier or more content, simply ask for it."

I gaped at him.

"What?" he asked, irritated.

I wasn't sure whether to laugh or cry over the fact that he wasn't going to make this easy for me.

"I have questions."

"Rake can help. Or Ghere. There are servants—"

"No, Cazz. I have questions *for you.*"

His jaw went tight. Then he sighed and opened an arm towards the bed. "Sit down and ask, then," he said through his teeth.

A small piece of me was thrilled that he was going to stay long enough to talk. But most of me was just sad. Something had happened last night. Something that drew us closer together. But he was acting more like a stranger today than he had since I'd met him.

Not knowing what else to do, I walked to the edge of the bed and sat down, staring at him.

"Ask," he said brusquely.

I sighed. "Cazz... last night... the claiming—"

"It is unimportant—"

I scoffed. "No, it's not. I may not understand everything that was happening, but I can feel it—can't you feel it?"

"Of course I can," he snapped.

"Why are you angry at me?" I broke out. "I was just following *your* orders!"

His eyes widened and he stormed over to stand over me, lowering his voice to a menacing hiss.

50. Claim This

~ JESSE ~

"You cornered me. You forced my hand. We would not be here today, except for you and your... agenda," he snarled.

"Agenda? Cazz, I didn't even know what the claiming *was!*"

"So you say..."

"Seriously? That's what you're telling yourself? That I've got some kind of master plan?"

"There are *countless* females who would give their lives to be claimed by me," he snarled.

"Good for you."

"I'm not going to indulge you if you're just going to be sarcastic."

"Indulge? Cazz, you haven't *indulged* me for a second since we met."

His jaw flexed. "I made no claims on you, I made no promises beyond our agreement. Yet you weep your way through the Palace this morning, crying on the shoulder of my cleric and revealing intimate details—"

"Your cleric is the only person who gave enough of a shit to come for me because he was worried—which is more than you did!"

"I sent you clothing and food, which is exactly what you needed!"

"Are you fucking kidding me?" I gasped, pushing to my feet. Because he was leaning over me, that put us nose to nose. "You think I need clothes and *breakfast?* After that... that... whatever it was last night, you think *that's* what I was aching for this morning?"

"What else could you need—you've just been positioned highest in the hierarchy below me!"

"I need *you*, Cazz! I need to understand! I need to feel like I haven't just lost everything that's important to me—like I can trust you not to become an abuser!"

"Abuser?! I fucked you silly and that makes me an abuser?"

"No, Cazz—you hurt me, then ignored me, *that* makes you an abuser!"

He growled and leaned in closer. I planted a hand in the center of his broad chest intending to shove him back a step because I was having trouble breathing. But the moment I touched him, something electric and powerful jolted through me, throwing my head back and fusing my hand to his sternum. I heard my name on a gasp, then the room around us disappeared.

I stood in that dark, dark tunnel again. Air whistled in the distance, a breeze fluttered in my hair. Confused and afraid, I turned around, then around again, but I couldn't see a thing. It was pitch black, cold, and damp. Fear trilled through me.

"Cazz... Cazz, what happened?!"

"I'm here."

Large, warm hands reached for me, and the moment he touched me, light flared, so bright and intense that I squinted and raised a hand to shield my eyes against it. The wind I'd heard rushed over us and chilled my skin.

"Cazz—"

"I'm here, Jesse. I'm here."

And he was, standing in front of me, pulling me into his chest, turning us so his body shielded me from the chill wind.

"I'm here, Jesse. I'll always be here. Please... don't leave."

Tears choked me as he tipped my chin up, forcing me to meet his eyes. And when our gazes met, that jolt happened again—flames roaring through my veins and igniting my entire body.

I lifted my hand, reached for his face, intending to pull him in, but the moment my hand left his chest the vision disappeared and I was left blinking in my dim room, standing between Cazz's feet, my wrist gripped in his hand like he shackled me.

But he was staring... his eyes searching mine, an expression on his handsome face that I didn't recognize.

"Cazz...?"

His brows knit together over his nose. His eyes went sad, then desperate. He opened his mouth and I thought he was going to say something—but instead, he groaned and descended on me.

And when our lips met, my body rose to find him.

He clawed both hands along my scalp, his palms bracketing my face, his fingers twisting into my hair and holding me there as he devoured my mouth.

The intensity of that kiss, the desperate groan that vibrated in his chest, tore me up. I threw my arms around his neck and pulled him in, gasping his name, shaking with the sudden jolt of need that rocked through me.

Tongue delving and teasing mine, he leaned down, his hands dragging down my back, then cupping my ass and pulling me against him. I gasped as I felt him, hard and insistent, then reached for his belt-buckle with shaking hands.

A small voice in the back of my head insisted that I needed to be careful, that he wasn't to be trusted. But the much larger part of me—body and soul—*ached* to be close to him. To have all of him.

He nudged me back the single step to the bed, following me when the backs of my calves hit it and I started to sit down, giving me no space, crawling up onto the bed, pulling me with him, groaning my name.

He dove for my neck, nuzzling and sucking. I arched against him—

The creak of the door was a startling jerk back to reality.

I gasped, ducking my head against his shoulder and flinching because I was about to be seen naked.

But Cazz threw himself over me, curling me into him, snarling over his shoulder in a guttural roar, *"GET OUT!"*

Whoever it was yelped and the door slammed home again.

Cazz had gone still, his head still turned over his shoulder, glowering at that door. We were both panting.

Then I realized he was shaking.

Letting my head fall back against the bed, I cupped his face in my hands and made him turn to look at me—gasping again when his eyes were...

His eyes were the blue, arctic eyes of a wolf.

"Cazz?" I whispered, beginning to tremble even harder.

He blinked, but nothing changed.

"Cazz, come back."

He blinked again, and then it was *his* eyes locked on mine. Neither of us moved for a moment, then I stroked his cheeks with my thumbs, my eyes blurring with tears, because he was open to me again. I could *feel* him. Feel what he was feeling—protection, anger, confusion, fear...

It was all there and tangled together, and Rake's words came back to me.

...he couldn't make that declaration for you without giving up a piece of himself. And now he's searching for it. He wants it back. It makes him feel vulnerable. And that's not a feeling he's accustomed to...

"Cazz," I breathed, blinking back the hopeful tears. "You're safe with me."

A shudder rocked through him, then he dove for my mouth.

Soundtrack for the next chapter is
Suffocate by Nathan Wagner

51. Don't Take My Soul

~ CASIMIR ~

"Cazz... you're safe with me."

A ball of *feeling* detonated in my gut, an eruption of need and heat that roared through me in a flood, coursing through my veins until my entire body trembled. And as that flash-flood reached my extremities, as the first surge of tide eased and the waters settled, the fading of power revealed something fragile in its wake.

A string, a thread tying me to her. So tenuous, so delicate. It glowed and sizzled, turning water to steam. And yet, one wrong move and it would snap.

But it pulled me in, twisted me up in her, tied me to her... undeniable.

When I took her mouth it was so electric, I twitched, gasping. My body quaked, unable to contain the rush.

"God, *Jesse.*"

She felt it too—that was the thing about that little thread. It was delicate, but it conducted—taking the explosion in me and feeding it to her, coursing in her veins, crackling where I touched, then rushing back to me expanded with her need to tumble me, head over heels until I could barely breathe.

Her hands started on my head, then she cupped my face, then I took her mouth.

I felt the moment she surrendered, the relief in her, the joy, the need. I almost gave in then, almost yielded—the craving for her was so strong my body fought to give and for a moment my grip slipped on my soul.

But in the split second when I might have retracted my soul's claws and fangs and released my hold, let myself be carried away in the flood of *her,* a single shriek of fear clanged through me.

Like a wolf scrabbling, hind legs hanging off the edge of a cliff, I dug in—clawing, growling, scraping, *fighting.*

As Jesse's head tipped back on the bed, jaw slack and breath tearing the quiet of the room, I fought—for control, for authority, for safety.

And my mind scrambled for the middle ground, because there was no denying that I needed her. Wanted her. Would *devour* her, swallow her, keep her within me if I could.

But the very thing that gave me strength was under threat—and she was the blade that would cut my vein. I couldn't let her. Couldn't let myself be weakened—worse, be leashed.

And so I gained clarity. And so I fought.

As Jesse reached for me, her fingers clawing into my back, I ground against her until she gasped, then pulled her hands down, clamping both her wrists in one hand and pinning them over her head on the bed so she was arched under me, ribs and breasts high, fingers curled and twitching, but useless to her.

Filling my free palm with her breast, pressing it up and high, I leaned down to take it in my mouth and she tensed, bowing under me, her breath coming in short pants as I sucked and nipped.

"Cazz... Cazz, let me touch you. I want to—*Oh!"*

I entered her in a single thrust of blinding pleasure, then drew out slowly and completely, dragging a low groan from her as I returned my attention to her breast, this time with my teeth.

My lungs heaved and I was already sweating, but I blinked away the fog of intoxication she'd forced on me and found myself again, turning my focus. There was a way to have her, to keep her, to addict her, without letting her collar me.

I could do it. I was certain.

She was inexperienced. She loved. She opened herself—fool that she was. Even if I couldn't use my power against her, I could compel her with need. She would fall to it...

So as I shook and shuddered and teased her, I wrestled first for my own control, then for hers.

"Cazz... Cazz, please—" she gasped.

I growled and closed my teeth on her nipple, just sharp enough to make her suck in and her body twitch. Then, when she was slick and whimpering, I pushed up on my knees to give myself better leverage to tease her properly.

With her hands clamped over her head, raising myself over her gave her more room to struggle, but also allowed me to drink my fill of the sight of her.

For a moment I did just that. Pinning her hip to the bed, I rubbed myself where she wanted me, *hard*, until she twitched and gasped, riding the line between pleasure and pain.

And as her tension increased, as she sought me and fought me in the same moment, as her body trembled and twitched, just when she might give up and begin fighting in earnest, I would enter again, thrust into her hard, groaning when she called my name and her entire body washed in goosebumps.

Then I teased her again, salivating at the sight of her writhing under me, small cries breaking in her throat. Her knees shook, her heels sliding as she looked for purchase to press back to meet me. But I gave her no chance. And she was weak, so weak, compared to me.

Utterly in my control

Enthralled with it. With *me.*

I gave a breathless chuckle when I pulled out of her to tease her swollen flesh once more and her eyes flew open and she tried to raise her head, fighting the binding I had, keeping her arms extended over her head and pinned to the bed.

"Cazz... *please!*" she gave a guttural groan, trembling and quivering, drumming her heels for a moment.

Locking eyes with her, I dropped my chin and smiled. "Please... what?"

"Please... please... do it."

"Do what, Jesse? *Be specific.*"

Color flooded her cheeks, but she didn't drop her gaze. She gritted her teeth and rolled her hips. "I want you inside me," she gasped.

I couldn't stop the smile. "So *demanding.*"

"Please... *Please!*"

Then I leaned into her ear, licking the shell of it, before growling, "Patience, Kitten. The King wants to play."

It was very gratifying when she bit her lip.

When I pulled back, her eyes widened as I reached between us to position myself, found her core and pressed into her. Her mouth dropped open and her eyes sparked, but I only gave her a slow inch, before I eased back out.

"Cazz!"

Without increasing my pace, or how much I gave her, I licked my thumb then found her with my hand, sliding the pad from where

I teased her flesh, up, up, up to that precious nub already slick and swollen. Then I lifted my thumb and returned to where we joined— barely—and repeated the process.

Jesse was twitching, her hips bucking, her legs peppered with goosebumps. She bent up her knees to open them wider as she thrust towards me, forcing me a little deeper than I had planned. I growled and shifted my hips, warning her with my eyes. But she wasn't even seeing me anymore. As I eased in and out of her, letting her feel me within and without, and slid my thumb up and down, her breath huffed in short, sharp pants as I found the rhythm— entering her so slightly, then, as I dragged back out, pressing up to her clitoris until her breath caught and held.

First one pleasure, then the other, without rest.

Jesse was left strangled and sucking at the air in gasps.

Soundtrack for the next chapter is
"Dirtier Thoughts" by Nation Haven.

52. Torture Me

~ *CASIMIR* ~

The sheer joy of watching her slowly fall apart was a drug. The control it took not to plunge all the way into her, to roar my own need and pump into her, was stunning. And addictive.

But she was clenching, sweating, whimpering, getting so close to climax. She was gasping for it, her eyes hooded, pupils dilated, but locked on me.

She couldn't get her tongue around words anymore, only guttural cries and calls. And that was how I wanted her, I realized: Surrendered, begging, wordless, and waiting... on me.

My chest heaved with my own panting. She was, without doubt, the hottest thing I'd ever seen. But I was back in control, thrilled and turned on, and ready to break her in half when it was my turn, but first...

First she had to come—whether she wanted to or not.

Well, fuck. Who was I kidding?

Of course she *wanted* to.

So, I would dance that line until she *had* to... or she might die.

*****

~ *JESSE* ~

Torture. Cazz was torturing me.

When he'd first kissed me, everything in me swelled. He groaned like he was giving in, desperate for me—and kissed me that way too. But as we tightened, clinging to each other, I could feel him fighting. Through the bond, and in the steel of his muscles, I could feel him struggling, feel the battle.

I grabbed for him, murmuring his name, because I was afraid he'd push himself off me and run. And I needed him. I *needed* him.

But he never left me, only rasped and growled and fought within himself.

When he took my hands and clamped them in one of his, forcing them over my head and holding them there, I thought he was going to leave me. I rocked my hips and tried to hook my heels behind his thighs so he couldn't move.

But I should have known.

He wasn't leaving. That's when he started torturing me.

Now, I didn't know how long he'd been teasing me, couldn't grasp time anymore. Could barely think. My body thrummed and hummed and shook—little explosions of pleasure where he entered me, easing slowly in and out, but never fully taking me. And then he added his touch and I lost control of my limbs.

And the longer he played my body like a musical instrument, the more he smiled and rasped my name, the more he teased me, the more I needed him. Desperately. Frantically. Illogically.

He had me begging—gladly. But it was so much more than just the desire for physical pleasure. Did he know that? Was he aware? I wasn't just surrendering my body to him, I had lost control of my heart.

And the longer he made me want, the less I cared about anything that wasn't him—his body against mine, his breath in my ear, his *presence.*

I flung my heart at him, begging him to take it. To take me.

Nothing else mattered.

Nothing.

It should have been frightening. He held me so tightly he might as well have bound me. I couldn't move beyond the twitching, spluttering shiver of need. He filled me with sparkling, driving pleasure and I swallowed it and wanted more.

I should have been embarrassed—I couldn't even say his name anymore. The world had disappeared. We might be watched and I wouldn't even know. I could see nothing but him. Hear nothing, feel nothing, but *him.*

And then he reared over me, smiling, and it was devastating.

Something deep inside me broke—the last of my will. The last of my *self.*

Then everything happened at once.

He entered me—still slowly, still barely an inch. Then he stroked me, pulling his thumb up the seam of me, hitting the center of my pleasure at the exact moment that my body shuddered and reached for that glittering wave of promise.

My back arched and I screamed as my body detonated.

"Caaaaazzzz!"

With a roar of satisfaction, my mate finally released my hands to grasp both my hips, pulling my ass up onto his thighs as he plunged into me to the hilt, and the first pulse of my orgasm was swiftly followed by a second wave of nearly equal pleasure.

I wasn't breathing, couldn't move. I'd thrown my hands down to find him, to anchor myself, as he plowed into me, pulling me against him, grunting and hissing through his teeth.

I gripped his forearms, my nails clawing for purchase, pleading with him not to stop as he pounded every ounce of pleasure from my body. And then, just as my pleasure broke and I sucked in a rasping breath, he bellowed his own climax and pulled me onto him again with such force I felt my body vibrate.

For seconds we hung there, vibrating with pleasure and need, with the shock of climax.

Then he collapsed over me like he'd been shot, covering me, panting in my ear, his weight pressing me into the bed until I struggled to inhale properly.

I loved it.

My entire body trembled. Sweat coated me in a sheen. Then he sighed, our cheeks brushed and his hair dragged on my skin.

I lifted trembling hands to his back and at first, just held him there.

The waves of pleasure had left me tingling and shaky. But as reality returned the overwhelming feeling was *relief.* He was here. He was close. He had me…

His weight was a soothing pressure, a tangible measure that he hadn't left me. And the clenching ripples of pleasure still zapping through me were evidence that he hadn't shut me out.

Tentatively, I let my hand stroke, fingertips playing up and down that dip at his spine, enjoying the sensation of holding him, because he'd kept me from him that whole time.

I kept swallowing, trying to wet my throat so I could speak, but I was still panting, so it took a minute or more before I could manage it.

"Cazz… that was…"

He tensed and a jolt of adrenaline shot through me. But when he pushed up on his elbows it was to pull my hands from his back and slid his grip back up to my wrists, pinning both hands down on either side of my shoulders. Only then did he look down at me, his eyes searching mine, that saucy smile curling the corners of his gorgeous lips.

"Any time, Jess. Any time, any day. I live to serve. But next time I'll bring my ropes. I think I like you bound." The wicked grin he gave me made me huff a nervous laugh, but the trickle of unease didn't leave.

In an effort to reassure myself that he was with me, I pulled my hands out of his grip and reached up to push his hair back from his face—it was sticking to the sweat on his face. But he just turned his head to kiss my palm, then pushed up and away. His eyes dropped to my body and he dragged his palm down from my arm to my breast, then my side, kissing my stomach once, and muttering, "Eat more," before pulling out of me and leaving me there, empty, as he padded over to the bathing room without another word.

My breath got a little faster again, a sinking fear in my chest as I sat up and watched him disappear into the little room, closing the door without looking back.

I frowned, but there was little pulse in the bond and I put a hand to my chest, reaching for him there.

But it was as if his soul reflected his body.

A small smile, a fleeting look, then he disappeared behind that wall again and everything went dark.

53. How I Learned to Hate Myself

~ *JESSE* ~

The couple weeks after the claiming were some of the most confusing and unsteady of my life.

In the days immediately following that harrowing night, I was dragged to several meetings in which my duties as Queen and the ways I would need to be trained were discussed.

Time and again, with different audiences each time, my education, intelligence, and physical strength—or lack thereof—were discussed in perfunctory tones and analyzed with a ruthless eye. Cazz would list my deficiencies in a way that, had they been spoken with any tone at all, would have felt like he had nothing but contempt for me. Yet, he seemed… unconcerned. Listing off my failings like they were merely points on a board to be identified and then crossed off.

To hear him speak about it, these were simply the challenges of mating a human—I would be educated. I would be trained. And my physical weakness would be protected for me.

He didn't curl up his lip in a sneer when he mentioned the fact that I hadn't gone to college, only asked me if I had pursued further education, which subjects would have held my attention.

"Um… probably psychology. Or sociology. Something about… human nature," I said honestly.

That raised a few eyebrows in the room, but sparked a lengthy conversation about the need for me to study and understand pack hierarchy—and learn the tools of royal power.

Cazz agreed with that statement, ordered that at tutor be identified for me in the coming weeks, and we moved on.

When others were around in these servant roles, he looked at me like I was a specimen under a microscope. And yet, if the Alphas were present, or it was just us, he'd devour me with his eyes. He spoke to others about me, in my presence, as if we were intimate. Yet he would ignore me when asking for ideas about the best way to train me, and only check in with his servants.

Sometimes I felt like a prized pig. Other times, a child.

Rarely did I feel like a woman of power. Or even his friend. Though he did wink at me once when he told one of the female servants not to anger me. That my tongue was sharper than his fangs.

He sounded like it was a compliment.

During those times, with servants around, or sometimes the Alphas, Cazz was always protective, keeping me close to his side and putting himself between me and any males who were in attendance. And even though he had the bond mostly closed to me, there were glimpses of feeling, surges of protective concern, or downright possessive aggression in the case of one Alpha who got sly when he mentioned the Queen visiting the Den again soon.

But then the meeting would be done. Cazz would hand me off to someone—usually Rake, or Ghere—and turn away to other duties without so much as a backward glance.

We would spend hours, sometimes most of the day, apart. He would not check in with me or speak to me at all. I would be convinced that he couldn't have cared less about me.

Yet, multiple times per day I would be visited by servants with bundles of hot bread or cakes, rich sweets, fatty meats, and offers to bring anything that I wanted.

I made the mistake of mentioning my love for fried chicken to Ghere during what I thought was a casual conversation as we waited outside Cazz's audience chamber for when he would be ready for us. And for the next three days, I was fed fried chicken two out of three meals until I protested and begged for variety. Then I wasn't served the same meal twice in a month.

Most days I would eat dinner alone in my room, wait up late until I had given up on seeing Cazz and dress for bed, falling asleep fighting tears—then wake to the touch of his hand, to the scruff of his five o'clock shadow on my cheek, and the ecstasy of his touch.

Afterwards, I'd fall asleep again, relieved, and clinging. And yet when I woke the next morning, he was always gone. No matter how early I jolted awake.

Hours bled into days. Days bled into one week, then two, and still it was the same every day: A different routine every day of meetings or gatherings, but a very predictable pattern in attention from Cazz.

He wanted to fuck me.

He didn't want anyone else to touch me.

But beyond that, he couldn't care less—except that I ate and slept as much as possible. He seemed obsessed with fattening me up, and making sure I rested... except when he arrived in my bedchamber.

Three weeks after the claiming was the first time he broke the pattern and showed up in my rooms soon after dinner while it was still early enough for me to be dressed and awake.

It was such a shock, at first I just stared at him as he dismissed the servants and cleared the room.

When the door closed behind the last of them I was still sitting in my chair with my book in my lap, stomach tingling, waiting to see what he wanted. Unwilling to admit to myself what I hoped.

He turned from the door and his eyes went straight to mine. He grunted, then prowled across the room scanning me from head to toe.

"Hello?" I said as he came to stand in front of me, his muscular legs painted in perfectly fitting leather pants that emphasized the thickness of his thighs and trim of his waist. He was in shirtsleeves—a thick, loose, almost-black shirt with eyelets and laces down the front that he'd tugged open at his throat, revealing his collarbones and the wedge of firm flesh between his pecs.

"Good evening, Jesse," he said in a low purr that made the tingling in my stomach ratchet up.

"What's going on, Cazz?"

"Stand up, please."

"I—"

"I said... *Stand. Up.*"

54. The Indifferent Bastard

~ JESSE ~

I tipped my head, considering telling him to go fuck himself since I hadn't seen him all day. But in the end I was curious about why he was here. And if he was asking me to get up, maybe we were going to go do something?

So, hating myself a little bit for not challenging him, I stood up and put my book down on the table next to my chair, then turned to face him with my arms folded.

"Now what?"

His lips curled up on one side like I had pleased him. "Now take off your clothes, please."

My breath got faster. I tried to keep my face firm and unaffected, but by this time, the bastard knew that all he had to do was stare at me with those ice-cold eyes and I was already shivering. So, knowing that he could hear me, I muttered to myself about what a pain it was to submit to a narcissist as I started taking off my clothes.

I considered turning it into a tease, but I'd never stripped for a man before. And knowing me I'd end up tripping over my skirts and falling at his feet, or something else *really* embarrassing.

So I sat my ass back down on the chair and untied my boots, then took my clothes off like I was about to change.

When I was naked—and surprised by how little it bothered me to stand in front of him like that—I planted my hands on my hips and gave him a pointed look, hoping that since he had the bond shut down, he wouldn't notice the way my fingers trembled.

Cazz folded his arms then, but he looked like he was stifling a smile.

"Turn around," he said quietly.

I gave him a flat look, but then did as he asked, turning my back, looking at him over my shoulder and catching his eyes—surprised to see a flare of desire there as he scanned my body, but it quickly disappeared into dark disapproval.

"You haven't gained enough weight," he growled as I turned to face him again.

I shrugged. "I've been eating everything you've sent. I'm sure it'll happen."

"Have you been exercising a great deal? Are the servings too small?"

"No, and definitely not. I can't even finish them half the time."

"Finish them," he growled, then took my elbow and turned me around so he was scanning my back again. "Your bruises have faded, too. Good. Does anything still hurt?"

That was a tender subject I preferred not to think about. "No. I'm fine," I said flatly.

"Good. Then things should be progressing. We just need to give your body more resources," he said, his tone dismissive and unconcerned, like I was a cow he was preparing for slaughter.

Pulling my elbow from his grip, I turned back to face him, glaring. "Can I get dressed now?"

"Of course. Although it's getting late. You might want to put on your nightgown."

Then he let his eyes come up to meet mine and the flare of heat was there.

I did my best to keep my face blank, but my stomach panged and I wanted to curse because I *knew* he could smell it. That was one *really* uncomfortable fact I had learned by being around the wolves: It turned out, while they were very attentive to posture and expression and tone, just like humans. They relied more heavily on their sense of smell to identify emotion and mental state.

I didn't matter how I glared at him, or how defensive my posture was, or how angry my eyes looked. When he smelled whatever my body did that made that pang rush from behind my navel to between my thighs, he *knew*. And the smug bastard grinned every time.

Like he was right now.

He stepped forward, putting his hands to my hips and leaning down to nuzzle under my ear. "Is my Queen a little… frustrated?" he murmured before nipping at my earlobe.

That always made me flinch in the ticklish lovely way. I swatted at his chest and pinched my shoulder up to my ear to push him away, but the pang in my stomach was a simmer now and he could probably smell that too, dammit.

He chuckled, still holding my hips and keeping his rough jaw pressed against my neck. But then he went very still.

He pressed his nose against my neck and inhaled deeply, then straightened to stare down at me, his brows pinched hard over his nose.

"How many days has it been since you last started bleeding?" he asked gruffly.

I blinked, startled by the question—then nervous, because I hadn't been paying attention.

"I don't know... four weeks? Five?"

He grabbed a fistful of my hair and leaned down again, burying his nose in the strands and inhaling again.

Then he muttered a curse and dropped it like I had offended him.

"Cazz, what—"

"You're about to start bleeding again. Definitely not pregnant," he muttered. Then he stepped back from me, his eyes hooded and no longer focused on me. "I'll leave you for a few days."

The slice of rejection hurt and inwardly I flinched. "You don't have to—"'

"Yes, I do. You need rest. And besides, you'll be sore. Don't worry, I'll send the healer. She has herbs to make it easier."

"Cazz—" but he'd already turned on his heel and was stalking for the door, every inch of his tall frame tense, his steps jagged.

Then he just... left. I stared at the door for a long moment, somehow still believing he was going to come back and tell me it was all a joke. And he hadn't left me standing here naked and spluttering.

But he didn't come back. And it occurred to me that he'd said he would send the healer, which probably meant *right now,* because that's what he was like.

So, dashing away tears that frustrated me because they came far too easily these days, I hurried back to the closet to find a long nightgown.

And my sanity.

55. Come Together

~ JESSE ~

No matter how I tried, I couldn't figure out where I stood with Cazz.

I had grown up on alert. I knew a man's anger, and a man's control. I understood intimidation and manipulation. But this wild swinging between sweet thoughtfulness, undeniable passion, and intense indifference... It had my head spinning. And my heart aching. Every day I rode a roller coaster of signals that had me convinced he was in love with me one minute, and loathed me the next. And no way to tell which was right.

Because they couldn't both be true.

Could they?

The final blow came the next morning when I realized Cazz had been right and my cycle had started.

I definitely wasn't pregnant. And even though that was something of a relief, it was also a blow. Because if I *had* been, then at least maybe he would have just left me and my shredded, baffled heart alone. And we could have got on with the healing. But instead... instead I had to wait and see what was going to happen tomorrow. And the next day. And every day for the next month.

And maybe the months beyond as well.

I wished my heart didn't lift at that thought, peppered with nerves and hope.

And I wished I didn't cling to that.

Hope was a very, very dangerous thing when it came to the Wolf King. Even I could see that.

*****

Almost a week after that night he had come to my room, I lost patience in waiting for him to come back. I wasn't bleeding anymore, and I had dreamed about him the night before. I'd barely spoken to him in the days between—only seeing him when I ventured out looking and manipulated events so we would run into each other. Or I'd find a reason to have to ask for his help.

He hadn't visited my bed once. Hadn't even asked me any veiled questions about it.

That morning when I woke up, I was done waiting. I swore that if he didn't come to find me before lunch, that I was going to find him.

The morning dragged so badly, that in the end I gave up.

I was Queen, wasn't I? He always said that the servants were at my beck and call. And that if I needed anything, I only needed to tell him and he would provide it.

Well, great.

I needed my mate. I needed my husband. And I needed something to tell me that all was not lost between us.

So I took the time to wash and dry my hair. I put on my normal leather pants, but chose a flowing, feminine blouse with a low-cut V-neck. And then I went looking for him.

It didn't take long to find him since he was in the smaller cavern he called an office. The door into it was off the same hallway as his bedroom, though it was a very grand looking set of double doors, with a couple stairs up to them, and those steel strips holding them together.

When I had poked my head into his room and determined that he wasn't there, then I reached those doors next and leaned in to the crack between to listen.

Sure enough, I could hear male voices. The doors were thick, so I couldn't make out the words. But that was a good sign. Either Cazz was in there, or Ghere was—either way, I was going to find him.

So I took a deep breath, grabbed the ring on the door that was used to open it, and heaved—because these solid wood doors were *heavy*.

I had barely opened it enough to step through when all voices inside stopped and three sets of eyes turned to look at me.

Ghere, who stood to the left and looked curious. Rake, who sat in a chair on this side of Cazz's massive, carved desk, and whose gaze was worried. And in the center, seated at that monument of a piece of furniture, was Cazz, glowering at me with disapproval.

Had I seen his face before I stepped inside, I would have turned on my heel and left again—clearly I was interrupting something. But the others had seen me now. Ghere rushed forward, bowing and greeting me.

Rake had gotten to his feet.

Only Cazz remained in his seat, his eyes dark.

"Good morning, Highness!" Ghere said breathlessly, rushing forward to take my hand and draw me deeper into the chamber. "Is everything alright? Are you well? Do you need assistance?"

"I... yes, I am. Very well," I said pointedly, with a glance at Cazz to make sure he knew what I meant. "I have just been a little bored the last few days. I wondered if there was maybe something I could help *you* with, Cazz?"

It hadn't been what I intended to say. But he looked so irritated that I was there, I was suddenly unwilling to make any demands on him—and hating myself for how nervous I felt just because his jaw was tight.

"Thank you for checking, Jesse. But no, there's nothing. If you need some help, or would like some ideas on ways you could get involved in helping others in the pack, I'm sure Ghere could point you to some of the servants who could—"

"No, no. I just... I wanted to be near... My King," I said lamely.

Ghere fluttered and smiled kindly and ushered me forward to stand next to Cazz's chair where he apparently thought was the best place for the Queen to be, while Rake stared at me miserably.

Cazz didn't even turn his head. He glared at the papers in front of him, flipping a pen back and forth impatiently in his fingers while Ghere fluffed, then as soon as the man stepped away from me, continued what he'd been saying before I interrupted.

At least, I guessed that's what it was.

For the next few minutes I just stood there, feeling like a fool while he asked questions of Ghere—who was forever referring to a stack of papers he had clipped to a board—and asked Rake to give his input on what he believed would be best for the people, before issuing instructions that Ghere diligently noted on those papers, then flipped to the next one.

I wondered if he had forgotten I was there—and I felt so stupid for coming, and for not making an excuse to leave *immediately* when it was obvious Cazz didn't want me there, that I just got more and more tense, until I was on the verge of tears.

"... can't afford to let the Alphas stew in their own juices. It will only get worse," Cazz muttered, scratching a few words on a piece of paper like he was slicing it with a knife. "Rake, I think it's time for a round-table. The question is, do we bring in the outliers so everyone gets the same input. Or just inform those who aren't involved? I don't want to create more drama by dragging them all here, but there's no denying that having them in front of me means we'll have no chance of—*Jesse, perhaps you could use some fresh air?*" he snarled, turning on me suddenly.

56. No Prey

~ *JESSE* ~

I jerked back from where I had just softly placed my hand on his shoulder, feeling for him because it was clear that he was stressed about whatever this issue was with the Alphas and packs. But he acted as if I'd poked him with a needle.

"Sorry, I just—"

"Rake, would you mind? I think the Queen needs her freedom this morning."

Rake pushed to his feet immediately, nodding, not meeting my eyes.

I took a step back from Rake, saturated in embarrassment. He was asking Rake to *walk* me like I was a pesky pet?

"I'm... I'm sorry," I breathed, swallowing back the pinch of tears. "I didn't mean to interrupt."

"It's fine. Next time send a servant. I'll let them know if it's useful to have you near," he muttered, scratching on that paper again.

Poor Ghere was staring at his board of papers like he'd be struck by lightning if he so much as twitched an eyebrow.

Rake politely hurried around the desk and took my sleeve, tugging me towards the door.

Confused and hurt and embarrassed, and angry that I was embarrassed, I took one final look over my shoulder as we crossed the room, only to find Cazz still buried in his papers and not even looking up to see if I had left.

Rake tugged me out the door, and I almost sat down on the step in the hallway and cried.

But then I took a hold of myself.

And as I shook off the drenching humiliation, I discovered I was *furious*.

"That fucking, arrogant prick," I breathed, then looked up at Rake whose brows were pinched together in concern.

"He's just busy and stressed, Jesse—"

"No, Rake. He's not. He's the fucking King. And if he wanted to be near me, or have me around, or use my help or… or *anything,* he'd do it. Instead he's treating me like an obnoxious child!"

Rake sighed and looked miserable. "I'm sorry. There's just—"

"Don't apologize for him! Don't pretend that he wants you to—he's already forgotten I was even there. He's *relieved* that I'm gone!"

"No, Jesse, I'm sure—"

"Oh, shut it, Rake. I'm emotional, not stupid," I snarled, then started stomping down the hall, back toward my rooms.

Rake kept pace with me, but didn't say anything until we reached an intersection of hallways. I was about to turn left, back towards my rooms, but he caught my elbow, and when I looked up at him, he gave me an apologetic look and shrugged.

"He said you need some fresh air, and we haven't done that for a few days. It might help? And then I can tell him that I did as he asked, and…" he looked over his shoulder and in both directions in the hall. "It might be easier to talk?"

I almost yanked my arm out of his grip and told him to go fuck himself, but the truth was… if I went back to my rooms, I was just going to sit there, bored and alone. I was probably going to cry. And even if Cazz *did* come see me later, I'd be a mess.

Maybe he was right? Maybe I did need some fresh air and light. It certainly couldn't hurt.

"Well, hoo-fucking-ray," I muttered and turned, pulling my arm from Rake's grip and stomping down the first tunnel that would lead us up and out of the underground Palace. "Sure thing, Rake. Let's get out of this hellhole and go smell the flowers."

Rake sighed, but followed me as I stormed through the Palace. It took several minutes to get to the surface, and by the end, I had walked so fast, without slowing, that I was panting.

And it did feel good to smell the fresh air moving against my cheeks as we approached the entrance. And it did lift my heart a bit to step into the half-sun of a patchy-cloud day.

But it also stopped me in my tracks when I reached the edge of the dirt outside and my footsteps were softened and muffled by grass.

Because I realized... I was alone.

Utterly alone.

Even Rake was here because Cazz had told him to be.

And it hit me so hard and punched so fast, that I lost my breath. The tears rushed to the surface and I was blinking, blinking, blinking trying to keep them at bay.

"That bastard!" I hissed, then made myself keep walking. "What is his problem?"

It was a rhetorical question that I didn't expect Rake to answer, but he clawed a hand through his dark hair and sighed.

"The problem is, Jesse, he's a wolf."

"So?! So are you, and you don't act like a fucking asshole every time you turn around!"

"No, I don't, but..."

Rake was quiet for a moment. We had reached the meadow which was where I usually stopped, but today I decided to keep going. So I stomped my way across the grass towards the gap in the trees where it seemed like there might be a bit of a trail.

"He's a King, and my mate, and he *claims* that I'm important to all of this—then treats me like a fucking *child* when I show up to try and be a part of his day!" I hissed, still fighting tears.

Rake sighed again, but he didn't speak again until we were under the trees in the speckled shadows.

Then he took a deep breath and stopped walking, turning to face me. I stopped too because it seemed like whatever he was about to say was important, but after catching the look on his face I suddenly wasn't sure I wanted to hear it.

"What?" I asked, full of dread.

"Jesse... he doesn't think of you as a child, I promise," he said hesitantly.

I folded my arms. "But?"

He looked down, then met my eyes, his jaw tight. "But he's a wolf. A predator. So, if you really want this to work, if you really want him to want you around, you have to let him *hunt.*"

I gaped at the man I considered a friend, my jaw in the dirt.

What the *actual* fuck did he mean by *that?*

57. The Hunt

~ *JESSE* ~

"Rake, if you're going to stand here and tell me to let him go find other females—"

"Whoa, whoa, whoa! No! That's not... that's not what I meant," he said, wincing. "Not at all."

"Then what do you mean by *hunt?*"

Rake sighed and met my eyes like he was bracing for impact. "I mean... let *him* chase *you.*"

I waited, but it was obvious that was all he intended to say. "You're telling me to play hard to get? I don't play games, Rake."

"No, don't think of it as games... that's not what I mean. I don't mean to manipulate him. I mean... build a life here. Find other things that interest you. Build other relationships. Don't... *need* him so much. Let him come looking for you."

"He's my mate!"

"And he's King, and he's fucking busy, and if you want to be a Queen he'll actually listen to, show him your spine. Don't beg for whatever scraps he's willing to throw. Make him work for your heart, Jess."

I stared at him, wanting to tell him to go fuck himself. Wanting to deny that he was making any sense. Wanting it not to be true.

But if there was one thing in this world that I knew, it was asshole males. And even if Cazz and I were bonded so tightly...

I bit my lip, chewing on that thought. But Rake must have assumed I was arguing with him in my head, because he stepped forward, speaking quietly, but urgently.

"I don't mean you should pretend to be anything you're not. I mean… submission is one thing—he needs that. But throwing yourself in his path when he's pulled away… it won't achieve what you want it to, Jesse. I know him. That's just a part of him. Whether you're his mate, or his friend, or his servant, he can't stand people who can't stand on their own."

"He literally controls people's minds when they stand on their own," I growled.

"No, Jess. He takes control when people *oppose* him. But that's part of why he doesn't lose the hearts of the pack—he wants his people independent. He wants them to *choose* his way. He doesn't care if it's out of fear, or respect, or just pure greed—but he's happy when people do things the way he wants them, whether he's watching or not."

"So what, I'm just supposed to sit in my room and simmer all day until he decides to see me?"

"No! The opposite of that—go show him what you can do without him. Let him hear from others what you're up to. Make him curious. Be… busy without him. That's what he respects—wolves who know what they're good at, and make strides to be successful in it. Wolves who know how they're strong and use that to help the pack. Wolves who don't need his direction."

"I'm not a wolf."

"Not a shifter maybe, but you're a wolf now, Jesse. You're in the pack. And if you ever want him to see you as more than just a… a breeding bitch, you need to make a life here. A life that continues even when he's not there to see it."

"You said before, back at the beginning, that he won't care what I'm doing as long as it doesn't affect him. You said I could do whatever I want!"

"And you can. I just… you're asking why he was impatient today, and I'm telling you. Deep down, he wants you to challenge him, not cling to his thigh."

I snorted. "That man does *not* want a challenge. He shuts down any challenge the second it arises. You said so yourself, he controls those who oppose him."

"I did. But challenging and opposing aren't the same thing. You understand that he can have anyone he wants? Between his status, his appeal, and his power, he can *literally* have any wolf or human he wants. I can tell you, I've watched him get bored so fast...

"He wants a female that makes him work for it, and you're the first mate he's had that forces him to do that."

"Vulnerable, right. Something he clearly *despises.*"

Rake rolled his eyes. "I'm not talking about the emotions of it, Jess. I'm talking about how males think. What gets their blood pumping. And I can tell you, with Cazz, if you want to engage his heart, you have to challenge his mind first so he respects you. And if you want to challenge his mind, you have to either outsmart him, or... make him work. There's nothing that gets a male hotter faster than a female he wants, but isn't sure he can have."

"How do you know? Aren't you celibate?"

Rake shrugged. "I am... now."

"Only now?"

"I took the vow a few years ago. I was a normal male before that, Jesse," he said, trying to keep his voice flat and uninterested. But there was a flash in his gaze as he looked at me. "Trust me, I'm not guessing."

"So you... you've done all this... before?"

He nodded reluctantly.

I grinned. "Oh my... Rake... The provocative priest?"

His eyes flashed brighter and he smiled the way Cazz did sometimes that made my belly tingle. It stole my breath for a second and I had to turn away, pretend I hadn't noticed, because he was just being cheeky.

Rake was still chuckling, but then he shook his head. "Not the provocative priest. Maybe more like the... resigned shepherd. Anyway, this isn't about me. I'm telling you, don't *pursue* him, Jesse. Let him come find you."

I wanted to. I wanted to believe that I could. I wanted to believe that he *would*. But all this talk was pushing me to face the biggest fear I had in all this.

I looked away from Rake because I didn't think I could stand to see pity in his eyes when he answered this question.

"And if he has found someone else to chase in the meantime?"

Rake shook his head. "He hasn't. And I pray that he won't. For both your sakes."

58. The Good Man

~ *JESSE* ~

Rake's words washed over me and made me screw up my face because they weren't what I wanted to hear. I wanted to hear reassurance that I shouldn't even fear that Cazz would cheat. I wanted to hear that I was too strong, or too beautiful, or too valuable for that to happen.

But at the same time my stomach pinched because he hadn't said that, I was also grateful because it meant he was telling me the truth.

The truth was that Cazz might betray me. And if he did… if he did, that was going to hurt more than anything I'd ever experienced, I thought. But even if he didn't… it didn't mean that we were coming out of this with a *happy ever after.*

That was sobering. And not reassuring at all. My heart quavered—then plummeted because I hated that I was spending every second of every day swinging back and forth between fierce desire for Cazz, yearning for his approval, and a shaking, fragile insecurity that I thought I had left behind in high school. I *hated* that he was making me feel that way again when I had felt strong for years now.

"Is it my fault, Rake?" I asked quietly, pathetically, hating myself for the question, but unable to leave it unsaid because it wouldn't stop haunting me.

"Is what your fault?"

I swallowed hard. "Is it my fault if he strays?"

Rake grunted and stepped right up to my toes, his expression fierce and angry. "You know better than that, Jesse. I know you do. But I'm going to answer you anyway: Absolutely not."

It's exactly what I would have said if another woman came and asked me the same question about the man they loved, but...

"I'm new to all this and he's very *experienced,* and—"

"Jesse, I know you're here for a reason. Even now, even with all the bullshit, he's still treating you differently than the others. I can see why God brought you here. And I think you can too."

"I do, but this whole situation just fucks with my head."

"Don't let him do that to you. You're both adults. You're here with a purpose and you know it, I think you should do your best to fulfill it. But these choices aren't just yours. They're also his. And you are *not* responsible for what he chooses. Don't let yourself carry his decisions like you own them somehow. God doesn't."

I huffed. "God has a little bit more perspective than me, and—"

"Jesse, listen to me." Rake's voice was deep, and quiet, and intense. I met his gaze, nervous because he looked so stern. "What you're doing... what you're capable of... it is good and right. And it will help Cazz because trust me, he's never been loved that way before—like he's important for who he is, outside of his power."

"It doesn't matter what I think of him, if he doesn't believe me," I pointed out, struggling not to wail like a child. "If I leave him alone, I fear... I fear he's just going to walk away and I'll never see him again—unless he wants to hurt me. And then... *oh god,*" Images of Cazz taking another female and letting me feel it through the bond—or worse, making me watch—turned my stomach. I swallowed hard against the urge to gag.

But Rake growled. Those muscles at the corner of his jaw flexed and twitched. He leaned in, holding my eyes.

"Jess, there's something happening here, and I pray it works out for both of you. But if it doesn't... if he refuses to change or open his eyes... if he ever hurts you again, I will not let him use you that way again. I'll get you out of here safely. I vow it. As God's representative to the pack, I can do that. I can declare you a Devotee. I can get you out—and even Cazz can't touch you."

"I'm not asking you to go against him—"

"No, Jess. Hear me: I won't let him break you. I promise. If you need to escape, I'll get you out, okay?"

He stared at me, waiting for me to agree.

"Why would you do that?" I breathed.

"Because I'm called to help Cazz—just like you are. But that doesn't mean we enable his self-destruction. That means we give him what he needs, even when it's not what he wants. And if he's trying to destroy you because he doesn't trust himself... well, I'll help him see the light."

He gave a small smile to soften the firm growl of his voice.

"You don't have to be afraid, Jess. You're safe. Either way. With him or without him, you're safe. I promise."

My breath caught as those words fed something inside me. Swelled my chest and eased something that had been *so afraid.*

I was once again fighting tears, but this time I was determined not to give in. I blinked and swallowed and looked down at my hands until I had control of myself. Then I looked back up at Rake.

"Why are you so kind?"

"Trust me, I'm not always."

I ignored him. "And why do you keep working for Cazz if you're so sure he's wrong?"

Rake took longer to answer that one. His face went blank and he swallowed.

"Probably for the same reasons you chose to be his mate and made yourself submit. Sometimes... sometimes you just know."

Something flickered in his eyes then, but he looked away before I could identify what it was.

"You're a good man, Rake. A man of God."

He gave a skeptical huff. "Male," he said, shaking his head.

"I'm sorry, what?"

"I'm not a man, Jess. I'm a male. I'm a wolf. Just... just remember that. Remember that with all of us, okay? Now... let's walk. We're out here at the King's order. We might as well make the most of it, right?"

I knew he was changing the subject because it was making him uncomfortable, but I understood that. So I nodded my head and sighed.

"Sure."

59. Clingy

~ *CASIMIR* ~

I didn't leave Ghere and the servants until hours after dinner, and even when I was finally alone, I was left cursing under my breath because that fucking tension that had been raising my hackles since the moment I woke, didn't ease.

I had spent the entire day edgy and frustrated, and I wasn't even sure why. There were some tensions with the humans, a few scuffles between neighboring Alphas, but nothing significant. Nothing that warranted the tight muscles that made me want to roll my head to loosen my neck, and the itch between my shoulder blades.

I had thought it was the constant presence of servants and calls for my attention and decision-making. It was the life of an Alpha. Particularly a King. And it wearied me at times.

When I stepped out of the council chambers to walk back to my rooms, my heels beat a drum on the stone floor in the tunnels that echoed ahead and behind.

It was a relief to finally be alone. But it was growing late. Day had given way to night and I had worked without break. But something still niggled at me. What was it?

Frowning as I stalked through the halls, I mentally scanned back through the day, my duties, and the pressing issues of the pack, but found nothing I had forgotten or overlooked. Yet that tap on my shoulder would not stop.

I frowned harder.

Rolling my mind all the way back to the morning, waking at Ghere's appearance in my rooms because I'd overslept. That never happened. It had only been by minutes this morning, but the male was more reliable than any clock. When I hadn't moved within my chambers, or summoned him, or linked to warn him away, he had grown concerned. He had come to check on me in case there had been some kind of nefarious attack in the night.

Ridiculous.

I had laughed him off and gotten out of the furs, but I realized now, that was when the niggle started. At first I put it down to the same weariness that had kept me in sleep beyond my usual waking time. But that didn't quite explain it.

I had been sleeping deeper, alone in my bed. For a week.

Over a week.

That naturally brought memories of Jesse appearing in my office the day before. No longer bleeding. Looking for me...

Her cries as I took her... the way her knees shook and I had to catch her weight—

My dick was hard, pressed uncomfortably against the confines of my leather trousers. I frowned. She hadn't come to me today. Hadn't arranged a "chance" meeting in the halls. Hadn't sent a message, even. Why?

A small, feminine noise of approval broke in the tunnel ahead of me. I looked up, expecting to see her, my teeth gritted because she couldn't just let me be... but instead I found Toree.

She was a lush female, strong and desirable. Unmated. And she'd caught the scent of my desire.

As I watched, she prowled towards me, nostrils flared and eyes bright. Her body supple and inviting. If she'd been in her wolf, her tail would have been high...

She scratched at my mind, seeking the link, and I didn't even think. Just opened to her.

Does my King have need? Does he finally tire of the fluttering virgin?

Something about her tone—smug and belittling—made me snap my teeth and she flinched. Submitting. As she should.

I kept walking, but didn't miss the thrill in her scent. It reached me like perfume in the tunnel even after we passed each other. It made me harder, and that made me tense.

I turned to look at her over my shoulder and our eyes caught. She smiled.

I am your servant... should you ever need one, she sent carefully. Then disappeared around the corner.

I kept walking. But my body thrummed, and that itch between my shoulder blades became a flare.

I should have taken the flirtatious she-wolf. At any other time in my life I *would* have taken her.

Resentment and frustration made me growl.

I had never had to leash myself. The few times I had abstained, it had been for the purposes of honing my edge in preparation for a dominance challenge, or simply because I had been bored. Never once had I been driven for sex and denied myself.

Now it had been a week.

All because of a weak—though admittedly fascinating—human.

That niggle began in the back of my head again. Why?

Jesse *was* weak. Undeniably so. She couldn't fight off any female wolf over the age of sexual maturity. She'd struggle against a male barely a decade old.

She. Was. Weak.

I caught myself gritting my teeth, as if I argued with an adversary and snorted at my own ridiculousness.

I was tense because I was driven, and I had left my mate alone for her bleeding—as was right. But in the past I would have simply filled the days with other females.

Perhaps I truly was aging. My appetites waning? I had never chosen to spend this many days alone in a row.

But it was true, I hesitated to do anything that might weaken the power she offered me. Power greater, and more consistent than any female before her. Human or otherwise.

And it kept growing. The more she struggled with her enslavement, the more power she fed into my veins. Those surges when she submitted...

My breathing grew heavy and my balls tightened.

A weak and frail human she might be, but she *was* my mate. And willingly so. And now... now there was no longer a need to leave her untouched.

But she'd been so clingy... did I want to feed that need, or force her to submit further, and see if that power increased again?

I reached the intersection of tunnels to the royal quarters, and stopped. I had a choice to make.

Turn left to Jesse's rooms. Or right towards my own?

I stood there for a moment, rolling my shoulders against that pinch. But then it hit me...

I could not allow her to take any measure of control. I was a strong male. I could resist her, and I should be able to do so without this incessant *complaint* in my body.

My choice was made.

I sighed as I took the first step towards my rooms.

Soundtrack for the next chapter is
Outcast by Lexa Monaco.

60. The End of Tears

~ JESSE ~

It was an awful night.

I'd tried to go to sleep early, but I had laid in bed, staring at the ceiling, thinking about Cazz. And in the middle of that, something woke up inside me. Like hope, at first. It turned my mind to the bond—could I feel him getting closer? Or was that just wishful thinking?

He had kept himself closed to me, kept the bond dead for days. But every so often I'd get a sensation—like something slipped through without his permission. And for a moment my heart beat faster because it felt like he was coming closer.

And then there was a flare of need. Desire. Want.

He was horny.

The images that flashed in my mind were foggy and distant, but it was memories of us.

Desire for him curled in my belly like a waiting snake. I sat up, staring at the door, willing him to come. It had been almost two days since I'd seen him—the morning before was when I'd gone to his office and wished I hadn't. I hadn't seen or spoken to him since. But now I could feel him. And I could feel him wanting me.

Do it. Come to me.

I didn't know if he could actually hear me through the bond, but I prayed he'd at least feel that I wanted him.

But then… nothing. Tension twisted in my chest. An itch between my shoulder blades became a pinch. Something was happening. Something that wasn't good. Something that made me fear.

I threw the furs off like I was going to get up, but then I just sat there because I remembered what Rake had said.

Let him hunt.

But what if he was hunting someone else?

My heart yearned for him. I dropped my face in my hands and made myself breathe, and pray, and wait.

And nothing happened.

The bond went completely dead, like he had slammed that door again.

I don't know how long I sat there, blinking back tears. I don't know how long I stared at the door, wishing for him. But eventually I slumped back onto the pillows and pulled the furs back over my body. And I gave up and tried to sleep.

But even though sleep came pretty quickly, it was the horrific half-sleep where I was aware of thinking—mostly about Cazz—and yet those thoughts and wishes mingled with dreams.

A few times I thought he had come to me and I opened my eyes, smiling... only to find the room dark and cold and empty, except for me.

The hollow feeling in the pit of my stomach became an ache.

I tossed and turned and woke from half-sleep with tears on my cheeks.

It was the early hours of the morning before I was exhausted enough to finally slip into a deep sleep. But it didn't last.

The darkness of the underground palace meant I never knew what time it was when I woke, or when I got tired, for that matter. But my body ran on rhythms here. Rake had already said it would become reliable.

When I woke, with the sense that there was movement in the tunnels and the day was beginning, I wanted to feel hopeful for what might come. That Cazz might finally come to me. But I was left laying there, eyes stinging with tiredness, body weak with weariness, heart despairing.

I don't know how long I lay there, my mind slipping between memories of his touch and kiss, and even his rare smiles... to his anger, his rejection, his aggression...

I found myself lying on my stomach, crying, face buried in a pillow, chest aching with pain and...

What the fuck was wrong with me? Why the *hell* was I letting him do this to me?

My sight was still blurred with tears when I pushed up to sit and turned to look around at the room, wiping my eyes.

"Get it together, Jesse!" I hissed at myself. "If he doesn't want you, if he's going to breach the bond, that's *his* fucking problem!"

A quivering, pained voice in the back of my head wanted to keep wailing, to keep crying, to saturate in self-pity, but—

"No."

No. I wasn't going to do this. I wasn't going to finally get free of the assholes in my life, only to let one more asshole destroy me in worse ways.

I wasn't.

And suddenly, I was fucking *furious* with myself for wasting all this time on a smug bastard who couldn't see what I offered. And who was so stuck in his own pain and pride, he refused to let me love him.

The moment I thought that word, love, my chest panged again. I wanted to weep, but I shook my head.

I did love him. I did want him. I could admit that. I wasn't like him. I didn't see loving another person as a weakness. I thought the vulnerability that came with that was a beautiful thing. But if he refused to give anything back... well...

He was going to destroy himself. That wasn't *my* fault.

I was still shaky, but my body felt lighter than it had since the moment he'd claimed me. Why had I let him blind me like this? Why had I given in to that fear?

So, Cazz was probably a cheat and definitely a bastard. A beautiful one. But still... his heart wasn't faithful. Or at least, it hadn't been in the past. And if he betrayed me that way too... it was going to be *his* fucking loss.

Resolved, I pushed the furs back and crawled out of that huge bed, and for the first time in weeks, I smiled genuinely.

"If my mate is nothing but a walking dick, that's his problem."

I snorted, then giggled, a little unhinged. But it felt good.

I turned my back on the unmade bed and walked over to that incredible closet full of every item of clothing I could possibly hope for. And once I was appropriately dressed, I opened my bedroom door to look for the female servant who was always outside in the mornings, ready to take my breakfast order.

"Good morning, Sire," she said, bowing her head slightly. "What can I get you tod–"

"Who is the oldest female in the pack—at least, here in the Palace?" I asked her abruptly.

She raised her head, blinking. "It's, uh... I believe it would be the healer, Maya," she said, licking her lips. "Are you in need of a healer? I could call—"

"No, no. I don't care what her role is. I need her perspective," I said quickly, waving a hand to stop her. "Is Maya able to walk?"

"Yes, though slowly. But... Sire, Maya is... she carries a great mantle. Her time is extremely limited. And she is not... patient with... well, with criers."

I surprised myself by giving a little laugh. I should have been offended. But clearly word about the Queen was getting around. I *had* been doing little but wail and cry these past couple of weeks.

Well, that was going to change. And Maya sounded like *exactly* the kind of person I needed to help me do it.

"Perfect," I said. "Tell her the Queen wants to visit. In fact, no. Let's go get breakfast at the hall—send a messenger ahead to her now. I want her to clear her schedule this morning. Tell her I'm coming."

"I will, of course, Sire," the servant said carefully. "It's only that Maya—"

"She won't like it. I understand. But I am Queen. She is supposed to submit, correct?"

The servant's eyes went wide. "Technically yes, but... even the King is quite careful how he approaches her. She doesn't take well to... orders."

I shrugged. "That's fine. Phrase it however you think it should be phrased. But please make sure she understands that I'll arrive wherever she would like to meet me in an hour. And I would like to make use of her time until lunch."

The servant nodded tentatively. "I will... yes, Sire."

"Thank you."

She scurried off, obviously worried. But I walked towards the banquet hall smiling for the first time in too long.

61. Maya

~ *JESSE* ~

During my meal, the servant from my room returned looking pale to whisper to me that Maya had suggested that I should attend her in her rooms. I thanked her, then after I had finished breakfast—the first meal I had actually been able to taste in days—I asked one of the male guards to show me to Maya's quarters.

He looked startled, but bowed and led me into the tunnels.

I'm not sure what I expected, but it wasn't a twenty-five minute walk through the halls, deeper and deeper into the catacombs of the underground Palace.

After the first ten minutes we were further underground than I had ever been, even when Cazz had taken me to the Den. But it wasn't until we took a corner and there were long, deep shadows between the torches that were lit on the sides of the tunnel that for the first time it occurred to me that I was far away from anyone I knew who might care about what happened to me. If this guard wasn't trustworthy—something I hadn't even considered—he could be leading me to my death.

Then we took another corner, and not only was the tunnel dim, but the temperature dropped several degrees, and the air was damp. There were places that water actually trickled down the walls to puddle at the sides of the stone floor.

"Are you sure this is the right way to Maya's chambers?"

"I'm certain, Sire," the male said, his deep voice echoed in the cold tunnel. "She has kept these chambers for decades and refused to move, even when better rooms were offered."

I eyed the blue-black shimmer of water on the walls and wrinkled my nose at the damp. Was Maya a healer, or was I going to see a witch?

We took one more turn in the tunnel and I was just about to lose my nerve, when the man—male—stopped in the darkest portion of the cave between two torches that were fifty feet apart.

"The King knocks and won't enter until she invites him," the guard said, glancing at me sideways. I couldn't tell if he didn't like me, or if he was nervous about Maya.

That was when I realized the deep shadow in front of him held a doorway.

"Oh, okay. Thank you." I stepped forward as he stepped back, gesturing towards the dark wood.

There didn't seem to be anything else to do, so I knocked.

The voice that rose inside was muffled enough that I couldn't make out the words, but the tone was very clearly irritated. But then there was no further sound.

Had that been her telling me to come in and now she was waiting? Or was she on her way to the door? Apparently she moved slowly…

I frowned and looked a question at the guard. He shrugged, but looked nervous.

What was it about this woman that made the servants step so softly?

Gathering my resolve, I turned back the door and knocked again. But I'd only gotten to the second rap when the door creaked and swung open and I was faced with an old, hunched woman, one gnarled hand gripping the rounded top of a walking stick, the other on the door, glaring at me.

"Not an ounce of patience in pups anymore. You just couldn't stand there and give an old matriarch a moment to move aching bones?!"

I blinked and stared at her, shocked by her aggressive tone.

She was shorter than me—mostly because she stood hunched over, her spine bent in a way that looked like she couldn't straighten it even if she wanted to. Her skin was that soft, thin, papery kind of wrinkled where it hung in lines that framed every movement of her face. And her hair was pure white. She glared at me out from under busy gray brows, even her lips puckered by wrinkles. But her eyes held the keen edge of intelligence.

She might be old, but she was not stupid. And she very definitely wasn't pleased.

"You're Maya, I assume?" I said as sweetly as I could.

She scoffed and turned on her heel, using the stick to give herself something to lean on as she began hobbling back into the rooms.

"Clearly our new Queen is sharp as a fucking tack," she muttered as she hobbled away from me. "Let me *invite* you in, your Highness," she said sarcastically, cutting me a look over her hunched shoulder. "But for the sake of all that is holy, wipe your feet. Even the King doesn't stain my rugs, so don't think you'll be allowed to."

Then she disappeared into the deep gloom of her den and for a moment I lost sight of her completely, the dark was so impenetrable. But then her silhouette appeared, just rounding a corner towards a light emanating from behind a wall.

Apparently she expected me to follow, human eyes and all.

I looked back at the guard who still stood in the tunnel, his eyes a little too wide. He shrugged again, so I just sighed and did as she asked. I stepped over the threshold of the door, wiped my feet on the rug inside, then closed the door and followed her into that darkness praying that I hadn't bitten off more than I could chew.

I kept my eyes on the haze of dim light glowing softly from behind that wall, but it was the only light in the room. I couldn't even see where I set my feet, so I was moving slowly because what if there was furniture in here, or things to trip on?

"Girl, get your ass in here—you've already stolen my morning. For a female who doesn't have many of them left, that's a crime. At this rate I'll be dead before you give up, start crying, and flee."

I grimaced. Yes, she obviously had heard about me.

"My eyes aren't as sharp as yours," I said through my teeth. "So forgive me if it takes me a moment to navigate the…"

I trailed off because I had finally rounded the edge of that wall and could finally see the light shining from what was a wide, round room carved out of rock—by nature, or by wolves, I wasn't sure. But I stopped short because the room was so unexpectedly inviting.

It would have seemed like a comfortable spot in any home— thick rugs on the floor, low, wide coffee table at the center. A stuffed, leather couch, two thick chairs. There was even a grandfather clock against the wall behind the sitting area and a tapestry hanging that depicted wolves hunting in the forest.

Lamps were lit in a triangle around the room, none of them bright.

Maya had settled herself into one of the chairs and was leaning her stick up against the side of it.

"Stop gaping like a child," she snapped. "Sit down and tell me why I'm *requested* to give up my morning."

I weaved around the central coffee table to take the single chair at its opposite end, facing her. I settled myself as quickly as I could, but I could feel her eyes burning on me as I tried to find the best way to sit—the chair was too deep. If I sat back in it, my feet wouldn't touch the floor. I'd look like a child. But sitting so I could put my feet flat meant perching on the edge of it, like I was getting ready to run.

If I had been home, I would have taken off my shoes, leaned on the wide arm, and curled my legs up, let the chair cradle me. But somehow I doubted Maya was going to have a high opinion of that. So I did sit on the edge, fold my hands into my lap, then sigh.

"Thank you for seeing me," I started.

The woman didn't even blink. "I wasn't given any choice, *Sire*. So please, state your business so that we can resolve it and I can get back to my life. As I think you can see, there isn't much of it left."

Then she folded her hands in her lap and glared at me, waiting.

62. Immovable Object, Meet Unstoppable Force

~ JESSE ~

I swallowed hard. She didn't scare me in the sense that I knew I could outrun her—not how I usually felt with a wolf. But I was beginning to see why the servants had all been so nervous. She was the kind of person who looked at you, and it felt like she could see through your clothes and read your thoughts.

And she wasn't impressed by anything she found in either place.

"Thank you for seeing me—" I started, trying to be polite. But she growled.

"Girl, you *sent for me* as if I am a common wolf, submitted to your will. Even the King—your mate—does not do that."

"Can you explain why?"

Her eyes widened and she shook her head. "He made you Queen and you don't even know the dynamics of pack rank? What the fuck was he thinking?"

"Believe me, I've been wonder the same thing. A lot."

Nothing changed in her expression. But she didn't speak immediately, so I plowed out.

"I asked to speak with you this morning—"

She gave an unamused huff when I said "asked."

"—because I need someone with age and wisdom to help me. I need to understand my role—not just as a ruler, as Cazz's mate. But as a woman in this... pack. I need to understand the... the

259

dynamics that you mentioned. And I need to be taught by someone who isn't intimidated by my rank, or…" I trailed off, losing my courage just a little.

"Or?" she prompted slyly, as if she already knew what I was going to say, and she wanted to make me do it.

I pursed my lips, but made myself do it.

"I don't trust the other females not to… compete with me."

"Compete?"

I gave her a flat look, because it was clear she was quite delighted about this turn in the conversation.

"They want him," I said bluntly. "I can't be sure that they won't… misdirect me, just to see me fail."

"You think I wouldn't misdirect you? That I somehow want you to succeed?" she asked blithely, sitting back in the chair.

"I think that you will test me, and if you think I'm up to the job, you'll help me do it. And if I'm not… well. At least you won't try to steal my mate out from under my nose."

"Tail."

"I'm sorry, what?"

"You raise your tail to your mate, not your nose."

I blinked at the mental visual *that* brought to mind, but then shook it off. "You see, you're helping already."

She snorted like she didn't want to, but before she could speak, there was another rap at the door, and she cursed under her breath. I saw her hands tighten in her lap as if she was bracing, and realized she probably had terrible pain. Her knuckles were so swollen—from arthritis, if I had to guess. She was clearly *not* impressed with having to get up for another visitor, so I sprang to my feet.

"I'll get it."

"Sit down, girl. It's only your servant. Too frightened to link with me in case I bite his face off. Figuratively," she added with a snort. "Come in, dog, and do not mess my rugs!"

I blinked. I thought at some point Cazz had told me that calling a wolf a dog was an awful insult. But maybe I was remembering wrong.

A moment later I heard the thin creak of the door, then the hush of feet wiping on the mat, before the male appeared seconds later at the edge of the room.

"Sire, I do not wish to interrupt, but I need to know if you would prefer that I wait outside, or come back later—"

"You cut a fine specimen of a male, dog, but you'll never make Alpha when you act as if a human girl could emasculate you."

Horrified, I looked at the male sympathetically. "It's okay." I tried to keep my voice calm and soothing. "I don't mind if you check back later. I plan to be here for at least a couple of hours, if you want to go back up and return."

He bowed his head. "Thank you," he murmured. "I would prefer—"

"Stop shaking like a chihuahua and speak up. Or have your balls not dropped yet?" Maya snapped, sitting forward in her chair.

"My hearing isn't that bad, I heard him just fine," I said through my teeth as the male's head dropped like he was ashamed.

"That's not the point. God, males were never such kittens in my day. Son, take my advice and go back to your rooms, strip off, then stand before a mirror and locate your testicles. Report back on whether or not they have descended. We may need to neuter you."

Her words didn't seem any more harsh than plenty of insults I had heard the males toss at each other over a meal, or during meetings when they were ribbing each other. But this male who had seemed so tall and strong back at the dining room, kept trying to make himself smaller, as if her words were cutting him.

"Maya—"

"That isn't a euphemism, pup. I'll expect your report when you return for the Que—"

"You will do no such thing!" I snapped over her. Maya humphed, but the male looked shocked. I turned to the older woman. "I understand that I've irritated you this morning, but that is no reason to humiliate this male who only helped me find you. He has done nothing wrong, and the only one trying to emasculate him is *you.*"

Maya tipped her chin up to look at me down her nose, and her brows rose. "You stand for a *servant?*"

"I stand for any person—human or wolf, servant or King— who doesn't deserve what they're getting. And I don't give two shits who's handing it out. Maybe these wolves are blinded by your age, or maybe that's just how wolves work. But it's not right. He's only here because I asked him to help me. If you have a problem with that, take it up with me. You owe him an apology."

Her eyes flared, but I didn't drop my gaze.

262

63. True Strength

~ *JESSE* ~

The guard made a little whine in his throat, his eyes darting back and forth between us like he was uncertain who to listen to. But Maya ignored him. Her brows rose so high her forehead wrinkled even more.

"So our Queen *does* have fangs."

I scowled, wishing I had a snappy comeback, but before I could come up with one, the older woman turned away from me and her expression softened.

"You did well, Sven. Thank you. Return before the lunch hour. Our Queen will be ready to leave me by then, I'm certain," she said with an amused huff.

Sven—the guard—nodded and bowed again, then turned without making eye-contact and trotted back out of the cave.

For a moment I was confused, then I realized he'd lost all apparent fear of her the moment I snapped at him. I turned back to her. "Wait, that was a play for—?"

"I have heard about you, Jesse. You were right to come looking for me."

I blinked. "But... I thought—"

"I needed to know the truth of your character—what you would do when faced with someone of authority using power against another. Whether you would stop your tongue to avoid angering me—or worse, mimic my behavior. Don't worry, Sven has been assisting me for years. He knows I appreciate him greatly, and that I didn't mean it."

I frowned at her. "You set that up? It was a ruse?"

"It was a test, and you passed—much to my chagrin."

"Chagrin? You *didn't* want me to be a decent person?" I snapped.

"No dear."

"Why the hell not?!"

"Because it means that I am now obligated to help you, and frankly, I'm not sure I have the energy. You're a... how do the humans put it? You're a *train wreck.* And you've done nothing but undermine your own position with the pack. Tying myself to you at this point when my age begins to overwhelm me could be the end of *my* power if you aren't strong enough."

I clenched my hands to fists on my thighs and didn't break her unimpressed gaze. "I *am* strong enough."

"We'll see," she said darkly.

I huffed and opened my mouth, but she locked eyes with me and leaned forward.

"Jesse, you have been handed the most difficult and politically volatile position in the entire Lupine Kingdom. Two females before you—both with better education and resources behind them—failed spectacularly."

"They were weak—"

"No, dear, they were human."

"What's *that* supposed to mean?" I folded my arms and tipped my head.

But Maya cackled like I had made a joke. "What that means, *girl,* is that your people are not my people. Your ways are not our ways. And because human senses are dull and your priorities *unfathomably shallow,* your minds are brittle. You develop no resilience. So that when you are faced with true hardship you crumble."

"You don't have a clue what kind of hardship I've endured—"

"Like the rejection and abandonment of your mate, for example?" she offered quietly.

I went very still—rage roared in my chest, but fear crackled there too.

She definitely knew.

Was she saying that she didn't blame him? Was she saying—

"Jesse, I understand that you did not choose to be here. However, here you are. And now we have to decide what to do with you. Frankly, even with my help you are more likely to fail than not. Hence my reluctance to be connected with you in the eyes of our pack."

I swallowed hard, but didn't back down. "So... what you're saying is that your power is so frail at this point that simply being associated with me—a weak human—could topple you?"

Her lips tightened, but I sensed the reluctant respect in her eyes.

"I'm saying... I wonder if you know the difference between true strength and simply goading those with less self-discipline than you until they lash out?"

"I do."

"Really? Please explain."

I didn't even hesitate. If there was one thing I knew, it was the difference between brute force, and intelligent strength. The question was, did she?

"The truly strong aren't made smaller by giving to others. Because we have enough left over to not be... lessened. So we are not driven by pride because we don't need others' high opinions to know our own value."

Maya's eyes turned thoughtful. She sat back in her chair and brought one of those swollen hands up, tapping her mouth with one finger. "You say *we* as if you claim the trait."

"I already told you I do. I'm strong enough to do this. But you're right, this is a new world and a different set of rules. I have been... struggling. I need help—and I'm not scared to admit that. I know two heads are better than one. That's why I'm here. Now... are you going to help me? Or do you just want to play games?"

She didn't respond immediately, but then her lips curled up on one side and she gave a deep, husky chuckle.

"Oh, dear, Casimir... what *have* you unleashed among us?" she murmured.

I rolled my eyes, but nerves fluttered in my belly. "He hasn't unleashed me. Quite the opposite. He's desperately trying to keep both of us tied down to whatever stupid control it is that he thinks he has to keep. That's the problem. That's why I need your help. I need him to see me clearly. I need him to *trust* me."

"And if he won't?"

God, I wanted to cry, but I swallowed the lump back and shrugged. "If he won't, then the only other option is to find a life here without him. And I can't do that while everyone sees me like some weepy child."

Maya's gaze went flat. "Perhaps you should consider not whining and crying like one, then?"

I gritted my teeth, because I knew she was right. But it felt mean of her to say it. Still, I braced myself. "Why do you think I'm here?"

"Because with the right word from me, the rest of them will listen to you."

I blinked. "Is that… true?"

"It is," she said flatly. "But what is also true is that if I herald you to them, and *then* you fail, you'll take me down with you. Your position is just powerful enough to do that. Neither of us would survive it."

I stared at her. "That's a metaphor, right?"

But Maya just gave me a grim smile.

64. Time to Learn – Part 1

~ JESSE ~

"I can see that you grasp what true strength is," Maya said carefully a moment later, but her face was still firm, still skeptical. "But knowledge and understanding are not the same thing."

"That's why I need help. I know the pack functions in a hierarchy, but I don't understand how it works. I know Cazz has been wounded and that's why he lashes out, but I don't understand why he chose me if I trigger that. I know wolves are having conversations in their minds all the time that I can't hear, but I don't understand how the packmind works... or if I can access it without that stupid drink."

Maya frowned. "All things your mate should have explained and helped you understand," she grumbled. "It is a good sign that you were able to access the packmind with a little help. But it isn't a guarantee you'll ever be able to do it unaided. Or that you would want to."

I sighed. "I do wonder. I'm sure you heard. It was a complete disaster."

Maya's wrinkled lips thinned. "I am of the correct opinion that Cazz bears responsibility for that. It was... beyond irresponsible to bring you into that environment for your first foray into the link."

Rake had said something similar. And I assumed they were both right. But that didn't change the fact that since that night, Cazz had been so bitter and distant, apparently blaming me for what had gone on.

I sighed again. "Cazz seemed to think ahead of time that he could protect me if anything went wrong, but he had a different story to tell when they all came after us. He blamed me. I didn't even know they were seeing my thoughts."

Maya muttered something I didn't catch. "Why would you want to be a part of the pack mind? It is… part of our animal. It is a community you would find brutal. Very heartless at times. Though not always."

"Because I want to connect! With all of them, but especially with Cazz. When the bond is open, when our minds start to link, I can *see* him. And it all makes so much sense. I understand how he feels and why he's doing what he's doing—at least, better than I do without it."

"Work on your bond. Press into your mate. Your link is an entirely different beast to the packmind—"

"But what if he won't give in? If he rejects me, I'm still stuck here. And I refuse to sit in a corner and cry anymore. I refuse to sit here on my ass for the rest of my life, waiting to breed for a man who doesn't give a shit about me. I need a purpose! And if it isn't going to be him, and I am Queen, and the pack needs a Queen, there must be *something* I can do?"

I realized I was shouting when my voice rang through the room after that last word and I snapped my mouth closed. But I didn't look away. And I didn't back down. I cleared my throat and made myself speak more calmly.

"I can be useful to Cazz if he'll let me. I can help him heal. But if he won't… I want to be useful to other people—other wolves. I want to stay alive."

Maya's expression was thoughtful. So I waited.

"You want to lead. Yet, without physical strength to command attention, or an existing connection that invites loyalty, you will struggle—and that even before all the weeping," she said darkly. I frowned. "However, you have been placed here for a reason, no doubt… Perhaps… perhaps your way forward is not the usual way."

I nodded, a sliver of hope rising in my chest. "So, what is an unusual way?"

Maya stared at me like she could read my thoughts. "In my experience, most rulers lack one very important skill," she said quietly.

"Which is?"

"Humility."

Relief flooded through me. "I can give you that."

The older woman arched a skeptical brow. "Oh really?"

"Really. Try me."

Maya pursed her lips. "Very well... Submit to me. Everything. Give me no restrictions. I will teach you and guide you, but you must endure whatever I tell you is necessary, whether I have explained it to you beforehand or not. And I will not commend you to the pack until *I* determine you are ready—not you. Not even Cazz."

My heart beat faster and I nodded. "I will. I will submit like that—unless your orders contradict Cazz's. He's still my mate, and my King. And I vowed to him... I will submit to anything you instruct unless he's already given me a contradicting order, or he says no."

Maya nodded. "You didn't lose your backbone, then. Very good. I accept. Let's get started."

I blinked. It was that simple? "On what?"

"On etiquette. Hierarchy. And your role in it. Only after you understand all of that can we figure out if you're capable of actually *leading.*"

*****

The days following that conversation were difficult, but in a way that got me out of bed in the morning with a smile on my face—as long as I pushed away thoughts of how Cazz was avoiding me.

Maya was brutally honest, mostly impatient, and utterly unwilling to "coddle" me, as she put it. I spent every morning with her, then most of the afternoons practicing or studying what she'd shown me.

I'd never been a bad student, but this was an entirely new field for me. Pack politics were far more complicated than I ever imagined.

I had assumed the hierarchy of the wolves was simple—a ladder. These wolves over those wolves, over those and so on, with Cazz at the top, and the youngest child at the bottom. It turned out that was only true to a point.

I was left breathless by the nuances of it—the ways their positions could shift and change, and how easily.

"How do any of you ever keep it all straight?" I groaned on the third day, almost tearing out my hair as Maya kept drilling me on the hierarchy of the packs—and then the hierarchy within each— and how wolves determined their positions when they gathered.

"To a wolf this is instinct," Maya said irritably. "Even the children rarely get it wrong. We can... scent it on each other. The

269

other wolf's power and strength, and where it places us against them."

"But you said the Burnt Timber wolves outrank the Stone River wolves, and yet when I was learning the Alphas yesterday, Derk, the Stone River Alpha is stronger?"

"A pack's rank is collective. A strong Alpha will pull up the rank of the entire pack, but only to a point. And Stone River is a young pack, with few matriarchs. Give them twenty years and they'll be growling for a challenge."

I had to take her word for it. I was doing some growling of my own trying to get this all straight in my head.

"Okay... I'll try again. Just... be patient, please."

"Girl, do I look like I have time for patience?"

I sighed, but started the recitation again, encouraged when Maya only winced twice.

I was getting it. Slowly.

65. Time to Learn – Part 2

~ JESSE ~

After getting a grasp on the bare skeleton of the hierarchy, there was the whole issue of the dominance challenge. I had thought a challenge was just a physical fight. One wolf fighting another for dominance based on strength. But I'd been wrong about that too.

"A wolf's sheer will can take dominance without so much as anyone snapping teeth," Maya had sighed. "Your human way of seeing strength, of believing it is only brute force, is so narrow—"

"No, we don't see strength as only physical," I had argued. "But I thought that *wolves* did. I thought this whole submission and dominance thing was won by fighting and whoever wins is stronger?"

"That can be true, and Alphas usually resolve disputes by a physical clash, but only after the other aspects of their rank have been measured. Do not let yourself believe that dominance is earned through sheer intimidation. Wolves perceive an indomitable will. Where it exists, the wolf will reign. But that might only be for a time. Or only in certain areas... we all know each other's strengths.

"For example, I am a healer. When the Alphas come to me injured or sick, they concede their will to my knowledge and skill. They submit. I choose their treatment and restrictions. They do not dictate to me. While they stand in my chambers, I am dominant. But that does not mean I will walk outside of these walls and publicly dominate my King, or the Alphas. Their strength and intelligence has brought our pack to the pinnacle of health and good fortune. I would be an idiot to challenge that, believing that my greater knowledge in this area means I am better than them at what *they* do."

And that was yet another thing I didn't understand.

"What *do* Alphas do, exactly?" I asked her, looking up from the notes I was writing. "Cazz is extremely busy. Always meeting with someone, ordering servants, calling for information, seeing wolves in audiences... what's he doing all the time? Is it just constantly giving orders?"

Maya had settled down in her chair, shaking her head. "Your mate does you a great disservice by not bringing you alongside him in these matters," she muttered. "I do not like to speak out against others—"

I almost choked on my own tongue, because it seemed to me that Maya did little *but* identify how others constantly failed, or did not meet her expectations. But she cut me a sharp look, so I didn't say anything.

"—but were he to bring you into the tasks and responsibilities of rulers, not only would it help you grow, but it would ease his burden somewhat, as well." She sighed heavily. "But, it is his way and has always been his way. He will shorten his life if he is not careful. In any case, to answer your question, the Alpha—any Alpha, at any level—is... sort of a parent. They are the Overseer. Watchman. Protector. The best Alphas teach and train so that their pack becomes stronger and smarter, and serves them without constant supervision. But at its core, an Alpha's greatest role is to watch out for those beneath them, push them to grow, give them resources and education, and make the tough decisions when tough decisions must be made.

"As Alpha King, Cazz is the, er, father of a nation. *All* the Alphas, no matter their age, submit to him. They bring their disputes to him. He determines our level of interaction and boundaries with the human world. He oversees trade and makes judgment where commerce and pack politics overlap. He selects the young wolves for training that he believes could become members of strength in the future. And he ensures that those lowest in the ranks are not mistreated.

"He guides our entire people. All of us rely on him to watch for danger. He and his advisors are party to information and relationships we do not have. There are dangers in this world that may come and go without our knowledge that they even existed. And that is well and good—he will tell us if there is something which concerns us. In short, he is... like a father watching over his family. Not present in every moment, but we know we stand in the safety of his shadow at all times."

My heart ached at the picture she painted. I would love to see Cazz that way. *Yearned* to experience that with him. But... I shook my head and focused on the facts.

Then I blinked. Wait... Cazz did all that? I knew he took his job seriously and that he was often busy, but I had no idea...

Maya's voice turned smug. "You underestimated him?"

"Sort of," I admitted, still staring down at the paper in front of me, though I hadn't written any of that down. "I thought he was just making himself look busy to avoid me. I mean, I knew he was powerful and others listened, but I guess I didn't realize just how deep the pressure went."

She scoffed. "Casimir would not describe it as a pressure— Alphas rarely do. They carry a weight, a burden. Something that will drag at them if they do not do their jobs well. But something that also fulfills their purpose in this world. I do not know an Alpha that would choose any role but the one he has. That's *why* he's Alpha. God made him to lead."

I shook my head. This picture she described... that was a man I could happily stand behind. That was a man I *wanted* to support and follow. But that wasn't the man I saw in the few moments our paths crossed in the day.

The Cazz I saw wasn't reaching out to protect and guide. He was self-serving, arrogant, and indifferent to the feelings of others.

Well, mine, at least.

I went very still then and suddenly felt cold.

What if the pack's Cazz wasn't the Cazz I knew? What if he was gentle with others? Warm? Or at least... not cold? What if it was just me who—

"What have I said about allowing your thoughts to descend, Jesse?" Maya growled.

I blinked and looked at her.

Her lips pressed thin. "Our King is many things, but inauthentic is not one of them. The male you know is the male we all know. In fact... I believe the reason you feel his distance more than we do is because he has allowed you closer."

I snorted. "He hasn't touched me in almost two weeks."

She frowned harder. "He hasn't?"

I shook my head. "He couldn't keep his hands off me when we first mated, but as soon as he claimed me, everything just... fell apart."

Maya growled low and long in her throat, but she didn't offer any commentary on that.

Then I had another thought. "Wait… how did you know that's what I was thinking about?" I asked quickly.

For the first time that morning, Maya smiled. "You're getting closer to linking. I couldn't make out your thoughts, but I am sensing your emotions beyond what I can read in your body or scent. You are not good at masking," she said with a low chuckle. "So perhaps that is where the rest of our energy should be placed today. Set aside the papers, girl, it's time to work with your mind."

I groaned. My attempts at linking were so frustrating. If we spent the next hour doing this, even though all I'd do is sit here, by the end I would be exhausted, my body limp as a cooked noodle. And if it went like all the other sessions had, I wouldn't even succeed in linking with Maya. I'd just be sweating and weary with nothing to show for it.

But I had already learned there was no point trying to convince her to shift her focus. Once she'd chosen a topic, we stayed there until *she* was done.

So I did as she said and put the paper and ink pen aside, then folded my hands on the tabletop and met her eyes.

"Now, breathe easily," she said quietly. "Focus on me, and open yourself to me. Reach for me with your mind and if you sense even a flicker of my shadow, do not pounce, but lean closer. Offer yourself and so be received…"

It was the same little speech she gave me every time, so I just sighed and focused on her and prayed I wouldn't fail *completely*.

66. Elated

~ *JESSE* ~

On the sixth day meeting with Maya, I returned to my chambers later than usual. Usually I left her before lunch, but we'd been making progress, so she'd had food brought to us there at her rooms.

By the time I got back to the royal wing I was utterly exhausted, still slightly pissed at Maya, but also elated.

She had insisted that we spend the entire morning working on my awareness of the packmind and ability to link. Then she had proceeded to spend *hours* poking at me, goading me, and venting her frustration when I didn't make progress.

At first I had despaired. It was the closest I had come to giving up since she started meeting with me.

As if she knew that, she grew disdainful—and kept pressing.

"Is this what you believe a Queen should be? Flinching and self-pitying? Or is it a ruse? I know there is strength within you. Do you pretend weakness to disarm an opponent? Is that how you work?"

"Maya, you aren't my opponent!"

"Oh no? You fight the submission. You resist my contempt. You justify yourself in your mind, arguing with me when what I offer is difficult truth."

"I'm not fighting the submission, I want to learn—"

"You want to learn easily. You want to be carried and shown. You want to be treated as if you're fragile—that will not build you strength, and will not bring the wolves to you."

"I don't want to be carried! I'm trying to—"

"Submit your will—accept the hardship I push on you. Accept that I do not press without good reason."

"I do!"

"You are lying to yourself—give up your will, Jesse. Submit."

"But I am!"

"No, you are being obedient. With gritted teeth and resentment."

"So you want me to just give up my will? You said an indomitable will is respected by wolves—"

"I do not want you weak," she hissed. *"I want you to* choose *to follow my plan. I want you to choose to believe that I am molding you in a way that will benefit you."*

"I don't doubt that—"

"Yet, you resist!"

"I'm afraid of failing—or that you're going to do something that will hurt. That's all. I flinch—but I keep going."

"I'm tell you to trust me, Jesse," she said, firmly but gently. *"I'm telling you to put yourself in my hands. That's what submission is. I will give myself into your hands and trust that you see things I do not and I will follow, even into the dark."*

I hadn't really understood—but I wanted to try. So I did.

She stopped talking and watched me, waiting. And I tried... I sat in my mind as she had told me to do, instead of *"talking incessantly,"* as she put it. And I thought it through.

And somehow, in trying to wrap my mind around it, in wrestling with my submission to her, somehow I had opened the door between us.

I'd seen a flicker of her mind, like a door just barely cracked— I couldn't see the whole room, but I managed a glimpse.

She was pleased, and tired, worried about—

That door shut with a decisive click, but we were both smiling.

As I opened the actual door into my rooms, I realized I was smiling again—beaming, in fact. It was going to happen, I was going to be able to link with the wolves—

"Where have you been?"

I gave a shriek and jerked back a step, almost running into the door. Clutching a hand to my chest where my heart was now pounding, I looked up to find Cazz, dark and brooding, devastatingly handsome in leather pants, a dark shirt open at the throat, those necklaces and—

"I said, where have you been?!" he barked.

I blinked. "I've been with Maya," I said breathlessly, battling conflicting drives deep in my core. My body wanted to shrink from him—he was looming, dark, intimidating and his eyes gleamed with anger.

And yet... he was here. Something deep inside *sang* because he was close,and the way he strode towards me with his hands clenched spoke of a drive to touch me as deeply as mine to be touched.

He was fighting, I realized. Fighting the urge to *want* to be close to me.

Why was he fighting it?

"Maya? What for?" he growled, his chin coming up. "Did you need healing—"

"No, no, Cazz. Nothing like that. I'm... she's teaching me. Helping me. To understand the pack and—"

"If you have questions about the pack, you can ask me."

I blinked at him, my head jerking back. "You aren't... serious?"

"Of course I am. I'm your mate, and King. You think I can't instruct you in the packs?" He had halted just out of arms reach and now he folded his arms, glaring down at me.

"But... you're so busy. And she's a female, and—"

"You don't need to be taking Maya's time. She'll be dealing with you out of respect for me. It was wrong of you to—"

"Actually, she challenged me a lot before she agreed to help me—and now she's saying she'll only commend me to the pack if or when I've shown *her* that I'm strong enough—"

"What commendation do you need from Maya?" Cazz snarled. "I am King and *your mate.* You think that isn't enough to commend you to them?!"

"No, Cazz—because you don't commend me! You claim me, then ignore me and leave me alone and don't tell me what you're doing and don't explain and I'm... I'm *drowning.* I'm drowning and you're never here!"

"I am *busy.* My job—"

"I know, I know," I said as gently as I could, scrambling not to anger him. "I understand that better now. Maya explained. I didn't realize... when I interrupted you and... I won't do that again, Cazz. I'm—see, I'm trying to learn how to be a good Queen so that I'm an asset to you, instead of another drain—"

"If you want to be a good Queen, give me offspring!" he snapped. "That's what you are here to do!"

67. The Tool

~ *JESSE* ~

I gaped at him, my head screaming with protests. My chest roaring with anger. My whole body flinching with the unfairness of it all.

"You're saying it's my fault that I'm not pregnant? *You haven't touched me in two weeks.*"

His eyes narrowed and the fierce disapproval on his face cut me like a blade, right through the middle. Those fucking tears rose without my permission, and my vision of him blurred.

I cursed and turned my back on him, wiping at my face and biting my lip, trying desperately to get myself back under control, but *pissed* because I had thought I was getting stronger. I hadn't cried more than a minute since Maya started teaching me. Almost a week and I was feeling so much stronger.

Then he showed up and…

Why did he have this effect on me? Why did I have no defenses against him? Was it the claiming?

That yawning chasm of despair loomed once more, echoing in my chest and threatening to suck me away again. But I refused it.

Dashing away the tears as much as I could, I turned to face him, to find Cazz's jaw tight. He stepped forward, eyes blazing, like he was about to roar at me, and something inside me crumbled.

"What did you do to me?" I whispered.

He stopped short, his brows diving low. "What do you mean—
"

"When you claimed me… why did you do it? What did you gain? How did you steal my strength—why would you do that then just *leave me?!*"

All expression fell from Cazz's face. His eyes went flat. When he spoke it was through gritted teeth.

"Why are you crying?"

I gaped at him. He couldn't be serious? But then I realized, he was asking… he was asking a question and that meant I could answer it. And then it all came tumbling out.

"I thought when I came here you were different," I said, working desperately not to cry through the words. "I thought even if you were hard, even if you were arrogant, you *thought* differently. I thought our bond was different and that would make things different between us. I thought you would see *me* differently. But you don't.

"You're just like every other man who's ever been in my life: You're aggressive when you don't get your way, then possessive when I look for care from somewhere else. You reject me when it suits you, then act offended and needy when I take you at your word.

"Coming from anyone else I'm equipped for that. But you, Cazz? I have no defenses with you. You're my mate. I gave you my body. I fell in love with you. And now… now you won't even *look at me.* If I don't find something to do that is bigger than my hurt… you're going to break me."

Did I imagine the tiniest flinch? As if the words made him recoil?

His expression didn't change.

"I don't want to break you," he seethed. "I only expect you to give me my due as Alpha and King."

"You will always have your due from me, Cazz," I said sadly.

"But?" There was a warning in his words. I shook my head.

"But, nothing."

"Don't play games with me."

"I'm not." I wasn't. I didn't understand what had happened between us, but I couldn't control it. I loved him. He didn't deserve it. But it was true. And it left me… weak. My tears welled again and his upper lip peeled back from his teeth.

"God, you're just like the others. So fucking pathetic. So unflinchingly *wrong.*"

"Wrong? About *what?!*"

"I told you from the very first, but you didn't listen, did you?"

"What, Cazz? What didn't I listen to? What haven't I done?!"

But he drew his head back, eyes hooded, nose wrinkled like he smelled something bad. "Don't get your heart set, Jesse. It won't happen. I told you."

"What are you talking about?"

"I told you I will not love you. I told you you will have everything available to me to give, but love is not there, and you cannot expect it. You cannot fail me in that."

"I won't," I whispered, my heart sinking to my toes.

"You will if you walk into this with hope," he seethed, like I'd offended him. "There is no hope, do you understand?"

I nodded because I knew any other answer would send him into a rage, but something inside me screamed in pain. "I understand," I breathed, and started to turn my back so he wouldn't see my tears fall again.

But apparently my defeat angered him. He grabbed my elbow and whipped me around to face him, pulling me right up and leaning down into my face to snarl at me.

"I have been nothing but open and honest with you. But it clearly hasn't registered, so let's try again: You are my mate. You are my bitch. You will be the mother of my young. And you will receive everything you ever need or want in return. But you are not my princess. You are not my dream, and you most definitely are not—and will never be—my *love.* Do you understand?"

Even through the blur of tears, I felt the tension in him. Saw the shadows in his eyes. Felt the screaming fear and rage burning through the bond.

"Who hurt you?" I breathed. "Who convinced you that loving someone was weakness?"

"I SAID, *DO YOU UNDERSTAND?"* he roared so loudly I flinched. When I didn't immediately reply, he shook my arm. "Do you?!"

"Yes, Cazz. L-loud and clear."

"Say it." There was a definitive order in the words, him asserting his dominance and expecting me to respond. So I did.

"You'll never love me and I should never expect that," I whispered.

"And?"

"And... hope is only going to destroy me." *But you're going to destroy me anyway,* I added mentally.

He shoved air through his nose, but didn't let me go, and didn't move. We stood there for a long moment, staring at each other. I wished I knew what it meant when his eyes went dark.

Then he released me suddenly, like my skin burned him. He straightened, looming over me, glaring.

"Do you regret it?" he growled.

"Regret what?"

"Giving yourself to me."

God, I wanted to tell him yes. I wanted it to be true. I wanted to be *certain* he'd never love me because it would make all of this so much easier. But instead I swallowed and gave him the honesty he didn't deserve.

"No," I croaked.

His shoulders dropped a hair, but his blank expression didn't change. He shook his head as if I had disappointed him.

"You will."

68. Fury

~ *CASIMIR* ~

I stormed through the tunnels of the Palace, furious at her and furious at myself, and even more furious about *that* because I didn't understand it.

But one thing was becoming clear; I should never have claimed her. I should never have invoked the immutable bond. I should have known. I did know! But I'd been caught up, and the pack was descending and...

"Fucking fuck!" I muttered. One of the servants passing me squeaked and cowered.

I kept walking, muttering to myself, my mind closed like a steel trap so no one else could overhear it.

She is my mate. She is a breeder. She is Queen—but I do not *need her beyond that.*

So why had it been so hard to walk out of her chambers? Why had her tears cut me in a way no fang ever had?

Why, even now, did I *ache* to be closer to her—even though I knew the moment she was in front of me, I'd barely be able to stand the sight of her?

"Sire." The low, clipped tones of Ghere approaching from behind me were both a balm, and a burr under my skin.

The male would do anything he was told. His submission was always soothing. And yet... he said more with his eyes and posture than with his mouth, and his meaning was never unclear.

I kept up my pace and didn't turn. "What do you want, Ghere?"

"Only to find out if there is anything you need. The packmind is… alarmed."

I wanted to snap my teeth, but it would only serve to make Ghere sigh. We both knew he wasn't truly afraid of me.

"Bring Rake. My quarters. Now."

"Certainly, Sire."

I felt the question—I could link with Rake and call him myself. It would be faster. But I didn't care. And Ghere wouldn't openly challenge my decision, not unless he foresaw a threat or risk that I hadn't. So he peeled off down a different tunnel as I made a beeline for my chambers, my heels clicking on the stone floor and my teeth gritted so hard my jaw ached.

*****

By the time Rake arrived, I was pacing the floor, clawing hands through my hair and cursing.

"You took your time."

"I wasn't open to Ghere, it took him some time to find me. Perhaps if you would have linked with me I would have gotten here faster."

"It is entirely my perogative—"

"For God's sake, Cazz, save it for the Alphas. You don't need to dominate me. I am your servant." His tone rode the line between subservient and subversive.

I turned to look at him—glare at him—but he just met my gaze and waited.

I folded my arms. "What?"

His look went flat, like I'd disappointed him. "Admit it, Cazz, when you're struggling, you don't like to link. I get it. But you know it doesn't actually change anything, right?"

"What are you talking about?"

"The refusal to link. You're trying to avoid others knowing how you feel. But it doesn't change how you feel. You're still feeling it, whether others know it or not."

"Enough of the psychobabble—"

"Do you want me to help you, or just kneel and leave you in this state?"

I snarled at him, but Rake didn't even breathe faster. When there was crisis in the pack, his unflappability was something I loved about him. But when it was me in a fury, it drove me up the wall.

"Fine, say your piece," I spat at him. "Get it off your chest, then we'll move on."

He rolled his eyes, but we both knew he wasn't going to let up until he'd spoken his mind—and that was exactly why I'd vowed not to compel him.

He opened his hands towards me. "She's your mate. You claimed her. And now you're resisting her. Don't you realize that when you claimed her your souls...grafted?"

"Our souls were already tied by the bond and I didn't feel this—"

"That is a breakable link, and you know it—hell, you've snapped it yourself more than once. This is different, and you know that too. Stop fighting what you can't change."

"Which is?" I seethed.

"Have her. Take her. Comfort her. You will comfort yourself if you do. Stop keeping such distance. I'm not suggesting you have to be around her all the time. But stop avoiding her. What you give to her you are giving to yourself."

"That is such bullshit, I don't have time for—"

"No, Cazz. It's not. And until you accept it, you're just going to feel worse and worse. You rejecting her is like your body rejecting its own limb. You'll only destroy yourself."

"How would you know, you've never even bonded."

"God made the bonds, God speaks, I listen. That's my job. You can take my advice, or reject it. But it's true. And your response to it doesn't stop it being true."

I didn't feel like responding to that.

Rake sighed. "Fine. Whatever. You're only hurting yourself. There you go. I'm done."

He turned to leave, but then he stopped himself and turned back. "Actually, that's not the whole truth: The whole truth is that you're hurting her as well... but you're hurting yourself more."

I doubted that. "I'm not the one claiming love and weeping over *her.*"

"No. You're just walking around, ready to explode. Everyone is talking. They can feel your tension, even if they don't know where it came from. Mark my words, Cazz, if you don't do something about this, you'll start influencing the whole pack, bringing their mood down so they start snapping and biting at each other."

"They have nothing to do with my bond."

"They are linked to you as well, strengthened by you—and weakened if you're weakened."

"I am not weak!"

"Of course not, but they are. Weaker than you, anyway. The question is… could you be stronger? Are you denying yourself the very thing that would grow you? I say you are. But who am I? I'm just a lonely cleric. You're the mated, powerful King."

He met my gaze pointedly, then turned on his heel and walked out without looking back.

And I didn't stop him.

But that coiled pressure in my belly didn't ease.

69. The Boiling Pot

~ *JESSE* ~

The next morning I woke *feeling* pale. I didn't even have to look in the mirror, I knew what I would find, because it felt like my entire body was… less there. And when I forced myself to get up, it felt as if at any step the floor might fall out from under my feet.

I had barely slept, haunted by those images of Cazz, fierce and disapproving, *despising me.*

I had to scramble to push away the chittering fear at that thought, the desperate hurt, and make myself move. Make myself dress and brush my teeth, and be human. But my eyes ached with tiredness. I didn't want to eat.

Still, I forced myself to go to the dining room and consume something, because I had already learned that it didn't matter how tired I was, or what had happened, Maya would be merciless.

In fact, showing weakness only seemed to encourage her to push me harder.

So, I choked down food, then made my way to Maya's chambers, surprised to find not just Maya there, but a handful of other females that she introduced me to.

When we all stood in a circle after their introductions, their eyes on me, polite but skeptical, I turned to Maya, feeling shaky and nervous, like I was under scrutiny.

"What are we doing today?"

Maya smiled wickedly. "We're going to find out if you can link with the packmind when there are more minds nearby," she said, flashing a grin. "I know you're tired, Jesse, but it might work in your favor. Bring down your defenses. Let's get started and find out."

*****

Despite my tiredness, a couple hours later, I stalked the halls of the Palace, almost laughing with glee. I was panting a little, partly from the exertion because I had been walking so fast for over an hour, but also out of excitement, because it was working.

It turned out I *was* better at finding the link when there were more wolves present in a combined link. Maya had theorised that the greater numbers would strengthen my senses, and she was right.

It had taken her some time to explain the difference between a one-on-one link which was more like knocking on a single door and seeing if the other would open to you, and a group link. The closest analogy I had was an online group chat. There were several people who could invite me, and several ways I could access them. And for whatever reason, that made it easier.

While I wasn't yet able to actually read their thoughts, we soon discovered that with each of them open to me, I was able to sense them. And within minutes, I could discern the difference between their links as a group, and individually.

They were still formless to me—lumps of clay that had all been shoved together and didn't make anything yet. But the fact that I could sense them at all was a thrill.

Within an hour, Maya had sent them out, told them to hold the link open, but to scatter and hide. That I would spend the morning learning to hone in my senses by seeking each of them.

It sounded weird, but now that I had located three of the five of them, I was getting excited. It was getting easier and easier to sense them, and now they were growing excited that I was able to. It felt like we were in this together. A team sport. And I was enjoying myself.

Where are you? I sent along into that formless group chat. When I felt one of them trill with nerves nearby, I turned down the next hallway to the right, grinning.

The Queen is coming. She's almost there.

*****

~ *CASIMIR* ~

When I first sensed Jesse—opening herself to me and drawing closer—I thought she was coming to my office. Perhaps to cry, perhaps to seduce me. I had muttered to myself about not having time. But an hour passed, and though at times she drew closer, mostly she was pulling away.

I frowned over the papers I was reviewing on security recommendations from the scouts who patrolled the lands between us and the city.

As the weather warmed up, the humans were encroaching on our territory. It was usual for this time of year, but the scouts were under some concern that there were more than we'd seen in the past.

But just as I was digging into their speculations on why, there was a surge along the bond from my mate—she was thrilled. Delighted. *Excited.*

And it had nothing to do with me.

I found myself on my feet and prowling the halls before I even knew I'd left my chair. And I grew more and more confused as my mate wandered the Palace, up, down, and sideways.

What *was* she doing? And why was she experiencing flares of excitement?

Finally, as I drew close to the dining hall—empty at this time of day—and realized she was in there, I hurried my steps. She was moving a lot and I wanted to pin her down and ask her what was happening.

But as I strode into the wide space, I drew to a halt.

Jesse was there, but she wasn't alone.

She stood in the middle of a cluster of females, all around her age, all smiling and bouncing on their toes, like they were celebrating something.

One of them *hugged her.*

She turned, and in the split second before she saw me, she stole my breath—her eyes were sparkling, her cheeks pink, and she was *beaming.*

I took a step closer, drawn by the warmth and beauty of her, and the sense of joy brimming in her that I could feel through the bond. But in the same moment, she caught sight of me near the doors and her entire countenance fell.

All that bubbling warmth and thrill dissolved in a deluge of grief and fear.

She halted so suddenly, one of the others almost bumped her and had to catch themselves.

Why the hell did her face fall like that just because she'd seen *me?* Her reaction was so distinct, so *available* because she was open in the link, it angered me, and I growled as I started towards her.

And she shrank.

My mate.

Shrank away from me.
I wanted to snap my teeth!

70. Sure Footing

~ *CASIMIR* ~

"Where have you been?" I asked abruptly as the other wolves settled and stepped back to allow Jesse to greet me first as was our tradition. She was my mate. She had first right to my attentions. But she didn't seem to realize it was an honor they bestowed upon her and she blinked nervously, glancing at them over her shoulder before turning back to me.

"We were... playing hide and seek, I suppose. I'm learning to sense others. I was using a group link to find them."

My heart rose sharply—she was linking? I was stunned.

"You can access the packmind without an aid?"

She shrugged, but a hint of that light returned to her eyes. "Not yet, but I'm getting there."

I frowned. That made no sense. Could she link with them or not?

But the way she was keeping her head down and no longer meeting my eyes... it made me grit my teeth again. And here we were in public, under the eyes of several females who were watching me with various degrees of caution.

"Leave us," I snapped.

And to my utter shock, all five of them turned to look at Jesse before they moved.

I opened my mouth to warn them, but she hurriedly turned away from me to thank them, and told them to go, that she would be fine.

They moved immediately, hurrying to the door behind me. And they kept their eyes down, didn't challenge me, nodding to me as they passed, but still…

What the fuck was going on?

When the door closed behind the last of them, I whirled on her, furious. She was still standing there with her back to me and her head down, like she was scared to even look at me.

I growled. "Is this what you're doing all day—playing games with wolves who have better things to do? Is this why I'm not seeing you?"

Her shoulders tensed, but she shook her head. "No. You've known where I was, you could have come to me," she said simply.

She didn't turn around, which pissed me off because she had also closed herself to the bond—poorly, so that I would think I had a grip on her, what she was feeling, what she thought, then it would slip through my fingers like water.

I closed the space between us in a few short strides, putting myself at her back and leaning over her to keep her in submission—but the moment we were close, the heat from her skin drew me and my breath quickened.

Her skin was like a drug. I began to shake. And that made me even more angry.

"You haven't come to me since you bled." I snapped the word off with my teeth. "Perhaps the time has come for me to start looking elsewhere to feed my appetite? I did warn you that you might grow weary of it."

I felt her tense. Felt the trill of fear jolt through her. She still didn't turn, but she reached for the back of one of the chairs in front of her, gripping it so hard her knuckles turned white.

Seeing her tense like that washed me in relief—which also irritated me.

This woman was a storm of conflicting urges and I was not accustomed to feeling conflicted.

"Cazz… I tried to come to you, but you didn't want me near. You said that. So I've been waiting for you. And working. But… but I don't want you to go to others."

She wasn't good at blocking the bond. I felt the thread of fear twisting in her, and scented it on her skin. It was slightly thrilling.

I leaned in, hovering over her, inhaling her scent, and when I spoke, I let my breath flutter against her ear. "What do you want, then?"

She swallowed audibly. "I… I want you to play with me."

Those words landed like a blow, and it took me a moment to accommodate the rush that jolted through me, so I didn't respond immediately.

While I was still wrestling for my own control, I *felt* her heart sink and knew it was because she thought I would reject her.

That just made me more angry.

Cursing my own confusion and conflicting desires, I grabbed her hand and pulled her towards one of the doors on the short end of the dining hall, a storage room full of extra chairs and a few smaller tables.

The moment I got her into the shadows of it, I didn't turn on the light, even though she'd probably be close to blind in here, I could still see her clearly, and I proved it—grabbing her as she stumbled, hesitating on the threshold, and turning her, pushing her up against the wall.

And when she sank back against it, I clamped a hand to her throat—just gripping her, not applying pressure that would affect her breathing.

But she kept her eyes down, and though she couldn't see much, I could see her. I could see her fear—and her thrill.

My own desire flared, but that only made me angrier, because I didn't understand it. How could I want her and despise her in the same moment?

I leaned in, letting my harsh breathing imply that I was trying to whisper. "Stop," I rasped. "Just stop."

"Stop what?" she breathed.

"Stop... *drawing* me."

"I haven't—"

"You are weak, and desperate, and useless to me unless you bear young. Yet... no matter where I go, you burn at me. No matter what I do, I cannot be free of you. It makes me *rage*. What am I supposed to do with you?"

She licked her lips. "I told you... I'm your slave. Do whatever you want, Cazz." Then she set her jaw and looked me right in the eye.

Bitch.

A tidal wave of heat ripped through my belly and I gave a low, puttering growl.

"Are you certain, Jesse?" I purred. "Are you *sure?*"

Her eyes flashed. But rather than answer me with words, she lifted her hands and opened her palms, as if in surrender.

"I'm sure, Cazz."

And then she waited... with a challenge in her eyes.

The wolf inside me howled.

71. Stripped Back

~ *CASIMIR* ~

The flash in her eyes sent a zing of power and desire through me so shockingly potent, my breath shuddered.

I didn't break eye contact. I had one hand planted on the wall over her shoulder, the other gripping her throat. There was a fleeting urge to curl my fingers into her flesh and tear out her throat—a flash of threat and fear. But then she swallowed and I felt it under my hand.

With a low growl, I lifted the hand from her throat to trail a finger along her jaw, down the line of her elegant neck to her collarbone, then dipped my fingertips into the V between her breasts.

"And if I said strip… right here?" I rasped.

Jesse hesitated. Then to the delight of my wolf, she began unbuttoning the jeans she was wearing.

God, I wanted her. I could smell her desire rising, and it added fuel to the fire burning in my gut. But I didn't move, giving her no room, only dropped my eyes to watch her toe off her shoes, then unbutton her jeans, then shimmy them down, her breasts brushing my chest more than once until she was able to kick it all away.

She reached for the buttons at her chest under my fingers, but I hissed at her to stop.

She froze, fear flashing in her eyes, but I smiled and leaned down, letting my nose trail down her neck as I flicked the buttons of her shirt open, revealing her bra, then her stomach, until both sides of the shirt fell away, and she was open to my touch.

My breath was loud, harsh in the silent room, but I barely noticed as I trailed fingers down between her breasts, watching as her skin pebbled in the wake of my touch.

My cock was so hard I was worried the seams of my pants might injure me.

"Remove my pants. Now," I growled.

She fumbled at my leathers for a while, so slow and clumsy I almost snapped at her to let me do it. But just as my patience snapped, she got me free, and I sprang into her hands.

I sucked air through my teeth as she stroked me tentatively and dropped my forehead against her shoulder, watching her stroke me.

Dear *god,* this woman was a drug.

It had been weeks—the longest I'd gone without a female since I discovered sex—and my body was already thrumming.

Thrusting into her hands, I gritted my teeth against the orgasm rising so quickly I feared I might embarrass myself.

Lifting my head, I pumped one more time into her hands, then snarled at her. "Stop touching me."

She blinked and looked up at me uncertainly, but did as I asked, watching my face as I drank in the sight of her, cursing that she was still too lean—she hadn't been eating enough—but unable to stop devouring every inch of her skin with my eyes.

Both of us were panting, our breaths meeting and mingling, fluttering over our skins.

Then I felt her gather her courage and reach up to the neckline of her shirt and start to pull it off her shoulders to give me a better view.

I growled, catching her wrists and meeting her eyes to warn her not to fight me. Then I pulled her hands down to her sides, reached up for the sides of the shirt and drew it slowly down her arms.

She'd let her hands drop back so it would slide off, but I had a better idea.

Rubbing myself against her stomach as I pinned her to the wall, I tugged the bulk of the shirt back and down until the sleeves swathed her hands, then I reached down and gripped them, tying them, locking her hands behind her back.

Jesse blinked and gave an experimental tug at the shirt, but she couldn't get her hands loose.

I smiled.

She leaned back, shoulders against the wall, her hands bound at the small of her back, chest pushed up and out by the position of her arms.

Her breath was coming short and sharp. Fear mingled with need in her scent. And that made me smile more.

"Trust me," I growled as I lowered myself, kissing my way from her neck to her chest, curling my fingers under each of her bra straps, but only dropping them off her shoulders before I opened my mouth on the lacy center of her bra and bit through it.

Jesse sucked in and I looked up, caught her eyes wide and startled as I opened my teeth again and let the pieces of the bra fall aside, then slid the straps down her arms too, to hang off her tied wrists.

"Trust me," I growled again, then opened my mouth over one of those peaked nipples, groaning when her breast tightened and first one nipple, then the other when I switched sides, became a rivet under my tongue. I never broke eye contact, drinking in the sight of her skin beginning to flush, and the fascination in her eyes at watching me.

By the time I began kissing my way down her stomach, her breath was coming in short bursts, and she'd arched her back.

Then I dropped below her belly button and she tensed.

"Cazz, wait—"

But I'd already cupped a hand behind her knee and lifted it, hooking it over my shoulder as I crouched and slid my tongue against her.

"CAZZ!" she gasped, instinctively trying to grab for me, but her arms were caught in the shirt. I had to hold her, help her keep her balance for a moment—but I didn't stop licking, sucking, sliding... and moments later when she was no longer at risk of falling, she sighed and let her head sink back against the wall.

I knew the moment I entered her we'd begin the very short countdown to my own orgasm, so I took my time, curling a finger inside her as I slid my tongue against that nub over and over again, until her knees began to shake.

72. Once More

~ *CASIMIR* ~

"Cazz… *Cazz…*"

I was panting hard, fighting the urge to *bite* her, as she tensed and writhed, seeking my touch, my tongue, and the fleeting promise of her climax. But when she began pulsing around me, her breath stopping, I knew it was time, because I wasn't going to give her that satisfaction.

Not yet.

So, when she began to shake and her breath was catching and holding, I dropped her knee off my shoulder, but cupped her thighs as I stood, pulling her knees wide and high, hitching them over my hips as I straightened, lifting her, pressing her into that wall as I used both hands from the back to spread her as wide as possible and positioned her over me.

Her head had lolled forward as I lifted her, and she blinked her glazed eyes, confused by thwarted desire. "Cazz, what—"

I thrust to meet her at the same time I dropped her onto me, and we met with such force her heels dug into my ass and a cry was torn from her throat.

She tightened around me with such a grip I almost gave in and simply pounded us both to our climaxes. But I wasn't done torturing her. I kept her pressed into the wall so she couldn't move, could barely tilt her hips, and drummed into her, too fast, too shallow to bring her to climax immediately.

Then, the moment her head dropped back and her little cries grew higher as she promised to crest that wave again, I gritted my teeth and forced myself to pull out of her.

"Cazz, *no!*"

I gave a dark chuckle as I turned her, dropping her to the tabletop a couple feet to my left, then flipped her around and grasped the back of her neck to bend her over it.

She was gasping, squeaking with shock. But then I clawed that hand down her spine and she shivered. When I reached the hollow of her back, I gripped that knot of shirt that bound her hands at the top of her ass, and leaned on it, pinning her down on the table, then plunged into her again from behind.

She gave a moan as I entered her and tightened so beautifully around me I had to hold her there at the peak of my thrust for a moment while I regained control.

When she sucked in a breath and started to relax, thinking I wasn't going to move, I leaned over her and growled, *"Hold on, kitten."*

Then I began hammering into her so hard that the table thudded against the wall.

Jesse cried out, a guttural sound, torn from her with every thrust.

It was too fast, too much, but I hadn't had sex in over two weeks and my body would not be denied again.

With a desperate groan, I gripped her shoulder with my other hand and pulled her back against me with each thrust until she lifted her chin, and with a silent scream, clenched around me. And the feeling of her gripping me like a fist hit so hard, I exploded too.

My thrusts became erratic, but no weaker. And she was helpless under the onslaught. Unable to use her hands, and her toes no longer even brushing the ground because I had lifted her off her feet.

Once, and again, and again, my body shuddering, I dropped my face in her claiming mark and cupped a hand over her head, bellowing as the last wave of my orgasm crashed over me.

Something in my chest broke open like a dam giving way. And suddenly I was flooded with *her*—her joy, her relief, her pleasure, her *love.*

And as I pushed into her for the final time, nothing within me ever wanted to leave.

For a long, breathless moment, I stayed there, wallowing, driven into her, drinking her in, my heart sheltered and comforted and *fed.*

Then Jesse choked my name on a sob.

Panting, boneless, limbs heavy, but our bodies *united.* We collapsed together, every inch of me covering every inch of her and it was so right. So *necessary.*

I was shaking.

"Cazz…" she whispered. "Cazz, please… untie my hands. I want to touch you."

I blinked, my nose buried in her hair, my mouth open on her claiming marks, my tongue tasting the salt on her skin. When had I done that?

"Cazz, please… I want… I love you—"

Instinctively, I slammed the door closed on that bond, shrinking back, pulling from her and away, trembling from head to toe.

I'd pulled her up with me so she was taking her own weight on unsteady legs. With a curse, I tore into the knot on that shirt, clawing at it, snarling until finally it was free and I could turn away—the tails of my own shirt fluttering around me as I stuffed myself back into my leathers with shaking hands.

"Cazz—"

"Get dressed."

I could barely breathe. Couldn't think. Confusion, fear, anger, *need,* it was all there, a swirling, demanding mess in my head. And through it all, I could still sense her—I had slammed the door of the bond on her, but somehow, like a scent wafting through the cracks, I could sense her hope. And it made me rage.

She wouldn't listen!

I whirled around to bark at her, to remind her—but she'd just lifted her head from where she'd finished buttoning her shirt, and she was a vision—her hair messy from my hands, her skin flushed and eyes sparkling.

And she smiled.

I was raging and she *smiled?*

It stopped me in my tracks.

"We sh-should do this more often," she stammered breathlessly with a flash of promise in her eyes. Then she trotted past me to pick up her jeans and pull them on.

I stood there, stunned, as she didn't even bother with her shoes, but the moment her clothes were in place, swept them up from the floor, tucked them under her arm, and turned to practically run from the room leaving me standing there, alone and aching.

73. Hunt Me

~ JESSE ~

I stumbled out of that room in a blind panic.

For a moment there, I thought he'd given in. Surrendered. I'd had tears, it was so beautiful, so *thrilling* when he cupped his hand over my head and just held me. Those few seconds had touched a place within me his body could never reach. And I'd responded, unable to stop myself. I was *hungry* for him. Not just for his body, but for *him.* To be close. To be held. To be… together.

When he'd dived into the bond and held me so gently, I thought that was it. We were over whatever this barrier was between us.

Then, when I tried to talk to him, it was like he flipped a switch and the lights went out. He had shut down so completely for a second I thought the bond was severed.

And even after that, when there was only the barest hint—like seeing a shadow pass over the light coming through the crack under the door—I'd still had hope. Blessed, beautiful hope.

He'd almost rejected me. Almost sent me away. I could feel it in him—white-hot rage and determination to be done. He'd wanted away from me.

He had felt that singing in the bond, that rightness, and it *turned him away.*

I had pulled up my dignity like a pair of pants, strapped myself into my self-discipline, and made myself show him my smile.

Because the smile was real. It was the joy I felt when he was open to me. When he wanted me. When he wasn't holding back.

But even though it wasn't a lie, it felt like giving a gift to an animal that would stomp it into the dirt.

So I smiled, then I left. At pace.

And he watched me leave like I might be insane.

As I hurried out of the dining room and down the tunnel towards the royal quarters, heedless of servants or others watching, knowing they could probably smell what I'd been doing, but unable to even let myself think about it, I did my best to keep my face blank so they wouldn't start any rumors. But I could barely breathe. I was fighting so hard not to cry. Not to lose control. Not to let anyone see what had happened, but knowing it must be painted all over my face. I could just hear them, whispering to each other through the link...

The Queen loves the King, but he doesn't love her back.

In fact, it appears that he loathes her.

In my mind, I could hear the way they would laugh. I choked on a sob, swallowed it back, and leaped into a run.

When I made it to the mezzanine where my rooms were, my throat pinched harder, but relief washed through me. I'd get into my rooms, bar the door, and then bury my face in the pillow and pray no one passed close enough to the doors to hear me cry. Because I was going to cry. I could feel the grief and sense of injustice like a weight on my chest. I was—

I rounded the last corner before my room and for a moment I thought I had turned too fast and run straight into the wall.

I went face-first into something tall and hard. It wasn't until I was bouncing on my ass, my shoes spilling across the floor, that I realized I had run into a male body.

I cried out with the pain of landing on my tailbone, and looked up, ready to break, when I realized I was staring into the shocked face of Rake.

"Jesse! What—I'm so sorry! I didn't know you were... are you hurt?"

I gaped at him, speechless, in pain both in my body and my heart and... and I broke.

A terrible sound erupted from my throat—a cry of pure anguish.

Rake's eyes flew wide, then he darted down to reach for me.

"Don't cry. Don't cry. Oh sweet girl, don't cry—don't let them see," he whispered, hooking my arm around his neck and lifting me to my feet. But I was so hurt, so dead, so scared, I could barely see.

After a few seconds of stumbling together, he muttered something, then swept me up, off my feet, cradling me to his chest and practically running with me the last few feet to my doors. He pushed them open with his back, and stepped inside, kicking the doors closed, then hurrying me to the first chair to set me down.

"What happened? Did he injure you? Where? How—Jesse, talk to me!" he hissed, sitting me down, but scanning me from head to toe, growling about my clothing because it stopped him seeing whatever he thought he might find.

I tried to swallow the next sob, but it hurt going down and then I cried harder. "N-no, no," I choked out. "He didn't h-hurt me. N-not like that. But he was… he was w-wonderful and then… God, Rake… I thought we b-broke through. I thought… but I was wrong. I could feel him… he h-hates me. Rake, he fucking *hates me.*"

Rake looked alarmed, but when I curled forward, hugging myself, he muttered something else, then wrapped me in his arms, holding my face to his chest, stroking my back and hair and shushing me over and over.

But I couldn't do it. I couldn't be strong. I couldn't pretend Cazz hadn't *eviscerated* me back there. I crumpled forward to the floor, landing on all fours, hands clawing into the carpet.

"Jesse!"

"Why?" I sobbed. "Why does it hurt like this?" I rasped. "Why c-can't I defend myself against him? Why can't I be s-strong?" Rake knelt in front of me and I lifted my tearstained face to meet his eyes, even though mine were blurred with tears. "He doesn't w-want me, so why d-did he take me? Why can't I just let him g-go? Why do I feel like I'll d-die if he doesn't want me anymore? *What did he do to me?* Did he make me like this? Has he *compelled* me?"

Rake's face crumpled and he dropped to his knees, gathering me up again and carrying me to the couch. I didn't fight him. Didn't help him. I just lay in his arms until he sat down and let my ass slide to the couch as well. He'd placed me with the couch arm behind my back, but I just curled into a ball like a child.

I wasn't really aware of the passage of time. I wasn't even really sure where I was for a time. I was trying so hard to push the pain away, to get control of my body that wanted nothing except to sink into the floor and disappear. But eventually… eventually the wracking sobs that made my back ache stopped. They turned to small hitches and hiccups. Then even that stopped and I was only breathing deeply.

And then… at some point, I was just sitting there, my face buried in my knees, and I was breathing.

But a part of me wished I wasn't.

That was the scariest part of all.

74. Find Your Feet

~ JESSE ~

When I finally found the strength to raise my eyes and sit up, my legs were over Rake's thighs where he sat with one of his thick arms on the back of the couch, the other elbow leaning on the couch arm behind me, and his face... his face was a picture of worried grief.

I didn't realize his hand was on my back until he moved it, catching my hair in his fingers and pulling it back over my shoulder as he sighed.

"I'm so sorry, Jesse."

"Wh-what for?" I inhaled deeply, still trying to get control.

"Because I saw this coming and didn't stop it. I should have stopped it. I should have stepped in when he wanted to marry you and... I should have stopped it," he repeated dumbly.

I frowned and made myself sit up and look right at him.

My whole body felt weak. Deflated. Limp, with no strength to even move.

But this man... this good, godly man, was staring at me like he was the one who'd hurt me—and like he'd do anything to change it.

"Don't you dare take responsibility for what *he* did," I mumbled through numb lips.

"Oh, I don't," Rake said darkly. "I just... I wish I could change it. You aren't the first he's hurt this way and I wish... I wish I didn't stand by and let it happen."

I put a hand to his shoulder and stared right at him. "You've done more for me than any single other person—or wolf—here.

Rake please... don't apologize. And just... just don't leave me, okay?"

He sighed, but nodded, rubbing his hand up and down my spine the way a teacher at school had done once when I'd been sick and was waiting for my dad to come pick me up.

We stared at each other a second and I was just so grateful to him.

Then he curled me into his chest and hugged me. Nothing more. Just wrapped his arms around me and held me, and whispered that it was going to be okay. And that I didn't have to do it alone.

A vindictive, petty part of me wished suddenly that Cazz would walk in and see this—and kill us both, so I could be free.

But I knew that wasn't the answer.

So when Rake sat back and rubbed his eyes, then leaned his head on his fist, I tried to make myself calm.

"Tell me what happened," he said quietly, an edge of something in his voice like he was a little bit afraid of the answer.

I opened my mouth to tell him, but then I sighed. "Is there any point talking about it?"

"I think so. I think it might help if you just get it out."

I frowned and leaned my arms on my knees, then rested my chin on my arms.

Would it help?

There was only one way to find out.

"Well, I'm guessing you already know that he... that we..."

"Yes, I know."

I shrugged, so completely exhausted I couldn't even muster up embarrassment. "So, he wants my body. But he doesn't want *me*. Every time he takes me it rips my heart out because I give him everything, and it seems like he's drawing closer—giving himself. Then... then he closes the door. Every time. Slams it shut. Doesn't want to be close to me. So I'm just left there alone. It's like... it's like he shows me the sun, then hides it from me and says I can't ever have it back."

My tears wanted to return. My throat was closing and my eyes were stinging.

"Rake... he's going to break me."

"No, he's not."

The simple conviction in his voice made my breath stop. I blinked back the tears and looked up at him. I couldn't even speak.

He held my gaze. "No, Jesse, he's not," he said firmly. "Because you aren't alone in this. And God didn't put you here to

308

get you broken. You know that. I know that. So... it hurts. And I wish it didn't. I wish I could take that part away—or that Cazz would. But regardless... you aren't going to be broken. You're going to win this. You're going to win *him*."

"What if I can't?"

Rake stared at me very, very worried.

"Don't let him, Jess. I've seen him... don't let it happen."

"I don't have any choice! I keep giving myself. I keep telling him I'm here. I keep submitting. He's just... he pulls away every time—and it's not just a simple shrug and he's indifferent. He's *cold*. He's *angry*. He's mad at himself for even getting close to me."

Rake gathered me close again when my face crumpled. I swallowed the tears back and made myself keep breathing, but I was so damn tired. I slumped against his shoulder and just closed my eyes.

It wasn't fair. None of this was fair—on any of us. But most especially Rake who wasn't even in this relationship.

God, I was so pathetic! Maya was going to disown me if she heard about this.

I sighed and slumped and let myself drift towards the darkness that was beckoning...

...then woke at some point to Rake's urgent whispers as he slid out from under me and got to his feet.

"...have to wake up and clean your cheeks, Jess. He's coming."

"He... what?"

"Cazz is coming."

I leaped up from the couch, suddenly convinced I had to flee, but I was still blinking back sleep. Rake caught my shoulders and held me at arm's length, saying my name and waiting until I focused on him.

"You're going to get through this. And he's going to realize how lucky he is to have you. You can do this, Jess. I know you can. You're strong. And he does want you. The day will come when he's not scared anymore, and he'll give himself back to you. Until then... don't let him tear you down like this," he said fiercely, squeezing my shoulders. "Don't give him an inch. Just stand your ground. Give your love, but don't accept his abuse. Let him see you, but don't let him tear you down. You can do this."

I nodded, but inside I was terrified.

Rake straightened as, behind him, the door creaked. He nudged me under the chin with one finger in a very brotherly gesture as Cazz strode in, then stopped dead, staring at me, his face blank.

I just looked at him, didn't say anything.

Cazz turned his head towards Rake slowly, his eyes only slipping from me when he was already on quarter profile. "Thank you for warning me, brother," he said quietly, tonelessly. "You're released. But on the way, can you tell the others we won't be at dinner?"

"Sure." Rake nodded to him once. I saw the tightness in his jaw as he headed for the door, but Cazz was already turning back to me, staring at me like I was a puzzle to solve.

I was standing there, wondering what his first word would be. Wondering how I would respond—imagining everything from shrieking rage, to desperate pleas.

But then Rake disappeared and the door closed and Cazz just sighed. I wanted to squirm. I knew my face would be blotchy, and my eyes puffy. They always were after I cried. And how long had I slept on Rake's shoulder?

But I waited for him to speak first, to see what tone he would set. And then I was surprised. Because Cazz stepped towards me, took one of my hands, then started leading me towards the bathing room.

"Let's get you cleaned up," he said quietly.

And like the pathetic, desperate creature that I was, I let him.

75. Wash it Away – Part 1

~ CASIMIR ~

I was numb as I led her into the bathing room, my head spinning, but none of it touching me.

When she had left me back in the dining room I had felt relieved. But as the hours passed in the wake of her strange farewell, my uneasiness grew. Something wasn't right, and I wasn't sure what it was. The bond was dead—I kept it that way.

I was considering going to look for her, assuming she'd be in her chambers, or with Maya, but before I could make the decision—because in truth, I didn't know what I was going to say if I did find her—Rake scratched at my mind.

'What is it?' I growled.

He didn't even speak, just sent me an image of her curled over her own knees, her face buried… and a feeling of great grief.

Damn.

'Your mate needs you.'

'Has something happened?'

It took a moment before he answered. I got the impression of a breathless hesitation on his part. Then, *'Yes, Cazz. You happened. If you really want to keep this one, if you really want her to be able to breed, you need to find a way forward. Together. You don't have to love her, Cazz, but for God's sake, don't be* cruel.*'*

That niggle started again at the back of my neck, like water dripping. Slowy, steady, unwavering.

I'd spent the short minutes walking to her rooms telling myself that this was little more than an irritation. The sacrifice a male had to make to have a female. By the time I was pushing open her door I had resolved to be firm but kind, to make the boundaries between us clear—then seduce her so she knew I wasn't rejecting her.

But the scent of her… it hit me the moment I stepped through that door. The hint of our mating earlier overwhelmed by a thick, pungent grief. It was the scent of a dying animal, and it was utterly alarming.

It froze me in place.

And when she looked at me, fear flickering in her eyes like a kicked puppy just waiting for the next blow to land… God, I felt about two inches tall.

"Let's get you cleaned up," I said gruffly, taking her hand and leading her towards the bathing room, praying she wouldn't resist, and sighing with relief when she didn't.

I didn't know how to reassure a female when she was heartbroken. I didn't know how to mend a soul. But I knew how to take care of others. How to provide.

I knew how to make the path straight.

And the first thing she needed was to get rid of that stench.

When we stepped into the wide bathing room, I let go of her hand and she stopped right there, in the center of the floor. Uncertain what else to do, I turned on the faucets first to get the bath filling. Then I went to the cupboard and pulled out three or four thick towels, stacking them on a chair next to the bath.

Then I took hold of my balls and turned to face her.

She was just standing there. At first glance, she was utterly dejected. And even as my chest panged, there was a flare of anger within me too. But then, as I was about to growl at her to find her spine, I saw her hands.

She had both arms loose at her sides. But her hands were clenched to fists so tightly her knuckles were white.

There was a flash in my head of her gripping that chair earlier, of her telling me how she wanted me, and my cock twitched. But I pushed those thoughts away and made myself take a deep breath before I walked back to her and began to unbutton her shirt, sliding it off her shoulders and folding it, then tossing it next to the sink before turning back to her, intending to repeat the process with her pants.

But she was standing there, her bra straps still hooked over each shoulder, the pieces dangling to either side of her breasts

312

because I'd bitten through it earlier and something about that... something about that was as erotic as it was sickening.

I tried not to let her see any emotion on my face as I reached for those scraps, tugging them off her arms and letting them fall from my fingers before starting on her jeans.

I knelt in front of her to draw the thick denim down her legs and urged her to brace on my shoulders as she lifted each foot so I could draw them off.

Then she was naked and glorious in front of me and I had to decide what I was going to do with her.

In the end I took her fingers again and straightened, holding her hand while she stepped awkwardly into the bath, then urging her to sit while I undressed.

"You're getting in?" she asked, and her voice was hoarse. Husky.

I swallowed back a surge of need and nodded.

She frowned, but didn't argue, just lowered herself into the hot water, then drew her knees up and hugged them to her chest, staring at the water as the faucets continued to run.

Something about that posture felt very frightening. So I hurried to undress, made certain the tray across the end of the bath held soap and shampoo, then slipped into the back with her, sitting behind her so we didn't have to make eye contact, extending my legs past her and bracketing her with my knees.

Then I picked up the soap, a soft rag, and began to wash her.

I took my time, lathering my hands and running them over her skin, trying to ignore the call of her flesh, and how pink all of it became in the steamy heat of the bath. I dipped the cloth in the water again and again, squeezing it over her shoulders and arms to rinse the suds from her skin, then gently tugging at her shoulders to urge her to sit back against my chest so I could wash the rest of her.

76. Wash it Away – Part 2

~ *CASIMIR* ~

Jesse tensed at first, but slowly opened up, resting her forearms on my thighs and watching as I lathered, and rubbed, then used the cloth all over her.

"Scoot forward," I whispered. I meant it to sound stronger, but my voice was gone. Little more than a hoarse rasp. I cleared my throat and tried again. "Put more room between us so I can wash your hair."

She went very still. "You're going to… wash my hair?"

I grunted.

She did as I had asked and scooted her ass forward.

"Hold onto the sides and use my legs to lay back, tip your head back, so I can get water over it without getting it in your eyes."

There was a moment I thought she would refuse. She didn't move. But just as I was opening my mouth, she lifted her hands from my knees and gripped the sides of the bath, pulling herself even more forward. When I propped my knees up behind her, she leaned toward me, bending her neck back in the cradle of my knees and pulling her hair out to let it fall over my thighs and into the water.

As her face tipped back towards me I was relieved when her eyes were closed.

Once she was leaning back, chin tipped right up, I took the length of her hair, gripping it like a rope and twisting it once around my fist. Then I pulled it back into the water, and used my other hand to cup water up and pour it over her scalp, until all of it was saturated.

It was a strange intimacy to run my fingers through her hair, scrape nails on her scalp, and watch the thick strands begin to curl, then tendril out over my groin and thighs, rippling in the tide of my movement like the most beautiful, copper-colored seaweed.

I kept working the shampoo into her scalp and down the lengths of her hair. Then I rinsed it again and again, until the strands squeaked between my fingers.

Reluctantly, I put the soap and cloth aside and nudged her shoulder. "Sit up," I murmured.

Her eyes flew open and she rolled up to sit without a word, curling back over her knees again and not looking at me, her wet hair now a dark net that lay slick against her neck and back.

For a moment I just sat there, watching her. But it was clear she wasn't going to move or speak until I did. And I supposed I owed her that much.

So with a heavy sigh, I opened my knees again and reached forward to gather her in, sliding her back towards me.

She startled when I first pulled her, the water sloshing up the sides of the bath and against my stomach and legs, and her as well.

When I had her ass pressed right up in the V of my thighs and the water was no longer rippling against us, I pawed at her hair, pulling it away from her neck and face and back over her shoulder. Then I leaned in.

When she felt my breath on her shoulder she tensed.

I brushed my lips on the top of her shoulder, watching her profile, waiting to see how she would react.

When she didn't protest, I kissed my way along her shoulder, then up her neck-softly, just brushing lips and breathing against her wet skin.

She still hadn't moved.

"Jesse?"

"Yes?"

"Do you still want me?"

It wasn't the question I had intended to ask. Not in such broad terms. But it had just come out.

Her breath rushed out of her in a whoosh and her chin dropped.

"Yes, Cazz. That's the problem. I always want you." Her voice was cracked and hushed, tormented.

But all I could feel was relief. *Thank God.*

Suddenly overcome with a zinging need, I slid my hands up her sides then to her stomach, bringing them up to cup her breasts as I kissed her neck, harder this time. Open mouthed, laving my tongue on the sensitive skin.

Jesse gave a tortured little sigh, then let her head sink back and aside to give me more room and her back arched to press her breasts into my touch.

"I want you too, Jesse," I breathed.

Her breath caught and she bit her lip, her eyes still screwed tightly shut. Her expression was a strange mix of sadness and elation.

Then I lifted a hand to cup her chin, turning her towards me and taking her mouth in a deep, demanding kiss.

Her nails clawed into my thighs. She gripped me for traction to keep herself turned into the kiss. And by the time we broke it, I was hard against her back.

"Jesse—"

"Yes," she gasped.

I grunted, putting my hands to her waist and lifting her, the water tinkling and splashing as I straightened my legs under her and held her up until she got her legs over mine, straddling my thighs.

My breath was already getting heavier—a result of abstaining for so long, now I couldn't get enough of her. I wanted to curl my fist in her hair again and bend her backwards, take her with mouth and hands and dick all at the same time. But it would be too much. I would be giving too much.

So, I planted a hand between her shoulder blades and pushed, growling at her to bend forward.

Her little hands dropped to my knees, clamping there to brace as she tipped forward. And the moment her knees came back, I gripped her hips and pulled her back onto me.

She sobbed as I took her.

I cursed.

77. Wash it Away – Part 3

~ *CASIMIR* ~

The combined pleasures of her enveloping my body as the water washed against my skin, the ripple and splash under her soft cries, and the sigh of her pink skin in the haze of the steam all conspired to steal my wits.

Then she dropped her head and her hair parted, revealing the claiming scars, puckered and pink on the other shoulder and a jolt of need crackled through me.

But I had a grip on myself this time. I had prepared for this. I knew what to do.

Jesse and I were bonded, it was true. Claiming her had tied us together. We needed each other. It couldn't be denied.

But love? Love was no part of that. It would only complicate things and create tensions that didn't need to exist.

As I began to ease in and out of her slowly, letting her feel me enter each time, as she began to tremble and her skin pebbled with the pleasure I drew from her, my mind was finally clear.

This… this was what we needed. Pleasure. Joy. Thrill. Time away from other wolves. And safety.

That was key, I realized.

Jesse had come to me for safety, certainty that I would give her a family, and provide for them. Keep her from harm's way.

In return, I had asked for her body, and her submission.

Until now I had been fighting the bond, but now it was clear that I couldn't anymore. Not if I wanted her to survive.

I soothed myself with reminders that the bond made our union more likely to result in offspring. It helped me know where she was at all times, and thus fulfill *her* primary need for safety. And it also allowed a unique measure of pleasure when we joined like this.

I experimented, opening to the bond just a hairsbreadth, like eyes barely opened.

But even in that small measure, power surged in my veins as Jesse came alive. She tipped back her head and gasped my name.

I gripped her hips so tightly, my fingers dug into her flesh, and she goosebumped down her thighs and arched her back, grinding onto me.

Teeth gritted against the urge to come, I pulled out of her again, then plunged back in, pulling her back onto me with a deep, guttural groan that she echoed.

The water splashed, splattering over the floor, but neither of us cared.

I was determined to savor her this time. So I leaned back against the end of the tub and watched her ride me, her ass bouncing as I thrust harder and harder, her fingers digging into my knees.

Her panting grew short and rough, but she was only tensing on me. Not ready to come. So I sat up higher, reached around to find where she was spread wide over my thighs and slid two fingers against her, all the way down to where we joined, then back up.

She shuddered and threw her head back, mouth open and shoulders tensing as she tried desperately to ride me and my fingers at the same time.

I played and tested, teased, and grew hotter with every thrust, because she was losing all control.

And as her cries grew higher and thinner, more frantic, it struck me: She'd never done this before. Any of it. No other male had ever had her sweating and gasping like this, no other male had seen that particular shade of her skin when she flushed with an impending climax.

Probably, no other male had ever heard her beg.

"Please, Cazz... don't stop. *Please.*"

Leaning forward so her back brushed my chest and all the nerve endings on my torso lit up with delight, I rewarded her with quick rubs and teases as I picked up the pace of my thrusts.

"Oh, *Cazz...*"

She leaned back, reaching her arms behind her to find me, buried her hands in my hair and held me to her. For a moment we were one, hitching and climbing together. I flattened my finger against her, rubbing and sliding so she rode my hand as well as my cock.

Then finally, perfectly, she was clenching around me, calling out wordlessly, gasping her pleasure as her world exploded in light and heat, and the pulsing of her drew me right to the edge of my own cliff.

Time slowed as I hovered there in a surreal half-reality of pleasure and dissociation. Then I opened my mouth on her shoulder and bit down—not hard enough to break the skin, but to hold her to me as I finally launched into the freefall of my own orgasm and we were shaking and tumbling together.

And deep inside me, something screamed—something falling off that cliff, arms pinwheeling, legs peddling, with nothing left to hold.

Something plummeting to its death.

Something I could ill afford to lose.

But my body was in the throes.

Jesse was relaxing, panting, gulping at the air, trying to find her bearings again. My orgasm sucked away slowly, leaving me blinking and gasping. Then we were there...

She hunched forward, hands still gripping my knees, her shoulders rising and falling as she tried to find her breath.

I had collapsed over her, one hand still between her legs, the other gripping her breast, my mouth over the claiming marks.

Letting go of her seemed... impossible.

But there was no choice.

I lifted my hand from between her thighs first, water tinkling as I raised it and lay it flat on her back. Then, with a final, parting stroke of her nipple, I made myself let go of her breast and wrapped the arm around her stomach, helping her hold her weight, because her arms were shaking.

Then finally, I lifted my mouth from her skin, glad that there was no blood. I brushed a kiss to that bend between her neck and shoulder, and she shivered.

Then I sat back against the tub and pulled her back so she lay on my chest.

She tensed at first, but relaxed quickly when I urged her to lay her head on my shoulder and just be there.

Neither of us spoke.

The tendrils of steam rose in lazy curls around us. I wondered if she watched them like I was.

Then suddenly, her fingers landed on my arm that still rested across her stomach. She slid her hand over my wrist, then down the back of my hand until her fingers slipped between mine.

I almost didn't allow it. But that aching, hollow gap in my center, that piece of me that had died, it needed the contact.

So, when her fingers slipped between mine, I gripped them.

But I didn't speak.

And neither did she.

78. Take it Like a Man

~ JESSE ~

The next morning I lay in the meadow just beyond the cave entrance, in the grass, watching the clouds drift lazily overhead. It was bright, but the sun wasn't quite hot enough to remove the chill from the breeze.

Kind of like Cazz's desire, I thought dryly. *Plenty of blaze, but it doesn't quite beat back the shadows.*

When I had woken this morning—alone—it was to a messenger sent by Maya saying that she had to undertake healer duties and we would have to wait until the following day to meet, so I'd suddenly found myself with freetime.

After the day—and night—before, I decided that was a sign. I was still fortifying the chinks in my armor after the roller coaster with Cazz.

As they had every few minutes since I woke up, my thoughts turned to memories of the night before and that familiar tug of war began in my chest—so I pushed those thoughts away.

I wasn't here to wallow. Wallowing was weak. I was here to plan.

Yesterday I had almost let him break me. And when I'd woken this morning and found Cazz's side of the bed cold, my heart had immediately plummeted. Just as I had many mornings since the Claiming, I spent a few seconds resisting the urge to cry, then...

Then I was so disgusted with myself, I groaned at my own pathetic heart.

"Get it together, Jesse!" I hissed. And I heard my father's voice echoing back from my past...

You need to learn to take life like a man.

And that's when it hit me that I had been here before.

I had spent my entire childhood desperately trying to be the daughter my father could love. And it had almost killed me. Until I was fifteen, and there was a day I woke up with this same ache in my chest: The burning injustice and shame of unrequited love.

And back on that day it had become clear to me that I only had two choices: To keep trying to make my father be something he wasn't, or to accept that he would never love me the way I wanted him to.

That day I sat up in bed and made myself take a good, hard look in the mirror. And within hours I started living differently.

I started living *free.*

Then this morning, as that familiar wash of shame and pain saturated me, I had blinked and realized that without intending to, I had turned my back on my father and his narcissistic bullshit, only to put myself in the hands of a man so controlling and emotionally stunted that it might have been better if he was a narcissist. Because then I wouldn't have fallen for him.

But I had. Damn me, I had.

And so, years after I found freedom from the grip of my father's assholery by facing the fact that he would never *truly* love me, I was right back in that boat, yearning for the love of a man who wasn't capable of it.

I had been fifteen when I refused to let my father break me. So why, now, as a grown ass woman, was I giving Cazz that power?

The answer was, I wouldn't.

At least…that was the plan.

I sighed and brushed my hair back off my face, squinting into the blue sky.

With a free day on my hands, and a chest that was desperate to breathe, I had set myself the first challenge of finding my way to the surface without help.

It had taken twice as long as it should have. I had taken wrong turns three times. But I made it. And that small victory had buoyed my fragile heart.

The breeze blew up, fluttering my hair along with the grass around me. And even though it was cold, I sat up, hugging my knees, to let it play on my face.

Breathing deeply and slowly, I made myself focus and stop putting off the inevitable.

I had to accept that Cazz, for whatever reason, was never going to love me.

He would want me. He'd probably protect me. He'd definitely use me.

But he wasn't going to love me. And if I kept moping around in these tunnels waiting for him to start, I was only fooling myself.

I hated to admit it, but he had been right the night before when he told me he'd been honest and he'd warned me that he wouldn't love me. He had been angry and I thought he was an asshole. But he had been right.

So now I was at that crossroads again. I could continue to sit around crying and aching for something that would never be. Or I could accept my life the way it really was, and move forward.

Forward to what, though? that small, frightened voice in the back of my head whispered.

And that was the rub. Because I knew... I knew that being with Maya and learning the wolves wasn't enough. Because it would still be there, lingering in the back of my heart.

It wasn't like I could separate myself from him. Not really. He was going to continue to seek me out and try to impregnate me. If I tried to resist him, he'd just compel me.

I had avoided his power because I knew I'd truly lose myself if he did that.

But was it any better to lose myself and my strength to loving him?

At least the compulsion would steal my wits as well, so I didn't *know* how desperate I was.

I sighed heavily and ran a hand through my hair.

This was a time for being honest with myself. For meeting the world as it really was and figuring out the best way through it.

I rolled my shoulders back and looked out to the forest below.

"I am a grown woman. I didn't bow to my father's toxic bullshit, and I wont bow to Cazz's fucked up head, either," I reminded myself.

If I was completely honest, I wasn't going to let him compel me. And I would keep letting him touch me. So my body was going to keep singing every time he was close.

I needed to find a way to let myself enjoy that part of him, without losing myself in the rest.

What I needed was a purpose beyond Cazz. Something bigger than him. Something that I could throw myself into with all my heart and know I would see others respond. Something rewarding and thrilling, and—

"What the hell are you doing out here by yourself?"

79. Start Thinking

~ JESSE ~

I startled and whirled around to find Rake hurrying towards me, his face thunderous.

Before I could respond, he was at my side, glaring down at me. "How did you even find your way out?"

I blinked up at him, surprised by his anger. And a little irritated, too.

"What are you worried about?" I muttered. "You said yourself, Cazz won't care what I do as long as he gets his puppies."

"Safely, Jesse. As long as you do it *safely.* And trust me, there is no way on God's green earth that Cazz thinks his Queen being out here alone, where anyone could find her is safe."

"Cazz does not see me as his Queen," I muttered.

"What the hell has gotten into you, Jesse? I know yesterday was rough, but seriously? Running away? Hiding? I've been looking for you for an hour—I almost called the guard. I almost told *Cazz."*

"Oh, shit," I breathed. I hadn't even thought about if someone else looked for me, and that they might tell Cazz I was missing.

Rake nodded, his expression like I was an idiot. "Are you just trying to put yourself in harm's way?"

That pissed me off. "Of course not! I just wanted to be alone."

"The Queen of the wolves doesn't go out of the tunnels *alone.* Do you have any idea what Cazz would do to you if he knew? What he'd do to *me,* who is supposed to watch you for him?"

I shifted my seat, but shook my head. "I didn't think he would care."

"Of course he'd care! Our people cannot lose another Queen, Jesse!"

Something about that statement rang in my chest like a gong, but I was exhausted and sick of being spoken to like a child.

"They won't!" I snapped. "I came out here specifically to make certain of it."

Rake's eyebrows dove to pinch over his nose. "What do you mean?"

I rolled my eyes. "I meant I'm not trying to kill myself—or get myself killed. I just needed space and light to think."

"Then call for me and I'll bring you up here. Or call for some females if that's what you want, but you don't just *leave.*"

"I didn't leave! I went for a walk. Alone. To think."

"The Queen doesn't walk alone. And if she needs to think, she does it under guard!"

"Oh for fuck's sake! Let it go, Rake. I'm here and I'm fine. And the only attackers who ever took an interest in me were wolves!"

"Well, wake up, Jesse. You aren't just a poor girl from a rough side of town anymore. You are Queen. You have responsibilities. And first and foremost among them is—"

"Helping the King get his rocks off?"

"—staying alive for your people so they can stop worrying about a future where our bloodline loses power because there are no royal offspring!"

I pushed to my feet, furious. "I expect that bullshit from Cazz, but not from you, so back off! I am more than a fucking *womb!*"

"But that's exactly my point! You are more, Jesse. So much more. You're Queen for a start! Stop acting like you're nothing but Cazz's sex toy!"

I didn't even think. I slapped his face.

The crack rang out over the trees at the other end of the meadow where a couple small birds startled and took wing.

In contrast, Rake had gone utterly still, staring at me, eyes wide. I glared back, clenching my stinging hand into a fist, because I wasn't backing down.

"Don't *ever* refer to... or imply... don't ever, Rake. He already treats me like that. Don't you do it too."

Rake cleared his throat and rolled his jaw a little. "Jesse... I would never... I didn't mean that I saw you that way. I was..." he gave a low, dry chuckle. "I thought I needed to stop you looking that way at yourself."

I opened my mouth, but he raised his hands in defense, and spoke faster. "I was wrong. I can see I was wrong. I'm sorry. Don't kill me for the offense, Sire. Forgive me. I won't ever speak those words again. I swear it."

His lips quirked up on one side as I watched him warily. But he kept his hands up in surrender, so I blew out a breath and waved him off.

"Don't call me Sire, either," I muttered.

"But you are, Jesse. You are Queen. And one of these days you need to let them *all* see the woman who doesn't back down from a fight. Trust me. They'll love it."

And then it hit me as shockingly as if Rake had slapped me back. My jaw dropped. But Rake didn't notice. He kept talking, keeping his eyes down and his posture submissive.

"...just glad it was me who found you and not Cazz, or one of his servants—"

"Rake... that's it," I breathed.

He frowned. "What is what?"

"Queen, Rake. I'm *Queen*. The people need a Queen. And that's me!"

He looked a little bemused, but he nodded. "I thought we established that a while ago. Are you just now—"

I hissed at him. "No, you don't understand. I came up here today to get my head straight. To make a plan. To determine my purpose."

Rake frowned again. "But you already have a purpose. It's Cazz... right?"

I turned away from him, pacing, my head spinning. "Yes, yes, but this is.. this is more than that."

"More than Cazz?"

"Yes!"

Rake looked truly confused. "Jesse, I'm not sure—"

"Cazz is never going to love me, Rake. I've accepted that."

"But... you can't *leave*—"

"I'm not going to. I'm going to do the opposite."

Rake scratched the back of his neck, his expression dubious. "You're going to... stay?"

"Not just stay, Rake. I'm going to *rule*. I'm going to be a true Queen. I'm going to show these wolves that even if my body is weak compared to them, my mind isn't. I'm going to be the best damn Queen they've ever seen—whether Cazz gives two shits about me, or not."

80. Enter the Queen

~ JESSE ~

Rake's expression reminded me of a checkout guy I had once seen at the supermarket trying to help an old lady—he didn't want to discourage me, but he obviously thought I'd lost my mind.

I gave him a look. "I'm not being unrealistic. I know I have a lot to learn. I'm not going to start issuing edicts. But... but I'm going to show up, Rake. And over time.... Over time I'm going to make a difference."

His face softened. "I love that idea. I do. But... Jesse, wolves are very different from people. We don't think the same way. I mean, we can understand you, but... a wolf Queen isn't like your human queens."

That's good, because I knew exactly zero about human queens. "I'm not going to expect them to be like me. I want to learn to be like them—that's the whole point. I'll bring my different way of thinking, but adjust it to these people. Maybe I can help!"

"But... Why now? Why are you so excited about this *today.*"

I sighed. "Because I want my life to matter," I said honestly. "Not just to me, but to other people. I want to make life better for other people. I was going to try and do that for Cazz, but... well, you've seen what he's like."

Rake still looked uneasy, so I spent a few minutes explaining that I had been there all morning, being honest with myself. I even told him about my dad, which made him growl. But I waved him off.

My father's selfishness didn't hurt me anymore. But it made me want to be free. So I needed to find that kind of freedom with Cazz.

Something that would let me prove my worth in other ways, beyond my reproductive exploits.

Eventually, Rake looked thoughtful, then started nodding.

"That's a good idea, actually. The last two Queens have been little more than ornaments at Cazz's hip before they became... well... jokes." He grimaced, uncomfortable with the admission. But I didn't care. I was going to change all that.

"What are the Queen's core duties? What have the people been missing?"

Rake got thoughtful. "The nurturing," he said finally. "Cazz's mother... she used to care. She'd help them and cheer for them and—"

"I need to talk to Maya. She said she'd evaluate my strength, then see if I had what it took to lead. But that's bullshit. I do. I know I do. I'm going to talk to her about moving this whole training thing along."

Rake's brows popped up. "You're going to... *tell* Maya that your training is over? Please let me be there to see her face—"

"No, no, that's not what I meant. I meant... I'm going to tell her that what I need is to be training in the open. Doing things the people can see. So they start to trust me. Then when I'm actually trained, they're already coming to me. I can help right away."

Rake winced. "I'm not sure Cazz is going to be excited about—"

"Fuck Cazz and his need to control everything, I'll show him, too."

"Whoa there, Kujo, you might want to—"

"I'm serious, Rake," I said, taking the step to close the distance between us, so I stood right at his toes, my arms folded, glaring right into his warm, dark eyes. "Please. Help me. Help me figure this out. I need this, Rake. I need to be successful at *something* that has nothing to do with Cazz's orgasms."

Rake spluttered, but I didn't back down.

"Tell me! Tell me something a real queen would do that I can start doing. Right now. Today. Just one step into the crown. Please."

Rake's forehead furrowed. He clawed a hand through his glossy, brown hair and sighed. "I don't know, Jess. Maybe you should talk to Maya?"

I groaned. "Maya is just going to keep educating me like a child. And I need that. I get it. But while I'm doing that, I also need... I need to *do* something."

Rake turned his head, staring off into the trees, thinking. And when he turned back, he looked hesitantly hopeful.

"What?" I asked.

"There's a Selection coming up."

I blinked. "Selection? What's that?"

"It's the ceremony where the powerful, unmated males who are ready to take a mate step forward and select from the group of presented females."

I frowned. "Like some kind of messed up beauty pageant?"

"No, no. More like... semi-arranged marriages," he said with a half smile. "The female pool is chosen by powerful, mated wolves in the hierarchy. Each powerful wolf choses a female that they believe has all the attributes and strengths to match an Alpha. And they tell the males why they selected her. The males then choose from that pool.

"I mean, these days, the Alphas and rising wolves usually already know who will be offered, and who they want to take. But... but if you want to do something that will put you in front of the pack as a person of authority, that would do it. Usually the Queen would select a female separate from the King, so you won't step on Cazz's toes. You would just be... asserting your position. And the female you selected would hold a very high prestige. The chances of her not being selected would be very slim."

I clapped my hands. "Brilliant. You are a *genius,* Rake!" I leaped forward on my toes and hugged him, then dropped to my feet. "Let's go get started."

"Wait, you need to talk to Maya. She can advise you about which females—"

"Don't worry. She already has! I just didn't realize... Rake, thank you. Seriously. This is exactly what I needed. I know what to do now. If you think of anything else like this, things I can still do while I'm learning, you tell me, okay?"

"Well, of course, but—"

"No buts, Rake. Today I'm going to start showing the wolves that I am more than just Cazz's mate. I am a Queen. Remember this day. This is the beginning of something big. For all of us."

Then I squeezed his arm and darted back up the path towards the cave mouth, excited to get to work. And I knew exactly where to start.

I could hardly wait to talk to Maya in the morning.

Soundtrack for the next chapter is

Evil is My Middle Name by Society of Villains and Sam Tinnesz

81. Dream a Dream of You

~ CASIMIR (Later that night) ~

I stood half-crouched and poised to leap or shift, I wasn't sure which. Neither was going to help. But it was instinct to search for a way out.

My father stood a few feet away, arms folded and expression unimpressed. His eyes were the cold, cold blue of a winter snow cave when the sun shone behind it and bored into me, bright and piercing... and they were beginning to glow.

"No," I snarled. "GET OUT OF MY HEAD!"

"Make me," he muttered.

I fought him as surely as I would any wolf that came at me with fangs and claws—sweating, grunting, heart pounding—but my body barely twitched because this battle was all in the mind.

Dad's mental claws dragged down the back of my mind as painfully as real talons would tear through the flesh of my scalp— and I yelped, reflexively flinching, then snarled, but continued to fight.

"I'm not... I won't—"

"You're getting stronger, Cazz. But still not strong enough."

"Go fuck yourself, Dad."

"You'd like that, wouldn't you?"

My fingers clawed and I gulped at the air, struggling desperately for anything that would ground me so I could resist him. But it felt like he was gnawing through my skull and peeling back a window on my brain.

I felt the moment he won, like I'd suddenly become a hollow sack of flesh and he was the puppeteer, shoving his hand up my ass to make my mouth move.

Along with the rest of me.

He chuckled when I straightened, trembling, but my body no longer in a defensive stance, lips no longer peeled back from my teeth.

And I fought. I fought with everything I had, but it was like pounding my very real hands against the walls of a steel box.

I was still there, inside my own mind, but my body had been taken by him and I could do nothing but watch as he determined every step I would take. Every move. Every word.

"Kill her," my father growled.

My body turned immediately towards her as, inside, I screamed and fought and threw myself against the prison he'd placed me in, my wolf snarling and snapping, rabid.

But nothing helped. Nothing slowed my young, strong body. Nothing stopped my large hands from reaching for her throat. And no matter how wide her eyes went, no matter how she batted at my arms, clawed at my hands, and fought for her life, it didn't matter. Because I was stronger.

That was the whole point.

I was stronger. I should have killed my sister years ago for no more reason than to prove it. But she'd posed no threat.

And I loved her.

And that was why my father insisted that she died.

Inside, I sobbed as her wide eyes began to speckle with burst blood vessels that slowly turned the whites of her eyes a deep red... then the light went out in her gaze and those damaged eyes began to glaze.

Her struggles grew weak, her fingers clenched, no longer able to grasp even the thick of my arm.

'It's not your fault, Cazz. I don't blame you—!' she sent all in a rush.

Then her arms dropped. Then her knees gave.

And suddenly I wasn't the only useless sack of flesh in that room.

And of course, just as she became a literal deadweight, just as I was left holding her by her neck, that's when the bastard released control, just so I'd feel the full sensation, the weight of her, the strength I was having to apply to keep her upright, and the strange pliability of her skin under my fingers.

I cursed and let go, scrambling back as she crumpled to the floor, tripping on my own feet as I tried desperately to stop seeing, stop hearing, stop remembering how she felt in my hands.

But I couldn't shake it.

My father muttered insults as I dropped to all fours and vomited on the floor, my body heaving and retching against the feelings and images in my head. But no matter how hard I tried, I couldn't will her back to life. I couldn't apply my own *power and force the blood to course in her veins again.*

I couldn't bring light back to a dead soul.

"Cazz…?"

When there was nothing left in my stomach and I found myself gasping, panting on the floor, I felt something cold and wet on my face and reached a shaking hand up to wipe my cheek, terrified that somehow I was going to find her blood there.

But it was only tears.

"Cazz!"

I stared at that little blot of clear, pure water on my trembling fingers…

I lifted my eyes to meet my father's cold, disdainful gaze, and something inside me snapped.

"I'M GOING TO KILL YOU JUST LIKE YOU KILLED HER YOU EVIL FUCKING CUNT."

My father laughed as I threw myself into my wolf and launched straight for his throat, but I was too late—the strength went out of my legs as his compulsion took hold and my heart broke when—

"CAZZ, IT'S A DREAM! IT'S JUST A DREAM, WAKE UP!"

I sat bolt upright with a snarl, sending the furs flying because my instincts screamed that their weight was the grip of my father's control.

For a terrifying moment all I could see was darkness, and all I could hear was my own heart pounding so quickly in my ears I feared it might explode.

My father standing over me, smug and cruel… "You're getting stronger, Cazz. But still not strong enough…"

But then I blinked and sucked in a shuddering gasp of air and suddenly I could see.

I was on all fours in my bed, in my chambers. And Jesse was standing at the edge of the bed, hands on my shoulders, eyes wide—

—eyes so wide they're white all the way around, and she's crying my name, begging—

"Cazz, it's a dream. It's just a dream," she hushed, urgently. "It's not real. You're here… with me… please… wake up."

I blinked again.

Her skin looked warm in the glow of a small candle alight on the bedside table that she must have put there when she came to me.

She.

Her.

Jesse.

Mate. Wife. Mother. Soul—

I blinked again and made myself breathe, shaking my head to clear it. "What… what time is it?"

"It's the middle of the night," she whispered uncertainly, her expression worried and sad.

I cleared my throat and tried to stop panting. "What are you doing here, I wasn't—"

"You were calling for me."

82. Come to Me

~ CASIMIR ~
You were calling for me.

That stopped me cold. I sat back, staring at her. "I... called? For you?"

Jesse grimaced. "I mean, not with your voice... I felt something through the bond. I didn't know what it was at first, but it woke me up and... and it got stronger the closer I got to you. And then when I got in here you were thrashing around and you kept saying no, and it sounded like... like..." she swallowed audibly.

"What?" I snapped, not meaning to sound so cold, but I had a feeling I didn't want to hear the answer to the question. And yet...

She swallowed again. "You just felt *really* sad," she whispered, like she was afraid I'd be angry at her for saying it.

I huffed, trying to deny what I knew she'd really meant.

You were crying.

I pretended I was only raising my hands to claw back my hair from my face, but I made sure the palms of my hands wiped my cheeks and eyes on the way up. Something in my chest was pulsing, but I didn't pay attention. I was too busy figuring out how to get away.

When I dropped my hands to the bed again Jesse tensed. I turned my head away so I wouldn't have to meet her eyes and leaned back, pulling out her grip, intending to slip off the bed and get my robe since there would be no more sleeping tonight.

But as I pulled away, she grabbed for me again, one hand on my shoulder, the other cupping my jaw and pulling me back around to face her.

"Cazz… please. It sounded awful. I have nightmares too. I get it. I'm here. You wanted me here, I can feel it. Please… please, don't just shut me out again."

Don't shut her out… again?

That's when I realized, that pulsing in my chest… it was her. The bond. I'd been open to her in my sleep. Holy shit—

I slammed my block down on the bond, but Jesse made a pained little noise and crawled into my lap before I could shift my seat. I took hold of her wrists to stop her grabbing for me, but she didn't fight me, just sat on my thighs and stared at me, her pretty brows pinched over her nose, her eyes bright even in the dim light.

My heart was still pounding, my skin sheened in cold sweat, but she didn't seem to care, just straddled my thighs and stared.

A moment later, she asked the question with her eyes, then tugged her hands out of my grip and cupped my face, staring right into my eyes.

"I'm your mate, Cazz. I'm your *wife.* Please… let me help you."

When I didn't respond, her brows pinched tighter. Then she curled her fingers into the stubble on my jaw and kissed me like I was a dying man and she could give me breath.

I sucked in hard, hands coming up to claw at her back, intending to pull her away, to toss her to the floor and tell her to leave me the fuck alone… but somehow…

Somehow I was sighing into her mouth, tilting my head, taking her frantic kiss and giving it back.

At some point I plunged my hands into her hair, gripping it in both fists, holding her into the kiss, because the moment our lips touched, that power inside me had surged, fusing us together.

I was gasping for entirely new reasons, washed in need and relief and fear.

And she held me so tightly. *So* tightly.

And a still, small voice in the back of my pounding heart prayed that she'd never let go.

*****

~ *JESSE* ~

I almost wept with relief when he started kissing me back. I shivered, my whole skin tingling when he clawed hands down my back, then into my hair, then down my back again, turning us together and dropping me onto the bed.

340

I landed with my head on the bed with a *whoomph,* and Cazz pushed up on his arms.

For a moment I panicked, thinking he was going to shove away from me and leave me there. I gasped, and reached for his shoulders.

But he only planted a hand on the bed over my shoulder and pulled himself up to cover me, back arched so his hips settled between my thighs, and shoulders flexed and broad as he reared over me to stare down.

And then he hesitated, his eyes searching mine.

He was panting—had been panting since before I woke him—his hair falling down over those piercing eyes that were glittering in the low light, mouth open, and chest expanding and contracting as his muscles rippled in delicious ways.

His eyes were a little wild, like maybe the dream hadn't left him entirely. But his touch was gentle as he cupped my face and stared down at me like he was still trying to figure out who I was.

His intensity made me nervous that he was going to run—I'd seen the moment when he'd intended to and had thrown myself into his lap shamelessly. But it was obviously the right thing to do. Because he hadn't run. He was still here. And until the moment he'd thrown that block on the bond, I'd been able to feel how relieved he was that I was there.

So, as he stared at me, searching my eyes, I reached up to cup his face too, letting my thumb play up and down his hollow cheek.

"I'm here," I whispered. "I want to be here, Cazz. I want to be with you."

"Why?" His voice was hoarse, guttural. But not sharp.

I didn't have the right words. So I took his hand from my face and pulled it down, laying it flat on my chest, between my breasts, right where I felt the bond.

And when his palm rested there, the bond thrummed, as if his touch fed something in it.

I bit my lip and he twitched, sucking in a deep breath.

"That's why," I breathed.

He held back for another moment, still staring at me, his eyes still a little wild.

But then he groaned like he was giving in to a great weight, and he lowered himself to cover me, both hands in my hair, and kissed me like he'd die if he didn't.

83. Bonded

~ *CASIMIR* ~

The matebond between wolves is a unique and powerful thing. I'd never denied that. My bond with Jesse was my third, but she was the first I had claimed.

I told myself that was why I shivered when she whispered my name.

I had her pinned to the mattress, covered, my hips between her thighs, my hands planted on the bed to brace myself, still trying to decide if I was clear headed enough to take her.

I wanted her, desperately. The looming dark of that dream threatened to suck me back in if I slept. And having her warm softness nearby was soothing.

But I felt... fragile.

And uncertain if taking her would help that, or make it worse.

Perhaps I hadn't shut down the bond as completely as I thought, because Jesse seemed to know what I was thinking.

"I'm here," she whispered. "I want to be here, Cazz. I want to be with you."

"Why?" It was a genuine question. In an honest moment, I couldn't fathom why she would stare up at me with such adoration in her gaze when I hadn't compelled it.

But in the fascinating way she had of often surprising me, instead of answering with words, she took my hand and laid it flat on her chest, between her breasts, over the thin nightgown she was wearing. But it was as if the scrap of material didn't even exist.

The moment she put my hand to that place on her chest, my entire body jolted with the surge of power that coursed through me—as if she had plugged me directly into an electrical socket.

My jaw went slack.

"That's why," she breathed.

A voice in my head screamed that this way was danger, but I was too far gone. I descended on her like a dying man in the desert would plunge into an ice-cold pool.

But there was nothing cold about Jesse. She was all heat. And for the first time, instead of trying to guard myself from her flame, I just raised my hands to the fire and let it warm me.

I pulled back from the kiss, gasping, all instincts on alert, but throwing me towards her at the same time, in a confusing chaos of senses.

But when I just lay there, staring down at her, Jesse laced her fingers behind my neck and curled herself up to kiss my throat.

I jolted, panicked for a moment. Instincts screaming.

I'd never let any female open their mouth on my throat. Ever.

But before I could react, she'd already started kissing her way down my neck and chest, then slumped back onto the bed, pulling me down over her, as if that moment had meant nothing.

Tension and fierce desire roared through my veins. I clawed my fingers on her chest, taking hold of the neckline of her nightgown and pulling it down to bare one of her breasts, growling with pleasure as I lowered myself to it, opening my mouth over it wide, and sucking on that peak. Hard.

Jesse gasped and arched, both hands flying to my hair, gripping me and holding me to her.

I growled my approval when I tugged at that nipple and her hips bucked so we were brought together deliciously for one, teasing moment.

Then, still suckling at her, I reached down to the skirt of the nightgown to begin pulling it up. But it was pinned both by my weight and hers.

Frustrated, I was forced to draw up my knees and kneel, to take my weight from her and help her sit up, to pull the gown up the length of her body, growling again in delight as her legs, then hips, then stomach were bared to me.

"Lift your arms," I rasped, smiling when she did so and I lifted the nightgown. Then all of her delicious pink skin was revealed.

I stared a moment, drinking in the sight of her. And she stared up at me, measuring me with her eyes.

Knowing she was watching, I gave a sly smile as I reached for the breast that had been neglected so far, playing fingertips over it, teasing that ruched skin until it puckered and stood up for more.

Then I scooted far enough back on my knees that I could lean down to suck that beauty into my mouth too.

Jesse's breath caught and she twitched. But I just continued to suck and lave with my tongue, while I reached between her legs to find more of her heat.

She wrapped her arms around my head, her hips giving small rolls to meet my touch, her back arched to press her nipple into my mouth.

I didn't stop touching her, curling one finger inside her, beckoning her to me as I came off her breast and kissed my way up to her neck.

"Lay down," I rasped, my breathing already ragged. Then, when she did as I instructed, I followed her down, lowering myself over her.

And when our bodies were aligned, but not yet united, I reached up to curl my fingers into her hair, fisting those silky waves and pulling her head back, opening my mouth over her throat when she gasped, and grazing my teeth there as a reminder to her, both to the danger I posed, and also to the fact that she could trust me not to give in to it.

We kissed and touched, writhed and rubbed, until her breathing was as ragged as mine.

Then I slid a hand up the back of her leg, chasing the goosebumps that rushed ahead of me, until my hand was under her hip. And as I delved the perfect velvet of her mouth, I found her slick heat and, pulling up on her hip to position her, I plunged into her with a ragged cry.

A soft, cold echo of warning rang in my head when her hands clapped to my back and she pulled me closer. But I threw caution to the wind and left her hands free as I drew almost all the way out of her, then thrust back in with a howl of triumph.

84. A New World

~ *JESSE* ~

Something was happening, and it made me shake.

Being with Cazz had always been a pleasure, a pure, primal pleasure. And the animal in him was still there, growling approval and seeking me with clawed fingers and bright eyes.

But as Cazz kissed me, and stroked, and let his body play mine like music, he shuddered and murmured and... softened against me.

His kiss was desperate and deep. But his lips gave, rather than took. His touch was skilled and intentional, but at times he stroked with a tenderness I'd never felt from him before.

And as we began to move together, even though I felt him tense more than once, he didn't trap my hands, but let me touch him, grip his back, slide my palms over the firm rounds of muscle, dig nails into his skin and *hold on.*

But what left me breathless was the bond.

I hadn't lied to him when I said he had called me. I'd gotten better at recognizing the bond and links since Maya was working with me. And although I hadn't been able to hear his words, I had felt him tugging at me.

And now... now that feeling hadn't stopped. It was as if his body called me closer and closer. And when he entered me, he came alive in my chest. A glowing energy, light and heat, that was growing the longer we were together.

The power of it was breathtaking, stripping away my self-consciousness and fear, replacing it with a bold delight.

I stopped worrying that he would run, and instead felt myself drawn nearer and nearer. As if his soul sang to mine, crooning, applauding, and promising more. Always more.

Then there was a moment, when my climax beckoned, when our movements had become urgent and rhythmic, and Cazz buried his face in my neck and breathed my name against my skin, that I began to shake for real.

That barrier he'd thrown between us dissolved like vapor in the air. And I was left breathless with *knowing* him.

The sense of him was so clear, it was stunning.

The dregs of his fear hadn't disappeared entirely. Something in that nightmare still gripped him. But it was easing slowly away as we clung together, moving in an intimacy that threatened to bring tears to my eyes.

But behind the thin veil of that fading fear, a fierce fire burned: Strength, protectiveness, honor… but it was blown by a wind that threatened the flames. Self-loathing, disgust, and cold, cold defeat.

When I tried to reach through that curtain to pull him closer, he flinched from me, hiding himself in the shadows. And yet, for the first time, he didn't run.

To the contrary, as the glittering wave of pleasure he wrung from my body began to overwhelm thought, as we climbed towards that final peak together, it was as if he kept turning his face towards the flames we made together, letting the light reveal more and more of his handsome features.

One of his hands came up to cup the top of my head, bending my neck and pulling my chin high—and he kissed it, then my lips, then buried his nose under my jaw.

And as I grasped for him, grounding myself, as he thrust into me again and again, pushing me up and over that peak until finally we hung on the edge of nothing… then tumbled into freefall together, I heard my name over and over, ringing through the chamber in rough, tortured tones.

And my heart rang with it.

*****

~ *CASIMIR* ~

My entire body shuddered as I climaxed, and her name tore from my throat as the ghost of *something* left me.

Panting like I'd run a marathon, I collapsed over her, one hand fisted in her hair, the other flattened in the hollow of her back.

I was stunned. Floored. Speechless.

My instincts still screamed warning, still begged me to find space… but something else soothed them.

She did.

My own breath rushed back over my face because I was panting into her neck. But I was too scared to lift my head and meet her eyes, because deep down I knew she could feel... whatever this was.

I'd lost sight of her completely, falling into the bond and the flames that roared between us, turned and tumbled like a leaf in the waves until I didn't know which way was up... except that I did.

She was up. She was north. She was—

That chord of light and power between us, pulsing now in time with my racing blood, pumping me full of the power she offered, which was roaring at me in waves... I'd never felt anything like it.

"Cazz...?"

She sounded so uncertain. And so hopeful.

That warning flashed in my head again, but I stifled it, though it raised the small hairs on the back of my neck.

"Cazz, are you okay?"

I made myself take hold of my balls and pushed up on my elbows to look down on her, huffing in delight at the sight of her, sweaty, pink, and mussed.

"Are you?" I asked with the best smile I could manage, praying she wouldn't notice the deflection.

She nodded quickly, her smile growing. "That was... I'm so glad you stayed."

"Me too," I said, because it was true.

She combed her fingers into the hair on my forehead, pushing it back so it now longer fell between us.

"You are... heavenly to look at, Cazz," she said with a little shake of her head.

I arched one brow and let my smile pull up on one side. "You know what they say, the devil masquerades as an angel of light."

I winked, but she didn't smile.

Instead, I froze, because she put one hand to the center of my chest, right where that glowing ball of *her* resided.

"Don't do that," she whispered, her brow furrowing.

"Do what? Wink at you?"

"No, Cazz... I can feel you. I know you're afraid. It's okay, though. That's why I'm here."

I almost ran. Almost tore myself from her body and ran for my life. But she put her free hand to my shoulder and held me there.

"It's okay, Cazz. It's just you and me. And it's good. This is good. Right?"

I nodded slowly. Then made myself stroke her hair because women loved that. But I couldn't shake that chittering babble of warning in the back of my head.

I silenced it, but the weight of it remained.

Later, as we lay together and I could see the questions shadowing her eyes, I sighed.

"Give me your word," I said quietly.

"To what?"

"You tell no one of this. Not a soul."

She looked thoughtful for a minute. "Do you mean the nightmare? Or the... the way we were together?"

"Both," I said, then kissed away the protests I knew she wanted to make.

And just to be sure, I kissed them away for a long, long time.

85. Clear the Mind

~ *CASIMIR* ~

"*Oh!*"

I jolted awake the next morning, sitting up quickly, and felt the weight of Jesse tumble from my shoulder because she'd been laying her head there.

Still foggy and uncertain, I scanned the room to find Ghere standing a few steps inside the doorway, dry-washing his hands, an apologetic look on his face. "I'm sorry, Sire, but it's urgent."

I frowned. Why was he—

"What's going on?" Jesse's voice was disoriented and husky with sleep and desire bolted from behind my navel, straight to my groin.

But as Ghere averted his eyes, I realized why he'd apologized.

I quickly grabbed the quilt and pulled it up over her naked breasts, giving a little grunt when they rubbed my knuckles as they disappeared.

"What is it, Ghere?" I said without looking at him, my voice low and rough from screaming in the night… and other things.

Jesse blinked and our eyes caught. I left a sliver of the bond open so she'd be able to tell that I wasn't pleased about the interruption. But not enough that she would feel the relief.

"Sire, the guards are reporting humans near the cave entrances, both north and west."

Forgetting everything else, I snapped my head around to meet Ghere's gaze and immediately opened the link with him.

'They're present near the entrances, or they've already found them?'

'Only nearby,' he sent quickly. *'But worryingly close.'* He sent images of the landscape where they were and I sucked in a breath—worryingly close didn't cover it. *'They are young and clearly undertaking some kind of... activity. But we risk them finding us. We've posted guards looking like hikers and campers near each, but—'*

'Gather the council. Tell them I'll be there in ten minutes.'

Ghere nodded and bowed. He offered Jesse a small wave and smile as he backed quickly out of the room.

She returned the wave with a frown, then looked at me as I threw the furs off my lap and swung my legs over to get out of the bed.

"You're... you're leaving?"

"I have to," I muttered, the hair on my arms standing up. "We're at risk of humans finding the caves. It happens now and again. We can usually divert them, but it's up to me to determine how soon to intervene and they've gotten closer than they should have before we've located them."

I was already out of the bed and stalking across the floor to the clothes I'd thrown over a chair the night before because I'd been too lazy to put them away.

"You two were talking... in the link." It was a statement, not a question.

"It's the fastest way to communicate, and Ghere never interrupts my sleep unless it's truly urgent."

Jesse nodded and scratched her head, but her face fell. She was sitting up now, the furs pulled over her chest, her hair sticking up in a bird's nest that grew from one side of her skull and would have been hilarious if I had had time to tease.

"I was hoping... after last night... I wanted to talk this morning..."

I had just pulled on my leathers and stood up to button the fly. "There may be time later today. But I am sorry, Jesse, this is what it means to be King. I am—and you will be—at the beck and call of the needs of the pack."

She nodded, but she was crestfallen.

That space in my chest that was *her* pulsed with disappointment and the edge of fear.

I wanted to curse. I wanted to rant—did she think I had arranged this interruption? But in the same moment, the urge was there to comfort her.

That made me uneasy. As I pulled on my boots and buckled my belt I examined that desire closely... a product of the bond. But did it weaken me?

When I stood, stamping my feet to settle them in my boots, she was still sitting there in my bed, just watching me.

I took a breath and prowled to her side of the bed, leaning one fist on the plush mattress and cupping her face with the other, kissing her briefly.

"Thank you for... helping me last night," I said quietly.

One side of her pretty mouth tipped up. "I always want to help you if I can, Cazz. You know that, right?"

I shook my head slowly and she thought I was denying her. She frowned and opened her mouth to protest, but I put a finger to her lips.

"I know you're telling the truth. I can feel it," I said abruptly. "I shake my head because... you baffle me."

"Baffle you how?"

But that felt like the humans outside—just a touch too close for comfort, so I shook my head again.

"I don't have time now. But I'll find you later, when this is dealt with."

She sagged a little, but she nodded. "Okay. I hope... I hope it's not a big deal."

I growled and kissed her again, then turned on my heel and stormed out of there, my body fizzing with excess energy that made me agitated and kept me walking quickly until I reached the Council chambers and could put her out of my mind.

But even as I sat and urged my advisors to give their reports, even as I applied my mind to the problem and watched the footage they'd taken of humans running through our forest wearing ridiculously bright clothing that would only attract attention rather than hide them from sight, my mind continued to turn over the events of the night before.

I just wished I knew why the memories of her wouldn't leave me.

There were more important things to address today!

But one of the genuinely useful things I had learned from my asshole father was that often, when a problem could not be solved right away, it eased the mind to take a single step, one action that might aid me in addressing it. It allowed the mind to clear, at least for a time, so other issues could be addressed in the interim.

So, as my advisors argued over whether it would be easier to fake a law-enforcement intervention, or only monitor the dozens of humans apparently running some kind of athletic event in the woods below the southern cave, I linked with Ghere and asked him to take care of one, small detail.

And to my relief, it was easier to focus after that.

Until I started wondering what she would think.

86. Think it Through

~ JESSE ~

"...really just wondering if the females you connected me to the other day... do you consider them... trustworthy? Women you would commend?"

Maya frowned, her eyes somehow cloudy with age, and yet piercing as well. She cupped one hand over the other on the top of her walking stick, leaning forward in her chair—which meant her back was hurting—and fixed me with those eyes that were now shrewdly narrowed.

"Naturally, I would say yes. If our Cazz were here, challenging my decisions and questioning my judgment, I would, of course, make it very, *very* clear that I do not bring wolves into the Queen's sphere that I believe could be a risk to her wellbeing."

I swallowed. That sharp tone wasn't the reaction I had expected.

"But?" I asked, because clearly there was something more to what she was going to say.

"But... Jesse, if you truly want to rule rather than *attend* the pack, you cannot require my approval to do so."

I frowned. "I wasn't. I just wanted to talk to them and I thought you might have—"

"But you see, you are. And the truth is, no matter how loyal or good I might believe them to be, if you cannot draw that same loyalty from them, or if you cannot wear your own pants as the humans say, and determine for yourself whether someone is of good character, how do you expect to rule?"

I knew my eyes were flashing. I also knew Maya *liked* to piss me off to see how I would react, so I tipped my head and met her pointed-gaze-for-pointed-gaze.

"Any ruler worth their salt will have objective advisors and seek counsel," I said tightly. "Even my very arrogant—excuse me, *confident* mate has wolves he goes to for advice. You want me to believe I should just be an island to myself?"

"No," she said simply. "I want you to trust your own judgment for who is trustworthy, first and foremost. Because we all know anyone can be wrong—even me, even Cazz—but also that the right leader can gain loyalty or assurance that another wolf might not."

"But, I don't know these women!"

"Then get to know them!"

"I planned to, that's why I was asking—"

"No, Jesse. You wanted reassurance that your instincts about them were correct. Were you an adolescent, or even a wolf your age but lacking your status, I might entertain the conversation and guide you in assessing those around you. But you are Queen. You are Alpha Female—or at least, you plan to become so. If you are on the battlefield and a wolf appears to help, do you need to come rushing to me first to see if you should trust them?"

"Of course not! I wasn't asking for that—"

"Then, make the decisions. Think for yourself, girl. I will not be here forever to guide you—"

"Maya, it's been a month!"

"And we may not have a month more. Is this truly how you want to spend the hours that are presented to us?"

That stopped me. I frowned at her. "Maya, is something going on? Are you trying to tell me you aren't well, or—"

"Dear, *God,* girl, you are determined to find problems that do not exist," she sighed, rolling her eyes. "Meanwhile you ignore those that beg for your attention."

"But you said—"

"I merely meant that at my age no day can be taken for granted. I am grateful every morning when I open my eyes—until my body has to move. Then I am rather more sharp with God about His choice to keep me here. But that is not the point. The point is… I do you no favors, holding your hand in simple decisions, like who you might build relationships with. Not only would that practice encourage your dependence on me—which we have already established is rife with risk—but it does not allow me to best measure when you are ready for my commendation. Until I see you act independently, to think and choose for yourself, I cannot accurately measure your worth to the pack at large."

I gaped at her. "You're saying that me asking you if those women are good is somehow... me asking you to lead instead of me?"

"You are asking for my commendation."

"No, I'm not! I'm asking for your advice!"

"Jesse... you have instincts. Intuition. God-given sense. I would wager they were the measures by which you lived prior to arriving here. Use them. Do not let them waste away!"

"All I wanted to know was—"

"You wanted me to affirm your choices, and I'm telling you, you're a big girl. Work it out for yourself!" she snapped.

I jerked my head back, blinking. She seemed genuinely pissed off.

And me asking more questions only seemed to make her more angry.

I hadn't been asking her to affirm my choices... had I?

Well, I suppose I had. I was going to assess these women to see if I could approve one for the Selection, and I'd been planning to give Maya a chance to rule one out if she saw fit. But we hadn't even gotten that far in the conversation.

But as I chewed over what she was saying—because I didn't quite understand why she was angry—I thought I started to see what she was *really* saying.

She wanted me to be more independent.

She wanted me to function without her guidance, so she could see what kinds of choices I made without her.

Which must mean, she was beginning to think about commending me to the pack... right?

Maya still sat in her favorite chair, her knees wide, hands both propped on the top of her cane, glaring at me a little.

But I smiled.

"Okay, I see."

"I do not think you do."

"Yes, I do, Maya. I get it. Okay. Thank you. I'll... I'll handle this on my own."

She lifted her chin, looking down her nose at me, even though she was several inches shorter than me when we both stood—in part because she was always hunched. But there was a gleam in her eye.

"Are you certain?"

"I think so."

She rolled her eyes, and I threw up my hands. "It's just a turn of phrase—a polite way to say yes!"

"Eradicate it from your vocabulary. If you truly want to lead wolves, you cannot show an ounce of self-doubt, even flippantly."

"No problem," I muttered. "If unwavering self-belief is what you want, I'll just model myself after Cazz."

I would have sworn she snorted. But I was brushing my thighs in irritation, and by the time I got my eyes up to hers, her expression was blank.

I eyed her, suspicious. "You're goading me."

"No."

But her lips twitched.

87. Think of Me

~ JESSE ~

I shook my head at Maya, but she just stared blandly back at me.

"You should be ashamed of yourself," I said bluntly.

"I have no idea what you're talking about," she sniffed. "Now, have you finally gotten the ancestries clear in your head, or will you leave me with another headache, trying to help you straighten them out...?"

I groaned—the pack bloodlines were my least favorite subject and I knew her bringing them up now meant she was either punishing me, or distracting me. But it didn't really matter which it was, because I was submitted.

And if she wanted to spend the next week talking to me about who sired who, I was going to have to suck it up and learn it so she'd have no reason to bring it up again.

As I sat back in my chair, she smiled smugly and settled herself in hers. "Start with the Stone River bloodline—and do *not* ignore the cross-breeding with our urban brothers this time!"

I muttered a curse under my breath, but did as she asked and prayed I would get it right first time this time. I still wanted to talk to Cazz today...

*****

A couple hours later, I was only a few tunnels away from Maya's door when a messenger appeared, walking briskly and his eyes lit up when he saw me.

"Ah, Sire, I'm glad to have found you. The King sends his regards." Then he stopped in front of me, holding out a basket with a flip-lid on it.

I looked at it, curious and took it from him. "That's from Cazz—I mean, the King?"

"Yes, Sire. He said to mention that there's a note inside."

My heart fluttered even as my mind protested that this was just going to be one more set of snacks he was sending to try and fatten me up. But he'd never told the messengers to point out a note before. They were usually just perfunctory lines telling me why the particular snack he had sent was beneficial, or urging me not to hold to the human ways of "frail, undernourished women."

"Thank you," I said carefully, lifting the lid on the basket to see a piece of paper folded inside, over something else that was wrapped in tissue. "I'll take it from here. Let him know I received it and I'm grateful."

"Certainly, Sire." The messenger looked relieved as he turned on his heel and darted away. I didn't follow him, even though I knew he'd move a lot faster than me. I was still a little off-balance from Maya's disapproval earlier, and now... now I found myself nervous about what this might be from Cazz.

Talking to Maya had been a great distraction. But the truth was, I felt like something had shifted between Cazz and me last night. And fuck Maya and her talking about self-doubt because even though I was sure about the women she'd introduced me to, I definitely *wasn't* clear on where I stood with Cazz.

And I didn't want to get my hopes up. If this was a written scrawl about the nutritional and hormonal value of nuts as a food group I was going to throw this basket against the wall.

But when the messenger was gone and there was no one else in the tunnel, I pulled my big-girl pants up and squatted at the side of the cave with my back to the wall, and opened the lid, flipping it back to reveal the folded paper and the wrapped package beneath it.

Eyeing that tissue paper, though I couldn't see through it, I picked up the note first.

~

Jesse,

It is a tradition among the wolves that when one gives aid to another, a forfeit is offered.

I don't think the humans use this term the way we do, so I will explain:

Last night you helped me overcome a difficult moment, as well as offering me solace in the wake of it.

In return, I offer you a forfeit.

It is, in essence, a debt.

I am indebted to you.

So, should you find yourself in need at any time, you must call for me. I will aid you and comfort you in your trial, as you did in mine.

— Cazz

~

I stared at the note, then frowned and read it again. Then I frowned some more because I couldn't decide if it was a sweet gesture and a way that Cazz was tentatively offering himself, or if he just saw it as a way to turn what had happened last night into a transaction—and this *forfeit* was his escape hatch.

I'll pay you back so we're even.

I tucked the note into the pocket of my jeans, then remembered that the basket had something inside it.

Heart pattering pathetically with hope, I reached into the basket and pulled out the tissue-wrapped bundle, pulling the pieces of thin paper away and shoving them into the basket until I held a scrap of lace in my hands.

When I shook it out and another small piece of paper fluttered to the ground. I dove for it, and unfolded it quickly, but there was only a few words.

~

I told you I would rectify the sad lack of lace in your closet.

Consider this the beginning of your collection.

~

He hadn't even signed it.

I almost laughed—without humor—as I let the lace dangle from my hand and finally realized what was. My whole body slumped. I dropped my head into one hand, shaking it. This time I didn't know whether to laugh or cry.

The night he claimed me... before that shitshow started, when we were in the closet, he'd looked at all the clothes they'd brought and said there was no lingerie.

He'd given me lingerie?

The beginning of a collection?

That was how he thought we should memorialize what had happened last night? A debt, and a sexy scrap of clothing that he'd probably bite through the first time I wore it?

Lord, help me with this man!

I was laughing, but as it echoed around the tunnel, even I could hear the cracked, slightly unhinged nature of my voice.

My first instinct was to go to him, to confront him. Who cared if he was with his council, did he really think *this* was how we moved forward together?

But even as I stuffed the slick piece of satin and lace into the basket, something put a hand of caution to my chest.

Cazz had been truly disturbed this morning—I could feel it in the bond, and see it in his posture, the way he'd looked at Ghere. He was genuinely worried about whatever they thought was going on outside.

There would be no faster way to push him over the edge and away from me, than to shake his "gift" in his face and tell him he was an Alphahole.

That thought made me grind my teeth. I knew from living with my father and brothers, the fastest way to make a man set himself against you was to challenge him when he was already stressed or under threat.

So I might take a day and cool off and let this go—for now. But no way was I going to applaud him for it.

What was it they said about training dogs? Reward good behavior, and ignore bad?

"Well, Cazz, I hope you aren't expecting a gratitude parade for this… whatever it is," I muttered, shaking my head as I started back up the tunnel, towards the Palace. "Because this mate might be weak, but she's not going to feed the beast. That might have worked on other women, but it won't work on me."

I humphed, pushed away the sting of sadness that wanted to rise, and set my course for the Palace.

My mate might be a lost cause. But I wasn't. And that meant the first thing I needed to do was find those females and get them talking.

Maya wanted me to figure things out for myself?

Cazz wanted me thinking like a sex-kitten?

Well they could both just fuck right off.

If they wouldn't—or couldn't—help, I was just going to go and be the best Queen I knew how to be. I was going to *slay*.

Just, not the way wolves did, I added hurriedly to myself.

88. Not that Way

~ *CASIMIR* ~

"I'm sorry… she said what?" I asked, doing my best not to let the irritation and creeping anger seep into my tone. It wasn't this messenger's fault that he had been waiting two hours to tell me how my gift was received, because I was too busy to take a break… and now his news wasn't what I wanted to hear.

"She said, *let him know I received it and I'm grateful.*"

"Those exact words?"

"Yes, Sire."

With a disgruntled growl, I dismissed the messenger and turned away.

Rake and the others were all gathered in clusters around the room. The Gammas had been sent off with instructions and now we waited to see if our decisions had been the right ones. They had taken far too long to come to, in my opinion. And I feared we may be right back here in an hour or so, learning that the time we'd taken had ultimately changed the landscape of the problem.

I wasn't afraid that humans would enter our catacombs and hurt us—they were frail creatures, mostly, though their weapons were certainly a threat. But there had been no sight of weapons at all—unless we counted the sports gear, which could be used that way in a pinch. No, it was clear that this was a group of students who had come into the "woods" from the university to undertake some kind of game. They were wholly unprepared to find us, and hadn't presented—or sensed—any threat in the two or three occasions that guards had interacted in an effort to turn these overgrown children away from our territory.

But still…

I was much more concerned that the rumor mill would cause much greater problems for us in the future.

While these particular humans did not pose a likely threat, the information they might bring back to their peers and authority figures could. Law enforcement in the city had been on our tails since the last Reaping. And though the news of that investigation had slowed to a trickle—a good sign that they were losing interest—it had not stopped.

If one of these kids sensed what we really were and told the wrong person what they'd inadvertently seen…

I shook off the dark thoughts.

So far, no humans had made it to the actual cave mouths. And we now had a plan in place to ensure that did not happen. Anticipating failure did no one any good. We would deal with it if it happened. But for now… at least for the next hour or two, I was free.

And apparently, so was my mate. The messenger had seen her leaving Maya. Which meant I could do some investigations of my own.

Surely once she'd seen my gift her response had been… warmer?

My toys fell over themselves when I gave them expensive clothing. The poor ones, especially. Jesse had just either not opened the gift before the messenger left, or been too embarrassed to send any message about it through him.

In fact… perhaps she was back at her chambers, already wearing it?

I smiled and stalked out of the council chamber and down the main tunnel towards the royal quarters. I would stop briefly at the dining hall to get some food—she still needed to gain weight. And I was thinking that if our strategy with the humans worked and I wasn't called back to judge next steps, perhaps Jesse and I could take the entire evening together…

But as I slipped into the dining hall, crossing towards the kitchens discreetly because it was late lunch hour, and there were many wolves milling around in there that I didn't want to get distracted by, something in my chest spasmed.

I drew to a halt instinctively, turning until that space in my chest sang, like a compass pointing north.

Jesse was nearby.

Had she been coming to find me at the same moment I was coming to find her?

I found myself torn—titillated by the idea that she might have draped herself in a shroud of clothing to cover the gift she was wearing, hoping to tempt me because no one else would know. But also irritated when it occurred to me that she might be back in that place of needy clinging, searching for me with those pleading eyes.

I ground my teeth and started in the direction that I could feel her, opening myself more to the bond when it became clear she was neither sneaking, nor cowering. In fact the feelings within her were a riot of conflicts—determination, queasy self-doubt, thrill, and unease...

I frowned, trotting through the tunnels until I was out of the royal quarters completely and prowling down one of the visitors' wings.

What was she doing down here? She could send a messenger to bring any servant she needed, even without being able to link. But who could be visiting that she would even know?

My confusion—and curiosity—got the better of me. And as I felt her drawing nearer, I reached through the bond to see if I could make her aware of my presence.

She'd claimed to feel me calling her last night. Would she still sense it when she wasn't still and in silence?

There was a burst of something in her that I couldn't quite read, then the door halfway down the tunnel opened and her fire-wood hair shone under the torches as she looked up and down until she saw me coming.

"I felt you!" she said brightly, running out of the room and straight to me. "I felt you, Cazz! You were calling me!"

I nodded, my irritation and confusion derailed by her clear joy. "I thought I would try it and see if you could feel it," I said quietly as I stopped walking and she came to stand in front of me.

Her eyes were wide and shining, her expression bright and happy—but just as she opened her mouth to say something else, her eyes clouded and she blinked. Her hands that had been rising as if to reach for me, stopped.

Then she frowned.

"What are you doing here?"

I frowned harder. *She* disapproved of *me* coming here, into the visitors wing? When we had no visitors that I was aware of?

"I was about to ask you the same thing," I said sharply.

She blinked again and her head pulled back. "I'm here talking with one of the wom—females. I've been practicing my linking and finding people and... anyway, we were just talking. Why are you here?"

I opened my mouth, but just then a female from the High Servants hurried out of the room. She saw me and bowed immediately, but kept moving.

"I'm very sorry if I kept the Queen from you, Sire," she muttered as she hurried past.

I watched her, glaring, because she looked guilty, but she scuttled away and I turned back to find Jesse standing with her arms folded, her brows pinched, and a distinct sense of *irate female* through the bond. And yet, with her arms like that it pressed her breasts up high. And maybe she had her gift on under that tunic?

"Cazz... what are you doing?" she asked suspiciously. "Are you... checking on me?"

I spluttered. "I was coming to find you, because I could feel you, and you being here made no sense!"

Her expression softened a hair. "Well... I mean, if you were worried about me..."

I *almost* shot her down. Almost told her that I was only worried she was in here making some stupid, human mistake and I had come to make sure she didn't embarrass herself... but something held my tongue.

In the bond I could still feel all those emotions churning within her, as if she couldn't choose how she felt.

God, what a mess it must be to be female.

I sighed and raked my hand through my hair. "I was curious what you thought of my message and my gift?" I said simply. Honestly. "You didn't send a return message and..."

I put my hands on my hips and frowned, feeling off-balance and uncertain why. I did not *like* feeling uneasy.

Her eyes shuttered and her folded arms tightened. "That's because I didn't know *how* to feel about it, Cazz."

I stared at her, baffled.

What the fuck did that mean?

89. Broken Life

~ JESSE ~

Cazz's brows drew down sharply over his nose and his eyes narrowed. "What do you mean, you don't know how to feel about it?"

I looked back and forth, up and down the tunnel. I hadn't planned to have this conversation with him so soon. I'd been busy hunting down my new friends. But Cazz's appearance had frightened Wylde, who thought he was going to be angry with her for talking to me while she was supposed to be working, so I didn't call her back when she darted away. I knew I could find her later.

The truth was, feeling that sudden tug behind my ribs, that call that could only be him, had excited me—then stepping into the hallway to see Cazz prowling towards me had been *thrilling*.

He was hunting.

At least, that's what I thought when I first saw him. Now, I wasn't so sure. He looked pissy and imperious, and I was remembering that I was kind of pissed off about the lingerie.

But I made myself drop the defensive stance and took Cazz's hand, leading him into the room we had just vacated. I knew it was empty because I had asked Wylde to take me somewhere we could talk alone, and she'd taken me there, saying there was no plan for its use in the near future, so no staff would be coming because it was already clean.

When we got inside, I closed the door and locked it for good measure.

Cazz's lips were pursed with disapproval. He had folded his arms and was staring at me when I turned from the door. He was obviously waiting for an explanation, but I hesitated because there was a moment I was struck by the pure, animal *presence* of him.

Tall and broad, his hair tumbling around his ears and dusting the back of his collar, that dark, linen shirt open at the throat to give me a peek at his collarbones. His trim waist, and strong legs, hugged tightly by the leather that let me see every muscle and…

He stood there, tense and glowering, his sleeves rolled to just above his elbows, looming over me.

My mouth went dry.

And a few seconds later, a low rumble started in his chest.

"Are you *certain* you don't know how to feel, Jesse?" Cazz purred, and his full lips tipped up on one side in the most stunning, lopsided smile.

"Do wolves use OnlyFans?" I asked breathlessly, my eyes dragging back down his beautiful body to those arms. "Because you do forearm porn better than anyone I've ever seen," I gulped.

Cazz blinked, then threw his head back in a mouth-open gasp of belly laughter, deep and rich. It didn't last long, but when he returned his eyes to me, they were shining and he had unfolded his arms so he could wipe one of them with a finger.

"Dear, *god*, woman. You surprise me every day."

"Is that a good thing?"

"Yes, Jesse. Yes, it is," he said, his voice low and rough. He came to stand at my toes. His smile had faded but the light in his eyes was still there. "Tell me," he said, more softly this time. "Tell me why my gift didn't please you."

I bit my lip and a low growl puttered out of him. I felt a zing of heat through the bond, and suddenly I couldn't breathe right.

When I looked up at him, our eyes locked. I swallowed as he leaned in like he was going to kiss me, but I shook my head and darted past him because I wasn't going to let him deflect me with sex again.

"No, no no no… I need to… *we* need to have this conversation," I said breathlessly.

Cazz turned to face me, his expression more serious. "What? What was wrong with my offering?"

"It wasn't that it was wrong. It was more…" I raised my chin and pressed my thighs together to ease the ache and told myself I wasn't going there. Not yet. "I wonder why you chose... those things," I said lamely.

Cazz's brows dove down over his nose again. "A forfeit from a King is an extremely valuable concession, Jesse. I know you don't understand all of our ways yet, but—"

"No, no. That's not... I mean, I know that. I get that you were trying to... give me something," I said carefully. "But the way you phrased it... you said you were in my debt. Like... like as long as you paid me back we were all good and then there was nothing more to worry about."

Cazz frowned harder. "Yes. I do believe that's how debts work. I was recognizing that you offered yourself last night—"

"But that's the thing, Cazz. You're my mate. I'll... I'd happily offer myself anytime. If it helped you. Especially when you're struggling. I don't feel like that's something you need to pay back."

He stared at me, his gaze sharp, but thoughtful. It was clear he was trying to *understand.* I didn't know whether to be encouraged, or to lose hope.

He took a step towards me, his expression strange. "I did not think I incurred a debt to you that could be paid in currency—"

"No, no. Exactly. But you still see it as a debt. Like... like I've got this hold over you or something."

Cazz's jaw rolled. "I was taught that with my great wealth and privilege it would be *impolite* to simply take from someone and not offer anything in return. I would have thought that you'd agree."

I almost rolled my eyes. "Well, sure, if you're taking firewood from the wood guy, or... I don't know. I mean, if it's someone's stuff, then yeah. But people... relationships... Cazz..." blinked then and a shocking thought landed in my head.

"Cazz... have you ever had a girlfriend? Or like... someone you were close to, just because you liked them?"

His lips thinned. "I have had many friends in my life. That's not what we're—"

"No, no, I meant... people who don't work for you. Or haven't got a role. People—wolves, females—who didn't have to be there."

His expression went flat. "Ghere told me it was rude to speak with you about my prior conquests, because you'll feel inadequate—"

I raised my hands to stop him, closing my eyes for a second because he was right, that's *not* what I was going for.

"No, Cazz, please... when you were young, or before you were King maybe, I don't know. Did you ever have a girl who... who maybe didn't know what you were and just *liked* you?"

His eyes went wary and he folded his arms again, but he didn't back away. "My role in the hierarchy has followed me since the day of my birth. It is... impossible to meet anyone in my world who is unaware of it. Nor would I want them to. The hierarchy is our lifeline. To ignore it? That's not how we wolves work."

"Okay, okay, fair enough." I was scrambling. "So maybe not unaware but... uncaring—about your role, I mean. Did you ever have a girl you liked, and she liked you, and the two of you just got along. And you had inside jokes and... you know, a girlfriend? Wolves must have *some* relationships before they get mated as adults, don't they?"

I made a mental note to ask Maya about that, because it was something we hadn't covered. I had just assumed.

"Wolves do have... relationships that aren't mated pairs," Cazz said tightly. "And I did, as a young wolf. Before taking the throne."

"Okay, cool, so, like... with those women—females—did you ever do things for them that were just... I mean, you just did it, because you knew they'd like it?"

"Like sending a note after a night of thoughtful passion?" he asked dryly, arching one brow.

I gave him a flat look in return. "Yes, like that. Except... without expecting—or wanting—anything in return."

His lips went thin again. "I am King, Jesse. I was *heir*. And before that, a potential heir. There has not been a day in my life that I have not possessed more, had more expected from me, and achieved more than every peer in the pack. That is precisely *why* I am King." He shook his head. "I thought Maya was teaching you this—"

"She is!" I snapped, frustrated. "But I'm trying to get at something and you're either playing dumb or..."

Oh shit.

I blinked.

His eyes narrowed. "What? What just made your heart pinch?" he muttered.

"Cazz... have you seriously never had a relationship that was just... for the pure joy of it?"

90. Broken Man

~ *JESSE* ~

Cazz was right. My heart *did* pinch. For him. My heart went out to him. I wanted to gather him in and hug him and pat his chest and soothe him, and promise him that it wasn't his fault. But the way he bristled, it was very obvious that he had exactly *zero* interest in my pity.

"I am royal. I do not have the luxury of *any* relationship for the sheer joy of it," he seethed.

Dear Lord, this poor man.

So much of how he dealt with me—and with others—was becoming clear.

I took a deep breath, instinctively wanting to get close to him and protect him from the blow he had to be feeling. But as I swayed towards him his gaze went suspicious and I realized he still didn't understand what I meant.

But how *did* you explain this to someone who had only ever been viewed as an asset, or a status, or a tool?

God help me, I needed to say something, because he was getting twitchy.

So I swallowed my pride and stepped right up to him, putting my hands on his chest and holding his shirt—not even sliding my hand under his shirt to feel the warm planes of his pecs, or the rounds of his shoulders, which were my favorite part and...

Holy shit, I was doing it to him too.

He was so primal, so fierce, so sexual, and so powerful... it was hard to think of him as just... a man.

His brows were low and pinched over his nose. His eyes darted back and forth between mine. He was confused by my reaction, his nostrils flaring, which meant he was drawing in my scent, but something about it didn't make sense to him.

Through the bond I could feel the tension in him rising and realized I needed to do something or he was going to run.

So just when his eyes got wary and his body tensed for flight, I held onto his shirt and locked eyes with him and made myself speak clearly, without hesitation.

Confidence. That's what Maya had said. Know your instincts and follow them.

Well, here we go, Cazz.

"I want you to know that if I met you in my world, and I didn't have a clue who you were, if I just saw you walking down the street, or in a bar, I wouldn't be able to stop watching you."

His eyes were still narrow, but his lips curled up in a smug smile. "I know."

I rolled my eyes. "No, Cazz, listen to me: You could be poor. You could be ugly. You could be *nobody*... but I wouldn't be able to take my eyes off you."

"That's bullshit. You are drawn to my appearance—as you should be, it's—"

"Cazz, seriously. Listen. Please?"

He pursed his lips and I tried again.

"You have a presence. You are... *So* strong. Sometimes that scares me, and sometimes it drives me up the wall. But mostly... mostly I admire that about you. I love that when someone comes to you with a problem, your first instinct is to care and to fix it. I love that when I'm nervous about something, the first thing you want to do is drag me into it and show me not to be scared. I love that... I love that when you touch me, you're thinking about whether I will like it. Those are... those are good things about you. And if I knew them and I saw you, and you weren't the King, or you weren't even a wolf... I would want to know you better. I'd want to be close to you. I think... I think I would like you."

If you weren't so fucking arrogant, I thought, but didn't say it because I was starting to understand something about my mate, and I needed him to hear me.

"Cazz... there are things about you that I would like and respect even if you weren't King, and couldn't compel people."

He blinked. Twice. "Well... that's good. But you see, Jesse... I *am* King. And I *can* compel people. And honestly, you don't have a fucking clue how you would feel about me without that."

"Bullshit," I said bluntly.

He huffed, but I didn't let him deflect.

"That's bullshit, Cazz, because you don't compel me."

"But I could," he said with a dark warning in his tone.

I shook my head. "Then I would *lose* respect for you. But I don't think you will. Because you gave me your word, and I'm starting to notice that even when you huff and prickle about it, you still do what you say you'll do."

"Huff and... *prickle?*" he growled.

"Seriously? That's the part of that statement that landed for you?"

"I am not a hedgehog, Jesse."

"No, you aren't. You're a handsome, powerful wolf, who's apparently never experienced the pure joy of having someone care about you just because they like you!"

He bristled again. "What does any of this have to do with my gift?"

I sighed, discouraged. "I wanted you to know that you aren't indebted to me. You're my mate. I care about you. And last night... Last night I could feel you and I wanted to help. I don't know if you want to talk about your dreams, or—"

"I do *not.*"

"—anything, but I just want you to know... if you ever have another dream like that. Or anything else that makes you feel that way. Just call me like that. Anytime you call me like that I will come, Cazz. I will always come. Whether you're king, or rich, or powerful, or not. That's all. I just wanted you to know that."

He stared down at me. "Um. Great."

I groaned and dropped my face into his chest, sighing. It was like talking to a brick wall! I felt for him, how horrible it must be to never know what it was like to have someone care about you just because they thought you were cool, and—

His fingers hooked under my chin and he lifted my head, his neck craned down so he could look right into my eyes.

"Thank you, Jesse. No one has ever told me that before."

A tiny spark of hope lit in my chest.

Cazz cleared his throat. "Now, I'm almost afraid to ask, but... what the fuck was wrong with the lingerie?"

91. Begin to Breathe

~ *CASIMIR* ~

Jesse was still talking. Something about connections being about a lot more than just having sex.

No kidding. There was *all kinds* of play and anticipation that could improve the bond between a pair when both wolves were engaged. I had always prided myself on never compelling an orgasm. I may have eased the path for females into my bed, but once they were there…

Well, I learned fast, and applied myself to learning them. I had had no complaints.

But my mind was only half on those thoughts—they flitted through, barely registering. Because I was too busy analyzing the bond to really hear her or want to argue. There was something strange going on in her, something I had never sensed before and I was struggling to identify what it was. A warm, solid strength—but not from her. As if the bond itself was growing thicker. But that was the wrong word…

The bond was growing more… resilient.

Interesting.

As she continued speaking earnestly, her pretty brows jumping up and down, her hands gesturing, I wondered whether that new strength came from me, or her?

I knew she was strong. At least in some ways. Stronger than the other females I mated. And yet, there was a strange vulnerability to her as well. A paper-thin shield between her and the world that sparked my Alpha protective instincts, and pissed me off in the same moment.

I *did* want her to be safe.

I *didn't* want her to cower in the face of danger. I certainly didn't want her scrambling for my attention. And yet…

This thing, thrumming in the bond, it wasn't her strength. Or mine. It came from her to me and bolstered me somehow, but it was something I'd never felt before…

"…it's the only way I can really trust you. I want to trust you, Cazz. But if you insist on—"

"I'm sorry, what did you say?"

Her forehead furrowed. "I said… I *want* to trust you."

Trust. Dear god, that's what it was.

Trust.

Something inside me shrieked, but I pushed it away and smiled. "You already do."

Her lips thinned. "In some things, yes. But—"

"You can trust me, Jesse. You're my mate. I will protect you. I will provide for you. I will punish anyone who so much as looks at you in a way that displeases you. What more could you ask for?"

Her mouth opened like she would answer, but then she closed it and pressed her lips thin. "That's great, Cazz. I mean that. I like it. I just… I feel like there's some stuff we could do to… get to know each other better. And when we do that, other things will get better, too."

"I agree wholeheartedly," I growled.

"You do?" Her voice tipped up at the end, hopeful.

"I do." I tipped my head and let my smile turn sly.

She tried not to smile, but she was. I took hold of her arms and started walking her backwards, towards the bed in the room.

This was a guest room—grand, in the way any royal room would be. But nothing like mine or even hers. Yet she'd said she would like me even if I was poor.

I arched a brow.

"Cazz, what are you doing?"

"Playing a game."

"I don't want to play a game—"

"This isn't that kind of game, Jesse. This is… something we can do to build trust."

She tipped her head, a warning in her gaze, but we were almost at the bed, and I needed to position her.

But in order to do that, she would need to trust me.

So I stopped walking her and took her hands. "You said you want to trust me?"

"Yes, I do," she murmured. I could hear her heart beating faster, her breath quickening too. But still… still that thread of fear in her.

It offended me, somehow.

"If it's trust you want, then… put yourself in my hands."

"I already do, Cazz. I'm here, aren't I? Submitted?"

I smiled at her. "Oh, Kitten. It wasn't a metaphor."

Then I reached out for the curtain on the closest of the four poster bed columns and examined it.

Smooth, soft, a little thicker than I would have liked, but it would cushion her skin well. I smiled.

"Cazz… what—?"

I could scent her nerves and gritted my teeth, made myself breathe slowly, bring my eyes up to meet hers with a heated smile.

"I will never harm you, Jesse."

She eyed that curtain in my hand warily. "But?"

"No buts. I want to show you that anything I would choose for you will be… for your benefit."

"Unless you breach the bond with another female."

Those words struck that cord between us, throwing sparks, as if steel had met steel. It stole my breath. And when I could exhale, it was all in a rush.

I had to make myself smile when her eyes returned to me. "Let's assume neither of us will betray the other. You're my mate, and as such, I will do everything in my power to help you grow and thrive. And to learn that I can be trusted."

"Trusted to do what?" she asked uneasily, her eyes flicking to that curtain again.

I began rotating my wrist, turning it, twisting it into a silky rope—pleased when the fabric compressed much thinner than I'd expected.

"Put yourself in my hands and let me show you," I rumbled.

She looked at the long, fabric rope I had made, then back up to me. "Will this help you to trust me, too?"

"Anytime you submit to me, our bond grows stronger, Jesse. I will not force you—it's clear that the power you offer does not come by that route. You're safe. I will persuade you. I will seduce you. I will *ask*."

I leaned right down until we were almost nose-to-nose. Her eyes were wide and shining, and I was smiling, my body thrumming with anticipation of the moment she—"

"Yes," she breathed.

Power crackled through me with such potency, I groaned.

Soundtrack for the next few chapters is
Breathe by Kansh

92. Bound – Part 1

~ *CASIMIR* ~

"Promise me you won't hurt me, Cazz."

"Kitten, I'm going to give you nothing but pleasure so that the next time we're together, you'll remember. And you'll ask for more."

Her heart raced even faster, but there was a simmering heat in her too. "Okay then. Okay. Show me."

To answer, I took the curtain rope and wound it twice around the bedpost, then yanked it tight, before folding the long end in half and reaching for her arm.

Jesse's eyes widened, but she gave me her hand, extending it so I could loop the fabric around her wrist in quick efficient tugs that ended with her wrist knotted expertly in the curtain-rope, positioning her hand higher than her head, but still able to move the limb up and down so it wouldn't grow too tired.

Then I turned her to face the foot of the bed and reached for the curtain on the other side.

When I looped that around the opposite post, Jesse watched me nervously. So I slipped up behind her, warming her back with my body as I extended her other arm and began the same process of ensuring she was securely tied and unable to escape, ensuring that the knots would not slip, but could be released quickly.

When I was done, she stood, feet shoulder-width apart, but arms extended and securely bound.

Already breathing heavily, I pulled her hair back over her shoulder, then leaned in to nuzzle the side of her neck, under her ear.

"Are you ready, *mate?*"

"I guess we're about to find out," she breathed.

The chuckle that broke in my throat was rich and husky, already colored with heat, because my body was already rising to seek her. Just seeing her bound like that sent shivers of pleasure through my belly.

I showed her how to position her hands so she could comfortably hold the curtain-ropes and give herself some leverage.

She tugged experimentally on each one and I felt the jolt of fear that sizzled in her when she realized she really couldn't get free.

I murmured reassurance, anticipation, seduction as I reached around to begin unbuttoning her clothes, kissing her neck and whispering to her as my fingers made quick work of stripping her naked, except for the shirt that fell down her back because I'd forgotten to remove it before we started.

Oh well, I grinned to myself.

Using my teeth, I split the shoulder seams on each side, then drew the shirt off the sleeves and began twisting it softly into a thick roll that I then placed over her eyes.

She gasped when I lifted it over her head and blocked her sight, her body trembling.

"Cazz… I don't know…"

I paused, halfway through tying it, and pulled it away from her face, analyzing her scent and considering what we were going to do.

"Is that a no, Jesse? Or an *I don't know?*"

"I… I don't know."

With a warm rumble in my chest I leaned into her ear again. "Trust me. Give yourself into my hands. Let me prove to you that I won't harm you. But if at any point I do, if at any moment it becomes too much, just say…" I hesitated. "I need a word. Tell me a word that will mean I release you immediately. The moment you say it, I'll stop and untie you. I give you my word."

She took a deep breath, then blew it out. "How about… love? It seems like that's… that's something that won't just come up, right?" She gave a nervous chuckle and for a moment I balked.

But then I realized… she was joking. She was playing with me. Good girl. *Very* good girl.

"*Love* it is," I said without a hint of irony. Then I pulled the blindfold up against her eyes and began tying it at the back of her hair. When I was sure it was secure, I leaned into her ear again, stroking my fingertips up the front of her thigh and letting my breath flutter in her hair.

"Now, are you ready?"

She gave a quick nod, but her breath was too fast.

"Good girl," I growled.

She bit her lip as I opened my mouth on her neck and reached around to touch her, just like I had our first time—letting her feel my hands slide over her body, letting my fingers slowly be wetted by her need, then run over her most sensitive flesh until her knees began to twitch.

She was breathing harder now and my blood was fire, her scent rising higher and higher as her body remembered past pleasure and she eased away from her fear.

It was difficult to hold myself back at first. This was one of my favorite ways to play, and the more she gave, the fiercer the roar in my veins of need and want and crackling pleasure. But I knew if we were going to do this together, if she was going to learn to want me this way, it had to be good for her. So I made myself take it slow and savor her.

I dropped to kneel, planting a kiss at the base of her spine at the same time I cupped her ankles, then drew soft fingertips up her calves, then the backs of her thighs.

I repeated the gesture, touching so softly I could feel each little hair and how it rose to meet me.

I chuckled happily, then stood up, letting my cock catch at the apex of her thighs, but not using it yet, letting that thick hardness be a taste of promise on her flesh, still stroking her thighs, and sides with my fingertips until she was goosebumping everywhere and her quick breathing had become a rasp.

Only when she was starting to lean and sway against the bonds, trying desperately to get closer to my touch, to press in, but lacking the leverage to do so, only then did I flatten my hands on her body and begin to stroke in earnest, cupping her, pressing into her skin, sliding against her flesh.

And when she began to whimper, I lifted her, bending one knee to plant my foot on the footboard of the bed, then lowering her to my thigh with one hand between her legs.

She was higher there, so had more slack and could let her hands down, reach back for me, though her fingers only brushed against my hair, sending a wave of goosebumps down my spine.

Bracketing her with my arms, I cupped and kneaded her breast with my free hand as I rocked her, and she gasped as she realized all of her weight pressed her body down on my thigh and fingers.

And as she wrapped her knees around my thigh and began to roll her hips, riding my fingers and the heel of my hand, her breathing grew urgent.

I tweaked her nipple, stroking and pinching, rolling it between my thumb and forefinger in time with her hips. And I felt her starting to come apart.

"Cazz, that's… that's… I've never felt…"

"That's my girl… my beautiful mate," I rasped. "Find your pleasure, Queen."

She could not fall from between my arms and she was such a little thing, it wasn't difficult to keep her balanced. I growled with approval as she relaxed and began to move with more urgency, believing that I would not let her fall even when her movements became stronger and more confident.

Watching her body writhe was thrilling. I hadn't even entered her yet, but I was hard as a rock and aching for her.

But there was a purpose to this—and important learning for her. So I made myself hold back, enjoying the anticipation of what was to come.

And as her cries grew harsher and her body tightened on my fingers, I tipped my head between her shoulders, my breath rushing down her spine as she began to shake, then cry out at the peak of each roll.

"Cazz… *Cazz—*"

"Let yourself go, Jesse. I have you." They were simple words, low and harsh, a succinct reassurance, but I felt her clench on my fingers. Then she stopped breathing and her body bowed. I dropped her breast to wrap that arm around her middle and hold her down, grinding onto my hand and thigh.

And as her first orgasm tore through her, I chuckled through my own heavy breath, and thanked God for making the female of the species.

Then her breath rushed out of her and her body began to tremble.

"Cazz…" she gasped, breathless and sweating. "That was—"

"One down, three to go," I growled.

She gave a breathless laugh, then a little squeak as I dropped my leg and lowered her to the ground.

"Cazz! I—"

"Don't worry, I've got you. I won't let you fall," I rumbled. "Just hold on and let me show you the way."

I smiled when her hands gripped the bonds until her knuckles turned white.

93. Bound - Part 2

~ *CASIMIR* ~

For a moment I stood there, gathering my self-control. She was beautiful—open and trembling from her orgasm, her skin flushed and warm, her breasts rising and falling with her heavy breath.

I stroked her slowly, but with full palms, playing hands up and down her body, kissing her neck and shoulder. I was preparing to change our position... But first I had to steady those weak knees, make certain she was ready to take her own weight again.

When she'd found her feet again and her legs were no longer shaking, I began stroking her body again—though staying away from anywhere too sacred. I didn't want her overstimulated.

"Are you going to untie me now?" she asked hesitantly, turning her head though she was still blindfolded.

I chuckled, filling both hands with her breasts and giving her peaked nipples a gentle pinch. "Not yet."

She sucked in a breath and arched into my touch. "But... I can't touch you."

"Yes you can," I said, my voice deep and rough with growing desire. "Use your body. Feel me, Kitten. Not with your hands, with the rest of you."

And to my eternal delight, she did. I'd positioned myself at her back, my erection resting in the cleft of her buttocks. And as I kneaded and played with her breasts, she bit her lip and began to experiment, leaning back against the bonds that kept her hands up so that her shoulders brushed my chest, but with her back arched so that her breasts were pushed up, into my hands.

She took a half-step back with one foot, bringing us closer together at the hip, then undulated her body against me in a way that was clumsy, but highly effective.

"Like that?" she asked breathlessly.

"Yes… just like that…" My breath hissed out through my teeth when she hollowed her lower back so her buttocks rose, then rubbed against me, up and down as she tried to keep her shoulders against my chest.

I looked down at her, shaking my head in disbelief. I could sense her nerves—she was still uncertain, but willing to try. And she took delight in getting a reaction from me.

But if I was going to make this last, really give her something to soothe her fears, I couldn't explode all over her back, so I took hold of her hips, holding her in place, then dropped slowly, letting my body drag along hers, until I was kneeling behind her.

Hands still on her hips, eye level with her lower-back, I smiled. There were so many options. Which to try first?

But it was clear that I couldn't enter her yet. We'd be finished far too quickly if I did.

So, letting my hands trail down her legs, I dropped to all fours and crawled between her knees.

She giggled and bounced on my back like a child playing horses, but I was only getting in position. I turned, still kneeling, arching back, my head practically resting on the footboard of the bed because there was very little room between her and it, then I dragged fingers up the insides of her legs, her thighs, stroking that swollen flesh and teasing her as I spoke, because this one was going to feel less secure for her.

"I'm strong, Jesse," I said quietly, kissing my way up her belly, dipping my tongue into her navel. "I need you to remember that—and trust that I won't let you fall."

"Why?" she asked quickly. "What are you—oh!"

I'd brought my arms together between her legs and cupped them underneath her so she straddled my elbows. And I began to lift her.

"Cazz! I'm going to fall!" she wobbled, gasping.

"Lean back against the restraints, use them for balance," I instructed her quietly, still lifting her until I could get her knees level with my shoulders.

At first she kept trying to balance herself, gasping and wobbling, but with gentle urging, eventually she came to understand that by leaning back, she'd gain leverage. And once she was more comfortable, I urged her to hook her knees over my shoulders so she sat on my chest and hung from her wrist restraints, and my shoulders. Only then could I brace her ass on my upper arms and looped my arms back to grip her thighs and hold her securely.

"Open your thighs, Kitten," I purred, pressing my hands and turning my face to kiss the inside of that soft flesh and encourage her to relax and let me take her weight. "I've got you."

She made a little noise in her throat, but as I kissed my way up the inside of her thigh, she relaxed, and then she opened to me.

With a low groan, I used my fingers to spread her, then bracing her as securely as I could, I buried my face in her flesh and kissed her right at her core.

She tensed, but as I began to apply my tongue to that fleshy little bundle of nerves, she sighed and eased back, letting herself hang from the restraints and beginning to roll her hips again.

It was, I knew, an entirely different experience than I'd given her before. And as sensitive as she was, she twitched and gasped, wriggling and arching until I found just the right spot and rhythm.

"Yes, Cazz…" she panted. "There… Oh god…" Then she began to pant again.

Knees hooked over my shoulders, ankles locked behind me, and her thighs pinned in my arms, Jesse gave the most beautiful groan and her head fell back. She finally fully let the restraints take her weight as she hung back, her breasts pointed to the ceiling, and rocked very slightly in rhythm with my lapping.

Her breath was coming in short puffs, her knees tightening and loosening on my shoulders as she sought that peak again. I couldn't speak to her, urge her on, but I groaned against her flesh, teasing her with my tongue faster and faster until her pants became cries.

She arched her back, not breathing at all, pressing into my kiss, and her feet lifted so that she almost unhooked from my shoulders, and even her cries stopped as her entire body tensed in a stunning climax.

94. Bound – Part 3

~ *CASIMIR* ~

I had to hold her thighs tightly, sliding and teasing rapidly with my tongue until her breath rushed out of her and her knees tightened against my jaw.

"Stop! Stop!" she hissed, jerking and bucking.

I chuckled and pulled back far enough to speak. "That's only two. We're still—"

"Cazz, please… please…" she panted. "I want to touch you."

"Soon, Kitten," I rasped, fighting my own battle then. The scent of her was rich and heavy in the room and my body was urgent. *Demanding* her.

I'd wanted women before, but there was something about her—each time she gave up her own will, each moment she trusted me… the power that coursed through me grew. And the need for her increased right along with it.

She was trembling, shaking in my arms, her skin flushed and rosy. Her hands gripping the restraints. With whispered reassurances that she was safe, I lifted her enough that she could unhook from my shoulders and lower her legs, then helped her stand again on knees as unsteady as a newborn colt's. She stood, legs wide, feet planted either side of me, her belly at eye level, hands still extended over her head and wide. I stayed there for a moment looking at her…

Dear god, the need that tore through me. I growled.

"What—what is it?" she panted looking down at me.

"Nothing," I said hoarsely as I pushed to my feet, my own knees a little weak as well.

"Cazz? What's wrong?"

"Nothing," I breathed. "Only… I want you."

"Oh, Cazz… I want you too. Untie me and let me—"

"Soon," I huffed, blinking, pushing away the uneasiness that rose when I thought of how she affected me. "Trust me."

She bit her lip, but nodded. I watched her for a moment because I could sense her unease—was she only uncertain about remaining bound, or was there something more to it? But she didn't use the safe word, and she wasn't struggling against the bonds.

My breathing picked up with anticipation as I stood over her, staring down the valley between her breasts, watching them rise and fall with her breathing.

I'd been holding her hips, making certain she was steady before I let her go, but now that we were both back on our feet I began to stroke again.

Jesse sighed and let her head loll forward this time, leaning into my touch, but her forehead was pinched as if she was unhappy.

"What's wrong?" I asked her, surprised by how hoarse I sounded.

"I want to touch you," she whispered.

"You will," I murmured back but I saw how she slumped.

The blindfold still covered her eyes, but a portion of the shirt had fallen loose and made a flap over her cheekbone. Instinctively I reached out to tuck it back in, then changed my mind and pulled the whole thing off to reward her for continuing to trust.

She blinked several times, then she lifted her head and her eyes found mine and she gave a hesitant smile.

"Hi," she said, a little shyly.

"Hi." I smiled back at her, stroking fingertips up her sides, then dragging them along the sensitive skin inside her arm. "Does anything hurt?"

She snorted. "Not right now. My whole body is just… pulsing. But I think I'm going to feel this in my shoulders later."

I nodded. Likely she would. I made a mental note to rub her with the herbed oils tonight, then took the half-step back to sit on the end of the bed, pulling her to stand between my knees.

With her arms extended up and her body slightly bowed, her breasts were presented to me like a feast I couldn't resist.

I ran both hands up her sides, to her ribs, cupped her breasts, stroking, playing my thumbs over her nipples that were rivet-hard. Then I pushed one to the side with the pad of my thumb, letting it pop up again and rumbling in my chest when the rosy little peak sprang back.

I couldn't resist. Looping one arm behind her lower back, I pulled her up onto her toes and against me, cupping one breast with my free hand, while I opened my mouth to taste the other.

Jesse leaned back over my arm and shivered, twitching, her breath catching when I nipped with my teeth.

I smiled and did it again. And again.

I spent minutes tasting and sucking, dragging my nose along her collarbones, cupping her ass and kissing her neck—anything to delay diving between her legs again because I knew it was important to give that part of her body time to desensitize—to keep her blood pumping, but stimulate other areas so that when I entered her she'd get that rush again.

But I was so needy, my own body aching for her.

Still, I waited, teasing and tasting, kissing and humming against her skin until her breathing was short and shallow again, and her hips began to bump, seeking me.

Then I lifted my head to meet her eyes and took her hair in my fist, wrapping it around my wrist and pulling her head back so her mouth was open for my kiss.

Her tongue tasted like honey.

I sipped and teased and sucked until her head dropped back and I could nuzzle her throat, let my teeth graze her skin there. I was about to urge her to climb into my lap when she sighed heavily.

And not happily.

I froze, one arm locked at her back, the other hand full of her plump ass, and my face buried in her neck.

My heart pounded faster. "What is it?" I asked, my voice much rougher than I intended.

"Cazz... I really want to touch you."

Relief flooded through me and I squeezed her more tightly. "Soon," I repeated, dropping both hands down to cup her ass and pull her up into my lap. "Soon, Kitten. Just... trust me."

95. Bound – Part 4

My entire body hummed, pulsing in time with my heartbeat that was pounding rapidly, thudding in my ears and thrumming in my skin.

I'd never felt so alive—or vulnerable. It was a strange and heady mix. I wanted to be there with Cazz. There was something different in him today. Because of the night we'd had last night? Or because we were doing… this?

I didn't know and that bothered me. But when he took off the blindfold I was reassured because his eyes were bright and his expression awed. He stared, drinking in the sight of me. With my hands bound, he pawed all over me, teasing, tasting, making every inch of my skin tingle. It was incredible.

He sat on the end of the bed with his knees wide. He had pulled me to stand between his feet and for a while he'd just been playing and kissing. But the truth was I'd come twice, but I still didn't feel satisfied.

I wanted him. I wanted him inside me. I wanted his kiss on my mouth. I wanted him to hold me—and I wanted to hold him.

At the beginning, having him tie my hands felt a little naughty, and watching him be so attentive to my body was thrilling. I could definitely understand the appeal. But I was still so unsure of him and… I wanted more.

But I knew I couldn't ask for it.

I shouldn't have told him the safe word was love. I had been sarcastic, but he'd smiled like I had pleased him, and that hurt.

And yet... there was no doubt that even though he'd tied me, he was also being more gentle than he'd been before last night— and there was something more present in him. As if he was really here with *me*. So hope and fear both climbed from my chest to my throat.

It was a shock to me that I didn't feel self-conscious standing in front of him naked like this. It helped that there was nothing but heat and approval in his eyes when he scanned me. But still, I would have expected to feel more wary of his eyes...

Then he started stroking me again and I stopped thinking at all. He bent me back over his arm and I let myself just give in to the attention. By the time he had finished playing with me I was panting.

Then he lifted his head from my neck and our eyes locked for a moment. His eyes flashed as he reached back and gripped my hair, then he pulled my head back again and to my relief he finally kissed me properly.

I was lost in that kiss, fighting the bonds that stopped me wrapping arms around him, but my entire body shivering at the sensation of his tongue drawing along mine again and again.

But when he left my mouth and continued kissing his way down my neck, it was reflex to try and reach for him, to bury hands in his hair and I met the resistance of the bonds and sighed.

Cazz froze—which scared me so I stopped moving too.

He didn't lift his head, but spoke against my neck. "What is it?"

"Cazz... I really want to touch you."

I felt him relax against me like he'd been scared I was going to say something else, and his hands tightened on me.

"Soon," he murmured again, his hands sliding down to grab my ass on both sides, then he started lifting me. "Soon, Kitten. Just... trust me."

I wobbled a bit before I remembered to lean into the bonds to take the weight of my upper body as Cazz lifted my legs, then he urged me wrap my legs around his waist and I hooked my ankles at his lower back, pulling myself against him—and we both exhaled heavily.

We weren't kissing, but he kept his head up, our cheeks brushing, his hair tickling my nose, our twin breaths fluttering on each other's faces as I tried to find my balance. I was still shifting, finding the most comfortable way to sit on his thighs, but he groaned and pulled me against him, rubbing himself against me.

I was so sensitive, I twitched and gasped—the zing of pleasure so intense, it was almost painful. Cazz felt my body jolt and gave a grunting little huff that was probably the sexiest sound I'd ever heard. His jaw brushed my temple and my hardened nipples brushed his chest, and just like that, my body was humming again, aching deep inside with the yearning for him.

His fingers clawed into my thighs and he flicked his hair back as he pulled back just far enough to meet my eyes—and we locked in.

It was a stunning moment, coated in pleasure. The room, the palace, the *world* disappeared. All I was aware of was *him*—his hands on my body, the promising nudge of his arousal between my legs. He was smiling, but I saw the trickle of sweat down his brow. But it was his arctic eyes, bright and piercing, unwavering as he leaned in so close that his lips brushed mine as he spoke.

"Ready, Kitten?"

"Don't call me Kitten."

He arched a brow, but his smile widened. "Oh?"

"My name is Jesse."

He nodded once, his breath coming short and fast. "I ache for you, *Jesse.* Are you ready?"

"Yes, Cazz," I choked out, my breath getting faster and shallower too. "I'm ready."

I thought he'd kiss me. Or bend me back over his arm again, or something.

Instead, he didn't even blink. His eyes remained locked on mine as he gripped my hips and lifted me, positioning me over him, then pulled me down onto him in a single, slow slide.

My eyes wanted to flutter closed, but I didn't want to lose that connection with him, so I forced myself to stay in that gaze, groaning as he took me, my entire body coming alive as if he'd injected my bloodstream with heated joy, raising the small hairs all over my body as he shuddered and his jaw went slack.

And as he filled me, he never broke eye-contact.

Then, when I was seated on him, he kept me there for a moment, fingers gripping my thighs, his chest rising and falling quickly, both of us panting. His brows twitched and he searched my eyes, but I didn't know what to say, because everything I was thinking would scare him away. So I remained completely silent, but never even blinked.

Then Cazz, my mate, and the Alpha King, grabbed for my hips like he was grounding himself and we began to move together… and I was lost.

96. Bound – Part 5

~ JESSE ~

"Cazz… *please,*" I hissed through my teeth minutes later, my head sinking back as I fought to speed him up, but he resisted.

He chuckled mercilessly—and breathlessly—holding my hips tightly and keeping the steady pace, lifting and guiding me, thwarting all my attempts to force him to move faster, digging my heels into his back, pulling him with my legs. But he was too strong.

He was fighting for control, though. I could see it. Feel it in him. His hold on the bond had slipped and I was feeling him clearly—I could measure the rising tide of his pleasure—which only increased mine—his determination to hold himself back, and his battle with the call of something primal in him that wanted to give me exactly what I wanted.

But so far, he was winning that fight.

Both our bodies were slick with sweat, and the only sound in the room that was louder than my ragged breath was his. As we moved together I could feel the glittering promise of another orgasm blinking on the horizon, but I'd already had two, and he was going *too damn slow.*

"Cazz—"

I pulled my head up intending to give him a piece of my mind, but found him gazing down at me, his stubbled jaw tight, his sweaty hair falling over his eyes that gleamed with a white-hot light. I saw his throat bob and bit my lip, leaning back into the restraints to change the angle and try to get more leverage to force him faster, but gasping instead when he reached a place within me that made the glittering promise on the horizon surge to the threat of a crashing wave.

"Cazz... *Cazz...*"

"Let yourself go, Jesse. I have you—ah, *fuck!*" he cursed as his fingers dug into my hips and he unleashed for a moment, pounding into me hard and fast so that my breasts bounced and my eyes rolled back in my head.

I wanted to call to him, needed to tell him how heavenly it was, but my lungs had frozen as another orgasm crashed over me, starting where we joined and spiraling out to every limb and nerve-ending.

Cazz moaned and cursed, his fingers tight on me and his body shuddering as he forced himself to slow and wring the last pulse of pleasure from me, then stop altogether when I slumped.

I tried to fall forward over him, to hold onto him, to ground myself, but my hands were still tied, so I could only tip my head forward and pant, my chest heaving and knees shaking. I was disoriented and confused... I didn't think he'd come, but he was trembling, holding me, his head down, his forehead on my shoulder and his chest heaving.

"Cazz," I gasped. "Did you—"

"No," he grunted on an exhale. "Just... give me a moment."

"But—"

"Three down," he rasped. "We're almost there, Jesse."

The sound that broke from me was half-laugh, half-sob. I was still trembling. My entire body pulsing in time with my heartbeat. My skin felt two sizes too small, and like it might actually split with the pressure of all this pleasure.

"Cazz... I can't... Three is plenty. Please, just... untie me. Let me touch you. Please. You can... it's your turn—"

I cut off because even though he didn't lift his head, and didn't respond to my words, one of his hands finally left my hip and slid up my body.

With his head still resting on my shoulder, he palmed his way up to my breast, tweaking my nipple as he passed over it, making me jolt, which made him groan. But then he followed my arm, sliding his hand up the inside of my arm to my wrist where it was bound where he fumbled for a moment, then there was a startling yank and suddenly my hand was free.

Folding forward, I buried my face in that place where his shoulder met his neck and clapped the hand to his back, clinging, almost crying with relief when he slid the other hand up my other arm, and then that limb was free too.

My shoulders gave a zing of pain, each time I lowered my arms, but I didn't care. I just wrapped myself around him, clinging like a fucking barnacle—no pun intended.

And to my relief, Cazz returned the gesture, wrapping me in his arms and pulling me up against him, moving inside me so that I bit my lip again, but didn't dare lift my head or let him go, because he was finally letting me touch him.

For a long moment we did nothing but hold each other and the pinch of emotion tightened in my chest and in my throat, because *Cazz was holding me.* But then he exhaled all in a rush and raised his head to look down at me, nudging me with his shoulder to urge me to lift my head as well.

And when I did, his eyes were near-black with need, those little muscles at the back of his jaw flexing.

He didn't speak, but I could feel something in the bond—a resonance that flooded from me to him and rebounded back, as he reached one hand up to comb my hair back from my face with his fingers.

I wondered if he knew his hand was shaking.

Then he cupped the back of my head and kissed me, groaning into my mouth.

And then he turned us both over, holding me to him as he rolled onto all fours and crawled up the bed, carrying me with him.

When he pressed me into the mattress, I almost cried with relief to be in his arms and holding him. I kissed him back with fervor, trembling. It felt like my bones were vibrating.

Cazz pumped his hips slowly, and I arched to meet him. But just when I thought this would be it, we'd finally make love, he tore himself out of the kiss and pushed up on hands and knees.

"Cazz, what—"

"I need you, *now.*"

I was confused when the weight of him disappeared for a moment, but then big, strong hands took hold of me, and flipped me over. Then he slid his hand under my stomach and pulled up on my belly. And when I got my knees under me, still disoriented, the warmth of him reappeared at my back.

Tender hands caressed my body, following the lines of my waist and breasts, then he positioned himself, then plunged into me with a guttural groan.

I gasped and sank down on my elbows. But Cazz folded over me, one hand sliding down my arm to twine our fingers and fist the pillow together.

His mouth opened on my neck just under my ear and he rasped my name, and then he began to move.

The position was new and I was uncertain at first, but every hair on the back of my neck rose, every prickle and tingle in my skin danced down my spine as he covered me and touched me and took me, grasping, growling, and pounding until I found the rhythm of it and discovered the joy of resistance, in the slide of his chest against my back, of our thighs slapping, and I began to climb and climb and climb...Then fell, pinwheeling into the ultimate bliss, my body jolting with pleasure, his name tearing from my throat—and almost weeping with joy when he followed me seconds later, growling and rasping my name, his knuckles white, squeezing my fingers between his to anchor us both.

Then he collapsed over me, his chest heaving, his weight a delicious, welcome blanket pressing me into the mattress, and his breath fluttering against my damp neck.

And as I lay there under him, boneless and depleted—utterly sated—there was nothing in the world but him—that thick, warm cord of light that connected us at the heart.

It pulsed in time with our heartbeats, sending little shocks of something warm and weighty back and forth between us.

97. Little Spoon

~ *CASIMIR* ~

Without leaving her body, I had rolled Jesse onto her side and buried my face in her hair... I took a moment to simply breathe and let the thrumming in my veins ease, tracing fingers up and down the dips and valleys of her side feeling more sated and content than I could remember in a good long while.

As she lay panting in my arms, I reached for her in the bond, inhaling her scent, measuring her for stress—it had been her first time bound and she had been nervous. But I was pleased to find her relaxed, her scent unhindered by fear. Instead, she smelled of contentment, like a cat stretching in the sun. And in the bond... in the bond she *pulsed.*

Memories of her pulsing around me jolted through me and I smiled. I wanted to purr. For her first time, she'd proved bold. She had been... delicious.

I flattened my hand on Jesse's waist, stroking it down her side, down to her knee, then letting my fingertips trail slowly up the seam between her thighs and my heartrate picked up again for a moment. I turned my thoughts inward, considering my body. It likely wouldn't be long before I could take her again. But just as I reached the apex of her thighs and leaned into her ear to whisper the suggestion, Jesse sighed and reached for my wrist, pulling my arm up and over her waist and twining our fingers on her stomach... then promptly fell asleep.

I smiled. *Kitten is tired. It's been a big day.*

Then the room was so quiet and still, I was left… uneasy. A tiny twist of tension appeared in my chest.

I inhaled deeply, tasting her scent, telling myself there was no reason for aggravation, then let my breath ease out of my throat as I considered a nap of my own.

If my advisors and I hadn't taken too long to get the Gammas out to interfere with the humans, I probably had hours before anyone would look for me. I hadn't slept long enough last night. And that little session, while delicious, had taken a great deal of control. If I wanted to try it again, it was probably wise to curl up and rest with her.

Feeling indulgent, trying to ignore the bubbling tension in my chest, I shifted my weight, buried my nose in her hair, and let my body lean into hers, tightening my grip on her fingers to keep her hand there on her belly while I curled myself around her until my body cradled hers from shoulders to knees.

The room was silent beyond our breaths and my spent body sagged into weariness. I reminded myself that it had been a helluva week. It would be lovely to just lay here with her in the afterglow of… that.

My eyes dragged closed and I smiled again, inhaling her as her breath evened out. There was an itch between my shoulder blades, an urge to move. But I reminded myself that we were here for a purpose. It was good for her chances to conceive if she just lay here. So I could let her relax into the mattress.

Into me.

I turned my eyes inward again, snapping back the shadows and instead letting myself be pleased. The bond between us still pulsed, glowing and growing, that cord between us becoming a rope that burned brightly as the power she offered flowed into me in bright little waves.

I could feel myself increasing. It was intoxicating. *She* was intoxicating. Of course, that did not mean that she would succeed, I warned myself. While she showed great strength in some areas— her bold and adventurous spirit, for example—I still had concerns that she may ultimately prove too weak.

Maya was reluctantly optimistic about her chances of truly molding into a Queen. When I'd asked my great aunt how she measured Jesse, the matriarch's eyes had flashed.

"What? What are you thinking?" I had insisted because Maya kept her mind closed like a steel trap, though that wasn't unusual. It had always been her way.

"She may surprise you, Cazz. She surprises me—both in her strengths, and her weaknesses."

"What are her strengths as you see them?"

Maya was quiet for a moment, then she turned away, smiling as she spoke. "Jesse doesn't fall in the petty conflicts that many females do which shows a strength of character and mind I do not usually see in one so young."

I frowned, not entirely convinced that Jesse was an independent thinker—she might just be human, and appearing willing to be different because she didn't know how else to be. But I kept those thoughts to myself.

"I still worry that when push comes to shove she'll be too soft to really take Alpha. And then where will I be? I cannot let my offspring be weak."

"Cazz, if your offspring with her are weak, I will eat my cane."

I had huffed and laughed her off, pleased that she wasn't dismissing Jesse as a true Alpha, but now that I lay here in silence... my doubts came rushing back.

If I were to have children with Jesse, would they follow my strength? Or would they offer themselves as she did?

The mere thought of one of mine humbling themselves to a lesser wolf chilled my blood and I almost let Jesse go and rolled away. But I recognized that to be an overreaction.

And still, the tension in my chest would not ease.

I would just have to take any child in hand as soon as they weren't dependent on her—especially if they were male. Not let her have too much influence until the strongest of them rose to the top. While I had despised my own father's "training," perhaps there was a balance. Perhaps I could find a way to help my children grow in strength without... breaking them to do it.

I shied away from the dark thoughts that rose in the wake of that and pushed away all thoughts of the future and even the problems outside of this room.

She was here. She was warm. She was willing, and she was delicious.

A new image flashed in my mind and my smile returned: It was Jesse, her back arched and mouth open, calling for me as she pulled against the restraints and fought for leverage and position to find her peak.

A rumble of pleasure began in my chest and I let go of her fingers to begin stroking her side again.

It could not be denied that she was the best mate I had taken so far, with that oddly alluring mix of innocence and sass.

She had challenged me earlier, but then given in when I asserted myself. And not because she feared my reaction—that was the part that delighted me—but because she was *choosing* to please me.

There were other things she'd done in the past twenty-four hours, other questions and uncertainties that my mind wanted to conjure, but I pushed them away to focus on this act of submission. This building of *trust.*

My breath shuddered a little at all the ways *that* would serve us.

Given how she had enjoyed this impromptu interlude, perhaps I could introduce her to the true nature of the alcoves in the Den sooner than I had anticipated.

That thought had my blood thrilling, which wasn't going to help me rest. But laying here, still inside her, it was suddenly hard to want to rest. If she wasn't too sore, there was always my favorite alcove—

'Cazz...'

I startled. Then breathed a curse.

Ghere was reaching for me. Scratching at my mind. *Dammit.*

All thoughts of having Jesse bent over that pommel horse, her wrists and ankles tied down, fled my mind as I reluctantly opened to my manservant, careful to keep memories and scents of what had just occurred, blocked from him.

'I'm busy. What is it?'

'Where are you?'

'Still in the palace, but—what's going on?'

'There's something here I think you need to see. Remember that footage I told you about, the recording of the Reapers that was being investigated?'

'Yes... but they haven't asked pertinent questions in weeks.'

Ghere hesitated, which was so unlike him, every one of my senses leaped to alert.

'Ghere, what—'

'Lawr caught something. The humans in the wood may not be as innocent as we thought. You need to see this.'

98. Deal

~ CASIMIR ~

Images flooded my mind from Ghere—his memories of the grainy, human footage from CCTV in a human city street as a team of Reapers swept a woman up and into one of the vans, while a group of human men looked on from across the road—

—then much clearer, colorful video that appeared to be from a phone but taken from a distance so it was shaky and blurred, zooming in on one of the clusters of young men out in the forest… And one of them looked very similar to one of those men on the street in the other video.

It was hard to tell because the clothing was different. But the set of his shoulders, and that backwards baseball cap…

Were they the same man?

Fuck. Fuck fuck fuck. *'Twenty minutes,'* I growled through the link. *'Have food and drink brought to the Council rooms, I haven't had time to eat yet.'*

'Yes, Si—'

I slammed the link closed between us, cutting him off as I reluctantly drew out of Jesse's body and rolled away. There was a small bathing room off these quarters, I would—

"Cazz… what…?"

Drowsy and pink-cheeked, Jesse half-rolled towards me, her eyes squinting and blinking away sleep as she looked for me.

I hesitated, mid-step, urged to rush back to her, to crawl over her, to take her again—frantic, desperate, quickly—before I had to leave her again. But I couldn't. There wasn't time. And besides—

"Cazz, what's going on?" she said more clearly, pushing her hair back as she sat up and turned to look at me, her forehead lined with worry. "You're leaving?"

"I have no choice," I growled. "There's an urgent matter. An emergency."

Her eyes locked on mine, and I held her gaze.

She sighed and flopped back down to the pillows, her breasts bouncing in a way that made me swallow a groan.

"Seriously?"

"Yes, seriously," I growled. "We were slow to address the issue of the humans outside because we don't want to *draw* attention. But now it looks as if they may not be as unaware of us as we thought. If that is true, our current strategy will not work. And the decision of how to move forward is ultimately mine."

I swept up my clothes from where I had tossed them on the floor and hurried towards the bathing room and inside without closing the door. I wet a cloth from under the sink quickly and began hurriedly washing myself before I would dress again. Who knew how many hours it would be before I could bathe properly. Much as I preferred having her scent on me, some of the unmated Alphas were still itchy. If we had to call a conclave...

It was close to a full minute before she spoke again, her voice raised just high enough to reach me through the open door.

"I'm disappointed you're leaving so fast. I thought maybe we could have dinner and..."

"Me too," I said through my teeth, though that jangle of unease turned me into a liar. I cursed, working on my buttons, my jaw growing tighter with every passing second as all the many and varied ways this could go horribly wrong began to file through my head—superimposed over flashes of Jesse, strung up on the bed, her mouth open and teeth bared and *holy shit*.

Of all the cursed luck.

I got my shirt buttoned and turned for the door, stopping dead when she was standing there, looking up at me, naked but holding her clothes over her arm, her eyes wide and searching mine the moment our gazes clashed.

Something in the bond went cold and that stopped me in my tracks.

"Do you really have to?" she asked quietly. "Or are you just... fleeing?"

Fleeing?!

My jaw went tight. "Yes, I really have to." Alarm bells rang in my head as her eyes went sad and wide. I gritted my teeth and strode to the door, nudging her aside until I could get back into the room beyond her.

I should have gone that second, but the pulse in the bond was jumping and erratic now and something held me back. Some instinct sang that this was a brittle moment to be handled with care.

I fought it—I couldn't afford to let her start clinging again. There were too many demands, too many needs. She *must* be able to walk on her own!

Growling with impatience, but still uneasy about those final steps to the door, I stalked over to the bed and began twitching at the curtains, tugging them loose from where they still lay in slack loops around the posts and shaking them out, pawing at the creases where they'd been knotted.

"I have to go. I have to be back in the council chambers in a few minutes."

There was a beat before she answered, but when she did, the strange, emotionless tone in her voice pulled me around to examine her face and scent—then stopped me cold.

"You're running from me," she said, and she sounded hurt. And *judgmental?*

I scoffed. "I assure you, I am not."

"You're lying."

"No, Jesse, I'm not lying—but I am… aggravated," I said sharply, turning on her.

She was still in the doorway of the bathroom, still staring at me, the shadow of an accusation in her eyes.

"What?" I barked. When she didn't reply, I shook my head and turned on my heel, starting for the door. "I don't have time for this."

"Cazz that was… amazing. Even I could tell… You're feeling something and you don't want to. You're running."

I stopped dead, the urge to snarl and intimidate crackling up my spine, *how dare she?!*

But I made myself bite it back and turn slowly, finding her with my eyes. Hers widened when she saw my face.

"I am a King, Jesse."

"And I'm your mate. I mean… if you don't breach the bond."
Her in my lap with her head thrown back.

Her laying on the bed, my nose buried in her hair.

Her fingers sliding between mine, tightening, pulling me closer—

I blinked.

My mother's shrieks behind closed doors.

The suck and drag of my previous mates shivering hearts, the accusations in their eyes.

The way they flinched from me—

"Cazz... Cazz, I'm not... I wasn't... what's wrong?" she breathed, dropping her clothes and hurrying towards me.

But I sucked in a breath and stepped back, away from her extended hand. "Nothing!"

Jesse halted in front of me, wilting like an unwatered flower, her eyes big and accusing.

I met that gaze and shook my head.

Her forehead pinched. "What are you afraid of?"

I cursed and turned on my heel, storming towards the door, ignoring the question.

"This isn't a little problem, I will probably be up most of the night. You shouldn't expect to see me again this evening."

"Cazz."

"I don't have time, Jesse," I muttered as I reached for the door.

"Cazz, please—"

"We'll speak tomorrow if I'm in the Palace."

"Cazz, I'm your mate! I trusted you—and you were true to your word. I'm true to mine as well. We could do this together!"

Her words were high and plaintive, pleading, but resolute. I stopped short, one foot already out the door but still holding it.

My heart was beating way too fast. I couldn't do this. Not now. Likely, not ever. But Ghere's words echoed in my head.

Don't do to her what you did to the others.

Fuck.

"Cazz... please. Let me in."

I swallowed back that chittering unease and turned to meet her eyes over my shoulder and resolved to tell her the truth. I supposed I owed her that much at least.

"I don't know how," I said quietly. Then stepped out and pulled the door closed behind me as a wave of pain surged through the bond.

99. Shake it Off

~ *CASIMIR* ~

As that wave of pain reached me through the bond, I slammed the wall down between us just as surely as I closed that door, and stalked up the corridor, clearing my mind of anything and everything to do with my mate.

This was not the time.

It could not be.

She was just going to have to live with that.

I'd already given her more of myself than anyone in my life. Ever. If it wasn't enough... well, she was just going to have to learn to deal—

Behind me, the door I'd just used clicked and creaked.

"Cazz!" Jesse hissed down the hall after me. "I don't have a shirt!"

I jerked to a halt, blinking, the two sides of my nature going to war—the King and Alpha growling that she was Queen and Alpha and could find a fucking shirt for herself, while the mate in me roared that she couldn't link and wanted to snap teeth at the mental image of her scuttling through the tunnels with her beautiful body bare.

I checked my blocks on the bond so I wasn't vulnerable to her tears, then turned and our eyes locked.

To my surprise, it wasn't the shine of tears in her eyes, but the blaze of anger. And disapproval.

I frowned. "I'll instruct a servant to bring you a change of clothes. Get cleaned up. They'll be waiting for you by the time you're done."

That was the moment to turn on my heel and stalk out, to show her that I was untouched by this. But I found myself frozen, still locked in her gaze.

Neither of us spoke, but I could feel her on the other side of the bond, trying to break through.

And that wheedling, insidious urge within me to give in to her. *Fuck.*

"Jesse, I have to go," I said, low and rough. "I'm not deceiving you about the urgency of this."

She took a deep breath, but her head didn't disappear back inside the room. "I'm not stopping you, Cazz."

Why did that make me want to flinch?

"Go back inside, I'll make sure there are clothes brought to you," I muttered, then tore my gaze from hers, turned on my heel, and stormed down the corridor again.

But the door didn't click, and I could feel her eyes on my back, like a laser, blistering my skin, until the moment I turned the corner and was out of sight.

*****

~ *JESSE* ~

Coward.

Fucking *coward.*

I felt him! I felt him feeling me and... damn!

Once Cazz disappeared into an adjoining hallway—without looking back—I pulled back into the room and stormed back to that bathing room, furious and flustered and... *ugh.* I was still naked, my clothes in a pile near that door, so I shut it and made myself focus on drawing a bath and getting clean while I tried to figure out the tangle of feelings inside.

Furious.

Hurt.

Scared.

Curious.

Thrilled.

And that inevitable thread of hope.

Cazz had been right when he'd said that hope was going to destroy me. I could feel it already, growing in my chest, sparking light and joy because he'd kept the bond so open and I could feel him being sucked in, just like I was. I'd felt his thrill and the part of him that fed on our connection coming alive.

He hadn't been able to hide it, not completely.

But he had fled again and where did that leave me now?

Weak kneed. I was sure of that much. But the rest?

Once again, washed up on the shore of tidal wave Cazz, I was left sprawled on the beach of his heart, choking and shaking the water out of my eyes. Panting.

Because he always left me panting.

That was half the problem. The moment he touched me—with fingers or his arctic gaze, it didn't matter—all I wanted to do was lean in. And that pissed me off. The bond drew me closer to him, while he tried to pull further away.

The bathwater tinkled and rippled as I washed myself, but my mind was barely on what I was doing.

I wanted to bristle at the memory of myself just giving in… but what choice did I have? I could submit willingly and hold onto my own control, or Cazz would compel me and I'd be lost.

It was the same roller coaster every time. He came for me, usually angry, then got that heat in his eyes, then took me and I got swept up—and so did he.

Then, just when I'd think he was going to be the one to surrender to whatever this was between us, he'd shut down. And I was left defeated and pulsing

But something had been different this time. He had awoken my body as he always did. But…

He used his teeth *to split the seams on my shirt and get it off me, then rolled it into a blindfold that he started to place over my eyes and tie behind my head—but when he did, I tensed and started shaking.*

"Cazz… I don't know…" Don't hurt me don't hurt me don't hurt me—

Suddenly the twisted fabric pulled away from my eyes and the light was back. Cazz leaned in from behind me and I heard him inhale.

"Is that a no, Jesse? Or an I don't know?"

I blinked. He was asking? *Hesitating? What would he do if I said no?*

Was he just giving me a chance to not *submit, so he could compel me?*

Or did he care?

Instinctively I reached for the bond to try and figure out what was going on in his mind, but he didn't feel angry. Just… on edge. Like he was impatient.

"I… I don't know."

Then he gave the most delicious rumble in his chest, leaning into my back, and murmuring in my ear with that deep gravel that never failed to give me goosebumps. "Trust me. Give yourself into my hands. Let me prove to you that I won't harm you..."

100. Stronger

~ *JESSE* ~

I swallowed hard and blinked out of the vivid memory.

It stunned me a little when Cazz hesitated—scared me that he might get aggressive like he had when I'd accidentally called the pack at the Den. And yet... he hadn't turned it on me. Hadn't blamed me. He had asked me a question like an adult, and then... *persuaded* me. And honestly, I had been nervous, but his assurances had given me hope that maybe this wouldn't be a bad experience. And now... now that I saw what he was doing, I would follow him over that particular cliff any day of the week.

There'd been something very unexpectedly intimate about being so helpless. And I could feel how it thrilled Cazz and somehow softened him. Of course it did—because I *had* been helpless and he loved nothing more than complete control.

Except, I had a hunch that perhaps he had gotten more than he bargained for, as well.

My eyes wanted to flutter closed, but I didn't want to lose that connection with him, so I forced myself to stay in that gaze, groaning as he took me, my entire body coming alive as if he'd injected my bloodstream with heated joy, raising the small hairs all over my body as he shuddered and his jaw went slack.

And as he filled me, he never broke eye-contact.

Then, when I was seated on him, he kept me there for a moment, fingers gripping my thighs, his chest rising and falling quickly, both of us panting. His brows twitched and he searched my eyes, but I didn't know what to say, because everything I was thinking would scare him away. So I remained completely silent, but never even blinked.

Then Cazz, my mate, and the Alpha King, grabbed for my hips like he was grounding himself and we began to move together... and I was lost.

I shouldn't be surprised that he'd run. We'd connected. I remembered his eyes in that moment—that long moment where we'd been connected at every level.

He'd *held me* afterwards. Curled his body around mine and... I'd fallen asleep because I was spent, but also because it was so quiet and it had felt like we were truly alone here. In a place no one was going to come looking for us. And I had sensed in him that same sense of contentment to just be there.

He'd flipped me onto my stomach and pulled my hips up. At first I had jolted, it seemed so impersonal after what we'd just been doing.

But then his tender hands caressed my body, following the lines of my waist and breasts as he positioned himself, then plunged into me with a guttural groan.

I gasped and sank down on my elbows. But Cazz folded over me, one hand sliding down my arm to twine our fingers and fist the pillow together...

I swallowed hard, stepped out of the bath with the hair on my arms standing up and my belly clenching again.

He did this to me. I couldn't escape it. It was so frustrating to me that I could never untangle how I *thought* from the feelings he wrung from my body.

He was like a drug—but I was starting to see the cracks. He wasn't untouched by this bond, either.

When I had found a towel and dried off, I opened the door to the bathroom and peered out, relieved to see a new set of clothes had been laid out on the bed.

I was relieved because it meant I didn't need to talk to anyone—but it was unnerving too. How had they come in here and made the bed and left my clothes without me hearing anything?

These wolves... Scary, scary creatures.

And he was the strongest of them.

An ache started in my stomach then that wasn't to do with sexual desire.

I could feel myself beginning to crumble and I shook my head.

"No... no, I'm not doing this again," I hissed at myself as I quickly dressed. "You felt that, Cazz. I know you did!"

I felt something tighten in the bond like a hand gripping tighter and I blinked.

Could he feel me? Did he hear me?

Cazz...?

I stood there for a second, listening, ears perked in the bond, but then my heart dropped.

Nothing.

I didn't move for a minute, breathing, bracing, feeling so brittle and fragile inside that if I took the wrong step, I'd shatter. But then...

"Fuck that, Cazz. Fuck you. Fuck you and your power and your fear. You're a coward. Telling me to trust when you won't even trust me not to hurt you. Well..."

I shook my head and raised my chin and strode for the door.

If he wasn't going to admit to what he was feeling, if he was too scared to let the light shine in and see what it revealed, well... that was on him.

And as I stalked down the hallway outside the room, reaching for the females I'd been working with through the link and clearly feeling them startle and...

'Sire?!'

I blinked. *'You can feel me?'*

'Yes!'

My breath rushed out of me. *'You can* hear *me?'*

'Yes!'

And then I felt it—felt them—rushing towards me. All five of them, clear as day. I could sense that Wylde was closest and would reach me in less than a minute. The others would take longer, but their voices tumbled over each other in my head.

'Oh, well done, Sire!'

'Maya will be so pleased!'

'You've been practicing!'

I stopped dead in my tracks, shaking my head. *'No, I haven't, I just...'*

I just... gave in to Cazz. Connected more deeply. And... holy shit, that power. *His* power. I felt it grow and pulse between us, but I assumed it was growing for *him.*

I looked down at myself, at my hands that were clenched to fists at my sides, at my now-clean and redressed body and...

I smiled.

'I'm just getting stronger,' I sent them all, letting them feel my grin. Then I made a decision. Wylde and I had been interrupted when Cazz showed up. But it was time to finish that conversation.

'Drop what you're doing and meet in my chambers as soon as you can get there,' I said quickly. *'I need your help. All of you.'*

The chorus of happy agreements that replied lifted my heart out of the shadow Cazz had left over it, and I smiled even wider.

I was getting stronger.

101. Girls Night In

~ *JESSE* ~

"…my mother always told me every male can only be led by two things—his stomach, and his prick. So there's little point trying to engage his heart before you've satisfied the other two."

I spluttered, choking on the mouthful of popcorn and leaning forward in my seat because I was afraid I might actually inhale it.

Around me, gales of giggles and snorts from the five women—females—I had gathered and eventually brought back to my room because I didn't know anywhere else we could just sit around without worrying about other people.

Wolves. Without worrying about other *wolves,* I reminded myself.

Brenna, the oldest of us, who I gathered was nearing fifty, just grinned and popped a berry into her mouth while the rest of us snickered.

Wylde, the servant I'd been speaking to in the visitors wing before Cazz found us, was laughing the hardest. She was a year younger than me and clearly enjoying being included in this circle of female wolves.

I was learning about all of them as quickly as I could, but I could tell there were a lot of dynamics going on here that I didn't really understand.

Wylde was a brunette. In our world she would have been described as cute and quiet, but the truth was, she was several inches taller than me, and only looked smaller compared to the others.

Reeca—pronounced *"Rees-ah"*—was also in her twenties and the tallest and most striking. She was stunning, with jet-black hair that had a streak of white that grew out of a scar above her right temple. She was clearly strong, and moved like an athlete, but she was the only one who I couldn't quite pin down on what she actually did. She did more listening than speaking, but her bright blue eyes were sharp with intelligence, and when she did speak, she was always very insightful. The others, even the older females, always paid attention when she spoke.

She looked at me now, smiling, but there was an intensity in her gaze that was unsettling.

"Your mother is a wise female," Brenna said dryly.

She was the oldest. Her fading brunette hair turning gray at the temples and peppered throughout. She had lines at the sides of her eyes when she smiled, and she acted like everyone's mother. Having lost my mother when I was young, I swung between finding her nurturing appealing, and uncomfortable. Sometimes I wanted to hug her. Sometimes I wanted her to stop looking at me.

"I mean, true," I snorted when the others had settled down. "I grew up with three men. Your mom nailed it."

"You have brothers?" Alys asked, blinking at me with a curious smile.

She was the only overweight wolf I'd seen so far. Shaped like a pear, in my world she would still have seemed intimidating because she was almost six feet tall. But next to the others she looked... soft.

She was a teacher, apparently. Mostly to young wolves. But Maya had told me she brought her in to help me because she was patient and "used to talking with dimwits."

I huffed at the memory.

"Yes," I answered her, kicking myself a little. I didn't want to talk about my brothers. So I kept my eyes down on the popcorn and tried to brush the comment off. "They aren't good men—males. But they can definitely be led by their stomachs and... other things."

Wylde snorted again, but Brenna and Alys both nodded sagely. I could feel Reeca's sharp eyes on me, like she was seeing more than I was saying.

Did the packlink work like that? I hurriedly checked my mental blocks. They had been giving me some more lessons today, especially since we were starting to be able to speak through it. I was still really inconsistent, but most of the time I could hear them if they offered to speak to me.

It was the weirdest thing. But also kind of cool.

I frowned. "So… can wolves talk in each other's heads even when they're kids?"

"Yes," they all chorused.

My eyebrows shot up. "Aren't they always scheming or something, then? If my brothers could talk telepathically, no one else would ever have been able to stop them pulling whatever shit they were planning that day."

Like selling me to the wolves… The thought made my stomach cold.

Alys shrugged. "Young wolves are mischievous, it's true. But they're also weaker in their shields. They learn early that we can reach them more easily than they can block us. It gives them some caution."

"Until they mature," Tynker muttered then bit into an apple like it had offended her. She was also a Palace servant and in her twenties, but she was much harder and sharper than Wylde. The kind of person you wanted on your side, because you didn't want to risk having to fight her. She was a great teacher when I needed help, but she had an edge of bitterness about her that made me curious about her life… and a little bit wary.

"What happens when they… mature?" I knew from my time with Maya that maturing happened for wolves around sixteen years of age. But it was a physical and mental development stage that happened slightly differently with every wolf. When the other wolves sensed that one of the youngsters had reached maturity, they entered the hierarchy and were treated as adults from that day forward.

No discussion. No transition.

According to Maya, it was usually the most difficult year or two of a wolf's life—because even though they were *capable* of being adults, they hadn't quite grasped it all yet. So they spent a lot of time getting challenged, or reprimanded by those above them in the hierarchy.

Which was pretty much everyone.

Tynker shrugged. "The males get very assertive," she said, rolling her eyes. "Especially those who are heirs to an Alpha. They'll lord their power over the other young ones."

Apparently the young wolves had a hierarchy within the hierarchy—those who were expected to grow into roles of strength and leadership taking that kind of role with their peers. While the others just struggled to keep themselves from being bullied into submission.

The whole system seemed very brutal to me, but the wolves assured me, it was completely natural to them, and the older they got, the fewer conflicts there were, unless you were an Alpha being challenged for your role.

"Trust me, you'll be grateful for that assertiveness when your mate is unafraid of a challenge," Brenna interjected with a pointed look.

Tynker didn't look impressed, but she didn't challenge the statement.

I was uncertain what was going on there, but there was no time to ask, because Wylde, apparently unaware of the others' tension, piped up.

"I can't wait until I find my mate," she sighed happily.

Tynker rolled her eyes while Alys nodded. Brenna watched me, which seemed odd. But it was Reeca who spoke up.

"You'll get there. Soon," she said quietly.

Wylde's eyes went wide. "Truly?!"

Reeca nodded and looked like she was about to say more, but Brenna turned and caught her eye, and the striking wolf closed her mouth and didn't expand.

I wondered what they knew that I didn't.

102. Imparting Power

~ *JESSE* ~

"That's…. that's interesting that you bring that up," I said carefully.

Tynker's eyes cut to me sharply.

Wylde's brows rose. "Oh?"

"Yes, I mean… I had heard about the Selection coming up and I wondered which of you were going in it, or already had mates, or… whatever…" I trailed off because Wylde's eyes went wide at the same time Tynker choked on her apple. I knew Brenna and Alys were already mated, but I wasn't sure about the other three.

Reeca stared at me like she'd never seen me before, and Brenna and Alys exchanged wary glances.

"What?" I asked them all, looking back and forth between them.

"None of us will be in the Selection," Brenna said briskly. "We either already have mates, or aren't high enough ranking to do so."

Oh. I frowned. "But… I thought it was the males who were ranked for this?"

"It is. Alphas and Betas, and a few heirs, probably. But understand that there are many, many wolves. They'll be drawn from every nearby pack for this, as well. Only the highest ranking or most valuable females will be presented," Brenna said.

"There's thousands of wolves, Sire," Alys added with an encouraging smile. "And more females than males in the numbers. Probably only a dozen or so of the males will be making Selections.

So only the best and brightest of the young, fertile females will be presented."

"So… what makes you best and brightest?" I asked carefully.

Alys folded her hands in her lap, which I had already learned meant she was going to start teaching.

"You'll have to forgive me if I'm a touch vague, Sire. It's—"

"You really need to stop calling me Sire. I keep telling you all, when we're alone like this just call me Jesse, or Jess."

Alys blinked. Tynker's eyes narrowed. Reeca and Brenna smiled. But Wylde looked scandalized.

"I mean it," I said firmly.

Alys swallowed, but nodded. "Very well, er, Jesse. You understand that this is just something we sense about each other as we grew up in the hierarchy. I'm not accustomed to explaining it in detail, but… at its foundation, the females who were born to Alphas or high ranking parents are most likely to be Selected by an Alpha. There are certain talents or skills that increase a female's value in the pack. So those with particular gifts may also be chosen. But mostly… mostly it is those whose bloodlines have already shown strength that will be highly prized. Sometimes, if a particularly strong female is presented, there will be challenges among the males to win her. But usually… usually the males come to the Selection already knowing who they want, and their families have already negotiated for their matches."

"Negotiated?" I asked, stunned. "Are you doing bride prices or something?"

"No, no!" Alys giggled. "I only meant that… well, it's better if the young, strong males don't tear each other apart, obviously. If the families have already agreed to a match, the male won't have to fight for her."

"So… this is like arranged marriages?"

Brenna shrugged. "Somewhat. There is a lot more to it, but yes, the parents usually make agreements before the actual ceremony."

"And do you all just show up and get married, or something?"

"No!" Wylde said breathlessly, laughing a little. "The presentation is first—all the males together and the females that are being offered are shown to them. Then there's a week where they can spend time together or discuss terms… then the actual Selection is made a week later. If any of the females are still being pursued by more than one male at that point, the weaker of the two will challenge the greater—or give her up. Or she can choose."

I sighed. "Survival of the fittest, huh?" I said. Sounded like something my brothers would be into.

"Survival of the strongest, which isn't the same thing," Brenna said mysteriously.

"So… it's just bloodlines and… skills? Do you mean like, your job? What kind of jobs would make a female valuable enough for an Alpha male?"

To my surprise, they all looked at Reeca, who looked like she wanted to sink into her chair. Her chin went low and her sharp eyes darted from one to the other of them as she clenched her hands in her lap.

"The gifts that make a female desirable above and beyond her rank are… God-given," she said uncomfortably.

I blinked. "Really? Like what?"

There was a moment of tense silence, then Alys spoke up again and Reeca looked at her gratefully.

"It can be anything from the ability to heal, to particular senses—perceptions, you would call them a sixth sense, I understand? Or a rare skill in any trade. In my mother's generation, one female was a particularly adept at battle strategy and her talents were so highly sought by the King, she was counted among the Guard, and presented for Selection, even though her parents were servants."

That made me uneasy. "So… being a servant's child means you can't be presented?" I asked, sad if this was going to be a barrier.

"Not unless you're Selected by a much higher ranking female because you possess a power or a skill that validates you raising in rank. A high ranking female can… impart her worth by commending a young female—but then the young female's rank is determined by who recommended her, and unless the female who spoke for her has a lot of power, the young female will be overlooked."

Commending. That's what Maya talked about doing for me. She'd explained it as putting your weight in the eyes of wolves behind someone else—so they saw your power in the other person.

Which was why, Maya said, she couldn't commend me to the packs until I was ready. Because if she laid her power on my shoulders and I failed, we'd both be taken down by it.

Maya made it *very* clear that if that were to happen, her only lack would be in having chosen me too soon.

"So… okay," I said. "I was talking to… I was thinking that one of the things I could do as Queen was present someone. And it sounds like I could choose a female who maybe wouldn't otherwise be considered for this kind of role. Am I—as Queen—high enough ranked to do that without causing problems?"

Wylde just about fell out of her chair. Tynker was staring at me with her mouth wide open, and Reeca kept blinking like I'd flicked water in her eyes.

103. Highest Quality

~ *JESSE* ~

Alys smiled at me and clasped her hands together at her chest, but it was Brenna who looked truly concerned.

"Sire—sorry, Jesse—I don't think you understand. When a high ranking female puts another forward in this way, the younger carries her reputation. If you were to select poorly—"

"I know a good female when I meet one," I said firmly. "Maya has been telling me to trust my instincts, and to start showing my leadership and initiative. Besides, you all came to me commended by Maya, which is the highest regard, right?"

They all nodded, though half their mouths were open like they were stunned.

I frowned. "I don't get it, what's the big deal?"

"It's just… someone like yourself… the mate to the King… the *Queen.* The Queen would usually present one of the highest ranking young females in the packs. Select someone of the highest quality. In terms of its attraction to the packs, your presentation would be second only to the King's."

"Okay, so am I wrong in thinking that if I present a female who might not usually get that kind of attention, it raises their position or value, or whatever? Can I give a female enough value that they'll actually be considered by the Alphas even if they aren't high born?"

All five nodded at me, but Brenna looked genuinely concerned.

"Yes, Jesse. You could. Without doubt. You would… you could change a female's life with that. But… you must understand… a female has to be born for leadership. Simply placing that mantle on her shoulders isn't enough—"

"I wasn't born for leadership, and I'm here," I pointed out.

Brenna tipped her head like she'd argue, but it was Reeca who answered, licking her lips, her voice slightly hushed.

"But your mate is *so* strong that… he could have a limp chicken as a mate and she'd still carry the role."

"Then we just have to make sure that whoever I present gets the strongest male… right?"

Wylde snorted. But Reeca stared at me like she was seeing a ghost.

"What?" I asked her. "Is there something I'm not seeing? Something I'm missing about how this works?"

Reeca shook her head, but she was still gaping at me. I turned to Brenna for her confirmation. She looked back and forth between me and Reeca, then put up her hands and shook her head,

"Jesse, if you're certain you want to… then no. The only one who could subvert your choice would be the King himself. Do you… would he wish to do so?"

"I don't know. I'll ask him."

"Ask me what?"

All of us startled and turned to find Cazz standing in the doorway, staring, clearly surprised to find me not alone. And obviously not pleased about it.

How had I not felt him coming? I turned inward to the bond, but it was still that cool, cold wall, nothing but his heartbeat vibrating in it when I reached for it.

My heart sank.

The women all got to their feet immediately, turning their heads down and rounding their shoulders a position of submission.

I frowned at the girls. "You're in my chambers at my invitation, you don't have to do th—"

"Yes, they do," Cazz growled as he strode forward, glaring between me and the rest of them. I ached at the cold tone in his voice, but the others didn't move.

Cazz stared down his nose at them, prowling forward until he stood at my side, glaring.

"Why are you angry?" I asked him—and heard one of the women's breath catch. "They didn't do anything wrong. I asked them to come talk to me. You said you'd be busy tonight."

Cazz bristled, his eyes cutting hard to me from the side, before he turned back to the rest of them. But at least when he spoke his voice was low and without heat.

"I have need of the Queen. Thank you for your service tonight. You may leave."

They all nodded once without meeting his eyes, then filed past me, Alys reaching out to squeeze my hand as she passed, and Reeca cutting me a single, pleading look that I thought I understood, but wasn't sure—she had been the most nervous about Cazz from the beginning.

But then they were gone and Cazz let out a deep breath, like he'd been holding it and turned on me.

"You're having meals... with *servants?*"

I folded my arms. "I'm eating snacks with females that were commended to me by Maya," I corrected him. "Besides, what's the problem? They're all very respectful. I'm having trouble getting them to call me by my name, instead of 'Sire.'"

Cazz's eyes bulged. "You told them to call you by your name?"

"Yes! Just like you and Rake and—I know Rake can't be the only wolf who calls you by your first name."

"He's not."

"Well, then, see, it's just—"

"But every other wolf who does so is either of high rank, or has been in my service for some time. They have earned their right to that kind of intimacy—unlike these females you've known for what, hours? You can't possibly know if they are trustworthy in that time, let alone if they should be intimate. It could be a plot, Jesse—I have enemies. Do not trust anyone who comes to you smiling. They're probably just trying to reach me."

I squelched the pang at the implication that no one would want to be close to me for my own sake, and gave him a flat look.

"Maya introduced us. Do you question her judgement, as well?"

Cazz growled.

I sighed. "Look, I'm just saying, just because someone isn't high ranking doesn't mean they can't be a good friend—"

"I am *King.* You are Queen—you shouldn't do this. I don't eat with the servants!"

I tipped my head. "Well, maybe you should try it sometime. One of them might have a tool strong enough to pry the stick out of your ass."

Cazz's jaw went tight and his eyes widened.

Dammit, dammit, dammit, dammit.

There was a flutter behind my ribs and an ache in my belly. I longed to throw myself into his chest and run my fingers through his hair, and beg him to go to bed with me and just hold me... I didn't *want* to antagonize him. But it was habit. A self-protective knee-jerk reaction I'd developed with my father. Whenever he was being a particularly aromatic asshole.

I took a deep breath, but didn't drop my eyes from Cazz's. "I was being funny."

"Hilarious," he seethed.

I shrugged. "I'm sorry they were here if that bothered you, but you did say you were going to be busy all night, and you didn't warn me you were coming."

His lips pursed and his jaw rolled. "That's because my evening is not over, but I find I have need of my mate."

I blinked. *Need?* I swallowed. "What kind of—"

"I need you to come and see if you can identify any of the humans who are near the caves. Or if you have any insight into what they're actually doing. We find ourselves... baffled."

"Baffled by what?"

"Come with me. You'll see." Then he turned on his heel and strode for the door, expecting me to follow as if *I* was the servant.

Clenching my hands at my sides, I took a deep breath and followed after him.

104. Cast Your Eye

~ CASIMIR ~

I shouldn't have come for her myself. I knew that. Ghere had almost swallowed his own tongue when I said I'd do it. But the truth was, it had been... uncomfortable keeping my space from her after that delicious time in the visitor's wing. I had needed to move, so I had said I would come for her myself. But I hadn't wanted to reach for her, to warn her that I was coming, because I had wanted to see what state she was truly in. And no matter how she might needle me, it was a relief to see her not shrinking after I left.

So why was it making my neck itch that she'd been... just fine? I had been braced for her shivering and pleading. To find her eating and talking with others was a welcome step forward from our previous separations. Yet, I couldn't shake that irritation, like a gnat buzzing at my ears.

And telling her not to eat with servants?

God, I had sounded like my father. Even *my* stomach had turned at that pompous declaration. But the truth was, she *didn't* know who she could trust—and neither did I, yet. I was concerned she might naively open herself to someone who did not have her strength and success as their deepest motives.

I was somewhat soothed by hearing that these females had been recommended by Maya, but still...

"Cazz, can you slow down please?" Jesse muttered next to me. "My legs aren't as long as yours."

I slowed immediately, biting back the urge to apologize.

"Is that better?" I asked her quietly.

"Yes, thank you."

I glanced at her from the side. She sounded so formal. I didn't like it.

Then I frowned. "What are you wearing?" It was a stupid question because I knew. But I hadn't paid attention.

"Pajamas," she said defensively. "I would have changed, but it seemed like you didn't want to wait."

I hesitated then—would the Advisors dismiss her, coming to them so informally? I hadn't even noticed, but then, my favorite outfit was nothing, so...

I huffed a little at my own joke. Jesse heard it and looked up at me.

"What?" she demanded.

"Nothing." I waved a hand at her, then shrugged off my jacket and slung it around her shoulders.

It dwarfed her, falling to the middle of her thighs and the seams sagging off her shoulders. It made her look small and vulnerable and... quite delicious.

There was a flash in my head of her naked and spread over me, her arms extended in the bonds, her breasts bouncing, and a jolt of desire crackled through me.

Jesse's brows popped up. "Seriously, Cazz? *Now?*"

I grunted and turned away, leading her down a tunnel off to the left. "You're a beautiful woman, Jesse. And my mate. It's right that I should want you."

She gave a little smile at that. "I thought you wished you didn't. You always seem a little pissed off after."

Understatement of the century.

I blinked. That thought hadn't come from me. I snapped my head around to look at her, my mouth dropping open and she shrank back.

"What? I wasn't—"

"Sire, there's been a new message!"

We both turned to find Ghere hurrying towards us—his thinning hair flying in five directions as he trotted down the hallway.

Instinctively, I pulled Jesse closer to me. "What is it?"

Ghere was panting, which means he'd been running. Ghere *never* ran unless it absolutely could not be avoided.

"The guards... they have a newer... much better image. Of that one man—"

"Show me."

"The device is back at the chambers. I didn't want to risk missing you on your path so that it wasn't waiting for you."

I nodded, lips tight and closed my hand on Jesse's. "Lead the way, Ghere."

"What images? What's going on?" Jesse asked quietly as we walked as quickly as she was able towards the council chambers.

"We have images of some of the humans that have been spending a great deal of time in the woods nearby—and continuing to circle back to the areas near our cave entrances. We need to see if you recognize any of them, or can tell us what activity they're engaged in. It is... odd."

As we walked I explained to her that the human devices, cellphones and so forth, didn't work here under the mountain. So the guards and scouts kept them above ground, using them to communicate with each other if they were too far to link, but brought them down to us when there was new information or activity.

"...we have both videos and still images. But the humans are doing something strange and we aren't certain what it is. We can't tell if it's a simple game, or some kind of maneuver. I need to know if you recognize it."

Jesse frowned, but nodded.

When we reached the council chambers, everyone looked up as we strode in. Jesse balked for a moment as all those eyes turned on her, but I pulled her forward, urging her towards the table at the side of the room where we had printed out images and kept the devices for review.

"This," I said, picking up several of the printed photographs. "What are they doing?" I spread the images out over the table that all showed young humans, probably Jesse's age, running and sneaking through the forest—sometimes hiding themselves, other times seeming to race. Each was in camouflage clothing, but had long, brightly colored ribbons hanging from their hips that made no sense. If they wanted to hide themselves, why wear the bright colors?

Jesse leaned over the table, frowning at the photos, her brows pinching over her nose.

But she was smiling.

"What?" I snapped. "Why are you smiling?"

"You're concerned that they're... doing something they shouldn't?"

"We're *concerned* that they're running reconnaissance on our caves and activity. Humans rarely come this far out, and when they do, generally they are just passing through to hike the trails up the mountain, or towards the camping area that's miles from here. But these humans have been in the area for two straight days."

Jesse covered her hand with her mouth and when she looked up at me, her eyes were sparkling. "They're, um, playing a game."

I looked at her sternly. "Are you certain? What kind of game?"

"They're playing Capture the Flag. The university… they usually do this over in the State Park, but they must have moved to this area this year. It's a tradition. They do it every year. It's like… a tournament. That's why they keep coming back. They do rounds—as one set of teams gets knocked out, the winners start to play each other. There are no boundaries on it, they can spread out as much as they want. I know… I know it looks suspicious with the clothes, but… but it's a game, Cazz. I really don't think you need to worry about this. They run it for a week. They'll be gone after the weekend. My brother used to compete. They're stupid about it—there's a trophy and everything. And the guys get… look, just trust me. It's not a… a reconnaissance mission. I promise!"

105. The Mission

~ *CASIMIR* ~

Jesse looked up at me, her face tight but smooth, like she was stifling laughter.

My advisors rumbled behind us and Jesse's smile faded when she looked over her shoulder at them, but I was too busy discussing this in the link with them.

'A game would explain why they are noisy at times,' Rake sent carefully. I nodded. We'd been confused by that—why sneak and hide, only to cheer and scream every few hours so that the entire wood heard you?

'But it could be a ruse? She said they don't usually do it in this area—and we know that's true,' Ghere offered.

'It also explains why they're all so young. The humans usually use their more mature males when they're preparing to attack. The young ones lack discipline.' Rory was my General. It had taken years to get him to trust me after my father deceived him, but there was no sharper mind in the packs for battle and combat.

'I'm not certain we can trust the Queen's judgment of this. She seems to lack strategic vision—has she even seen battle?' Alpha Cayn had been a peer of my father's and was reluctantly preparing to release his pack to his son—who I couldn't stand. I would keep Cayn on my council even after his son Drayk took over their pack.

'Go gently on the girl. We would not expect a young female who had been promoted and in her first days of mating to have mastered her mate's entire world so soon.' That was Harn, the

431

oldest of my advisors, and a good friend to Maya. He was a decade younger than her, which she constantly pointed out. A former Alpha, he had retired when his son grew the strength to command, and now spent most of his time counseling younger wolves. Including me. When I let him.

'I sense no uncertainty in her,' I told them, opening the bond a hair to assess her more deeply.

Jesse was still looking at the photos, tipping her head, and fighting that smile. I couldn't tell if she thought it was funny that we'd taken a game as a threat, or if she was merely being nostalgic about her past with her peers.

She kept shuffling through the images, shaking her head or pointing at certain things, then moving to others. Her hair was twisted into a messy bun on top of her head, but small wisps of hair had fallen down at her temples and in front of her ears, softening her face. She looked very pretty when she was unguarded like this.

I cleared my throat.

'Where are the new images?' I asked Ghere gruffly. *'Do they show anything we haven't seen here?'*

'Not in their activities, no, but...' Ghere stepped forward to join us at the table and picked up one of the tablets that had been left on the tabletop. He frowned at the device, tapping it several times, then turning it to hand it to me.

"We're wondering if it's the same man," he said solemnly.

I took the tablet and looked at it. It was a much closer, much clearer image. Whoever had captured it had obviously been quite close to the humans, which made my teeth grind. But it was too late to do anything about it now.

The man in the photo did look similar to the one we had seen in those videos. But once again, I wasn't sure. There was growth on his cheeks which shadowed his face, and the light was flatter—

Jesse sucked in a breath and snatched the device out of my hands.

I growled instinctively, but when I turned on her, she was staring at the tablet, her mouth open and hands gripping it so tightly her knuckles were white.

"Where did you get this?" she asked breathlessly.

"In the woods," Ghere told her calmly. "He's one of the males we've been seeing. We think we may have caught him in previous images—"

"He's..." She blinked, then looked up at me, fear painted all over her face.

I frowned as my instincts crackled alarm. "What? You recognize him?"

She nodded slowly.

A slow coil of dread appeared in my stomach. "Jesse, what is it? Who is he?"

She swallowed and looked down at the image again, then bit her lip. "He's... my brother."

Tension crackled around the room and the link came alive with urgent chatter from my advisors. But I silenced all of them as the pieces of this puzzle began to click into place, one by one.

I had meant to follow this up with the Reapers, and...

"Be clear, Jesse," I said darkly. "This is one of the brothers who sold you to the Reapers? He's definitely aware of us?"

Jesse nodded, her eyes never leaving that image. "If he's... I mean, he used to do this when he was at college, but he's not anymore and..." She looked up at me, her face wide with fear. "Cazz, if he's getting close to the caves then it seems like that's a huge coincidence. He's the oldest. He hasn't been at college for four years. And he's... he's the one my other brothers listen to."

Her head snapped right then, towards the table, and she started sorting through the images again.

Her hands were shaking.

"Jesse—"

"I need to see if the others are here," she said in a faint voice. "I need to see if it's just him or... all of them."

I still had the bond open, so I felt her heart plummet, felt her fear rise in a wave that threatened to overwhelm her. Yet, she didn't show it, except in her urgency and trembling fingers. There were no tears, no wringing hands, no shrieking.

"Ghere?" I said quietly, never taking my eyes from her.

"Yes, Sire."

"Khush led the foray of Reapers that brought the Queen to us, yes?"

"Yes, Sire."

I nodded once, my teeth grinding. "Bring him, please. Immediately." *'And don't warn him why,'* I added through the link.

'Yes, Sire.'

106. Make Sense of It

~ JESSE ~

It was stupid. Stupid to be so scared. Cazz could tear out Ryan's throat before my brother could blink, I was certain of it. But, seeing his face...

My heart was thumping and my fingers had started to tremble. It was so dumb! If Ryan was here, even if he was looking for me, it wasn't like he was coming to kill me, or anything. For fuck's sake, he *sold me* to the wolves. He didn't give two shits about me. So why did my body feel like he was creeping up behind me, holding a gun to my head?

Because coming here was supposed to be the escape.

I kept flipping through the photographs spread out over the table, but I wasn't really seeing any of them, and I wasn't being organized in how I filtered through, so I kept looking at the same photographs over and over.

I could feel Cazz's eyes on me. The wolves were murmuring to each other, and probably talking in their heads. I didn't know who half these males were... but why did I feel safer here than I did in my own home?

Because of my mate.

The thought made me look up at him suddenly and Cazz caught the movement and turned his head, locking eyes with me.

His face was tight, but blank. He'd kept the bond open a little, so I could feel the simmering tension in him as well. But not really anything else. It was a relief to have him there, though. Which was also dumb. He was angry with me—

'I am not angry at you, I'm angry at the situation in which we find ourselves—'

I sucked in a shocked breath as Cazz's voice in my head cut off and the bond went quiet again. But his eyes had widened and the other wolves could obviously tell that something was happening, because they were all looking at us.

"Was that…?" I breathed.

Cazz blinked, then his face went blank again and he turned back to the men, talking as if nothing had happened. But while I stared at his back, frozen, his voice bloomed in my head again.

'Don't say it out loud, don't let them know. It gives us an advantage if they assume we can't speak this way.'

I swallowed and started to nod, then realized that wouldn't make sense to anyone watching, so I turned the movement into dropping my eyes and turning around robotically to go back to the images and devices on the table. But my heart was pounding even harder now.

Cazz could talk in my head.

Did that mean I could talk in his?

I'd been practicing with the girls today and felt like I was getting closer to being able to actually share thoughts with them. This was like that. Cazz felt different, though. Closer.

Pretending to keep my focus on the images in my hands, I tried to reach out to Cazz through the bond. He'd kept it slightly open, so I could feel him.

But it was like sliding my arm through a gap in a door. I couldn't see what was on the other side, so I was just flailing around trying to find something—

'Stop grasping,' he said, his voice short in my head. *'Your mental voice is not like your physical one. Nothing has to move to make it work. All you need is intention—you want me to hear, so I will.'*

He was so impatient! Even though I was scared, it pissed me off. *'You could offer a little grace, you know. I'm just trying to figure out—'*

I gasped, then froze as Cazz whirled and I realized that he'd heard me. We stared at each other for a moment, the other wolves all watching curiously.

'Give them a reason for your shock. Quickly.'

"It's just occurred to me…" I blurted out, then trailed off, because of course, nothing had occurred to me.

"What?" Cazz asked, biting the word off.

My brother. He sold me. Now I was here, alone. What could he possibly want? Why would he go hunting for the wolves? Ryan was an asshole, but he wasn't stupid. He had to know that the wolves were deadly...

"He probably wants more money," I said weakly.

Cazz's brows pressed down, shadowing his eyes. "I'm not sure—"

"What I mean is... you called this a... a reconnaissance, right? You think they're out there trying to find where the wolves live? I'm thinking... if he was paid for me and it was a lot of money, he might be thinking he can find a... a den, or something. Like... a place he can rob."

But if that was the case, why try to hide it behind the college games? Wouldn't he be a lot more stealthy and just come out here searching? And how the hell did he get the college to move their entire tournament out here? And to what purpose?

While we were at it, how did he even know to come out this way? He'd sold me to them in the city.

I frowned.

'What is it?'

'None of this makes sense. He sold me. He doesn't care about me. So he's not here looking for me. Yet, he's obviously up to something—but why would he want to find the home of the wolves?'

'You tell me. My first thought is that he has come for you.'

I shook my head. Ryan was toxic and strong and pretty fearless. But he wasn't dumb. He would know the wolves could kill him. He wasn't out here to pick a fight. He didn't want to die. So that meant, either he was going to gain something by locating them. Or...

'Cazz... which wolves would my brothers have dealt with when they were planning to sell me? How would they even have found out they could? *How would they have even known that you wanted me?'*

I felt something sharp and nervy in Cazz, like a blade sliding against skin. *'I've been meaning to ask that, myself,'* he growled in my head. *'I've been a little... distracted.'*

I looked up at him and our eyes caught again.

107. Wrestle with That

~ JESSE ~

As our eyes held, the bond came alive—heat, fear, anger, and something frantic under it all that I couldn't quite define.

I instinctively took a step towards Cazz, but his head jerked back and he tensed, so I froze again.

Then the door to the chamber opened and Ghere trotted in, ushering a huge wolf-man behind him.

My first impression of this creature was that he reminded me of a professional wrestler—so I found myself swallowing back a nervous giggle and trying to keep my face straight.

I'd never seen this guy before, but as Ghere melted into the background, the man strode forward. He was a complete beefcake—dark hair, heavy brows, a square jaw shadowed in stubble, his shoulders were even broader than Cazz's and his muscles so inflated, it made his neck look short. But he moved with a lot more grace than any human guy I had ever seen who was that big.

He stalked right up to Cazz, then went down on one knee, one meaty arm and fist to his chest.

"Sire? You summoned me?"

At the sound of his voice, the entire world sucked away. There was no room. There were no photographs. There was no council, no cave-chamber. No light...

I was blindfolded, gagged, and curled up in the back of a moving vehicle, spots on my arms and shoulders singing with pain where I had been grasped in huge hands and thrown bodily into this rumbling box that stank of gasoline fumes and mildew. And that voice...

That voice was growling at me, pissed off and impatient, and without a hint of warmth or compassion.

"...Now keep your head down and don't make any more trouble, or the King will have one less toy to play with in his little harem, do you understand?"

Harem? King?

What the hell was going on?

But I couldn't ask—I'd already fought those hands, tried to scream around the gag. The side of my head throbbed where someone had struck me and growled at me to shut up.

I thought I'd been thrown in the trunk of a car, but the sound of the slamming doors echoed through a much larger space—a van? A truck? I was laying on carpet—and there were chuckles and several low male voices murmuring around me.

I was struggling to breathe around the gag and terrified that my nose would clog completely from the tears leaking down my cheeks and then I'd suffocate.

Even more terrified that these men were taking me somewhere to—

"Yes, Khush. I have questions about the Reaping that I've been meaning to ask," Cazz drawled.

I blinked back to the present, my breath fast and shallow. A pile of photos clutched in my hands wrinkling under my too-tight grip.

'Breathe, Jesse.'

'I know him. I know that voice. He's—'

'Just breathe. They can all smell your fear.' But I felt the jagged rip of anger in Cazz as he turned his full attention on Khush.

Khush, who looked like a tan-skinned Hulk, was still kneeling but now looking up at Cazz with a smug smile on his face, clearly expecting to be commended.

I wanted to do some growling of my own.

'That's better. Hold onto that.'

"How can I help, Sire?" Khush asked with a smile.

Cazz's upper lip twitched like he was fighting a sneer. "You can start by explaining the process of the Reaping. My Queen wishes to know how she was identified and... obtained."

Khush gave me a measuring look from the side, but kept his attention on Cazz. "Well, as you know, we first watch areas where the right kind of women can be found, and when we think we have found an appropriate target, we set a team on them to ensure they're both fertile and… not likely to be deeply missed," he said, raising his brows.

"How can you tell?" I asked quickly.

Cazz shot me a disapproving look, but Khush turned his head and met my gaze boldly. "Which part?" he asked me, his voice not nearly as meek towards me as he had been towards Cazz.

I supposed it was easy to feel superior to a small woman you'd manhandled and forced to shit in a bucket.

I folded my arms and spoke through gritted teeth. "How about you start at the beginning of the whole process and keep talking. I'll tell you when it's been enough."

I *felt* Cazz laughing in my head. I looked at him quickly—he couldn't undermine me here, or these males were never going to listen to a thing I said.

But to my surprise, he looked *pleased.* And a little amused. And he didn't speak up in Khush's defense, even when the male looked at him, presumably to check whether Cazz was going to let me speak to him like that.

Khush's mountainous shoulders rose and fell once, then he turned and spoke to me with the slow patience I'd give an obstinant child.

I wasn't impressed.

"Our first forays are simply to identify women of appropriate age and stage in life. They must be virgins, attractive, and not deeply entrenched with their families or acquaintances in a way that will make those in their lives… persistent in trying to find them if they disappear."

"How would you even know if a woman was a virgin?"

'We can smell it, Jesse—or rather, smell the lack of a certain quality in your scent. It's subtle, but it's there if you're looking for it. We're rarely wrong.'

Khush was explaining that as well, but in much more patronizing tones. I arched an eyebrow at him.

"…when we have found eight or ten that we think are right, and we're certain their cycles are healthy and regular, then we strategize. We take the final selection of women over the course of forty-eight hours so that there's little chance of escape or discovery."

"Take them?" I prompted.

"I think you already know how that part works," Khush said, arching one of his eyebrows right back.

Smug fucker.

108. Get to the Bottom

~ JESSE ~

The tension in the room ratcheted up another notch.

"Yes, I do," I seethed. "So, did you buy all of us, or just me?"

Khush didn't even blink. "We take whatever approach is most likely to be successful with the least consequence. In your case, it was clear that the males in your family were open to… negotiation. They saw it as something like an arranged marriage," he said with a shrug.

"That's not marriage, that's trafficking!" I hissed.

'Don't let him see your emotion. It will only weaken you in his eyes.'

'He's so fucking smug—'

'Leave that to me.'

"I wasn't aware that we were purchasing females as part of the Reaping," Cazz said casually. "How many of the women in Jesse's Reaping were purchased?"

"In this round, only her. Abduction is easier when they're poor. Everyone just thinks they ran away."

"Why was I the special one?" I growled.

Khush's head snapped back to me, his eyes flashing. "Because, as I said, we assessed the males in your life and determined that they would be open to the idea. Though they take longer, purchases are always preferred because it makes the others complicit in the act—which means less chance of a nasty surprise. Your law enforcement are dull in their senses, but their weapons are just as effective against a wolf as a man. We avoid them if we can."

I shook my head. "All of my brothers carry weapons," I snapped. "Your assessments are for shit." I didn't want to admit that he was right, that my brothers wouldn't call the Police. They had no need to. They were a law unto themselves.

Khush huffed. "We were well aware of their arms. But your brothers were *eager* to negotiate with us. And look, it was a success. Everyone is happy."

Khush looked back at Cazz on that point, like he'd finally realized that maybe he hadn't been brought here for a commendation and he was reminding Cazz that he'd chosen me. Cazz's expression didn't even flicker from the bored stare he'd been using since the male arrived, but I felt the flare of anger in him.

"You think everyone is *happy?*" I started, but Cazz hissed at me through the bond to keep me quiet, and he stepped in.

"How did you approach her males?" Cazz asked quietly. "How did they learn that they could sell their sister? How was the connection forged?"

Khush blinked, then frowned. That obviously wasn't a question he'd expected. Was he trying to remember? Or scanning back to figure out what he needed to lie about?

"Sire, is there a concern about—"

"Answer the question, Khush," Cazz growled. "Leave nothing out."

Khush rubbed his jaw, scratching the stubble there. "I didn't make the initial contact. But believe her brothers were distantly known to us. They'd had dealings with us in previous years for… other goods."

I looked at Cazz. *'What goods?'*

Cazz never moved or reacted. "Dealings with whom?" he asked slowly. The hair on the back of my neck stood up because I could feel the tension in him growing and I wondered if this guy knew that Cazz was *livid.* Was I just sensing that through the bond, or could they all tell?

"I don't know. It wasn't important to know. One of the scouts was familiar with the family, had contacts with one or two of the brothers." Khush shrugged like it was no big deal. "We reached out and negotiated a mutually beneficial agreement. Apart from her shrieking, it was the easiest of the reapings in this round, honestly."

My whole body went cold.

I was in the backseat of Ryan's car because we'd just pulled up to my favorite truck-stop waffle place. My brothers did this every once in a while—decided we needed to have a family meeting about something. There was no arguing, I was just informed when it was happening and expected to attend. And it meant I got a free breakfast, so I didn't care.

I was still half-asleep because I'd worked late the night before, so I wasn't paying attention to what they were needling each other about.

I didn't even realize anything was happening until we got out of the car. It seemed weird that they walked so close to me—usually I hung back and followed them while they ribbed and teased each other. But this time they bracketed me.

I had my head down and was rubbing my eyes, so I didn't see the guys coming from the other side of the parking lot until my brothers grabbed my elbows and pulled me around the side of the restaurant, to where the dumpsters were.

I still thought they were just being stupid—it wasn't until these huge guys crowded in behind us and Ryan started barking about "cash first" that I realized something was happening. And even then my first thought was that Ryan was dealing again, and they were just dragging me along on some stupid deal.

It wasn't until Ryan took the envelope and his eyes lit up as he fingered through the stack inside it then turned to look at me and his eyes...

His eyes gleamed.

"She's yours," he said. And he smiled.

I frowned. "What are you—"

I started screaming the second one of my brothers planted a hand between my shoulderblades and shoved me forward so hard I almost lost my feet. I was caught in a firm, warm grip and for a second I thought these strangers were helping me.

Then the guy who caught me tipped up my chin and smiled the same smile Ryan had just given me.

"He's going to like you," he said in a low, rumbling voice.

I screamed.

A meaty hand clapped over my mouth and male arms and bodies caged me.

I screamed and I fought so hard there were lights flashing at the edges of my vision.

The world became shadows and light, fingers pinching my skin, male grunts when my fists or feet connected. But I lost. I lost quickly. There were too many of them, and they were too strong.

Something soft but dirty was shoved into my mouth. Thick arms held me immobile while someone tied a blindfold over my eyes.

And the only person who heard me scream after that, was me. I couldn't see, so wasn't sure how they got me to their vehicle without anyone seeing, but then I was tumbling into that space and that voice—

"If the transaction went so smoothly, why did she and the others all arrive bruised and with torn clothing?" Cazz asked, his voice quiet and slow, but even I could hear the blade-edge in it.

Khush's brows dropped. "You asked for those who'd seen darkness. Lived it. The poor ones are more... scrappy," he grumbled. "In the past we've taken from the more affluent, educated areas. It's harder to find girls who fit our needs, but when we do, they're more easily intimidated. These ones didn't freeze. We had no choice but to physically restrain them."

"And yet, so many bruises and tears? And not just on my mate."

"You never asked us to be gentle," Khush said with a casual shrug.

I didn't think I'd ever seen a man be so utterly *undisturbed* by the idea of women physically harmed. Even my father and brothers understood the rules and had become very good at pretending concern when it was needed.

But Khush met Cazz's eyes without any apparent worry. He expected Cazz to think about this the same way he did.

Did he?

I turned to Cazz in horror. His gaze flicked to meet mine for the barest second, but the bond throbbed in that moment.

"Rake?" Cazz said quietly, his eyes still on mine.

"Yes?"

"Please join the Queen. And in case there's any confusion, if it becomes relevant, I'm asking you to be gentle with her."

Khush tensed, never taking his eyes off of Cazz as Rake got out of his chair and hurried towards me.

'What are you doing?' I sent warily.

'Don't be afraid,' Cazz replied as Rake reached my side.

I thought he was talking about Khush and was about to scoff at him—I couldn't control the way my body reacted at the sound of his voice—until Cazz's eyes dropped back to the massive male who was still kneeling, and the air in the room suddenly felt like it had taken on weight.

I gasped and flinched, crowding Rake back a step as thick, black power began to gather behind Cazz like boiling storm clouds sucked out of hell itself.

Soundtrack for the following chapter is
Seven Nation Army by Future Royalty

109. Be Gentle

~ CASIMIR ~

It was the first time I'd drawn on the power in full since I'd claimed her and it almost washed me away. My body *thrummed* with it. A tsunami of strength and compulsion and sheer might. I sucked in a breath and had to work to keep myself from dropping to my knees in submission to *myself.*

Feet planted on the stone floor for a moment I ignored Khush and all the others, just let it hum through my veins as I wrestled it under control.

I was panting, I realized, my skin throbbing as the power coursed through me like electricity in my veins.

Dear *god,* I knew she'd fed my power, but this…

I almost staggered under it.

I could feel my heartbeat in my palms.

'Cazz!' Her voice in my head was high and urgent.

Bridling the waves pounding at me, my eyes flew open to find her, half-expecting that Khush had launched himself for her in an attempt to stop me reaching him. But no, she remained on her feet, her eyes wide and frightened and fixed on whatever she saw around me as I pulled at that waterfall of cataclysmic power.

Holy shit.

Khush remained kneeling, his eyes now wary and flicking back and forth between my face and the power he could see gathering around me as I pulled it over my shoulders like a cloak.

But the arrogant fuck was only barely nervous. Did he think this was all for show? That I *truly* didn't care if he was rough on females being brought to me as potential mates?

449

'Keep hold of Jesse,' I sent to Rake, and even I could hear the strange echo in my voice. *'The power makes her nervous.'*

'Cazz, you're making me *nervous.'*

I cut him a look and examined him in the link as best I could with that torrent of power rushing through me.

'Need help finding your testicles, Rake?'

'No, Cazz... look at yourself.'

He sent me an image then—myself in his eyes.

The power had swelled in my veins, making me appear even larger, and my eyes glowed almost-white from the roiling black clouds of it that rose behind me like demonic wings.

I had to choke back a laugh.

'Well, how dramatic,' I drawled in Rake's head. *'What was it you said once, Rake? What God gives the Devil corrupts?'*

'Cazz—'

'Don't worry, brother. I think even your God would be proud of this.'

I felt the flash of curiosity from him, and alarm from Jesse, but I was done waiting, so I set them aside in my mind to ensure they wouldn't be touched and turned my attention back to the others.

With an exhale, I spread the power out in the room like a flood, rushing to fill every gap, saturating every body. I wanted it seeping into their *hair*.

But for once, I wouldn't use the bulk of it to override their minds. No, if I were to unleash this torrent of power in only compulsion, it would sweep away more than just their will. They'd lose their minds. Become empty shells good only for following orders.

Instead, I used only tendrils of compulsion to keep them still, and let the rest of the power appear to solidify and close them off from each other, and from me.

Khush stumbled to his feet as a slick wall of power, black as tar, shiny as water, rose from every side, surrounding him and me.

At first, he whirled, staring at the darkness like it was coming for him, but once I had us completely surrounded he froze, then he slowly turned to face me, his eyes wide and wary as he saw his doom coming.

"Cazz... what are you doing?" he asked hesitantly.

I smiled.

And I let him sweat.

Opening myself further to Rake and Jesse individually, I let them see through my eyes, praying that Jesse wouldn't find the onslaught too frightening.

Nothing like a trial by fire.

She sucked in a gasp as she saw me and Khush within that black dome, but I reached for her mind, as if I were spreading a hand at the back of her skull and cradling her head.

'Don't fear. My anger is for him, not you.'

'Cazz, what are you doing?' Her voice was high and thin, but I just smiled.

'We're getting to the bottom of this. Watch and see.'

Khush tensed the moment my eyes cut back to him and he let his weight settle, lowering his center of gravity as if we were about to fight physically.

I laughed in his face, but not for long.

'Tell me which goods the Queen's brothers purchased from us in the past?' I said in his head, letting my voice boom and echo in his skull.

His Adam's apple bobbed. But he held my eyes. *'The women,'* he said. *'We knew they weren't above that kind of transaction because they'd bought access to the women you discarded in the past.'*

I felt Jesse's stomach plunge, then I *felt* her turn her mind to me with a question that sickened her. It made my jaw clench.

'I did not tell you to sell them,' I hissed at Khush, making certain she heard and saw the exchange.

'You didn't say we couldn't.'

God, I wanted to snap my teeth, but I wouldn't let him see how he'd gotten under my skin.

"A mistake I will make certain not to repeat," I growled.

Khush only nodded, his eyes still wary. He wasn't backing down, but he knew he was in danger. If he'd been in his wolf his ears and hackles would have been high, his body poised to leap aside if I came for him.

If, because I had a reputation for keeping my males on their toes—challenging them just to see how they'd react. Khush was smart enough to remember that sometimes all I wanted to see was a male's submission. So he was giving it.

But the fucking idiot had no clue what he was dealing with.

110. The Threat

~ *CASIMIR* ~

Mind still open to Rake and Jesse so they'd hear every word, I stepped forward to put myself right in front of Khush. The male was larger than me by at least fifty pounds. If we'd been men, I would have needed to use skill rather than brute strength to defeat him.

But we were not men. And he did not stand a chance.

Snapping a thread of compulsion at him like a whiplash, I smiled as Khush's eyes glazed, then he blinked and focused on me again.

"Tell me the things you're holding back—the things you think I wouldn't approve of, or that protect someone else's interests," I said casually. I kept the others in the room ignorant to the conversation, their ears stopped so they wouldn't hear it, or move from their places.

Khush nodded quickly. "I'm concerned that these brothers might be involved in the activities outside. They were very eager for information about us when we've dealt with them in the past. Their interest seems driven by titillation—they believe we live a hedonistic life—but even so, they lack the care many humans have for law enforcement. They openly flaunt the laws of their land, and laugh at those who would warn them. It gave us a great deal of freedom in dealing with them, but in light of the recent humans in the area, I worry."

"Have you had contact with them since you took the Queen?"

"No, but Andras has cell phone numbers."

I felt Jesse tense and sent her a wave of soothing along the bond. *'I will handle this.'*

"If you were concerned they were involved in the activity outside, why didn't you raise it with me earlier?"

"Because I'm hoping you'll get humbled by this. I'm sick of getting passed over for raising. If we shake up the hierarchy, I know I can defeat enough above me to take a pack."

My jaw ached, I clenched it so hard at that. The compulsion held him in thrall—kept his instincts from warning him or cautioning his words. What he spoke was what he believed.

"It takes more than brute strength to lead a pack," I seethed.

The male shrugged. "I have more to offer than you realize. But you take too strong a hand in forming the packs now. You should let us handle ourselves and only step in if a wolf is hurting the Kingdom."

The male met my gaze unwaveringly. He was being honest. At least, as he saw it.

I sneered. "Are you rebelling, Khush?" I asked quietly. "Do you scheme against me?"

The fact that he hesitated before answering meant he was aware of betraying himself. I shoved a hair more of the power into the compulsion, elated to find that with the greater reach to my power, I was also finding a more delicate control. It was important to give him no wiggle room to fight me, but not wash his mind. I needed him just as strong and just as certain of himself when he left this conversation as he was when he walked into it.

"Khush, answer me," I growled. "Do you scheme for my downfall?"

"Not yet." The male swallowed hard again. "I have ideas, though."

Yet. Not *yet.*

My wolf snarled and leaped, pushing for release, urging me to take his throat.

I clenched my fists and made myself wait. "Do your ideas include using the humans somehow?"

"If they can put pressure on you, your attention will be taken by them, so it will be easier to achieve things without you learning about them."

A growl puttered in my chest.

'Holy shit, Cazz,' Rake breathed in my head. *'Is he—?'*

"Tell me," I ordered Khush, holding the compulsion on his mind tightly. "Tell me every plan and action you've taken that could even be perceived as being against me."

Khush frowned. "I didn't tell you my suspicions about the humans. I spoke to Andras to make certain he had kept their numbers so we could contact them if needed. I've spoken to your toys. And gathered loyalty from wolves who should be ranked higher and are growing impatient. They're willing to follow if it will benefit them."

"You plan an uprising?"

"Not necessarily. We know how strong you are. We're... looking for opportunity."

I almost tore out his throat on the spot. He wanted *opportunity?* He would get it.

"You've spoken to my toys about what?" I demanded as calmly as I was able.

"The Queen."

I felt the jolt in Jesse and instinctively raised a hand to stop her speaking out, but then realized he wouldn't hear her even if she did. So I sent a rush of soothing, but kept my attention on Khush.

"They're struggling, Cazz. They haven't seen you in weeks and you're the only thing they care about."

"How would you use them against the Queen?"

Khush hesitated again and I almost growled, but then he spoke without me adding to the power against him.

"They're like me. They know how strong you are, and they don't want to hurt you. But they'll take an opportunity if they can find one. They watch for her. If they can seed doubt, they will. If they can draw you away from her, they will. And if they learn anything that could help us, they'll tell me."

"How could they work against me if they're compelled to please me?" I snarled, scrambling to remember how I'd left them, what weaknesses might have been present, what flaws in the compulsion I needed to fix quickly—

"They won't work against you. At all. They'll only work against *her*. They don't know that I want to see you brought down."

And there it was. I saw the flare in his eyes as he realized what he'd said, the small part of him that was still in control of his own thoughts screamed alarm, but the compulsion had such a grip, he couldn't remember why it was a problem.

I let him see me smile, because this fucker was *going down.* And he was going to help me find any others who might even consider following his lead.

111. Commendations

~ CASIMIR ~

'Very good, Khush. You've pleased me.'

His large body relaxed, the compulsion keeping his mind away from the apparent contradiction in that statement.

'Now you're going to please me even more.'

'Tell me. I'll do it,' he replied as my power surged in his veins and the talons of it sank into his consciousness.

I felt Rake and Jesse both tense and alarmed—confused—but they would see.

I took the final steps to completely close the distance between Khush and I. My power was a hammer, but it was also a scalpel, and a needle… and a fucking nuclear bomb.

I put my hand on his shoulder because touching him gave me even more precision, then I began to wash his mind clean—only of this conversation.

'You won't remember anything we've spoken about since you told me that I hadn't given the order to be gentle on the women.'

Khush nodded eagerly, his eyes glazed again.

'You believe that I accepted your explanation, and commended you for handling the affairs as they were needed. You'll tell all your… loyal wolves as much. You will feel extremely confident that you have successfully pulled the wool over my eyes. This will embolden you in taking the first steps in your schemes.'

'Yesssss,' the male hissed back through the link.

God, I wanted to tear his face off.

'You will retain your natural caution, but you'll begin to select those you believe can help you—whoever will willingly help you—

in the event that I'm weakened or distracted. You'll begin the planning and organization, but you will not pull the trigger on acting against me.'

'No. Not yet.'

I nodded grimly. *'You'll get the phone numbers of the human males who sold my mate from Andras—tell him you're thinking about a side hustle. You might take some women just to sell them to other humans and pocket the funds for yourself. You're planning a foray into the human world just for the sheer enjoyment of it,'* I snapped the words off in my mind like my teeth were closing on them. *'When you have the numbers, you'll feel compelled to write them down and give them to me—but you'll tell no one that you've done it, and the moment I have them, you'll forget that you gave them to me.'*

"Yes," he rumbled, nodding as if he thought this was an excellent plan.

Stupid, weak-minded *fuck*.

My nose wrinkled in disgust. *'You will never actually take a step against me, but you will plan and organize and gather others as if you are. And at every turn, you will feed me the names of those who support and strengthen your cause.'*

Khush nodded again, smiling.

'Any information you receive about these human men, or others, who would work against me, or against our Kingdom, you will provide to me personally, without the knowledge of any other wolves, and the moment you've shared it with me, you'll forget that you have done so.'

Khush continued nodding. My contempt for the asshole grew.

'While you might be seen by your treasonous comrades to work against me, or my mate, you will secretly protect both of us with your life. If it requires that you die in order to stop another wolf from harming me, or my mate, you will do so without question.'

"Of course."

'And if you hear even a hint of a plot from another wolf that could harm me or her, you'll make certain I hear of it immediately—but forget that you have informed me.'

"Yes."

'You will continue your talks with my former Toys, and make them any promises necessary to draw out their true intentions and plans. But you will not take any actual step against me, or my mate. *And you will not allow them to do so either. When any scheme or plot becomes a reality, you will give me every detail you know and allow me to thwart it. But you will not remember informing me, and*

you will believe yourself to be acting independently, and all your subversive or treasonous intentions will remain within you.'

"Yes, Sire."

Rake sucked in a breath at that, but I nudged him to keep him quiet and continued.

Looking Khush directly in the eye, I held the threads of compulsion around him as I cupped his neck with both my hands.

"To any other wolf who would join you, you will appear to be a great threat to me and my mate," I growled. "But in truth, you will guard both of us with your life, and see nothing as more important than keeping us safe. Even if it means losing your own life to do so."

Khush nodded. I stroked his jawline with my thumbs.

"And the moment that you are no longer useful to me, your heart will stop, and you will die."

Jesse's entire body screamed alarm, but I didn't stop.

"So make certain you remain undetected and useful to me, Khush. Do you understand?"

I felt the goosebumps rise on his neck. His instincts fought his mind, which I controlled, but I couldn't cut him off from his instincts entirely—he needed them to hunt down my other enemies in the pack. And in the human world. So I waited.

"I understand," he replied hoarsely.

I nodded, clapping my hand to his neck time and again. "You are my hound now, Khush. No one will know it but you and I, my mate, and my Cleric. In the event that you cannot get word to me, you will find one of them, then forget it the moment your message is delivered."

Khush smiled like I'd given him a gift. "Yes, Sire. Thank you."

"Now, think about what you're to do. Make a plan for who and how you will draw information out from my enemies, until I call on you again."

"Yes, Sire."

With a huff of disdain, I pulled the weaves of compulsion tight enough on his mind that he couldn't resist them, but left enough room to allow him to think for himself, and be unaware of his own motives.

Khush stepped back when I let him go, his expression thoughtful as I strode away from him, through that wall of power, to stand in front of the others who'd been gathered to advise me.

112. The Best Mate

~ *CASIMIR* ~

I regarded my council of Advisors for a moment, considering my options. They were all far too important for me to wash their minds clean and risk taking parts of them or limiting their capacity, so I'd only used the compulsion to keep them still and silent. And unaware of my conversation with Khush.

But now I spoke to them through the link we'd maintained, letting that thread thicken slightly to take a small, needle-like path into their minds.

'You'll remember nothing except that Khush was brought to me and we discussed the Reaping. I am unhappy with how he went about it, but pleased that he did not subvert me, only took the most efficient route to find the Queen.'

Realizing what I was doing, Rake tensed. *'Cazz, the risk—'*

I growled at him through the link, letting the power Jesse had given me course in my veins—heightening every sense and awareness until my body thrummed with it.

He was right that delicate, specific compulsion was very difficult. Or had been. Especially on a group.

But he couldn't feel this, didn't know what she'd given me.

I was breathless with it—the precision, the strength, the sheer *power.* God, I was getting hard.

'When you think back on this meeting, you'll remember that Khush had my approval, and you will suspect nothing of his motives, and have no concerns that I suspect him. He is an asset to the crown, and a strong male who should be considered for raising in the years to come.'

The Advisors eyes were glazed, but they nodded and rumbled their agreement with that.

'And you will see my mate as an asset as well,' I sent, smiling when Jesse tensed again. *'Her knowledge of the human world is something we can use—and we should regularly call on her to do so. Let the other wolves see you rely on her for her insight. And let them see you offer her the respect any wolf Queen would be due.'*

They all nodded, a few of them even beginning to drop into a kneel—perhaps I'd turned the compulsion on them just a little too thickly. I eased back.

'Khush will be spoken of as the wolf who identified and successfully took the best Queen I have ever mated, and the only one I have claimed. He will be applauded as if it was his instinct all along that she would be Chosen. He will increase in his power in the pack, and be trusted for his judgment. Most importantly: He will be seen to be trusted by me. And you will ensure that others note that fact.'

They were all nodding, in complete submission. I ground my teeth knowing it was going to physically *hurt* to treat the male as if he were an asset to me. But also knowing it would be the very best weapon in my arsenal against my enemies.

Their pride would lead them straight to my hound—who would bite out their throats and forget he'd even done it.

I smiled. "Are we clear?" I asked the entire group of Advisors.

"Yes, Sire!"

"Very good. Now cleanse your minds of any point that would contradict what I've told you."

Then, leaving them a moment to allow the compulsion to travel their minds and find every memory or thought that didn't comply with what I'd told them and eradicate it, I stepped through the power wall again and strode over to where Rake held Jesse by the elbow, both of them staring at me wide-eyed when I appeared from out of that onyx wall of power.

Jesse's face was pale.

Rake was wary, but I could feel his approval, as well.

"No one will remember what's happened here today, except you two," I said calmly. "I am trusting you both never to share a word of this with anyone—not even the wolves we trust."

Rake nodded slowly, but Jesse folded her arms. "Why would you do that? You're empowering him!"

"Because if he truly believes he has retained his independence, *and* that I've commended him, he'll be more effective. Smug because he's fooled me. The others who are drawn to his ideas, but scared of my power, will be more likely to show themselves if they think he's truly deceived me and become one of my inner circle."

Jesse frowned, looking past me in the direction where he'd still be standing if she could see through the wall of my power. "He's... Cazz, he makes my skin crawl. He wasn't kind. And he's..." she shuddered.

Something panged deep inside me. I vowed that when this was over the male would die and she'd see it and know she was safe from him.

"Don't worry, Jesse. They'll all keep you safe. *Especially* Khush," I said with an amused rumble.

"But... they... they really won't remember all of this?"

"Not until I tell them to. And if it would make you feel better— before I kill him, I'll make sure he remembers every moment. Every word. Every time he helped you without his own knowledge. I could make him kneel to you now, if you wish?"

"N-no, that's not... I don't need that," she said uncomfortably, with a glance at Rake. Then she swallowed. "If you're sure he won't remember until you tell him to. But what about the others?"

"They haven't heard a word since I pulled the power around them, and their minds are currently burning away anything that happened after he said I didn't ask them to be gentle. When they leave this room, it will be as if none of this happened."

She blinked and I felt her flinch, rather than saw her do it.

Rake's eyes cut to her—did he feel it too, or did he just know she wouldn't like remembering that?

Itching between my shoulder blades, I offered my hand, and was surprised how much more easily I breathed when Jesse took it.

"Now, if you're ready, we're going to stand in front of the council so we can commend Khush, and you're going to thank him for bringing you to me, and then you're going to receive the loyalty of my Advisors. Are you ready?"

Jesse's brows pinched over her nose. "I... I guess?"

As I drew her through that wall of power, she flinched. But she didn't give in to her fear.

She stood next to me, proud and calm, even her scent revealing little more than tension, as she nodded along while I commended Khush, then thanked the Advisors when they all vowed their loyalty, and commended my choice of mate.

I could see that the whole scene made her uncomfortable, but I couldn't stop smiling.

I was the wolf, on the trail of the fox.

And I was going to shake him until his neck snapped.

113. Rising Queen

~ *CASIMIR* ~

When the whole scene had finally played out and Khush was excused, Jesse stood at my side with folded arms, smelling a little uneasy.

"Rake, would you please escort the Queen back to her chambers?" I asked quietly. "Then come back here. We need to determine the best and fastest way to remove those who are a threat—"

"No, Cazz, don't!"

Rake was nodding and beginning to pull at Jesse's elbow, but she ignored him and stepped towards me.

My hackles rose. I had to swallow back the urge to bark at her not to interrupt me—or contradict me in front of others when her opinion hadn't been sought.

"I will come to you as soon as we're done here," I told her quietly, surprised by how warm the thought made me—and impatient.

"No, that's not… you can't just take Ryan or any of the others out. That's the fastest way to bring all of them down on you."

I gave her my most predatory smile and a flash of warning through the bond. "You'd be surprised how discreet we can be when we choose. Any of us could take even the strongest human out before they even knew—"

"No, Cazz, you're not listening. I'm not saying you're not capable of taking them out. I'm saying if I'm right and that's not a police operation out there, but my brother working some scheme, right now, no one else is aware of where they are or what's happening. But if you go making people disappear—someone's going to sound the alarm and then *lots* of humans will be actually hunting around here. Too many for you to just keep killing them all."

My jaw ached from grinding my teeth because she kept interrupting me, but she was making sense, and I'd just told the Council we needed to listen to her insights on the humans.

I opened the bond a little further to give her a more substantial nudge of caution, but put my hand up to Rake not to try and take her away.

"What do you suggest?" I asked as calmly as I could. "We cannot allow your brother or his associates, whoever they might be, to surveil us, or worse, actually find his way into our homes—"

"The tournament runs all week. They'll still be around for days. Didn't you say you have, um, friends in law enforcement? Could you ask them to do some digging about whether the Police are involved in this at all? Because if they aren't, then my brother's up to no good. And that means the last thing he wants is cops showing up. You can deal with him a lot differently from that place, than if he's actually working with the Sheriff."

My ears perked at that. "You believe he might be?"

Jesse frowned. "I highly doubt that he's working with them *officially,*" she said with a snort. "But it's worth checking, isn't it? If they are, they'll make problems for you if you start killing people. Or even just scaring them. But if he isn't... then he's just on his own mission, and then it's a lot safer for you to... intervene."

I tipped my head and caught Rake's eyes over her shoulder.

'She's making sense,' he said. I agreed, but it frustrated me.

"You're certain you don't know what his plan is."

"I didn't even know he knew the wolves existed," Jesse grumbled. "Let alone that he'd been... doing business with you." She gave a shiver, and I felt her go cold.

It was instinct to reach out, to offer some comfort, some sense of protection.

'Jesse, I was not aware those... transactions were occuring. I would never... that wasn't... that wasn't from me,' I sent her, keeping my eyes on her until she returned her gaze to me and our eyes locked.

'Isn't that what you do though, Cazz? Bring women who didn't ask to be here, then either use them or discard them?' she sent bluntly.

I was breathless with the combined fury and startling respect for her sheer balls to just put it to me like that.

Rake coughed, so I realized he was still in this link as well. I sighed. *'Frankly, no,'* I said, though a niggle in the back of my head wanted to argue. *'I keep no one who doesn't wish to stay, and certainly never suggested those who left should be* sold.*'*

Jesse's brows pinched. *'After you compelled them, though... right?'*

'I don't follow.'

'You gave them the choice to stay or go... after *you compelled them?'*

'I wasn't compelling them when they were given the choice. I don't see what that has to do with—'

'I do,' she sent simply. And stared at me with fear in her eyes.

The feeling that danced up my spine then was... uncomfortable.

But it got immeasurably worse when I saw flickers, foggy snippets of what was in her head—and felt the horror coursing through her...

...her brothers throwing her to the wolves—literally—but instead of being brought safely into our dens, she never made it to my chamber. She was taken and used by Khush and some of the others...

...or she made it to my audience, but I overwhelmed her with the compulsion, and she folded like paper. I rejected her, and then she was handed to them...

...or she didn't give in to the compulsion, but I rejected her proposal and she was discarded and picked up by them to be sold—

There was a terrifying, gut-wrenching moment when I saw, with crystal clarity, the nightmare she imagined then and my entire being went cold with fear, then white-hot with rage.

'Jesse, I would never—'

'You didn't have to, Cazz. You just had to not care enough to see that they already were.'

I blinked, my chest suddenly hollow.

'This isn't the time for this conversation,' I growled in the bond, then turned back to my Council who were watching us curiously, obviously trying to figure out if I was linking with Rake or Jesse, or both. Damn. I hadn't wanted to plant that seed.

I turned to Rake in my mind. But something stopped me from closing the bond on Jesse. I let her hear me issue him orders.

'Tell them all that we agree that her plan is solid. Our first step will be to access our contacts in law enforcement. Show them the brother's image and see if there's any of their presence in this. Check in with the packs in both districts for reports on any

movement near their dens. Then, *if we're sure he's working alone, then we'll take him out.'*

Rake nodded and immediately turned to address the Council, while I reached for Jesse's hand and pulled her from the room, setting my teeth against the chill I could feel in her because the bond was open.

'And we are not to be disturbed for the rest of the evening unless circumstances outside change,' I added to Rake. *'If there is no activity tonight, we will meet again in the morning and I will be left alone until then.'*

'Sure, Cazz,' Rake answered on a sigh.

I didn't link with the council again, instead speaking to them as I marched from the room.

"I am assisting my mate back to her chambers and will speak with you all tomorrow," I rumbled, leading a surprised Jesse from the room.

None of them contradicted me of course—or interrupted me. They were far more respectful than my mate had been.

Jesse and I needed to discuss that. She couldn't be undermining me that way. But this wasn't the place. Not in front of the Council. And it was already late. We were going to seek intelligence on her brother. And... and my mate had averted her eyes in a way that made my teeth clench.

I needed to get out of there.

Soundtrack for the next chapter is
The World in My Eyes by AG and Kate York.

114. The Bond

~ *JESSE* ~

Cazz wasn't happy, but what else was new?

But then I realized, what was actually new was that I could tell he was unhappy without looking at him. He was carrying a tension and disapproval that was reaching me through the bond. Because for the first time I could remember, he was keeping the bond open. He'd held it since we started talking and he hadn't let it go. Hadn't shut me down.

My heart beat faster.

It had been thrilling—and a little bit scary—to discover that we could talk in each other's heads. But then he opened the bond further and started letting me *feel* him... I didn't know whether to fistpump, or cry happy tears. Of course, it wasn't all smiles and fun. At first I realized he'd only done it because he was using it to warn me off—a sensation in the bond reached me, like yanking on a leash. But then...

I felt the wave of irritation in him the second time I interrupted him.

And the begrudging respect when I confronted him about the women. But it was cold comfort. Because everything in that conversation suddenly brought home how close I had come to ending up in a very, very different place than here in Cazz's hands and under his protection.

The moment I let myself think about the fact that my brothers had *bought women* from the wolves—women that had been part of the very same process I was, just a year or two earlier... I didn't just feel sick. I felt *panic*.

It had been bad enough before that. The sound of Khush's voice had brought back the fear of that first day and night when the Reapers were collecting all of us and we didn't know why. The confusion and terror and instinct to survive that I'd lived in for those hours. The desperate terror, when I'd done everything I could to stay calm and listen and even ask careful questions to figure out what was going on...

But now I was here and... what had happened to those other six or seven women? Were they still here? Were they dead? Had they been sold to someone as callous and self-serving as my brothers?

What had my brothers done with the women they'd purchased in the past?

I couldn't stop imagining what might have happened to me if even one set of circumstances had been different—and with a sinking feeling, knowing that those things were probably happening to those other women because of my proposal to Cazz.

I'd been here, weeping about him rejecting me, feeling sorry for myself because my mate didn't want me as much as I wanted him, pouting because I was being treated like a child... and all the while they were out there, either in the dens, or in our world being treated like commodities...

Oh God, I was going to be sick—

'Jesse, please be calm. You're safe.'

'I know I am, Cazz. At least for now. But—'

'There are no buts. *You are safe. I will ensure it. Always.'*

A skeptical huff burst in my throat before I could even think about how he might read it. We were almost back to the royal wing, I was waiting to see whether Cazz was going to lead me back to my room or his.

When that sound broke out of me, Cazz's head snapped towards me and his grip on my hand tightened. He hesitated, then pulled me forward, walking so quickly I had to trot to keep up.

"Cazz, I didn't mean you wouldn't protect me physically, I know you—"

'Be quiet. This isn't the place,' he muttered in my head.

My heart rose a little bit when we reached the royal corridor and he turned right towards his chambers, instead of left towards mine. Then moments later he was pushing his door open and pulling me in behind him, his face a mask of tension.

Had he only brought me here because it was closer?

I decided it didn't matter, because Cazz was growling and locking the door behind us, and turning on me.

"You are the Queen of the Wolves, Jesse," he snarled, stepping up to loom over me. "No matter what you might think, I have given you a great honor—and I don't regret it. I will not remove it from you," he said, his eyes intense and locked on mine. "If anyone attempts to hurt you or take you against your will, *I will end them—*"

"That's not why I huffed, Cazz," I said sadly.

"I felt it in you—skepticism, resistance—"

"Not that you'd be protective, but…"

He waited, his eyes flashing. And when I didn't continue, he hissed the words through snapping teeth.

"But. *What?*"

Uneasiness bubbled in my chest, but I took hold of myself and told him the truth.

"You always care about my physical wellbeing—making sure I eat and rest and that my body is… that I enjoy things." I swallowed hard because he started to smile then and I saw flashes in my mind of what *he* was seeing in his—namely, me tied up on that bed.

My stomach started thrumming, and he felt it or smelled it, because he did that thing where his body kind of rippled and his hips pushed forward. He put a hand on my back and started to pull me in, but I shook my head and pushed down the rising arousal, because this was important.

Cazz froze when I put a hand to his chest and that connection crackled between us. I curled my fingers into his shirt, gripping him there, but didn't drop my eyes.

"Cazz, you always take great care of my body, but you completely ignore me as a person."

"That's impossible," he hissed. "One is the other."

I arched an eyebrow at him. "Seriously? That's how you're going to play this?"

"I assure you, I am not *playing.*" He snapped his mouth shut and glared at me. And when I didn't start talking, but let us sit in silence, he turned his head slightly but his eyes remained on mine, like a wary animal.

I waited.

But he didn't give in. He didn't relax. Instead I felt him tense and start to turn away.

No!

115. Hold On Tight

~ JESSE ~

"Cazz, please!" I tightened my grip on his shirt and he froze. "I don't want you to leave. I don't want to be away from you. I love it when we're together," I admitted carefully. "But… a few hours ago you did incredible things to me that made me *feel* for you. And then you just walked away! And you keep doing that. Every time we're together you leave me like a bad smell."

"I am King, Jesse. It is my life to serve the pack and Ghere had found—"

"That's not what I meant and you know it!"

Cazz's jaw was tight, his eyes wary. I was still getting the hang of this mind thing, but he'd been able to show me images, so I must be able to as well. I concentrated, dragging up the memory of earlier that day, after he'd had me tied and made my body hum *four times.* For a while there, just a few minutes, he had held me, curled his body around mine and stroked me and… it was wonderful. Yet then, just like all the other times, he just… left.

I made myself see that moment in my head again when I'd gone to confront him after he walked to the bathing room, then got aggressive when I asked him not to leave.

My stomach clenched as I remembered…

I was standing in that bedroom naked and pleading… and he was going to just walk away.

"Cazz… please. Let me in."

His shoulders hunched towards his ears, but he turned to look at me over his shoulder and his jaw was tight.

"I don't know how," he said quietly.

It was a very real admission, I realized. But then, instead of talking about it, he just stepped out and closed the door firmly behind him as if to tell me not to follow.

Pain ricocheted through me.

Cazz obviously saw it too, because his eyes got wider and he pulled his head back looking at me down his nose. I was encouraged because he hadn't closed the bond, so I could feel the tension in him. But it felt like he was swaying away from me, preparing to pull out of my grip.

"Cazz, I'm not asking you to fall in love with me," I whispered, though I would have given anything to see it happen, because I suspected he'd be an *incredible* husband when he wasn't afraid. "I'm asking you to stop denying that you care about me. And… and I want you to let *me* care for *you*."

He blinked, then snorted. I could feel his defenses rising, feel him beginning to lean into the bond like he would a door he had a grip on and could swing shut.

"Don't," I said quietly. "Don't do that."

"Do what? I said nothing," he growled.

"Don't do that thing where you feel something and flinch away from it and pretend you didn't, then get mad at me because I made you feel. Don't shut me out."

Cazz exhaled heavily. "That's not—"

"I'm not asking for your slavering devotion, Cazz. I know you think that's the only way it's possible to give to someone, but that's not it. I don't need you to tell me pretty words, or gush on me. I just need you to stop pretending you don't feel *anything*. That's why I huffed when you said you'd protect me—because you're really good at protecting my body, but you *suck* at protecting my heart."

He'd gone tense as a rock under my hand, his gaze intense— and fearful. "Jesse, your heart is not my concern—we've covered this. I told you that I will not fall in love. I *can't*—"

The deepest part of me recoiled from that, but Maya had been working with me on strengthening my mental defenses. I did my best to keep that covered from him as I rushed in to interrupt him again.

"I'm not asking for your love, Cazz. I'm asking for your compassion."

He didn't look away, but through the bond I could feel him pulling in on himself. And he didn't respond. I swallowed hard and made myself very consciously remember that moment when he had spooned me on that bed and curled his body around mine… I felt him tense and threw caution to the wind.

"Compassion isn't something you just give your mate," I said hoarsely. "You don't have to see it as... as something unique to us—"

"I know what compassion is, Jesse."

I nodded. "Then... then I'm asking you to give me what you'd give someone who was just... important to the pack. To you, maybe. Someone you wanted to protect. I'm asking you to... to stop pretending that we don't have... *this.*"

Then I focused on that cord between us, the one that pulsed and sang when he touched me. The place where I *felt* him and he felt me. Maya had made a few small mentions of how the bond could be used by mated pairs, but it was all theory. I'd never had a chance to try it with him. But I tried to remember what she said.

I imagined taking hold of it, embracing it, hugging it... and I stopped holding myself back and let him feel all the things I was feeling—the joy of having been close to him, the satisfaction of the Council listening to me, the jittery nerves about what my brother might be up to, the fierce certainty that Cazz was stronger than Ryan so whatever was coming, he'd win it and... and the fear.

Cazz sucked in a breath, his hands coming up to grip my upper arms and hold me there.

"Why?" he growled. "Why are you afraid? I made your body sing. I brought you to the Council. I *trusted* you with knowledge I didn't even give them! I stood for you even when you interrupted me—you're here in my fucking chambers! For God's sake, what do you have to be afraid of?"

I didn't even know how to start answering that, but it all flickered through my head in a movie too quick for me to even try to explain...

116. All the Ways You Were

~ JESSE ~

Cazz in that very first moment I'd ever seen him, walking towards me out of the dark like an apparition manifesting out of hell itself—tall, broad, so strong, and so cold...

...Cazz, staring at me intently, his arctic eyes chill and his tone so full of self-satisfaction. "Kitten, I can make them do anything. I can heal—or I can stop their hearts with a word. I could, if I wished, tell you to die, right here. Right now. And you would..."

...Cazz standing with his head dropped between his arms, and his hands so tight on the bar in that room off the Den, his knuckles were white. The door shuddered with another barrage on the other side. Then a moment later, still breathing hard, he turned around to stare at me. The thunder against that door seemed fitting when I saw that his eyes were glowing again. That incandescent blue, so bright. But his face was a mask of rage...

...With a roar, Cazz grabbed my shoulders and turned me around, frog-marching me towards the door. He grabbed my hands and planted my palms on the door, flattening his hands over them so I couldn't pull away. I gasped as the pounding, vibrations, and rattles threatened to break through and my entire body wanted to recoil, but he held me there as he snapped off the words like ice cubes between his teeth. "You made them want you, gave them reason to think they could take you from me. You took power from me and handed it to them."

"I d-didn't mean to—"

"And yet, you did..."

....Cazz, grabbing my elbow and whipping me around to face him, pulling me right up and leaning down into my face to snarl at me.

"I have been nothing but open and honest with you. But it clearly hasn't registered, so let's try again: You are my mate. You are my bitch. You will be the mother of my young. And you will receive everything you ever need or want in return. But you are not my princess. You are not my dream, and you most definitely are not—and will never be—my love. Do you understand?"

"Who hurt you?" I breathed. "Who convinced you that loving someone was weakness?"

"I SAID, DO YOU UNDERST—"

Cazz shuddered and pushed away from me, recoiling, eyes wide but locked on mine. And as I felt the horror jolting through him I realized he'd seen it all—all of it through my eyes.

"I'm not... that isn't... I would never have *hurt* you—"

It was ruthless, but I held onto the bond and our link in it and made myself remember standing in front of that mirror after the claiming, examining my body for bruises—

'*Stop,*' he hissed in my head.

"Cazz, you're terrifying when you're angry."

"I told you, I vowed to you that I would never—"

"But how can I know? How do I know you haven't already? I burn for you—I ache for you even after all the ways you've rejected me. I want you and it *kills me* when you turn your back on me. You don't deserve that kind of devotion, but you have it—did you already compel me and just make me forget?"

His eyes widened. "No! I keep my word—I vowed I wouldn't compel you and I haven't. Trust me, the past month would have been far fucking easier on *me* if I had! I can't believe you think I would—"

"That very first day I saw you strip the wills of two women in seconds, Cazz. They were terrified one second, then desperate for you the next. And even when you stopped putting that power out there, they still tried to get close to you. I saw it."

"You saw weak minds that held onto the compulsion because it was easier than facing the truth: That they couldn't stop me from controlling them if I wanted to," he growled.

I shook my head. "I just watched you compel an entire group of males that you said are some of your strongest and wisest, and they don't even know you've done it!"

His expression darkened. "I rarely use that kind of compulsion—it was extremely precise, and mostly it was to keep *you* safe. Keep Khush from figuring out that I'm onto him so he'll lead us to your brother and any wolves that might be working against me. And I let you stay aware of all of it! I kept you in the truth!"

"And I'm grateful, but don't look at me like it's somehow baffling to you that I would think you were capable of shifting my memories and not telling me."

"I don't want to change who you are, Jesse, I just want to stop feeling like you could rip the foundations out from under my fucking feet!"

We both froze as those words echoed through the chamber, in my mind and his. And it occurred to me that it was possibly the most honest he'd ever been.

I swallowed hard, not wanting to push, but needing to understand.

"Foundations?" I breathed. "Foundations of what?"

"Everything, Jesse. Don't you realize? Don't you get it yet? *Everything* could fall over with one wrong step. Your brother isn't the only male in this world that would tear me down if he could. Khush isn't the only wolf that will steal my power if he can find a way past it. You are not the only female who would chain me like a pet if she could—"

"What? Cazz, I don't want to *chain* you!"

"—but that is the life of an Alpha King. It is a constant battle. Warfare. The strongest survives. And no one can stay the strongest forever. So I refuse to face the day when I have to submit myself to someone else—or die—as a… a shivering pet. I will walk to my doom with my teeth bared and knowing I fought to the very last moment to hold my crown."

I stared at him, forcing myself not to shake my head as it came home to me that my screwed up, messy mate was so convinced that feeling anything was a sign that he was about to be taken advantage of.

He was so deeply, desperately *broken.*

"Cazz… I don't want to chain you," I repeated.

My heart sank when he shook his head.

117. Stronger You

~ JESSE ~

He sighed. "Perhaps not. Or, perhaps your heart wants something you have no words for?"

"No, Cazz... I'm serious. I didn't offer myself to you because I thought I could beat you."

"Why *did* you offer yourself? Truly?"

"Because you were the first man I met who it seemed like could genuinely protect me from the others."

A wave of feeling came through the bond then. That shriek in him. That hollow pain that cried out to be soothed.

He had already pulled away from me, so he just stood there, staring at me.

Yet, he hadn't shut down the bond.

Holy shit. Did he not know he was still open to me? Was he going to do it again the moment he realized? I scrambled mentally to keep him talking, opening myself to the bond as fully as I knew how, pulling at him, praying he wouldn't shut me down so I could see where he was really at.

"Cazz, I don't want you for your power, I want you for your strength," I whispered.

His eyes narrowed. "That's bullshit. They're one and the same."

"No. No, they aren't." I swallowed hard, holding that bond so gently, but so desperately. "Because power... power is about other people. Who you can order around. Who you can influence. But strength... strength is who you are. Cazz... You don't lose it no matter how powerless you might be in the eyes of others. And you're the strongest person I've ever met."

I felt the smug satisfaction ripple through him and wanted to roll my eyes, but I kept going to keep him distracted from how open he was to me.

"I love that you possess that stubborn streak. When it's applied to doing what's right, it's going to be incredible. But you have a really fucked up way of using what God gave you," I said honestly.

Everything in him went still. His face blank, eyes locked on mine.

"No one speaks to me that way. Except, perhaps, Rake."

I snorted. "That's because everyone else is afraid you're going to change their minds for them," I muttered.

That brought us back to *my* fear that he'd compelled me without my knowledge, and the chill trickled down my spine again.

He didn't like it. He took a step closer, his face stern, but when he reached for me his touch was gentle.

"So, tell me, mate," he said dryly. "How do I prove to you that I haven't broken my word?"

That was an excellent question. It made me frown and look away, because... he was right. How *did* he prove it?

I sighed. "I guess... I guess you can't. I guess I have to trust you."

He lifted a hand, nudging my chin with his fingers to make me look at him again. And as I did, my heart tore again.

I yearned to just lean into his chest so he'd wrap his arms around me and kiss me and take me and we could forget about every other fucked up thing that was going on... but I also wanted to keep him talking, keep looking at his heart through the bond. I was *hungry* to understand him.

His eyes cut back and forth between mine, his expression growing more intense. "What is it that you want? I can't quite define it," he rumbled.

"Probably because I want more than one thing, and they don't really go together," I said honestly. "Cazz... I want you. That's real. Sometimes I wish it wasn't, but it is. I want you. I want to understand you. I want to be with you. And I want you to want me. It's all jumbled up together and—"

"You have all of those things!" he growled and I felt that twist of frustration in him again.

But I shook my head. "No, Cazz. I have your... management."

He frowned. "What the fuck does that mean?"

I sighed. "It means that you watch out for me. Like I'm on your staff, or something. You make sure I'm provided for. But you don't... you don't..."

He tipped his head like a puppy trying to understand, his brows pinched over his nose. But I didn't have the words. I didn't know how to say what I was feeling, so I just grabbed the bond and thrust my heart at him—all that aching, yearning uncertainty. All that desire to have the part of him that he defended and protected so vigorously.

Because I knew he burned for me. I knew he wanted my body—and I suspected that went a lot deeper than just the desire for kids. But he also hated me for making him feel things, and that scared me because it *clearly* scared him.

My feelings were only growing. And from what I could tell, his were too. Was he going to get more and more angry? Push me further and further away until he finally gave in and breached the bond like he had before?

And if he did, would it kill me literally, or metaphorically?

Cazz was leaning in, his pupils growing wider, darker, his breathing speeding up.

He crowded me, stepping right up into my space, his eyes still flicking back and forth, searching mine with the same intensity he gave everything else.

"Jesse..." he breathed.

"I don't want to pretend I'm okay with this, Cazz," I said, hating myself for the high, thin tone of my voice. "I don't want to pretend I don't want more from you—" I grabbed for his shirt again when he froze and made him stay there with me. "I'm not trying to take anything from you except... unity. I just want you to stop seeing me as an adversary. Because I don't want that. I don't want to resist you, or resist my feelings for you. I want to... I want to give you everything and do all of this *together.*"

His brows pinched tighter. "My life, my role, it doesn't allow for... togetherness."

"Bullshit," I hissed at him, swallowing back tears of frustration. "Maya's been teaching me, Cazz. About the pack and the hierarchy, and I don't pretend to know all of it yet, but I can already see it. I can see how I can be there and strengthen you and make *you* more. That's what I want—do you get that? I don't want to take from you, I want to add to you."

The bond pulsed then, throbbed with a jolt of electric emotion and my breath caught as a low, deep growl puttered in Cazz's chest, but there was a quality to it I'd never heard from him before.

He took hold of my shoulders and started walking me backwards—towards the bed—and my entire body throbbed, but I didn't drop eye contact, and I reached for him through the bond, praying he wouldn't shut me out.

'I want to make you stronger, Cazz. I want to watch you grow.'

He sucked in a breath, still walking me slowly backwards, and when he lifted one hand to my face it was shaking.

'I want to watch you get stronger, and stronger—'

His breath rushed out of him and my heart began to pound with that cursed hope.

'—and I want to watch you win. I want to be proud to be your mate,. I am proud to be your mate, Cazz—'

Cazz cursed and took my face in both hands, pulling me into a kiss so deep and needy that for a moment I couldn't breathe.

118. Need You – Part 1

~ *CASIMIR* ~

'I want to watch you get stronger, and stronger and I want to watch you win. I want to be proud to be your mate,. I am proud to be your mate, Cazz—'

I'd already had her, just hours earlier. But when she spoke those words it didn't just light a fire in my belly, it sent a bonfire through my veins. There wasn't time to consider *why,* because my wolf threw itself forward as if she were prey to be devoured.

I couldn't speak. Could barely think as I descended on her, forced to take a grip on myself or I might actually have bitten her delicious tongue, I was so desperate to consume her.

Something deep in my chest thrummed and flared, ached and called.

And she was answering... Dear God, she was answering. In the bond, in her body—she didn't have a wolf to howl to mine, but something deep within her lifted its voice and *sang to me.* Calling me closer as she grasped and clung and gasped my name.

The back of her legs hit the bed and we stumbled together, but as she put an arm back to catch herself, I growled, unwilling to wait.

I took the lapels of my jacket and shoved it open, off her shoulders, down her arms, flinging it away so it pinwheeled across my room then landed with a heavy slap on the floor. But I was already stripping her.

As she remained leaning back onto the bed, her chin tipped down, but eyes wide, watching me, I gripped the sides of her pajama shirt in either hand and didn't bother with the buttons, just tore it open, buttons pinging against my chest and pattering to the floor, ignored as she gave a little squeak, but laughed breathlessly too.

"Cazz…"

"I can get you a dozen of these in minutes," I growled as I tugged the shirt off, baring her to the waist, my wolf snarling as we realized she'd been in that room with all those males and no bra.

I shuddered and felt the jolt of concern from her.

She eased off the bed, her hands appearing at my chest and fumbling with my buttons as she laughed shakily again.

She was quick, my shirt more than halfway unbuttoned by the time I pushed her pajama bottoms down to bare her completely, leaning down to drag them off her legs and throw them across the room to join the jacket.

"Get my pants," I rumbled as I straightened up and reached for my own shirt. She was on my belt in a second, but it was too slow.

I didn't bother with the seduction of it, just grabbed my own shirt and tore it off as she tugged my belt out of the loops on my trousers. The long tongue of the belt slapped against my thigh in a way that made my blood fizz. The moment I had my shirt flying, I grabbed for the pants and gave them the same treatment—tearing them open and shoving them down my legs as Jesse gave a breathless giggle.

But then we were both bare and I was desperate for her in a way I'd never felt for any female before.

She gave a little shriek as I reached down and picked her up, cradling her to my chest, then tossing her onto the bed with perhaps a little more force than was necessary. She bounced and her eyes went wide, but then I was on her, a deep growl of desire rumbling in my chest as I covered her and took her face in my hands, took her velvet mouth and teased her tongue, sighing with the relief of finally being skin-to-skin.

I want to watch you get stronger, and stronger…

I had to force myself to gentleness as I clawed a hand up from her hip to her side, to her breast and pushed it up, leaning down to open my mouth over that gorgeous nipple, desire jolting through me when she sucked in and her body bowed.

I want to watch you win…

I shuddered and arched my back, rubbing myself against her, still sucking on that breast, then switching to the other, using tongue and teeth to tease her as she gasped and writhed under me, her nails digging into my back as she clung.

"Cazz…"

I want to be proud to be your mate. I am *proud to be your mate, Cazz.*

With a groan that any wolf would have heard two doors away, I dropped my hand down to cup the back of her knee and gripped it, pulling it up towards her chest, opening her even though I gave her no room to move.

She was slick, but was that from her or me? I could barely keep my thoughts straight as my wolf snarled and jumped, howled and growled, pushing me to her. I was already gasping like a fish out of water, my body overwhelmed with need and thrill and—*fuck.*

"Jesse, I need you," I groaned, flexing my hips to draw myself against her much harder than I should have. But she arched to meet me and I almost took her by accident, both of us holding our breaths until I passed over her.

"It's okay, Cazz. I'm ready. I want you."

Plunging a shaking hand into her hair, I gripped those thick waves as I thrust into her in a single, long slide.

Her head snapped back and I dove for her throat, locking lips and tongue over that soft flesh and sucking so hard I knew it would leave a mark. But my wolf still wasn't satisfied, and neither was I.

Teeth grazing her skin, tongue laving, I pulled almost all the way out of her, then braced my free hand on the bed, elbow bent back and arm shaking as I held all my weight there so she'd have room to breathe, then plunged into her again.

"Cazz!" she gasped, one hand slapping to my back, the other fisted in the furs to ground her.

I want to watch you get stronger, and stronger…

A small whine broke in my throat and my body shivered with need. Keeping that hand in her hair, her head back so her neck arched towards me, I began to take her, over and over, in a punishing rhythm.

119. Need You – Part 2

~ CASIMIR ~

Jesse's eyes were closed, but her mouth was wide, her breath tearing in and out of her extended throat. As our bodies joined again and again, she gave small, sharp cries of joy. And just when I worried I might be too rough, her hand clawed down my back to grip my ass and pull me in harder.

Oh fuck.

"Jesse… Jesse, say it… say it again—"

"S-say what?" she gasped.

I shivered, my body flinching from the embarrassment, but my heart rushing towards it. But I couldn't say it.

'Open your eyes,' I sent desperately, thrusting into her.

Her eyes flew open and locked with mine and I was jolted again with a rush of power and need and—

'Say it.'

'Say what, Cazz? Tell me. I will.'

'What you said… right before I kissed you.'

Her jaw was slack and her eyes beginning to glaze, but there was a moment when confusion flickered across her features. But then she blinked. I saw it in her mind before she sent it, but it came with such a wave of bliss I couldn't speak.

'You mean… I want to see you stronger?'

Oh, god. Yes.

'Cazz… I want to see you win—'

My body was alive, electric, shimmering, *shaking* with need for her. I was incoherent with it. I pounded into her like my life depended on it and she cried out with it.

"Cazz… Cazz… oh god—"

It felt as if my body expanded. As if my chest swelled and my heart grew. Still fisting her hair, I raised myself on my arms, braced myself over her so I could look down on her, watch her breasts bounce, watch her eyes roll back in her head, watch her body flush and sweat.

But then she reached for me in the bond again.

'I want to be proud to be your mate.'

My jaw dropped and my body *throbbed.*

Jesse was arching her back, pulling herself up on my back, my shoulders, trying to reach me, but I had a grip on her hair, so she couldn't lift her head, only her body.

"Oh, god, Jesse—"

"Let go, Cazz. Let go. I'm here, I'm *here—"*

The moment I released her hair, she gave a little gasp and rolled up my body, pulling herself right against me, one arm braced around my neck, the other clinging to my back, holding me so close her chest was pressed against mine, her face buried in *my* throat.

She didn't speak, but reached for me in the bond.

'This, Cazz… this is… I need you. I need you so mu—oh fuck—
,

She stopped breathing and her body tensed to offer resistance as I unleashed and began to pound into her with abandon, holding her ass and keeping her there, curled up on me as her body began to tighten around me and those words she'd given me, that precious gift, echoed in my head again.

'I am proud to be your mate, Cazz.'

Oh shit oh shit oh shit oh shit—

Unable to hold her any longer because it wasn't close enough, I flipped us over so I was sitting and she was in my lap, my hands clawing at her back and in her hair.

Jesse gave a little yelp, but then clenched around me again as the angle changed and now *she* was riding *me.*

I looped my arms in the hollow of her back and my wolf called to her as she let herself drop back, her breasts high and bouncing with the force of my thrusts—but she met me at the peak every time, tiny cries breaking in her throat.

As her head began to loll, I hissed a curse and clapped one hand up over her shoulder, pulling her down onto me—and as she ground against me, the added pressure finally broke her.

Her head fell back and a gorgeous, ragged cry erupted from her as she clamped down on me and her body went rigid in my arms.

"Jesse! Jesse!"

"Cazz I'm here—"

The waves of her orgasm overwhelmed her—and she clamped down on me so hard, my own climax burst like a dam under pressure and I was sucked down, spiraling into that vortex of ecstacy.

I lost all sense of time or place. There was nothing but her— her warmth, her cries, her body taking mine. Everything disappeared, even the oxygen from the air. And for those few short moments I would have given it all. I would have given *everything* to stay there with her, hanging in nothing, but together.

The bond swelled, crashing over both of us just as surely as the pleasure, tumbling and turning us until I didn't know which way was up. But she was under my hands, over my body, *with me.* And I clung.

I clung like she was a log in a stormy sea.

I inhaled her, like air.

And I drank her in.

By the time reality returned, I was laying over her on the bed, crushing her with my weight. We were both panting and my face was buried in her neck.

She'd wrapped me in her arms and was holding me so tightly, it made it hard to breathe.

But I didn't care.

I trembled from head to toe, my body overwhelmed and my heart… my heart pounding so hard and fast, I wondered if it would explode.

I should have moved. Should have done *something,* but I could only lay there with my nose against her skin, breathing in her scent, every inch of my skin throbbing in time with my pulse.

And then I felt a tiny, cold trickle down my cheek.

For a moment it confused me, but then there was a second, and I lifted my head—was she bleeding?!

But no… no… my mate didn't bleed. She stared at me with eyes wide and shining with tears.

"Did I hurt you?" I rasped, horrified.

But she shook her head. "No, Cazz. No. I just…" she swallowed hard and brought both her hands up to hold my face, keeping me there, locked into her gaze.

I just love you. I just love you and there's nothing better than when you give yourself to me. It's… beautiful.

I froze. My body tense. But her nails dug into my cheeks and scalp.

"Don't do it, Cazz, please," she breathed, her brows pinching and forehead furrowed. My skin screamed under her nails, like she might actually puncture it. But I was frozen there with her.

I swallowed hard, my chest going cold even as my body wanted to sink into her.

"Don't do it, Cazz. Don't be afraid of me. I only want to see you have more. More of everything. I swear it," she whispered through trembling lips. "Believe me, please. You can feel me—I can feel you too. Test me. Feel me. I'm telling you the truth."

I was shivering, but I felt her in the body—throwing her heart wide. Completely defenseless. Utterly submitted. *Offering herself.*

I punched a hand into the furs, gripping them to ground me, and threw back my head and howled as power erupted out of her and poured into me.

120. You Grow Me – Part 1

~ JESSE ~

I just love you. I just love you and there's nothing better than when you give yourself to me. It's… beautiful.

I hadn't meant to just blurt it out like that, but it was there and it was true, and the bond was so deep and close, it just came out.

I knew it was a terrible mistake the moment Cazz froze up. Desperation and fear rocketed through me and I held onto him, gripping him, one hand on his beautiful, square jaw, the other buried in his hair.

"Don't do it, Cazz, please," I breathed, panicking. He didn't move. His eyes were locked on mine and he stared like he was trying to see *inside* me.

And he could. He could!

"Don't do it, Cazz. Don't be afraid of me. I only want to see you have more. More of everything. I swear it." I swallowed to try and stop the tears that wanted to come because everything felt so raw, so deep. "Believe me, please. You can feel me—I can feel you too. Test me. Feel me. I'm telling you the truth."

He was shaking under my hands, but he blinked and I felt him, deep inside, measuring me. Taking the bond and turning it, examining it, looking at it and me and us together. So I let him see. I did what Maya had been trying to train out of me and threw my heart wide like doors to the sun—let him see me, see everything. Everything I wanted for us—everything I wanted for *him.*

And in that moment when he was staring at me and I was offering myself, something happened. A volcano in my heart, erupting, filling me with a torrent of heat and power.

I sucked in a breath as Cazz's entire body went rigid. He slapped a hand to the furs like he was grabbing for salvation, then threw his head back and roared—the tendons on his neck standing proud, every muscle in his beautiful torso tense and shaking with the force of what was coursing through us—like I'd just grounded him to mainline electric current.

I held him by my nails, terrified I was going to be torn from him, everything inside me burning up. But I felt this *fire* flood from me and into him at the same time cooling, soothing water rushed back to me in a tidal wave to calm the blistering inside my veins.

We both arched. I couldn't breathe.

Cazz's long cry broke off like he'd lost his air, but his body didn't relax. He was trembling like he fought for his life—but his head dropped and his eyes…

His eyes were the wolf again. Glowing so bright the blue was almost white.

I would have been afraid, but I could feel him. In the bond I could feel him—he hadn't closed off from me—he was flailing, desperate, ragged, hopeful, and terrified.

"C-Cazz…" I tried to call for him, but my lips were numb and my body thundering with this torrent of power that I didn't understand.

But when I spoke, he gave a guttural groan and dropped to his elbows, his shaking hands cupping over my head as if he tried to shield me in the circle of his trembling, steel arms.

He dropped his forehead to mine and closed his eyes. I threw my arms around his neck and held him there, calling through the bond, pleading with him not to leave, and pleading with God not to kill us with… whatever this was.

And then… just like something had powered through a lake and tossed huge waves on the shore, but now the water settled, that ocean of power retreated.

We were both left there, gasping and shaking… and stronger.

When I could breathe without a fight, I blinked my eyes open and kept holding him there to me, but turned my attention inwards, examining myself. Because something had changed. Something I didn't understand, but I felt… stronger. Like all that electricity hadn't burned me out, but it had been stored inside me.

"Cazz?" I rasped, lifting my hands to his hair, gripping him there, still terrified he was going to leave, even though he was still covering me, his arms still holding me like he'd use his body to shield me from an attack.

His breath came out in a rush that fluttered over my face.

He raised his head, and I grabbed for him, afraid he was going to leave me. But he didn't. He just raised himself on his elbows high enough to look down at me, searching my eyes, his expression awed, and afraid, and… stunned.

"Can you feel that?" he croaked.

I nodded, still clinging to him because he was trembling and my head was screaming that he was going to leave, but I needed him…

"What did you do?" His eyes wide and bloodshot, fixed on mine.

I shook my head. "I just love you, Cazz. It's not… it's not a bad thing. I just love you," I whispered, blinking back tears.

A thousand things flickered through his gaze then, too fast for me to read any of it, but the bond thrummed.

"Why?!" he rasped.

I couldn't help it, but I laughed—a wet, slightly unhinged little giggle, then clapped a hand over my mouth. But he didn't move, just kept staring at me.

'I don't know, Cazz. But something about you… you were made for me.' And I was made for him, too. I wanted to say it so badly, wanted him to see it. But I was too scared. I'd already gone so much further than I should have, I was terrified he was going to just snap and leave.

But his breath rushed out of him again like he'd been punched. He dropped his head so his forehead rested on the furs next to me, and his cheek lay against mine.

His lips brushed my ear when he whispered, "You grow me."

I nodded, biting my lip, praying he wouldn't flee. "And you grow me," I rasped back. "It's how it's supposed to be, Cazz. It's not a bad thing."

"Your power grew as well," he said, his voice wary.

I nodded again. "But not as strong as you, Cazz. I'm always… any power I get I'm always going to use to make you stronger. I promise."

His breath was shaky. But his fingers curled into my hair like he was holding on.

"Please, Cazz… please, don't leave," I breathed.

He lifted his head again and stared at me.

I made myself reach up and stroke his face, and I waited to see what he'd do. And I prayed.

Soundtrack for the next chapter is

Burn by Nathan Wagner.

121. You Grow Me – Part 2

~ CASIMIR ~

My entire body trembled as I worked to accommodate that torrent of power she'd imparted to me. My head was spinning, my heart was full, and the bond was *alive*. But it was overwhelming, all of it. So I shook, and I doubted and I tore in half, right down the middle of my soul.

Half of me was terrified—this was exactly what I'd been warned about. Exactly what I'd feared. The closer we got, the stronger she would become. And as Alpha female, her power would draw the wolves. She fed off of me, and whatever she gained would benefit her in their eyes.

It wasn't even a matter of loyalty. They sensed it in her, and the animals within followed that kind of power without thinking.

While she and I were aligned, it could be a great asset. But if or when our goals diverged…

And yet, as the cold chill of fear crackled through me, the other half of me sang. It *sang*. Like the core of me had been divided, half of my soul hungered for more. Half of my mind chittered with the thrill and joy of drawing her nearer. Half of my heart swelled to fill the new width and breadth of my chest that was expanding and contracting with an almost uncomfortable pressure of power.

I felt as if I could call the wind—and she was the one who'd taught me the language to do it.

It was stunning. I *shook* with it.

That side of me wanted nothing more than to plaster myself to her and never let her go. When she said she loved me, that side of my soul wept with joy—and leaped forward, begging for more.

But then the fear screamed.

She could betray me.

She could gather others against me.

She could break me and steal my power, outgrow me…

But there was a part of me that wanted that… a part that wanted to see what she'd become if I didn't hold her back. A part that wanted to lift her and use *my* power to increase *her.*

And that was the most terrifying thought I'd ever had. And so I plummeted again.

Back and forth. It was exhausting to swing so wildly between cold fear and warm hope.

Hope. Fucking hope. It was fuel to a dream, and it killed *everything.*

Jesse lay under me, breathing words that were beautiful and stunning and everything the warm side of my soul yearned to hear—if they were true.

And they were the cauterizing resolve the cold side of me needed.

Even after the rush of power had eased, my body trembled because I fought a war within myself. And she knew it.

My beautiful mate with her shocking power, lay under me and stroked my face, tangled her fingers in my hair, and *begged* me not to leave her.

And the larger part of me wanted to give her that much.

And the larger part of me was terrified to admit it.

"Jesse…" I croaked, staring down at her, our bodies still joined, her eyes shining with unshed tears and hope and fear, and mine… well, I didn't know what mine were doing. But I felt it, deep in my chest. The pull to her—and the pull away. It was exhausting.

"Please, Cazz," she whispered. "Please don't run."

I sighed so heavily it fluttered her hair.

When I finally rolled off of her, she sucked in a breath and pushed up to sit, but I was just rolling onto my back, hands over my face, trying to calm my mind and my racing heart. I wasn't leaving the bed. I wasn't leaving her. Not yet.

"Cazz—"

"I'm not leaving. I'm just… I just need to breathe," I murmured, tugging her back down to lay at my side.

She was tense, afraid. I could feel it through the bond, even as I fought not to cut her off there, because I knew it would make this battle easier to fight. But something deep down ached to hold onto her. To keep that connection that was pulsing between us, and feeding power into my veins—but also into hers.

Dear god, I couldn't win.

After a few seconds, she started to believe that I wasn't going to run, and she lay down in the crook of my arm, her head on my shoulder. We had lain this way a few times when I'd come to her in the night. But usually we both slept. I knew she was wide-awake now. I could feel her in the bond—just as alive and vibrant as I was because that fucking power was coursing through us both.

Shit.

Shit.

And then, with the impeccable timing he had always shown, memories of my father bloomed in my mind—one of his lectures on being Alpha. His instructions.

"...Humility is for the week, Casimir. And nothing will humble you faster than the female that holds your bond. No one can betray you more easily than the female who holds power over you."

I'd thought of my mother—her quiet dignity that disguised a timid, fearful heart. The way she could stand in audience and silence an Alpha with a look, but would cower under my father's disapproval.

"Mom wouldn't ever betray you," I had offered, uncertain if it was meant to be defense of my mother, or reassurance to him.

Dad smiled. "She'd never dare. Because she's learned to her own detriment how lightly she holds my bond. That is my job, and I did it—making certain she was precisely aware of how far she could push me without losing her life. Making certain she had no question that I would willingly tear out her throat myself.

"Unflinching, Casimir. You cannot waver. Let her have enough of you to keep her alive, but not an ounce more. She will be the gateway to your destruction if you empower her. Because in your absence, the packs will follow her. So, you'll have only yourself to blame if she manages it."

"But, she's Alpha female. They're supposed to follow her if something happens to you—"

Fury flared in his eyes. "Is that what you want to see, Casimir? Your mother on the throne?"

My blood ran cold.

122. You Grow Me – Part 3

~ CASIMIR ~

My father stared at me, power crackling and boiling in the air behind him.

I rushed to soothe his suspicions, raising my hands in surrender, which was the only kind of submission he'd accept.

"No, no, Dad! I just meant, that's the hierarchy—if the male dies, the Alpha female is supposed to be the one who leads until the next Alpha takes the—"

"And what do you think it does to her if she believes that's her due? What would you do if you knew that with one step you could snap my neck and take it all for yourself? Would that increase your loyalty, Casimir? Or would you seek to destroy me?" he asked in a quiet, cold tone that turned my blood to ice.

The point was valid and he knew it. I was fighting to be chosen Heir. My loyalty right now was to my father, because if he selected me his power would assist me in dominating my siblings to win the throne after his death. But if they were all gone? If it was just him and me, and I held all the power of the Heir?

He'd be fucked the first second I was capable of compelling him, and he knew it. And so did I.

He smiled to let me know that he knew exactly what I was thinking.

"The choice will be yours if you succeed me, Casimir. But what I tell you is true: Empowering those with the strength to overcome you is just working against yourself. It's simple mathematics. And I know you've got a good head for numbers, so don't stare at me like I'm confusing you."

"I'm not confused," I growled. "I'm just thinking about what you're saying."

"Do less thinking and more applying," he growled. He strode over the sidebar and poured himself a drink, shaking his head. "Your heart for others is a weakness, Casimir. The gateway by which you'll be defeated."

"If I'm stronger, they can't defeat me, even if they want to."

My father turned, his eyes narrowed. "What you're missing is the conviction that they want to. Would you simply stand aside and let Cuan take Heir?"

"No!" Cuan was the oldest of my siblings, and a sadistic asshole. I was looking forward to taking the birthright from him.

"Precisely! And yet I've seen you submit to him. Seen you smile and laugh and work with him against others—"

"Because it suited my purposes at the time."

"That is exactly my point, Cazz! Wake up! There is no one near you who seeks what's best for you beyond what you can do for them. They're only willing to work with you while your goals align. The moment you're at odds, they reveal that they have been an adversary all along. Just like you will to your brother!"

I sat back, rolling my jaw, turning his words over in my mind. I knew he was right about my siblings—and some of the other Alphas that carried sway and would want nothing more than to take the throne. We all knew that when the time came, we were at war.

But everyone?

A face bloomed in my mind. A smiling face. Warm skin. Quiet words in the dark of night, and a lush body that welcomed—

Swallowing hard, I quickly double-checked my mental defenses, ensuring there was no way my father had seen that in the link. But he was still staring into his scotch and shaking his head.

"Many will help you take the throne if they believe it will increase their portion, Casimir," he said darkly. "But none will keep you there if they believe they can take it from you."

He looked up from his drink to lock eyes with me. "Do not usher in your own downfall. Choose a mate who will empower you, then make her your slave. She cannot be free. She must be an extension of you—a limb that you command, but that has strength to do the tasks you set for her. Because if she's not, if she has any agency in her own life at all, the only thing between you and death is her finding the right way to kill you—"

The stroke of a small hand on my chest pulled me out of the memory, but left a nervous chill in my chest.

I caught Jesse's hand and held it, at first to stop her touching me, but then because holding it felt... right.

Shit.

I was so fucked.

"I wish you could just believe me, Cazz," she breathed, her words fluttering against my neck. "I wish you could see inside me and realize that I'm not hiding anything. I really want what's best for you. I want to see you win."

I took a deep breath, trying to ease the tension building behind my ribs as the two sides of me flew into combat again.

She wanted me to win... for the wolves? Or against her brothers? She'd admitted that she gave herself to me because she believed I was powerful enough to beat the males in her life. I'd been pleased to see that in her through the link—smug because she recognized my strength against her brother. But what then? What would happen if I removed the other threats in her life?

Would she still want to increase my strength *then?*

"I'm not... I don't doubt that you care, Jesse," I said carefully, staring at the ceiling. Because I knew that much was true. She'd fallen, despite my warnings not to. But I knew from experience that love could quickly chill to hate—or vengeance.

"Then what is it? Why can I feel you afraid—like your life depends on it?"

Unbidden, that face came to mind again—the sound of her laugh and the feeling of my own cheeks stretching into a smile—

Inwardly, I flinched from the memory and instinctively turned towards Jesse, curling her into my chest as I rolled to face her, and holding her there.

She buried her face in my neck—another astounding moment because I *never* let a female near my throat, and this was the third time I hadn't snapped at her about it. But she inhaled deeply, then sighed it all out like having my arms around her soothed something, and I just...

I just wanted to be there.

I drew my hand up her naked spine, buried my fingers in her hair, and held her to me.

"Your heart's beating so fast," she whispered, muffled against my skin.

I just tightened my hold on her and tried to breathe and calm.

I reminded myself that I was King. And she was only human. And no other wolf came close to me in power.

No one could take her from me this time.

No one was strong enough.

The question was… would she walk away of her own free will if I allowed her to have it?

Or worse…

Would she find a way to kick the throne out from under me and take it herself?

And was I going to let her?

"Cazz, *stop,*" she murmured, pushing out of my arms and up onto her own elbow, staring at me, her face serious and brows pinched.

"Stop what? Holding you? I thought that's what you—"

"Stop doubting me."

Fuck. She could feel it in the bond.

I reached for it, intending to close it between us, but her hand shot out to my chest, and that pulse of power jolted between us again as she *plugged in.*

I was gripping her wrist, but I didn't pull her hand away, because she stared at me, and I was frozen in that gaze.

"You felt me, Cazz," she whispered, looking down at me like I made her sad. "You felt how I feel about you and… that's more important than anything I could do with my body, or yours. The heart is always more important. The motives. Can't you see that?"

I considered deflecting. Considered pushing away and just leaving. And I considered remaining silent.

But in the end…

"I don't know," I said honestly. "I just don't know, Jess."

Her face kind of fell, but she sighed and slumped down, curling into my chest and holding me. So I held her back.

Because no matter what the future held, that felt good. For here and now… it felt *right.*

Volume 2 available summer 2024!
Or read ahead of the paperback volumes on Radish, Goodnovel, Webnovel, or Alphanovel!

Turn the page to find a list of other books by the author.
Or go to linktree.com/authoraimee

For announcements, giveaways, and laughter every day, join my Facebook group, Author Aimee's Reader Tribe: *www.facebook.com/groups/authoraimeetribe*

Follow me on Instagram: @author_aimee

Acknowledgements

I'll always thank Jesus first, because without You I wouldn't even be here. Thank you for saving my life more than once. Thank you for giving me these talents and passions. And thank you for making it possible to pursue them. Thank you for not shying away from the ugliness and darkness in life (and in me) so that I didn't have to either. I love you.

Thank you to my husband Alan for loving me so much you inspire romance, and for supporting me personally in pursing this very erratic career, and for your forearm porn. It's my favorite.

Thank you to my son Harry for putting up with sharing me with your fictional brothers and sisters since before you knew what they were. Thank you for trusting me with who you really are, and for never being too shy or cool to give your mother hugs and say "I love you." I love you, too. Now... *do not read this book until you're married.* Okay?

Thank you to every single one of my Reader Tribe (go to linktr.ee/authoraimee to join us!) You literally make every day a joy, every book a triumph, and every #AuthorFail a funny-rather-than-embarrassing moment. You have made my dreams come true and I'll never stop thanking God for you.

Thank you to every digital publisher (even the ones who ripped me off) for taking chances on my stories, promoting them, and helping me find my audience.

Thank you, finally, to every single reader, on every single app and in every book. Without you I couldn't do what I do. I hope you'll find me on social media and say hi. Because there's no one I'd rather meet! I've been wishing for you since I was seven years old. So, thank you. You *are* what they mean when they say "dreams come true."

You all changed my life. I will never not be grateful.

Aimee

Did you know?

Aimee Lynn is a bestselling and award-winning serial romance writer and has several books available right now on various reading apps! (Also writes as Aimee Lane and Aimee Lynn-Lane)

Available and complete on all your favorite reading apps:

The Anima Series (Webnovel and PocketFM):
Falling for the King of Beasts
Taming the Queen of Beasts
Rise of the Dark Alpha (spin off)
Mated to the Warrior Beast

Complete and available *only* on MyFavReads
(Pen name: Aimee Lynn-Lane):
Heart of Fire
The Guardian Alpha

Available and complete *only* on Dreame (Aimee Lane):
His Stolen Luna
(Also available as audiobook on DreameFM)

YA ROMANCES AVAILABLE ON AMAZON:

Breakable (Formerly known as Every Ugly Word,
the Amazon #1 Book for Teens, October 2015)
Under My Skin

AND MORE!
Find them all on:
Linktree.com/authoraimee

Made in the USA
Monee, IL
13 January 2025

76783911R00298